Betrayal

IVY SMOAK

ISBN: 9798409864668

Cover photo by Michelle Lancaster
www.michellelancaster.com

2023 Edition

To all those awkward high school moments.

Who knew they'd be useful?

CHAPTER 1

Saturday

Nunca.

With each step I took, the more determined I became. I couldn't let Isabella win. Not like this. Not ever. Someone needed to stand up to her. And that someone was going to be me.

I tried to ignore the cold autumn air biting at my skin. I tried to ignore the rough pavement on my bare feet. I tried to keep my head held high.

But when Isabella's limo sped off, splashing water all over me, my shoulders crumpled forward and my tears started to fall again.

Who was I kidding? I'd been given plenty of chances to stand up to Isabella, and all I had ever done was cower. Just because I was half Pruitt didn't mean I could play the same evil games as her. Isabella would always have the upper hand. She'd always win.

Stop it. My mom raised me to believe in myself. To believe that people could get through hard times. *Then why isn't she here with me? Why'd she have to die?*

My tears wouldn't stop. For some reason crying brought up all the memories. My last moments holding my mom's hand in her hospital bed. The image morphed in my head, and instead of my mom in a hospital bed it was my uncle.

What the hell was I fighting for when I'd already lost everything?

I swallowed hard. Matt. Kennedy. Myself. I was fighting for myself. I wiped away the stubborn tears off my cheeks. I was fighting for my freaking self.

I was still standing after everything that I'd been through. And I'd keep standing through this too. I just needed to figure out what to do next. I was naked in the middle of the city with no money.

Shit. What was I supposed to do all night? The bus station that Isabella had mentioned wasn't a bad option. If I could sneak into the terminal in my skivvies without being seen, then maybe I could hide in the bathroom all night. It would be warm and relatively safe. The only people that hung out in bus station terminals at night were homeless. And that was me. I'd fit right in. And I'd have plenty of time to figure out how I could make sure Kennedy was safe without alerting Isabella that I hadn't left town.

I opened up the soggy map that Isabella had dropped at my feet. *You horrible witch.* It was a map of the city, but she'd crossed out tons of landmarks to make it harder to figure out where I was. I didn't see a single bus station listed either. And even if there had been one, it would have been hard to decipher because across the map in big bolded letters, she'd written SORRY NOT SORRY.

What is wrong with her? I turned the map in my hands, trying to find something that made sense. She'd said 10 blocks, right? I scanned the map again, squinting in the dark. There was no bus station listed that I could make out. Unless it was one of the things she'd crossed out. And I didn't even know where the hell I was, so I had no idea which direction to start walking. Knowing Isabella, she probably dropped me in the middle of nowhere.

I heard a crashing noise behind me and spun around. "Hello?" I pulled the map in front of me, even though I was more worried about being murdered than showing off my underwear.

There was no response.

A bus station was fairly safe. An abandoned parking lot surrounded by rundown industrial buildings? Not so much. Another crashing noise made me turn around again. There was nothing there. But I'd heard it. I backed away slowly and tripped over something. Whatever it was sliced into my skin as I fell onto the hard pavement.

Damn it. I looked down at the line of blood on my ankle. I was naked and bleeding and now I had tetanus. I heard another loud noise and tried not to cry out. If there was someone out there, I didn't want them to know where I was. I'd already called hello like an idiot. I stayed low and crawled away from the spot. Staying low was good. That was a thing, I was pretty sure. Or was it serpentining? *Ow.* My left knee just nicked something too.

I looked down and something glinted in the moonlight. Peeking out the top of my bra was the keycard that James had given me. *Oh thank God.* It felt like a miracle. How had I forgotten about the keycard? James being an asshole was the best thing that had ever happened to me! Now I had somewhere to go that was safe. I could head back to the hotel.

How long had we been driving since leaving homecoming? Twenty minutes maybe? In New York traffic that was like…just a few miles, right? I could get back to the hotel and ask James for help. As far as I was concerned, he owed me. I could swear him to secrecy so he wouldn't tell Isabella I was still in New York. It was the perfect plan.

I didn't know where I was, but I'd recognize something eventually. I just needed to start moving. And I needed to get as far away from here as possible.

I looked behind me to make sure I couldn't see anyone. The coast was clear. I pushed myself up and started running as fast as I could. Luckily for me, I'd been training for my mile run in gym class. If I could just figure out how to get back to the hotel, everything would be fine. And maybe if I ran fast enough, I wouldn't get arrested for public indecency.

***

I ducked into an alley a few buildings away from the hotel. New York was nothing like Delaware. Apparently a girl running through the city in a makeshift dress made out of a soggy map in the middle of October wasn't such a strange sight. The lack of shoes and blood didn't phase them either. For the most part, everyone just ignored me. A few people laughed and rolled their eyes like I was the new crazy lady in town. A few men whistled at me, which made me increase my pace. But mostly, I was ignored. Or maybe they'd called the cops on me and I was just gone before they'd arrived. All I knew was that if I'd run around like this back home, I would have been arrested for sure.

I'd be sitting in a jail cell...*safely*. Crap, was that a better plan than sneaking into the hotel? At least I'd be safe and warm in jail. But I'd be in jail...

I tightened the map around my naked body as I peered around the corner at the hotel. I just needed to think this through. I couldn't run into anyone from the dance or they might alert Isabella. But as I tried to come up with a plan on how to get in, my mind felt as frozen as the rest of me. I shivered as I stared at the front entrance. Trying to get a cop to notice me and lock me up was looking like a pretty good choice as I stared at the ornate doors.

The doors. There were more entrances to the hotel than just the main lobby. The first time I'd been to this hotel, I'd gone around to the staff entrance. I wasn't sure why I hadn't thought of it before. Probably because I was exhausted and cold and minutes away from just curling up to cry myself to sleep in a dumpster. *Stop.* I was not dumpster diving tonight. I was going to go to James' room and demand he let me stay there for the night. Just until I knew for sure Kennedy was home safe. It was a great plan.

I tried to stand up a little straighter and the map slipped out of my hands. *Oops.* I pulled it back around me as I made my way out onto the sidewalk. I walked as fast as I could up to the hotel and then made a quick left down the side alley.

I almost started crying when I saw the door propped open. The last time I'd been in the kitchen it had been hot. They were probably excited to have the frigid autumn breeze coming in. I ducked inside. I wasn't surprised that I didn't see anyone. There'd only be a few stragglers on cleaning duty this late. I looked around for an apron or a chef jacket or something to cover myself better. But there was nothing in sight. My map dress would have to do.

I opened the door to the ballroom and immediately closed it. There were still students slow dancing. Was this the never-ending homecoming from hell? I took a deep breath and looked down the hall. This kitchen had to connect to more than just the ballroom. I made my way down the hall, checking door after door until I reached a staircase. *Thank God.*

As I climbed the stairs all I could think about was room 315. I kept saying it over and over again. My thighs screamed from overexertion. My body was still shaking from the cold even though the stairwell was warm. And when I reached the third floor I did everything I could to hold back my tears. I was so freaking close.

I pushed open the door but immediately pulled it shut when I saw someone I recognized. It was one of the football players that had danced with Matt. *I think.* I pushed the door open again, slower this time, and peered down the hall. The football player was opening up a door and the girl next to him was laughing.

Was this whole floor filled with students from Empire High? I bit the inside of my lip. If one of them saw me, it would ruin everything. Isabella couldn't know that I was here. I couldn't risk Kennedy's safety. Maybe it would be better to just stay in this stairwell all night. I looked behind me to see if there was anywhere I could hide out.

Oh my God. I'd left a trail of bloody footprints behind me. Leading from the kitchen all the way to this floor. It would only be a matter of time before someone followed this mess. I got down on my hands and knees and tried to wipe up the blood, but it just smeared everywhere. And more blood got onto the pristine floors from my knee.

It took every ounce of strength I had left to push myself back up to my feet. And now that I knew how cut up the soles of my feet were, each step hurt. But I couldn't stay here all night. I was a sitting duck. I peered into the third floor again. The football player and his date were still talking outside his hotel door.

Come on. Just get in there already! Didn't he know how to close the deal? He just needed to tell her how pretty she was. Promise not to lie to her or pretend she was invisible. Basically just act like Matt minus the whole Isabella blackmail thing. I stared daggers at the happy couple.

"Hello?" Someone's voice echoed in the stairwell. "Is someone in here?"

Shit balls!

I heard their footsteps getting louder as they made their way up to me.

I looked back out at the third floor. That stupid couple was still standing there. *Damn it.* I had to get to James' room right this second before I got kicked out of the hotel. I could only imagine how many students would see me as I was dragged out kicking and screaming.

Close the deal already! I silently cursed at the couple who didn't even see me.

The footsteps were getting closer.

God, it was now or never. I didn't know either of them. At least it wasn't one of Isabella's minions. Hopefully they wouldn't recognize me. Besides, I didn't exactly look like myself. I reached up and touched my hair. My loose curls had transformed into a messy rat's nest during my run. And I could only imagine what my face looked like. Justin's promise of my makeup lasting until midnight probably didn't take into account that I'd be crying and running around.

I took a deep breath and ran out onto the third floor, clutching my map dress to my skin. I ran as fast as I could, biting down on my lip so I wouldn't scream from how much my feet hurt.

They stared at me like I was crazy.

"Oh my God, is that a prostitute?" the girl said in a disgusted voice.

There was so much wrong with her statement. First…slut shaming. What a jerk. And second…didn't prostitutes look classy? I was literally bleeding on the floor with no clothes or shoes. I looked homeless. If anything, I was a beat-up prostitute. They should have been helping me, not staring at me like I was diseased. But if they thought I was a prostitute, at least they didn't know I was a fellow student. My best bet was to play along so they wouldn't recognize me.

"Yes, I'm a prostitute!" I said as I searched for room 315. "You caught me!" I glanced at the door next to me. 302. I was close. I picked up my pace. Fortunately room 315 was still pretty far away from them. I stopped in front of the door and pulled the keycard out of my bra. The map slipped again and I held it to my stomach, not even caring anymore. "I'm having sexy time with the gentleman in this room. So stop staring at me and let me do my job."

The football player laughed and the girl looked disgusted. But neither of them seemed to know who I was.

"Isn't that James' room?" the girl asked.

I ignored them. But I was relieved that I'd remembered the number correctly. I didn't waste any time knocking. Any second now they could figure out who I was. I slid the keycard into the door and shoved it open. I stumbled into the room.

But instead of breathing a sigh of relief for being safe, I threw my hand over my mouth at the scene in front of me. *Kill me now.*

CHAPTER 2

Saturday

Rachel was kneeling in front of James. His fingers were buried in her hair, guiding her head up and down as he lazily stared down at her. His shirt was still on, but the buttons were undone. He was basically fully clothed, his pants just unzipped enough for Rachel. But Rachel was completely naked.

My pain and exhaustion morphed to horror. *I shouldn't be seeing this. I can't be here.* But I stood there frozen. Where the hell else was I supposed to go? I opened my mouth, but no words came out.

The door closed with a thud behind me.

James looked up. For a second we just locked eyes and neither of us said a word. Rachel kept bobbing up and down.

James groaned, his fingers tightening in Rachel's hair. He closed his eyes, as if he thought he'd just envisioned me and I wasn't actually standing there. Which apparently just turned him on. Because his breathing grew heavier.

Oh God, why am I watching this? I backed up until my butt hit the door.

James opened his eyes. And then blinked. And blinked again. He suddenly didn't look so relaxed. He lowered both his eyebrows. "Brooklyn?"

I was pretty sure Rachel said, "What the fuck?" But it was mumbled because her mouth was full.

"What the hell!" James yelled, as he pulled away from Rachel. He grabbed himself and stared down at her. "Did you just bite me?"

Rachel stood up and poked him hard in the middle of his chest. "You said *her* name. Are you freaking kidding me? You were thinking about her when I was…"

"She's standing right there." He grimaced, still holding his junk.

I wanted to laugh. I wanted to cry. I wanted to be anywhere in the world rather than here as Rachel turned toward me and screamed at the top of her lungs. She flung herself on the bed, trying to wrap herself in the sheets.

"Shit," James said under his breath, looking down at himself.

"I'm so sorry," I croaked. "I'll just…" I couldn't leave. I didn't have anywhere else to go. I put my hand out in front of me, blocking them from my sight. But it was a little late for that.

"What the hell are you doing in here?" Rachel screamed. "Get out!"

"I'm sorry," I said again. "I…"

"How the hell did you even get in here? Oh my God, James, did you give her a key to our room?"

"I thought you slept with Matt," he said, his voice laced with pain.

"It was just one kiss. It didn't mean anything! I told you that! And instead of believing me, you were going to sleep with *her*? Are you kidding me right now?"

I lowered my hand slightly to make sure she wasn't about to attack me.

She had pulled the comforter around her and was staring at me like she was going to kill me. "Get out of here you slut!"

The word was a punch in my gut. First a prostitute. Now a slut? I was in pain. I could barely stand. How could she not see that? How could everyone have just ignored me on the street like I was nothing? It was all too much. Her unkind words made me burst into tears.

"Are you deaf?" she screamed.

I closed my eyes. Maybe if I closed them tight enough I could wake up somewhere else. Why did I think I could just come in here? Of course he'd be with Rachel. They'd made up. *Let this all be a dream. Please, please.*

"Rachel, cut it out," said James as he zipped his pants up.

"Excuse me?"

"She's hurt, Rachel."

"I don't care if she's…"

"She's bleeding," he said. "Just sit down and give me a minute to figure out what the hell is going on."

This isn't happening. It's just a bad dream. I didn't just see any of that.

"What happened?" James asked as he gripped my shoulders.

I jumped. I didn't realize he was right in front of me. I couldn't get the words out. I couldn't breathe through my tears.

"Brooklyn, what happened?" His hands were on my face, trying to get me to focus on him.

"Don't you dare touch her again, James," Rachel said. "I swear to God."

He didn't listen to her. He just stared at me, his hands still on my cheeks.

And for some reason his kindness made me cry harder.

"You're safe, Brooklyn," James said. "Talk to me." His hands were too gentle on my face. It was such a contrast to everything I'd experienced in the last hour.

I just wanted to go curl into a ball on the floor and sleep. I couldn't speak. The words wouldn't come. I tried to pull the map back up to cover my exposed bra. As if that would make this situation any better.

He was staring at me so intensely. "Did Matt do this?"

What? "No." I finally found my voice. "Isabella. It was Isabella."

"Jesus." He let go of my face. He stepped around me and grabbed the door handle.

"What are you doing? You can't leave. You can't tell Isabella I'm here. She has Kennedy. She said she'd kill Kennedy if I didn't leave town. She can't know I'm still here. She had a gun. And a bomb." It sounded so ridiculous that I thought he'd just laugh and tell me to leave and stop ruining his night. That he'd just ignore me like everyone else.

Instead, he shook his head. "Isabella's always been nuts, but she's officially lost her mind."

Had she ever had it? "I don't know what to do." I wiped the tears from my cheeks, but it was no use. My eyes weren't nearly as dehydrated as the rest of me. "I didn't have anywhere else to go. I'm so sorry, James. I didn't know that you'd be..." my voice trailed off.

"It's homecoming," Rachel said. "Of course he'd be with his girlfriend."

He ran his hand through his hair so roughly that I was surprised he didn't pull any out.

"Mr. Pruitt..." He took a step back. "Mr. Pruitt was in the lobby causing a scene right before we came up here. I didn't hear what he was yelling about. But he's probably still here. Let me call downstairs." He ran over to the hotel phone.

"Where the heck is my dress?" Rachel said as she looked under the bed. Then she turned to me. "Can't you wait outside?"

I shook my head. "I can't leave. I can't risk Isabella finding out that I'm still in town."

"James, do you seriously believe her?" Rachel asked. "She's probably just trying to get your attention. You led her on."

Oh come on. Like I'd do this to get James' attention, when I already had it fully clothed earlier tonight.

He was still on the phone and he held up his finger to her.

She cursed under her breath. "This is the freaking worst night ever," she said. She abandoned looking for her dress and walked over to the door. "Move."

I shook my head. "You can't leave."

"You don't get to tell me what to do," Rachel said. "You don't get to kiss my boyfriend at homecoming and then come in here demanding his attention. Haven't you already done enough damage for one night?"

Hadn't she? And she was being awfully territorial when she was the one that had cheated on him.

"Rachel, you can't go," James said. "This isn't a joke. She said Isabella had a gun and a bomb."

Rachel laughed and lifted her hands in the air. "A bomb? Seriously? Where would a prissy high school girl get a bomb? It doesn't even make any sense. I don't know Isabella very well, but she doesn't seem like some insane evil villain to me. I only hate her because your mother loves her and is always trying to gently nudge you two together. But that doesn't mean Isabella is a monster. It means your mom is. God, why are we even talking about this right now?"

I had no idea why we were talking about James' mother right now. This felt like a private conversation. Could tonight be any more awkward?

"You brought it up," James said. "You know I don't like Isabella. We've talked about this a million times."

Rachel glared at him. "All I know is that Brooklyn kissed you. And either she goes, or I do."

"Brooklyn isn't leaving. And neither are you," James said and grabbed her arm. "You're not even wearing any clothes, babe."

"Which is apparently your thing," she said and gestured toward me.

"Come on, Rachel."

"No." She took a step away from him. "I can't believe you're taking her side. This…you…ugh!" she screamed. She turned in a circle looking for her dress again. "And where is my dress?!"

"It's in the bathroom," James said.

Rachel started toward the bathroom door.

"Yeah, I kissed her," James said. "And I gave her a keycard to *my* room. Because you cheated on me, Rachel. And our relationship has nothing to do with the fact that Brooklyn's in trouble."

"You're full of shit. You're just trying to torture me." She shifted the comforter on her body so she could fit through the bathroom door and slammed it behind her.

James cringed.

"I'm sorry," I said. "I'm so..."

"Don't." James ran his hand through his hair. "Don't apologize when you haven't done anything wrong." He looked down at my bloody knee and grabbed a tissue from the table behind him. "The front desk said Mr. Pruitt was still there. He'll be up in just a minute." He leaned down and put the tissue against my knee. "I'd say we should clean up that cut, but I guess Rachel's hogging the bathroom." He laughed, but it sounded forced.

"James, I didn't mean to ruin your relationship. I..."

"You didn't ruin anything. We're going to be fine."

"It doesn't seem like you guys are fine."

He shrugged. "Well, maybe she shouldn't have cheated on me." He was acting like he didn't care, but I could tell that he did.

"I really do think it was just a kiss," I said. "I don't think she slept with Matt."

He shook his head. "Does it really matter? How would you feel if you found out Matt was kissing someone else while you were dating?"

I swallowed hard. I had kissed someone while I was kind of dating Matt. Was that the same as this? Rachel was upset and went to Matt. I was upset and went to Miller. My stomach churned. "It sounds like she's sorry. Maybe you should give her the benefit of the doubt. Besides, didn't you get even?"

"I love her. I love her so fucking much and she betrayed my trust. I'd have to do a lot more to get even."

"That doesn't sound very healthy."

"I didn't say I was going to do it." He lowered his eyebrows again. "Are you seriously analyzing my relationship right now? You're the one that came here instead of going to Matt. Maybe your relationship is as unhealthy as mine."

"Matt lives outside the city. It would have taken me forever to walk to his house."

James stared at me. "You still chose to come to me."

"Because I had your keycard."

"You still chose me."

I laughed.

"That," he said. He reached up and lightly touched the bottom of my chin. "That. Don't let Isabella ever take that away from you."

I swallowed hard. "Take what away?"

"Your happiness. Your hope." His eyes drifted to my lips. "Your innocence."

My heartbeat kicked up a notch.

He closed his eyes for a second, his eyebrows drawn together. "I want to kiss you again," he whispered. "And I don't know if it's because I like you. Or because I want to make Rachel feel like I did when she kissed Matt. Or because you remind me of what Rachel was like when we first met. Before my world corrupted her. Or because I'm still mad at her. Or if it's because you're hurt. I don't know why." He opened his eyes and they bore into mine. "But I want to."

I stared back at him. "Making a second mistake doesn't right the first one."

"Kissing you wasn't a mistake, Brooklyn."

Yes it was. "I was actually referring to Rachel kissing Matt."

"You really think it was just one kiss?" he asked. "You really believe him?"

"I do."

James' eyes travelled back to my lips. "I don't. I don't trust a word out of his mouth. And I still want to kiss you."

I knew he didn't mean it. He was just hurting. "I think you're just scared that Rachel doesn't love you back anymore," I said. I knew the feeling. I was currently worried that Matt wouldn't love me back once I told him about Miller. "And maybe you think I could fix that feeling. But I can't."

"Maybe you could."

I looked up at him. "I'm not going to kiss you again. But I won't turn down a hug. I could really use one."

He laughed. "Yeah. I can do that." He pulled me into his arms. "You're going to be okay, Brooklyn. I've got you. Everything is going to be okay."

I didn't know if anything would ever be okay again. A revenge kiss hadn't made James feel any better. Would revenge against Isabella be just as bitter? I wasn't sure if I cared if it was. I wanted her to feel the same way I had tonight. I wanted her to suffer.

"You're safe now," he whispered against my ear.

I wasn't safe. I wasn't sure I'd be safe unless Isabella died before she had a chance to kill me. But I wasn't a murderer. I wasn't her. So why did I so badly want her to die? I closed my eyes tight. I just wanted to wake up from this nightmare. I wanted to be back home with my mom. I wanted to rewind time.

A loud bang on the door made me jump. *Oh God. What if Isabella had already found me?*

CHAPTER 3

Saturday

I backed away from James and the door. "How did she find me?" It felt like my lungs wouldn't inflate. Was Kennedy okay? Had Isabella already gotten rid of her? *I can't breathe.*

James put his hands out like he was dealing with a crazy animal instead of me. "It's probably just Mr. Pruitt, Brooklyn. The front desk said he would be right up."

Whoever it was started knocking harder and I jumped.

"It's okay," James said.

It sounded like someone was hitting the door with a gun. "No, it's her. James, don't answer. Please just let me spend the night. Please." I was gasping for air. I shouldn't have let him call downstairs. Isabella had eyes and ears everywhere. She knew. She freaking knew.

He lowered his eyebrows. "Brooklyn, it's okay."

I tried to tighten my map around me, but instead it started to tear down the middle. *Shit.* I didn't want to die half-naked in James' hotel room. Everyone would actually remember me as a prostitute. I didn't want that to be my legacy.

James moved toward the door.

"No! You can't." *I couldn't breathe.*

He looked out the peephole. “It’s one of Mr. Pruitt’s bodyguards.”

Oh my God, it was probably Donnelley. Isabella must have sent him to finish me off. “Don’t answer it.”

“Brooklyn, you’re being ridiculous. He’s here to take you home.”

“I can’t go home! She’ll kill me!” How was he not getting this?

“It’s fine,” James said. And then he completely ignored my pleas and grabbed the door handle.

“Please, James. I’ll do whatever you want. Just don’t answer the door. I’ll kiss you, okay? Don’t answer the door and I’ll kiss you.”

“I’m not going to kiss you when you’re freaking out. Let’s put a pin in that for now.” He started to open the door.

Had he lost his damned mind? I would have run into the bathroom to hide if Rachel wasn’t already hiding out in there. So I did the first thing I could think of and ducked behind one of the curtains. My heart was beating so fast, I swore it was the only thing I could hear.

“Where is she?” said a deep voice.

Donnelley. I didn’t know him that well, but it sounded like him to me. Isabella had sent him to kill me. I threw my hand over my mouth so he wouldn’t hear me crying.

There was a long pause.

“I don’t know where she went,” James said. “She was right here a second ago. Brooklyn? It’s okay, you can come out."

Right into Donnelley’s trap? *No freaking way.* I felt behind me for the latch to the window, but I couldn’t find one. Wasn't this a fire hazard? What kind of fancy hotel made their rooms death traps?

"Brooklyn," Donnelley said. "You can come out. I'm not here to hurt you."

Like hell you're not. Why was he doing this? I let Isabella abandon me in that parking lot in part to keep his secret. I ran miles in my bra to protect him. And now he was going to kill me? *Fuck this guy.*

I could hear footsteps getting closer to my hiding spot.

No. No, no, no. I was too young to die. But I knew better than to believe that. Life could be cut short. And I was going to do my best to hold on a little longer. I tried to take a gulp of air and my throat made a squeaking noise. *Crap.*

The curtain flew open and Donnelley was standing there frowning at me with what I assumed was a murderous expression.

Not today. I did the first thing I could think of and threw my map at his face.

He yelled and I slipped past him.

"What are you doing?!" James yelled.

Donnelley lunged for me and I dodged him by hopping onto the bed.

"Brooklyn, he's here to help," James said. He was staring at me like I was crazy.

And maybe I was. I was jumping on James' bed in my underwear. I looked over at James and he was staring at my breasts as I jumped. *What the hell is happening?* I had no idea how my night had turned into this. But I couldn't trust Donnelley. He was an extension of Isabella. That conclusion wasn't crazy. It just made logical sense.

Donnelley tore the map from his face and ran to the side of the bed. I bounced to the other side and tossed a pillow at him to slow him down.

"Get down," James said, his eyes still focused on only one part of me.

Good idea. I threw another pillow at Donnelley and then leapt off the bed. James sidestepped and caught me in his arms.

"Calm down," he said.

His voice was so calm. Normally I would have found it soothing. But not when I was about to die.

I pushed him off of me, knocking him back into Donnelley.

"Brooklyn!" James yelled.

"What is going on out here?" Rachel shrieked as she reemerged from the bathroom fully dressed.

"Get back in there! Save yourself!" I gasped as I ran past Rachel and out into the hall.

"Stop telling me what to do!" she yelled back. "James! Don't you dare go after her!"

I looked both ways to see which way I should make my escape. That stupid football player who couldn't close the deal was still standing there with his girlfriend. It didn't really matter if they saw me again.

The girl gasped. "What did James do to her?"

High school gossip was the last thing on my mind as I sprinted down the hall. Let them think the worst. They already thought I was a prostitute.

"Stop!" Donnelley yelled from behind me.

"Brooklyn come back!" James said from somewhere closer behind me.

I looked over my shoulder. James was running down the hall after me. I felt bad for running from him. But if I stopped for him, I stopped for Donnelley.

"Brooklyn!" James yelled. "What the hell are you doing? I'm trying to help you!"

His voice was so close. He was going to catch me. I ran toward the stairs, gasping for air. Everything hurt, but my chest hurt the most. I tried to take a deep breath like Rob had told me to do when I was panicking earlier tonight. But I couldn't. My vision was starting to blur.

I ran into the stairwell. Someone was cleaning up my bloody footprints. They didn't look pleased that I was leaving a trail of more footprints. But they could have also been frowning at me for running around in my underwear. I didn't freaking know and I didn't freaking care.

I heard his bucket topple over and I just hoped it was Donnelley tripping over it instead of James.

I picked up my pace and ran down the stairs as fast as I could. When I reached the first floor, there was someone dressed in a rent-a-cop outfit coming toward me from the kitchen hall. I couldn't trust a hotel security guard any more than I could trust Donnelley.

But I hesitated a moment too long.

James grabbed my arm. "What are you running from? Donnelley came to take you home."

"He's in on it, James. He's the one that was driving. He left me there."

"Fuck."

We both looked up the stairs. We could hear Donnelley's footsteps, but we couldn't see him.

"This way." James opened the door to the main part of the hotel. His hand slipped into mine as we ran down the hall. We turned left and his fingers tightened around mine. We ran down another hall until we ended up running into the lobby.

Shit. "Someone from school will see us," I said and tried to take a step back. But then I saw the only face that I knew for sure would help me. Mr. Pruitt was arguing with the man at the front desk. His suit coat was wrinkled and his hair was askew. He looked a mess. And I said the first thing that popped into my head. "Dad." My voice cracked as my tears spilled down my cheeks.

His eyes softened at the name.

I let go of James' hand and ran into the lobby.

He ran over to me. "Sweetheart." He pulled me into his arms. "I thought you were dead." His voice was raspy, like he'd been crying too. "I thought I lost you." He kissed the top of my head as he held me tight. "Thank God you're alright."

I buried my face in his chest. "Dad." It was suddenly the only word I knew.

"You're okay." He kissed the top of my head again. "I'm here now."

I knew I was safe as long as I was with him. But I wasn't worried about me. "She's going to kill Kennedy. She's going to kill Kennedy." I kept saying it over and over again.

He must have seen the bloody footprints, because he yelled, "Someone call an ambulance!"

"No." I wiggled out of his grip. "Isabella can't know. She'll kill Kennedy. She'll kill her if she knows I'm still here."

"Isabella's not going to hurt anyone," he said. He turned his attention to James. "Why would you let her run around like this?" He pulled off his suit jacket and draped it over my shoulders.

"I'm sorry," James said.

"I said call an ambulance!" my dad snapped at the man staring at us from the front desk.

"She has Kennedy," I said. "I can't go to a hospital. She can't know I'm here. She'll know."

"Mr. Pruitt," James said. "Brooklyn said Isabella had a gun. And a bomb."

"I'm taking care of it," replied my dad.

Donnelley ran into the lobby too. "There you guys are."

I took a step back. "Stay away from me! He's in on it! He's in on it." I leaned over. "I can't breathe."

"She's having a panic attack," James said.

"Donnelley, you're scaring her." My dad stepped in front of me, blocking Donnelley from my view. "You're okay, sweetheart. I'm here. I'll never let anything happen to you."

"Let me help," Donnelley said.

"You've done enough," Mr. Pruitt said. "I'll deal with you later."

"But…"

"Go home right now if you want to be breathing in the morning." The kind voice he'd used with me was completely gone.

"The ambulance is ten minutes away," the man at the front desk said.

A few students started filtering out of the ballroom to see what all the commotion was about. All their eyes were on me.

"She can't know that I'm here," I said. "They'll tell her. She'll kill Kennedy."

"You're okay, sweetheart. You're okay now."

"She can't." I was gasping for air.

"Okay." Mr. Pruitt lifted me up in his arms. "I'll get you out of here." He pulled his phone out of his pocket and handed it to James. "Call number three on my speed dial."

I closed my eyes tight. I just wanted to be invisible again.

"You're okay now, princess," my dad said.

Princess. It was his nickname for Isabella. For his legitimate daughter. And for some reason, him using it for me made me feel so loved. Maybe I didn't want to be invisible to him. I could get used to having a dad. As long as number three on his speed dial wasn't something terrible.

CHAPTER 4

Saturday

The elevator doors dinged open. My dad carried me into his secret apartment. The only other time I'd been here had been when I first learned that I was a Pruitt. I'd spent the entire night completely terrified. But it didn't seem scary this time. I'd choose to be here any day over his actual apartment. The naked walls and sterile feel of everything was comforting as long as Isabella wasn't allowed in here. Maybe he'd just let me stay.

"Where are we?" James asked.

"Somewhere safe," replied my dad.

I kept waiting for him to tell James to get lost, but he didn't. And I was a little relieved James was still here. The whole car ride over, James had held my hand and told me to breathe while my dad drove like a mad man. *Just breathe.* I wasn't sure why James had come with us. He should have been fixing things with Rachel, not worrying about me.

My dad carried me down the hall and into the bathroom.

"James, will you stay with her? I need to make a few calls." He'd already talked to whoever was number three on his speed dial. But I hadn't been able to make out any of their conversation on the ride over here, because I'd been gasping for air.

"Yeah," James said. "No problem."

My dad set me down on my feet and I cringed.

"It's going to be okay," my dad said and lightly touched my cheek. "Just keep taking deep breaths like James said. I'll take care of everything." His hand fell from my cheek.

"You mean Kennedy? You'll make sure she's okay?" I asked.

"I won't let anything happen to your friend. You have my word."

I trusted his word. I just didn't trust that Isabella hadn't already done something terrible. He pulled out his phone and left James and me alone in the bathroom.

James reached into the shower to turn it on.

"Can I have a minute?" I said. My voice was barely a whisper. The last thing I needed was for James to actually see me naked. I was already mortified enough.

"Of course." James walked to the door. "I'll be right outside. Call for me if you need anything."

I nodded and he disappeared out the door, leaving it open a crack.

I didn't wait for the water to warm up. I just needed this day off of me. I pushed my dad's suit jacket off my shoulders and walked into the water with my bra and panties still on. I pressed my back against the wall and let myself cry. The water burned the scratches on my knee and the gash on the back of my ankle. And the bottoms of my feet. I whimpered and slid down the wall until my butt hit the cold tiled floor.

I didn't know if Kennedy was okay. I didn't know if Isabella knew I was still in the city. I didn't know how my dad had found me. I didn't even know if I was okay. Everything hurt. My muscles ached. The water in my cuts burned. I put my hand over my mouth to stifle my sobs. How the hell did I wind up here?

Just breathe. Of all the things that hurt, my chest ached the most. I wasn't sure if it was my lungs or my heart. I just felt broken. I let the water cascade down on top of me, washing away my tears. The water ran red with blood down the drain. I hugged my knees to my chest and let myself cry.

I heard a noise and looked up.

James climbed into the shower fully clothed and sat down next to me. He was even wearing his shiny dress shoes. His arm brushed against mine. "You're okay, Brooklyn."

"Why are you helping me?"

He smiled, not at all phased by the water falling on us. "I think I already made it clear that I like you."

"You're in love with Rachel."

He sighed and leaned his head back against the tile wall. He didn't have to say it. I knew what he was thinking. That maybe she didn't love him.

"And maybe I still feel bad about what happened at lunch when Isabella told everyone you were related to Jim. It was your secret to share if you wanted to. I had no right to tell Isabella. Especially since I knew she'd tell the whole school." He looked over at me. "I swear I didn't know about your mom. Not that that's an excuse. I shouldn't have threatened you."

"You already apologized for that."

"It doesn't mean I stopped feeling bad about it. I feel like shit." He laughed. "I always feel like shit." He hit his head against the tile wall again and sighed.

"Well, I think you've more than made up for it." I laughed, but it sounded strange in my throat. "You don't have to sit here with me. You should go back to the hotel and try to fix things with Rachel. She's probably furious with you."

He shrugged, his arm brushing against mine again. "That can wait. My friend needs me."

I looked over at him. "Friend?"

"Yeah, I guess. Since you won't kiss me." He smiled at me. "Besides, it just so happens I have an opening for some new friends."

Matt and Mason. Thinking about the Caldwells and Hunters fighting just made my chest ache even more.

He reached up and grabbed a bar of soap. "Do friends soap each other up naked in the shower?" He raised his left eyebrow.

I laughed for real this time. "No they do not." I grabbed the soap from him and looked down at my scratched knees. This was going to be painful.

"Maybe they soap each other up clothed then." He took the bar of soap back from me. "Take a deep breath, this is going to hurt."

I pressed my lips together and he ran a soapy hand across my knee. For some reason it wasn't so bad when he did it for me. He ran the soap down my legs. The bottoms of my feet stung the worst.

"You're okay," he whispered. I barely heard his words over the falling water. "You're okay."

It had been a long time since I had felt so cared for. Probably not since the last time I was sick when my mom was still healthy. She used to let me rest my head on her lap as she combed her fingers through my hair. I was glad we were in the shower so that my tears mixed with the water. She used to sing to me. And I could barely remember what her voice sounded like. How could I forget her voice? How could my mind be missing such an important piece of information? It was like she was drifting farther away every day.

"All clean," James said. "Unless you want me to get your upper half." He raised his eyebrow again.

I laughed. "I think I can handle that." I took the soap back and dropped my head to make sure he couldn't see me crying. For some reason my arms were tired too. The soap felt like a brick in my hands. "Who was number three on my dad's speed dial?"

"Some doctor. You said you didn't want to go to the hospital. So I think he's having the hospital come to you."

That was sweet of him. And I was already emotional, so it just made me cry harder.

James tapped the bottom of my chin so I'd look up at him. "Come here."

"Come where?"

He patted his lap and then opened up his arms. His shirt was soaking wet, clinging to the muscles in his chest and arms. "Let's be miserable together."

Misery did love company. But instead of crawling onto his lap, which it seemed like he wanted, I rested my head against his shoulder. He pulled me closer. And we sat like that until the water ran cold. Him just holding me.

***

I pulled on the pair of pajama bottoms and a tank top that my dad must have left for me. They fit me perfectly. The pajamas were fuzzy and warm and comforting. There were cute little squirrels on them. My mom had loved squirrels. We used to name the ones in our yard. Had she always loved them? Did my dad know that about her too? Was that why he brought me these?

A knock at the door made me jump. "Yes?" I knew I was safe here, but I still pictured Isabella on the other side of the door with a gun.

My dad opened the door. He smiled at my pajamas. "I'm glad they fit. Is there anything else you need?"

I wrapped my arms around myself. I wasn't sure what would make me feel better. But I had a million questions. Was Kennedy okay? Was James still here? Where the hell was Miller?

But before I said anything, Dr. Wilson appeared at the door.

"Dr. Wilson's here to check out your injuries," my dad said. "Do you mind if he comes in?"

I shook my head.

"You should be sitting down," Dr. Wilson said as he walked into the room. "I heard you had quite the night."

You could say that. I sat down on the edge of my bed. For some reason, I felt uneasy around him. The last time I'd seen him, I'd been terrified. But my dad came into the room too and sat down on the bed next to me. Him being here too was reassuring.

"The bottom of her feet are cut up pretty badly," my dad said. "There's another cut on the back of her ankle and her knees were badly scratched. Is she going to be alright?"

"Let's take a look." Dr. Wilson pulled some things out of his bag.

"And James mentioned that she was having a panic attack. He said she couldn't catch her breath. Is that common for someone her age?"

Normally, I would have been horrified by someone talking about my health. But I was exhausted. And something about the way my dad did it made me feel cared for. He knew I was still shaken. I needed him here.

Dr. Wilson put his stethoscope against my chest. "Take a deep breath for me, Brooklyn."

I followed his instructions.

"And another."

I took another deep breath, glad that my lungs seemed to be working again.

"Do you have panic attacks often?" Dr. Wilson asked.

I shook my head. *Not until today.* I was pretty sure I'd had one while I was dancing with Rob, when I was worried Isabella might be planning on killing me. And then again in the lobby when I was worried about Kennedy. I guess Isabella had a way of making me freak out. "No. Just today."

Dr. Wilson nodded. "Have you been under a lot of stress recently?"

"Isabella tried to have her killed," my dad said.

"Ah. Well, that would do it."

I laughed because I didn't know what else to do. Dr. Wilson didn't have much of a reaction to the statement though. Why wasn't he horrified? I swallowed hard. *Oh.* Because he was my dad's doctor. He probably dealt with things like this all the time. Maybe even things like this that had happened because of Isabella.

He pulled the stethoscope down around his neck. "Your heart is racing right now. Are you nervous that I'm here?"

"No, I'm worried." I turned to my dad. "I'm worried about Kennedy. Have you found her?"

"She's safe. When Donnelley brought Isabella and Kennedy home, he pulled me aside right away and told me what happened. Isabella gave Kennedy a pretty strong sedative, and I was hoping she'd wake up before we had this conversation. Last I heard, she's still unresponsive. But she'll wake up soon."

Dr. Wilson nodded. "I was just with her before I came here. I'm sure she'll wake up in a few hours."

I breathed a sigh of relief, suddenly even more tired. Kennedy was okay. She was safe.

My dad patted my knee, keeping his hand there to comfort me. "Right now all you need to know is that Miller is guarding her room. She's perfectly safe. And I promise to tell you as soon as she wakes up."

I tried to hide how relieved I was. Miller was safe. I'd been worried about him too, but I couldn't ask my dad about him without raising suspicion. "And Isabella?"

"I'll deal with her myself." My dad looked back at Dr. Wilson, as if that was the end of the discussion.

Deal with her how?

"Is there anything we can do to make the panic attacks go away?" my dad asked.

"I'd rather start with preventative measures. Maybe you can start keeping a journal when you have panic attacks? Find out what's leading you to…"

"It's Isabella," I said. "I can't breathe when I think about what she's planning. I'm scared all the time."

My dad looked so defeated. "But we'll keep a journal just in case. Yes, princess?"

I nodded. I didn't want him to look so sad. And when he called me that, my chest ached a little less. "Yeah. I can do that."

"Good, good." Dr. Wilson pulled out some bandages from his bag. "I'm going to get you all fixed up." He looked at the cut on the back of my ankle. "Actually that might need stitches. Let me take a better look."

My dad held my hand as I got my stitches. And when I got my tetanus shot, he didn't mind at all when I squeezed his hand so tight that it must have hurt.

"That should do it," Dr. Wilson said as he placed the last bandage along the sole of my foot. "Try to take it easy the next few days. No stress."

"That won't be a problem," my dad said. "She'll be staying here for the foreseeable future."

The foreseeable future? What did he mean by that? I had school on Monday.

"Very well. Make sure to keep that journal, Brooklyn. I'll see myself out." Dr. Wilson's shoes echoed in the empty hall.

"Does it still hurt?" my dad asked.

I wasn't sure what he was talking about specifically. My cuts? My heart?

But then he reached down and inspected the bandage on the back of my ankle.

I knew what he needed to hear. And I knew it would help if he heard the truth. "Everything hurts a little less now than it did before."

He nodded, but he didn't look reassured. "I thought I could protect you." He lifted his hand away from my bandage and ran it down his face. "I never meant to put you in danger. You were safer without me."

I'd never seen him like this. He was always so put together. But tonight? He just seemed…human. I liked this side of him a whole lot better. "I'm glad you found out about me." I was just getting used to him. And I was a little sorry it had taken me so long. He was a good person. I could tell.

He cleared his throat and stood up. "You need to get some rest. And I have a few more things I need to take care of."

"You're not leaving, are you?"

He smiled down at me. "No, I'm not leaving." He pulled the comforter back on the bed, holding it up for me to climb under.

Was he tucking me in? I wasn't a kid anymore, but it warmed my heart. I had a weird feeling that despite having a daughter already, he didn't really know what he was doing. I lay down and he pulled the covers over me. I was reminded of my mom again, tucking me in when I was little. Only he was way more awkward about it. *Is it normal to literally tuck the sides in around my body?* He was wrapping me up like a sausage. But the fact that he had no idea what he was doing just made it that much sweeter.

"Is there anything else you need?" he asked. "Anything at all? Are you hungry? Or…"

"Is James still here?" I wanted to thank him for everything.

He lowered his eyebrows slightly. "No, I sent him home."

That was probably a good thing. James needed to be focusing on his relationship with Rachel.

"Do you want him to come back?" he asked. "I can have someone go pick him up. Just say the word."

I shook my head. "No." I didn't need James right now. "But could you maybe get Matt?" I needed him. I just needed him to hold me like he had the nights after my uncle passed away. I needed his comfort. I wanted him back.

My dad nodded. "I'll make sure he comes." He leaned over and placed a kiss on my forehead. Instead of walking away, he pushed a loose strand of hair out of my face. His fingers slowly ran through my hair.

Even though the pads of his fingers were rough, where my mom's had been soft, it still reminded me of her. I blinked fast, holding back my tears. Had she done this to him too? Comforted him when he was feeling scared or down? "Dad?"

He smiled when I called him that. "Yes?"

"Can you sit with me until I fall asleep?"

He sat down next to me on the bed, his fingers lazily brushing my hair again. "Of course."

I closed my eyes.

It was silly, but it was almost like I could feel my mom next to me. If I focused on it hard enough, I could even smell her perfume. I started to nod off with my dad's fingers untangling my messy hair.

"Go to sleep, princess," he whispered.

If I was his princess, that meant Isabella wasn't. I smiled to myself. I was going to take everything from her.

CHAPTER 5

Sunday

I opened my eyes as the light streamed in through the blinds. I felt disoriented and still tired. But something had woken me. And the first thing that popped into my head was that Isabella was here.

A door squeaked as if the hinges were rusty.

I sat up in bed. Everything in the apartment seemed brand new. So what door could have sounded that way? My heart was pounding as I threw off the covers. I rolled out of bed and stepped down onto the floor. *Ow.* How could my feet possibly hurt more today?

I cringed as I opened the door of my bedroom and peered out. The locked door at the end of the hall was wide open. It felt like my heart was beating in my throat as I tiptoed down the hall. I expected to see Isabella in the room. What I didn't expect was to see a room packed full of furniture and clothes and knickknacks. And my dad sitting on an old couch, his hand on his forehead, the sound of him crying softly.

Richard Pruitt was crumbling. And for some reason it made me more terrified than ever. Was he scared of the monster he created too?

But then the smell hit me harder than it had last night. My mother's perfume. I took a deep breath and my dad looked up.

He turned away from me, wiping at his eyes. "Sorry," he said and stood up. "I was just looking for a journal for you to write in like Dr. Wilson suggested." He picked a journal up off the couch he'd been sitting on.

"What is this?" I walked into the room. It was stuff from a lifetime ago. The couch had a hole in it and was worn from use. Outdated clothes hung on a rack. There was a crochet blanket folded on an end table. I swallowed hard. My mom loved to crochet. And her smell. It was everywhere. It was like I'd walked into the past. Where my mom was still alive. I looked up at Mr. Pruitt.

He was looking down at the journal in his hands. I looked behind me at the completely empty, stark apartment. The stuff in here could have filled this place. It would have made it warm and homey.

"When we were together, your mom lived here," Mr. Pruitt said.

"You kept all her stuff?"

"Just the things she left behind."

The things she left when you paid her to have an abortion. Maybe I should have been mad at him. But how could I be when I thought I just lost every possession my mom ever had? My Keds and her favorite blue dress were in a disgusting abandoned parking lot. This room held so much of her. Pieces of her I never even knew about. I looked down at the squirrel pajamas. They were hers. That's why they smelled like her. I blinked away my tears. "Does anyone else know about this apartment?"

"Just a few members of our staff."

I reached out and touched the blanket. "So not your wife or Isabella?"

He shook his head. "No. This was your mother's place. I couldn't bring them here."

My mom had lived here. Probably thinking she and my dad had a future. He'd said my mother didn't know he was married. She was waiting for him. Starting their lives without realizing he'd never be hers. "Why didn't you sell it when she left?"

He tapped the journal against his thigh. "I thought she might come back."

I pressed my lips together. He still loved her. It felt comforting to know that I wasn't the only one missing her every day. "And what about now? That she's gone?"

"I kind of thought you might want it."

He wanted me to live here? Tucked away? Hidden like he'd hidden my mother from his family? I folded my arms across my chest, suddenly cold. "Did you bring other women here? After my mom left?"

He lowered his eyebrows. "No. Brooklyn, I loved your mom. I never made a habit of straying from my responsibilities. She was…she was it for me." He looked down at the journal in his hands. "But I understand if you don't want it."

"I want it." Of course I wanted it. It felt like my mom was here with me.

"Yeah?" He looked up.

"Mhm." I bit the inside of my lip. "Does that mean you don't want me to come back to your home?"

He smiled. "Our home, princess. No, that's not what I meant at all. I'm adding extra security measures. And hiring a few new staff members."

My mind instantly went to Miller. Was my dad replacing people? Or just adding more members because he was worried about my safety?

"But I'll want you to stay here for a little while until everything's done. If that's okay with you?"

I nodded.

"It'll just be a few days. But I need to make sure I can keep you safe before you return." He handed me the journal that he'd been holding. "Speaking of which, make sure you keep that journal Dr. Wilson requested. Just in case we can pinpoint something else that's causing you to stress."

He didn't want it to be Isabella. But it was. I held the journal to my chest, comforted by the fact that it had belonged to my mom, even if she'd never used it. I nodded my head. "Is Kennedy awake?"

"Yes, and she's already back with Mrs. Alcaraz. She doesn't remember much about last night, which is probably for the best. But she'll be okay. I'll have Dr. Wilson check up on her again today."

"And what about Matt?" I had kind of been expecting him to be here when I woke up.

My dad put his hands in his pockets. "I sent for Matthew like you asked, but when he arrived he was so inebriated that I wouldn't let him up here to our apartment."

Oh God. I forgot about how drunk he'd been at the dance.

"Are you sure you don't like Mason?" he asked. "I really think he's more put together than his brother."

I laughed. "Yes, I'm sure." I doubted my dad knew about Masons' sexual escapades. Not that any of that mattered. I loved Matt. I knew it. I'd seen everything so clearly last night. Felix and Miller would always have a piece of my shattered heart. But Matt? He'd healed it. He was the one who made it easier for me to breathe. I didn't feel like I was drowning when I was with him. He was the light I desperately needed. He made me feel alive. I needed him. I'd always needed him.

"All right. Well, Matthew is waiting downstairs. He refused to leave even though I wouldn't let him up."

That was so sweet. I knew he'd done the same thing after his fallout with James. He'd told me he was worried about him so he'd camped out outside his house. He didn't want him to be alone. But now he was choosing me. He was putting me first.

"Hopefully he's not too hungover," my dad said. "I made it clear to him that he's never allowed to get intoxicated like that around you again. That he needs to always put you first."

Dad.

"I think he got the message since I wouldn't let him up. If you'd like I can make an amendment to the relationship contract that states…"

"That's definitely not necessary." That conversation sounded embarrassing enough. And really Matt was only drunk because I'd made him wait all night for a dance. He'd just been staring at me dancing with tons of other people. I'd never seen Matt drunk before. And honestly, it had been endearing. In his drunkenness, he'd finally given me some answers I needed.

"Alright, princess. But let me know if he gets out of line again and we can circle back to it. Are you hungry? I'm a terrible cook, but I think I can manage to make some eggs. Does that sound okay?"

"That sounds great."

"How about you get back into bed and I'll bring them to you? You really should still be resting."

"Do you mind if I stay in here?"

He gave me a sad smile. "Of course. This couch is actually pretty comfortable."

I sat down on it and took a deep breath. "It smells like her."

My dad lifted up a bottle of perfume off a dresser. "It's her perfume." He handed it to me.

I had no idea what perfume my mom had worn. It was like a little bottle of her. It was the greatest gift he could possibly give me. I spritzed some on my arm and almost cried. It smelled like she was hugging me.

"I didn't know that she still wore it," my dad said.

I looked up at him. "Yeah. I never knew what it was, but she always smelled like this."

He nodded, but he looked so sad. "I bought it for her."

I stared up at him. I wished my mom had told me about him. I wished she'd followed her heart. She had clearly still loved him. And he loved her too. Thinking about how they never crossed paths again broke my heart. Especially because I was the reason that they had a falling out.

He cleared his throat. "Eggs. Well, probably burnt eggs. They'll be right up." He chuckled at his own joke and then left me alone in the room.

I took a deep breath of the perfume. My mom had been here. She'd sat on this very couch. I ran my fingers along the worn fabric. She'd lived here before she had me. Before she got pregnant and moved in with my uncle. Before she ran away to Delaware. Why didn't she want me to know about this part of her life? I looked around the room at all her abandoned memories. She'd given it all up for me. Why?

"Brooklyn?"

I looked up at Matt in the doorway. It was like he didn't realize we were in a time capsule. His bloodshot eyes were focused solely on me. His hair was pushed up in every direction. He looked terrible.

"I'm so sorry." His voice was hoarse. "I'm so sorry that I wasn't there to protect you. I'm so fucking sorry." He stood there like he didn't know what to do. When all I wanted was for him to hold me. He put his fist against his mouth like he was holding back tears.

"It wasn't your fault."

He winced. "I was freaking drunk and you needed me. I'm never there when you need me."

"It's okay."

"It's not." He sat down next to me and stared at me with all the hurt in the world in his eyes. "I keep letting you down."

"You're here now." I hated seeing him upset. Especially over this. None of what happened last night was his fault. Just Isabella's.

"Tell me where it hurts." He was looking at the bandages on my feet. "Tell me everything that happened. Tell me I can make it better." His Adam's apple rose and then fell.

Matt had put me through hell. And I think maybe I had put him through hell too. But us torturing each other ended today. I was just glad he was here. I was glad he was choosing me back. Out loud. Not hidden anymore. Not like my dad had treated my mom.

I climbed onto his lap. "Can you just hold me?" I rested my head against his chest and breathed in his familiar scent. It mixed in the air with my mom's perfume and made me feel so content. I was exactly where I was supposed to be.

I knew I needed to tell him about the past week. About Miller. Even about James. But not right now. I just wanted one minute where I didn't feel awful. And when he held me, I no longer felt like I was sinking. I was all in with him. I just hoped he felt the same way after he knew the truth.

"I'm going to fucking kill her," Matt said.

I believed him. I should have been scared of his words. But I wasn't. The threat was comforting. He finally had my back. I just wasn't sure I deserved it now.

"If she even breathes your name, she's dead." He held me tighter.

I hoped it was a promise. Because even though I felt safe in his arms, I wasn't sure I'd ever truly feel safe as long as Isabella was still breathing.

CHAPTER 6

Sunday

Despite my dad's reservations, he and Matt were getting along well. The three of us were watching the Giants game together. Matt and I were curled up on the couch and Mr. Pruitt had pulled out my mom's old couch so that there was enough seating. It looked weird for my dad to be sitting on it when he was usually so formal. The floral couch also looked weird against all the pristine white. The first thing that I'd do once I moved in was paint all the walls yellow. My mom would have liked that. And I wouldn't have been surprised if they'd been yellow in the first place.

Matt grabbed another slice of pizza. My dad had burned the eggs terribly, but luckily pizza was a perfect back up. Everything about this afternoon just felt...normal.

Except the fact that it wasn't real. This wasn't my dad's real home. I wasn't his real family. And Matt didn't know that I'd kissed Miller. The perfection of this afternoon was just a façade. But I wasn't ready to say goodbye.

"Touchdown!" my dad yelled and high-fived me and Matt.

I smiled and rested my head on Matt's shoulder. Today reminded me of the time Matt met my uncle. We'd all watched a movie together. It had just felt...right. For just a moment everything had been perfect. Right before my whole world had shattered again.

"Are you okay?" Matt whispered.

"Just tired." I wanted to freeze time. I wanted to stay in this safe little bubble forever.

My dad's phone buzzed. He pulled it out. "I should take this. I'll be right back." He got up off the couch.

"Here, you should lie down," Matt said. He shifted on the couch and I lay down, resting my head on his lap. But instead of looking at the TV, I stared up at him.

He traced the dark circles under my eyes. Or maybe he was thinking about how he hadn't been there to wipe my tears away last night. Because the expression on his face was pained.

"I love you," I said.

He smiled, but it looked forced. "I love you too." He ran his hand down the side of my neck. "I don't want you to have to go back to their apartment. I know he's your dad," he whispered. "But I don't trust him. I don't trust them."

My stomach churned. *All the Pruitts are toxic.* That's what he'd said before. Is that what he saw now when he looked at me?

"Come live with me," he said.

Whoa, what? "I can't move in with you."

"Why not?"

"Well, first of all you still live with your parents."

"My mom already loves you."

I laughed. "She doesn't even know me."

"She knows that I love you." His fingers traced my collarbone. "She knows you make me happy."

"I haven't been making you happy recently."

He ran his thumb along my bottom lip. "It's my own fault that I've been unhappy. I didn't put you first. But I won't make that mistake again."

"You said it was because you knew I was strong."

"You are strong. You're the strongest person I know." His hand settled on my cheek. "But I don't remember saying that."

I laughed. "You said it last night when you were drunk."

He laughed. "Well at least I was honest. What else did I say?"

"Oh all sorts of things." I looked up into his chocolaty brown eyes. "You also told me you were secretly in love with Rob."

"What?!"

I laughed. "I'm just kidding." I couldn't resist messing with him. I reached up and ran my hand along the scruff on his jawline. I liked it. He was usually cleanly shaven.

He shook his head. "What did I really say?"

"You said you loved me. You said you were sorry. You explained what really happened with Rachel. You kept saying I was yours."

"You are mine." He lowered his eyebrows as he studied my face. "You're mine, Brooklyn."

I nodded. "You had a whole list of reasons why you loved me. I really liked that list."

"Hmm. I think I remember a few of those things."

"Just a few?"

"A million things is kind of hard to remember."

I felt my cheeks blush. "You also really wanted to sing to me again. And you kept making farting noises with your mouth."

"Well that's another lie. I definitely didn't make farting noises with my mouth in front of you when I was trying to win you back."

"No, all of that was true."

He laughed. "Well, I guess it worked."

I smiled up at him. "It did." I shifted my head and felt him beneath me. I locked eyes with him. "You also said if I wanted to, I could take advantage of you and you wouldn't press charges."

He laughed again. "What the hell is wrong with me?"

"It's probably because of all those naughty dreams you have of me. And all those cold showers you have to take because of me." I could feel the heat in his gaze at my words.

"Well, that's true." His fingers played with the strap of my tank top.

"Yeah?"

"You drive me crazy, Brooklyn. Whenever we're not together, I'm thinking of you."

My stomach churned. I needed to tell him about Miller. I'd tried to tell him last night, but Mason interrupted us. "We also promised that there wouldn't be any more secrets between us," I said.

"That sounds like a good plan." He looked over at my dad talking in the kitchen. "Full disclosure…I'm pretty sure Mr. Pruitt hates me."

"I think it takes him a little while to warm up to people."

"That's one way to put it."

I laughed. "He's just protective of me."

"Pretty sure he just hates me. Last night is fuzzy, but I think he said something about how I should go home and send Mason." He shook his head.

Now I knew what it was like to have an overprotective father. "I don't want to be with your brother. I want to be with you." I swallowed the lump in my throat. "But I need to tell you something."

"Please don't tell me you kissed Mason. I already lost my two best friends. I don't want to fight with my brother too." He rubbed his thumb along my cheek. "I love your freckles."

I smiled underneath his hand. "I didn't kiss Mason. And I love your 5-o'clock shadow."

He lifted his hand and ran it across his jaw. "Yeah?"

"It looks good on you."

"I guess I'll keep it then." He smiled down at me.

"So you really don't remember our conversation at all last night?"

"Just bits and pieces."

"Do you remember that I kissed James?" I cringed as I said it.

"That's a little hard to forget."

This seemed like the best place to start. It was easier to tackle than the Miller thing. I'd gone to James for help. Matt would understand that.

"Did they score again?" my dad asked as he sat back down on the couch.

"Yeah," Matt said, even though he hadn't been watching the game. "Mr. Pruitt?" He looked over at him.

"Yes, Matthew?"

"While you're fixing up the security at your place, could Brooklyn come stay at my house?"

"I don't think that's a good idea."

As much as I loved being surrounded by my mom's old things…I wanted to go with Matt. Mr. Pruitt didn't let boys spend the night. It was one of the only rules I knew. But I had a feeling Matt's house would be different. I missed falling asleep in his arms. I didn't want to have to spend the night here without him. "Please, Dad?"

His eyes softened. "Is that what you want?" he asked.

I nodded.

Mr. Pruitt looked back at Matt. "Do you still have that security system?"

"Yes," Matt said.

"And you'll let me send a few of my own people?"

"I'm sure that will be fine."

"Well, let me call your mother to make sure it's okay. Separate beds though, yes?"

"Of course, sir," Matt said.

I hoped he was lying.

"I'm serious about the sleeping arrangements," Mr. Pruitt said, as if he could read my thoughts.

"As am I," Matt said.

Mr. Pruitt nodded. "I'll call your mother then. Maybe we can head over after the game?"

"That would be great," I said. "And maybe we can swing by Kennedy's to check on her?"

"She's resting. How about you wait to chat with her until tomorrow when she's feeling better?"

"Oh. Okay." I wanted to press it, but he was already letting me stay with Matt. I had to take that win. I just hoped Kennedy was feeling better soon because I missed her terribly.

My father pulled his phone out of his pocket and stood up. "I'll be right back."

"Separate beds?" I whispered up to Matt.

"No. I'm not letting you out of my sight after last night. I just knew your dad wouldn't approve."

A little white lie was worth getting to be back in his arms where I belonged.

He ran his fingers across my bottom lip again. "I swear I'm going to protect you, Brooklyn. Nothing bad is ever going to happen to you again. I promise."

I believed him. He used to lie to me. But there was nothing to lie about now. And as soon as I told him about Miller, we'd have no secrets.

"Miller and Donnelley will be here to drive you over," my dad said.

Oh God.

"I'll want them both to secure the perimeter for the night."

I wasn't sure which was worse. Miller having to escort me to Matt's before I'd had a chance to talk to him, or Donnelley because he was freaking in Isabella's pocket. "But Donnelley..."

"Has been taught a lesson," my dad said. "He won't let anything bad happen to you ever again. And he had valuable information about Isabella's plans. You can trust him. He knows the consequences if he steps out of line again."

I had no idea what he meant by any of that. But I didn't like the sound of it. Especially the fact that *plans* was plural. What else had Isabella been planning?

"You okay?" Matt asked.

"Mhm." But my voice came out weird and high-pitched. I couldn't tell Matt about Miller in front of my dad. Or else Miller would get fired. And I wouldn't get a chance to tell Miller that I was choosing Matt before seeing him. It was a disaster.

***

Oh my God. I stared at Miller who was leaning against the car. His face was barely recognizable. There were so many bruises and cuts. He stared at me like he was dying. And I didn't know if it was because of his physical pain, or if it was just killing him to see me with Matt.

I looked at Donnelley in the driver seat. If anything, he looked worse. *Is that what it looks like when Mr. Pruitt teaches someone a lesson?* A chill ran down my spine. And why had he done it to Miller? Or had someone else done that to Miller last night? He'd disappeared. I'd thought he was mad at me…but what if he'd been in trouble? He'd needed me and I hadn't been there.

"You okay?" Matt asked and slipped his hand into mine.

The look on Miller's face said it all. He was angry and sad and hurt. So freaking hurt.

I looked down at my feet. "Yeah."

"Miller and Donnelley, check out the Caldwells' security system," my dad said. "If there are any weak points, notify me right away. Otherwise, I expect you to do surveillance for the evening. And Brooklyn needs her rest, so she won't be going to school tomorrow. You bring her right back here in the morning."

"I'm skipping school tomorrow," Matt said. "To take care of her."

My dad nodded and turned back to Miller. "Very well. I'll have someone switch out with you two in the morning. Got it?"

"Yes sir," Miller said.

My dad leaned down and hugged me. "If you need anything, call me," he said. "Anything at all, okay?"

"Okay." My voice sounded strangled. I wanted to yell at him for what he had done to Donnelley and maybe Miller too. But I didn't know what to say.

He kissed my cheek and then climbed into his town car.

Matt grabbed the back door and opened it when Miller didn't move. "After you," he said with a smile.

I didn't move. I couldn't move. "Did my dad do that to you?" I asked Miller.

"Your dad?" He seemed confused by what I'd called Mr. Pruitt. And then he looked down at my hand in Matt's. He shook his head. For a few seconds, he didn't say anything at all. But his silence was loud and clear.

"Miller…"

"Miss Pruitt, please get in," Miller said, cutting me off. "And make sure to buckle your seatbelt."

Miss Pruitt. The words felt like a knife in my chest.

"Come on, Brooklyn," Matt said. "I'll help you." He lifted me into his arms like the reason I wasn't moving was because I was in pain.

I was. Just not the way he thought. I blinked away the tears in my eyes.

Miller slammed the door behind us.

Miss Pruitt. Did Miller seriously think I was like them? I was still a Sanders. I was. *Right?*

I looked at the front seat where Donnelley was sitting. He flinched under my gaze. Was he scared of me?

Matt put his arm around my shoulders, oblivious to how Donnelley and Miller were acting. If this was what it felt like to be elite, I didn't want anything to do with it.

CHAPTER 7

Sunday

The car came to a stop on the circular driveway. I looked out the window. The first time I'd been to Matt's mansion, everything had seemed sinister. The gargoyles didn't look quite as menacing during the day. Besides, he was here with me. I looked at the front seat. And Miller. My stomach twisted in knots.

"Ready to meet my parents?" Matt asked.

Not really. I felt like I was going to be sick. How could I meet his parents when I had been in Miller's bed just a couple days ago? And I was wearing my mom's squirrel pajamas. I'd added a jean jacket to it that had been in the room with all my mom's things. But none of it could be classified as ready to meet the parents attire.

I wanted to ask for a moment alone with Miller. But then Donnelley would be suspicious. And I couldn't ask for Matt to go for a walk so I could tell him about Miller. I could barely even stand on my stupid feet.

"I'm going to go check out the security system," Miller said and unbuckled his seatbelt. "Donnelley will stay with you."

I swallowed hard.

"You have nothing to be nervous about," Matt said as Miller climbed out of the car. "My parents are going to love you."

Are they? Matt hated the Pruitts. He said his father used to be in business with my dad but they'd had a falling out. Did his parents think the Pruitts were as toxic as their son did?

Matt opened up the back door and held out his hand for me. I grabbed his hand and immediately felt a little calmer. Before I could step down, he lifted me up in his arms and I laughed as he spun me in a circle.

He carried me up to the front door, past the bushes trimmed to look like gargoyles. The inside of his house was just as spooky as I remembered. It really seemed like whoever had decorated my dad's apartment had also done the decorating for this one. Dark marble floors. Dark red wallpaper. Black and white pictures on the walls in what were probably pure gold frames.

I trained my eyes on Matt instead of the chandelier above us. And I swore he winced when he walked beneath it. What a cruel daily reminder of losing his aunt. How could his family stay here after that? How could they keep the chandelier?

But my thoughts trailed away as Matt pushed through a door down the dark hallway. The light was suddenly blinding. A complete contrast to the horrifying foyer, ballroom, and bedrooms of this place. We were standing in a light and airy kitchen. Everything was still ornate, but the colors were more white and gray instead of blood red. There were skylights in the ceiling, letting in the final rays of the setting sun. And there was music filtering through a sound system.

Mrs. Caldwell was humming to the music as she watched something on the stove.

"Hey, Mom," Matt said.

She spun around with a huge smile on her face. "You must be Brooklyn," Mrs. Caldwell said as Matt set me down on my feet. "I'm Matthew's mom."

"It's so nice to meet you." I put out my hand.

"Don't be ridiculous." She wrapped me up in a hug. A real one. Like the kind Mrs. Alcaraz gave. I closed my eyes for a moment. Like the kind my mom used to give me.

"Matthew mentioned that you love hot chocolate," she said as she pulled away.

I smiled at him. He'd remembered my story of my mom always making it for me on snowy days. A cup right now sounded like the most comforting thing in the world. "I love hot chocolate."

"Give me one second. The milk is almost done heating. Sit down, sit down."

Matt grabbed my hand and pulled me over to their kitchen table. This room was not at all what I was expecting. It seemed a lot more like the staff's kitchen at my dad's place. It just felt…light.

Mrs. Caldwell started humming again as she stirred the milk in the saucepan.

It felt like a home. Mrs. Caldwell was in her element at the stove. This room felt like an extension of her. Which meant the rest of the house was an extension of her husband maybe?

"Where's your dad?" I asked.

"Probably finishing up some work," Matt said.

On a Sunday?

"And are you Donnelley or Miller?" Mrs. Caldwell asked, suddenly realizing there was another person in the room.

"Donnelley, ma'am," he said.

"Well, go on and take a seat too."

"I'm alright," he said. "I'm just going to stay right here."

"Nonsense. I've made plenty."

Donnelley looked over at me like he was asking my permission. So now he wanted to know my opinion? He didn't seem to care when there was a gun pointed at my head. But I couldn't be mad at him. I knew Isabella was blackmailing him. And he'd gone straight to my father after the fact. And his face looked absolutely awful. Was the rest of him that beat up?

I patted the seat beside me. I wasn't Isabella. I wasn't a monster. And it looked like he was in as much pain as me. The worst part was that I was pretty sure my father had done it to him. Donnelley smiled and made his way over.

Mason wandered into the kitchen. His plaid pajama bottoms made me suddenly feel a lot less out of place. "Something smells good, Mom" he said.

"It'll just be another minute." She continued to stir. "Brooklyn is here. Have the two of you already met?"

Mason smiled over at me. "Yeah, we've met." He patted Matt on the back before giving me a side hug. He sat down in the seat across from me. "You decided to come join us after all?"

"Mhm." I'd forgotten how nice he'd been last night. Standing up for me in front of Isabella. Inviting me to stay with them so that I could avoid her. I should have taken him up on the offer immediately. I could have avoided a half-naked run around the city.

"So..." he said, his voice trailing off. "Are you okay?"

Matt put his arm behind me, giving my shoulder a reassuring squeeze.

"Yeah, I'm okay," I said. "Last night was definitely a little scary."

"Are the rumors true?"

"What rumors?" I asked. Oh God, what were people already saying?

"Mason," his mom said and put down a tray of hot chocolate. "Don't antagonize Matthew's girlfriend."

I could feel my cheeks blushing. I kind of wanted to know what people were saying. But it probably involved the words whore or prostitute, so maybe it was better if I didn't know.

"What happened to your face?" Mason asked Donnelley.

"Mason," his mom scolded again. "Where are your manners?"

"It's okay, ma'am," Donnelley said. "I made a mistake last night." He looked down at me. "I'm really sorry, Brooklyn. It won't happen again."

"It wasn't your fault," I said.

"Either way. You're safe under my watch."

Mrs. Caldwell looked uncomfortable. Matt pulled me closer like he was the one in charge of protecting me. And Mason still looked really curious.

"A mistake?" Mason asked. "How did a mistake lead to your face getting beat in?"

"Well, Mr. Pruitt..." Donnelley's voice trailed off when someone cleared their throat behind us.

I turned to see a much older version of Matt staring at us. And he didn't look very pleased.

"Dad," Matt said. "This is my girlfriend Brooklyn. Brooklyn, this is my dad."

Even if I wasn't hurt, I wasn't sure I would have stood up. Because Matt's father didn't exactly look happy to see me. "Hi." My voice sounded so small.

"You told me her last name was Sanders," Mr. Caldwell said, not acknowledging me at all.

"Yeah," Matt said. "Brooklyn Sanders."

He shook his head. "Then what is one of Richard's watchdogs doing sitting in my kitchen?" He gestured toward Donnelley.

"Max!" Mrs. Caldwell said.

He held up his hand. "Brooklyn, I'm very sorry, but we are going to have to politely decline our previous offer of you staying here. My very charming wife and son have misled me. Please have your bodyguard show you out." He stepped to the side, dismissing me.

"Dad, Brooklyn is a Sanders. She..."

"Sanders? Really? You didn't think I'd find out who she really was? You don't think I heard the rumors of that asshole having an illegitimate daughter? It doesn't matter what her last name is, she has Pruitt blood in her veins." He turned to his wife. "Did you know about this?"

"Yes, but..."

"I won't have a Pruitt sleeping in our house. Or let his thugs stick their noses in my security system. Do you want to get us all killed?!"

"Maxwell!" Mrs. Caldwell yelled and stood up. "Enough." She walked over to him and grabbed his arm. "We'll discuss this in private. Not in front of the kids."

"I want her out of here," he said. "By the time I come back."

Mrs. Caldwell pulled him out of the kitchen back into the sinister portion of the house where he'd come from.

Donnelley cleared his throat. "I'm going to go check in with Miller. I'll be right back." He walked away before any of us even had a chance to protest.

"Cheers," Mason said and held up a cup of hot chocolate. "Welcome to the family, Brooklyn."

Matt groaned and leaned his head back on his chair. "Why does Dad have to be such a dick?"

"You didn't tell him I was a Pruitt?" I tried to search his face. I'd thought he was embarrassed of me when I was a nobody. But being a Pruitt somehow seemed worse.

"You're not a Pruitt," he said, lifting his head. "You're a Sanders, baby."

I wasn't entirely certain that was true. I was pretty sure my dad had changed my last name without my permission.

"Don't leave me hanging," Mason said, his cup still outstretched. "I've always thought having a little sister would be fun. You're already taking the heat off my back." He laughed and tapped his mug against the one in front of me, even though I hadn't lifted it up.

"This isn't funny," Matt said. "Dad can't make her leave. You saw what Mr. Pruitt does to people that go against him in some way. Brooklyn can't live with that nutcase."

"My dad would never hurt me," I said. I trusted him as much as I trusted Matt.

"Maybe not. But Isabella tried to freaking kill you last night. You're not going back to their apartment."

I didn't want to cause a mess with Matt and his family. But even though I wasn't scared of my dad, I was still scared of Isabella. He was right, I couldn't go back. Not until the new security was in place. And even then, I'd have a lot of questions about it before I'd ever feel safe there again. *Again?* I shook my head. I'd never felt safe there.

"Dad's not going to kick her out," Mason said. "Not if Mom doesn't want him to. Let's circle back to the rumors. Did you really run around homecoming completely naked?"

"What?" Matt and I both said at the same time.

"No," I added. "That's not..."

"And did you really dress up like a prostitute and go into James' hotel room?"

Oh fuck. "No. Well...yes." *God.* I could feel Matt's heated gaze. "No to the prostitute thing. But I did go to James for help." I turned to Matt. "He slipped me his keycard last night. I was never going to use it. Ever. But when Isabella abandoned me in my freaking underwear, the keycard was the only thing I had. I didn't have any money or my phone or clothes. It was my only choice. I would have come to you but your house was so far away. Trust me, I definitely would have preferred your help. You know that."

Matt reached out and tucked a loose strand of hair behind my ear. "I'm sorry I wasn't there for you."

He looked so hurt for letting me down. Hadn't he just heard what I said? It was just a proximity issue. It wasn't his fault.

Mason laughed. "Wait, so let me get this straight. You showed up to James' room in your underwear?"

"Well, I kind of made a makeshift dress out of a map."

He smiled. "So you showed up naked to his room. And then what happened?"

Actually, sharing this part might cheer Matt up. "I walked in on him and Rachel."

Mason spit out his sip of hot chocolate. "Really? Having sex?"

"No, she was…um…giving him…you know…"

"Head?" He cocked his eyebrow up. "You can say it you know. Oral. Sucking his cock. Blowing…"

"Cut it out, Mason," Matt said.

My face had to be bright red. "Yeah, that." I didn't want to say it out loud. I'd never even done it before. "Everyone completely freaked out and I ended up running through the lobby. But I was in my underwear. I'm pretty sure only a handful of students saw me." How had the rumors spread so quickly?

"This is amazing," Mason said. "What did James do when he saw you come in his room?"

"He said my name. And Rachel…bit him."

Even Matt laughed this time.

"Serves him right," Mason said. "Fucking asshole."

I didn't laugh. I didn't find it funny at all. James had been kind and sweet. I didn't feel comfortable telling Mason the rest of the story. I wanted to tell Matt in private. But I wanted to fix what I'd help break too. "James helped me," I said. "I think this crazy misunderstanding about Rachel...you could all clear it up, don't you think? If you just sat down and talked."

"What do you think I've been trying to do the past week?" Matt asked.

"I know, but..."

"The Hunters are dead to us," Mason said. "We tried to fight for them. And all they wanted to do was fight us."

It wasn't just them being stubborn. They were hurt. I looked at Matt. He had tried to fight for James. He'd tried to look after him. He'd worried and fretted over the blackmail because he cared about his friend. And all James wanted was to punch him in the face.

But James and I were friends now. Maybe I could convince him to try to fix things.

Matt lifted up my hot chocolate. "Aren't you even going to try it?"

I took the mug from him. It tasted just like my mom's. I sat in their warm kitchen, listening to the two of them laugh. And I hoped that I could stay. No one ever laughed at the Pruitts' apartment. I hadn't felt this at home since I'd lived with Kennedy.

But I had a feeling Mr. Caldwell wouldn't let me stay. And I understood why. I was a Pruitt. I was toxic. I laughed along with the Caldwell brothers, but I kept thinking about the fact that the hot chocolate always felt warm in my hands. No matter how much time went by. And I wondered if it was because my hands were permanently cold. Cold to the bone. Just like the Pruitts'. Was Mr. Caldwell right about me?

CHAPTER 8

Sunday

I sat down on the edge of Matt's four-poster bed. The last time I'd been in his room, Rob had pushed me inside and locked the door. I'd thought I was about to get the life sucked out of me by a vampire. But today I was just waiting to see if I'd get my hopes sucked out. Any minute now, I expected Mr. Caldwell to come through those doors and kick me out of his house.

"What's going through your head?" Matt asked as he sat down beside me.

I looked over to his closet. The one I'd stood in for what felt like an eternity, waiting for Matt to come back after he'd pushed me into it. He'd spent the rest of the night with Isabella, instead of with me. *Isabella.* My stomach twisted in knots as I looked up at Matt's eager face. "What if your dad's right? About...me."

Matt's eyebrows lowered. "He didn't say anything about you."

"I have Pruitt blood in my veins," I said and looked down at my hands. "You told me what that meant. That the Pruitts' whole family is a disease..."

"I didn't mean you."

"You called them toxic. I'm them, Matt."

"You're not..."

"I want her to die." I looked back up at him. "When she drove away in her stupid limo, that's what kept me going. I wanted to get back at her. But really…I think I'd be happy if she died. I'm a monster. I'm a Pruitt." I felt big tears roll down my cheeks.

"You're not a monster." He grabbed both sides of my face. "Baby."

My heart ached whenever he called me that.

"Look at me."

My eyes locked with his.

"Wanting revenge for this is a normal reaction. I want to fucking kill her myself for what she did to you." He wiped some of my tears away with this thumbs. "But you'd never actually do it. You're not evil. Isabella hurt you and you're hurting. That's the end of the story."

Was that the end of the story? I felt his love. And with it, there shouldn't have been any room for hate. But God I hated Isabella.

"You're better than her." He dropped his forehead to mine. "Your heart is too good to ever be like her."

I wanted to believe him. *I'm good. I'm not like Isabella.* And even though I trusted my dad, I'd never trust Isabella. "Please don't make me go back there." I felt lighter since stepping foot in Matt's house. Despite his dad hating me, I felt safe here. I felt like I'd shaken some kind of darkness off my shoulders. Maybe it was just because I was breathing in Matt's exhales. The familiar scent of cinnamon was calming and exhilarating at the same time.

I didn't want to be evil. I didn't want to kill anyone. That was crazy. I wasn't crazy. I lifted my leg, straddling

Matt on his bed. It was like the closer I got to him, the more I felt like myself.

His hands settled on my waist. "You're driving me crazy," he said against my lips.

I'd rather him be the crazy one than me. I pressed my lips against his and savored the groan I got from him. His fingers tightened on my waist as I deepened the kiss. I knew I should have been telling him about awkwardly showering with James. Or how I'd been spending most of my nights in Miller's bed. But I needed this. I needed him. And I could feel him beneath me. He needed me too.

For just a few minutes we were a happy couple. No ups and downs. No good or bad moments. Just us. I left a trail of kisses down his neck and got another delicious groan from him.

His hands splayed against the top of my thighs, his thumbs dangerously close to touching me where I'd dreamt about.

Normally we'd stay like this. He was patient with me. Always waiting.

But I'd told him my darkest fear and he'd washed it away. He knew me. He loved me. And I wanted to do for him what his brother so casually mentioned. What I'd literally seen Rachel do to James. Wasn't that what he needed from me?

I tried to move off his lap to get down on my knees.

"What are you doing?" he said, his fingers digging into my skin, not letting me move.

"I want to do that…thing."

"What thing?"

I ran my index finger along the waist of his jeans.

His lips brushed against my ear. "Say it."

"I want to show you how much I love you."

"How am I supposed to know that you're ready if you won't say it?" he whispered in my ear.

I swallowed hard. "I want to lick you."

"Where, baby?" The scruff of his 5 o'clock shadow was rough against my jaw.

"Here." I pressed my palm against his hardness and he groaned again. God, he was big. I wasn't experienced like Rachel. I had no idea what I was doing. But I wanted to do it for him. He'd been waiting for me. I didn't want to make him wait any longer.

"Say it," he groaned as he kissed me behind my ear.

I whimpered instead of responding.

"I want to hear you say the words."

I wasn't exactly sure what he wanted me to say. Everything that came to mind sounded very sex education class instead of sexy.

He kissed behind my ear again. "Say it, baby. Tell me you want my cock in your pretty little mouth."

Fuck. His words were dirtier than I expected them to be. But it was exactly what I wanted. "Yes. That."

"Say the words. And I'll give you whatever you want."

It felt like my heart was beating in my throat. "I want your cock in my mouth."

"God I love you." In one second flat, he'd spun us around and slammed my back against his plush mattress. His lips on mine were more frantic than before. "Let me taste you first." He kissed down my neck and collarbone as he pulled my tank top down. He lifted his head and locked eyes with me as he pulled it down the rest of the way, exposing my bra. "Tell me to stop and I will."

I had no idea what he was planning on doing to me. But I didn't want him to stop. I shifted beneath him instead of responding.

"Fuck," he hissed. He pulled down my bra cup and took one of my nipples in his mouth.

Oh God. "Please," I moaned. I wasn't even sure what I was begging him for. I just wanted more of…that. Why had I ever worn a shirt around him? Shirts were no longer necessary. I reached down to try to remove his too.

He laughed against my breast, but his laughter was mixed with someone else's. My eyes flew to the now opened door.

Mason laughed. "Having fun?"

What the hell? How long had Mason been standing in the doorway? I grabbed the front of my tank top.

Matt leaned forward and pulled my strap back in place before turning to his brother. "What the hell, man? Can't you knock?"

Mason shrugged. "Dad wants to talk to you guys," he said as he leaned against the doorjamb. "Should I tell him you two need a minute?"

"No." My voice came out squeaky and high-pitched. "We're ready now."

Mason laughed. "At least Matt didn't pull a Rachel and try to bite your nipple off when I walked in. Come on, it seems like Dad's in a significantly better mood now that Mom told him to be." He pushed himself off the doorjamb but didn't move.

Mason had seen my left boob. Now half the Caldwells had officially seen my left boob. Why was this happening? I could feel my face turning red.

"No need to be embarrassed," Mason said. "You have great tits."

"Get the fuck out," Matt said and threw a pillow in Mason's direction.

Mason laughed as he walked back into the hall.

Matt cupped my face in his hand. "I'm so sorry," he said. "Ignore him."

"It's okay." But I knew my cheeks had to be red.

"I'll lock the door next time." He climbed off the bed and put his hand out for me.

Next time. I put my hand into his. What if his dad made it so there would never be a next time? My body felt alive. More alive than it had ever felt. I wanted to spend the rest of my life in Matt's bed.

He put his arm around me. "Mason was right though."

About what? I looked up at Matt. Oh. *Oh.* He was referring to the comment about my breasts. Could my cheeks be any redder?

"Don't worry," Matt said. "My mom will have convinced my dad that you can stay. And we can pick up where we left off."

I hoped he was right.

We wandered down the creepy hallway and back downstairs to the kitchen.

Mr. Caldwell was sitting at the kitchen table drinking his hot chocolate. Mrs. Caldwell was sitting next to him. They both smiled when we walked in.

"Would you like another cup?" Mr. Caldwell asked and gestured to the hot chocolate. "There's plenty."

I shook my head. *Please don't kick me out. Please.*

"I called your father," he said.

That probably wasn't good if they didn't like each other.

"My wife and son kept the fact that you were related to Richard from me. All I knew was what Matt first told me. That you were new in town. And that you were living with your uncle."

I nodded.

"So you can imagine my surprise…"

Mrs. Caldwell cleared her throat.

"The funeral was very nice," he said.

I'd forgotten that he had been in attendance. "It was." It was until I had been taken away. I could feel tears welling in my eyes. I was getting closer to my dad. But suddenly the distance felt momentous. He'd kidnapped me during my uncle's funeral. I couldn't trust him. I wasn't a Pruitt. It was just like Matt said. I'd never be a monster. "Please don't make me leave," I said.

Mr. Caldwell smiled. "I would never make you go back to him."

Him. My dad. I should have wanted to defend him. But how could I? I didn't even know if Isabella was being punished for what she did. As far as I knew, she was just hanging out back at the apartment with her evil puppy and plotting her next murder. But at the same time, my dad had taken care of me. He'd made sure Kennedy was okay. He'd promised to keep me safe. I still wanted to stay here though. With Matt. With his family that knew how to smile for real.

"His bodyguards are to stay outside at all times," Mr. Caldwell said. "They won't interfere with our own security. I've told Richard as much. As long as they stay outside, you can stay here."

I blinked fast, forcing my tears to stay at bay. "Thank you." I walked over to him and hugged him.

He awkwardly patted my back for a second. But then he hugged me back. And it was stupid, but it felt like a hug from my uncle. Which made me tear up all over again.

I pulled away. "Actually, I'd love another cup of hot chocolate."

He smiled and nodded to the chair.

"How about a round of cards?" he asked. "Matt, go get your brother."

***

We spent hours together in the kitchen playing Canasta, a game I was apparently terrible at. But it was so much fun. Mrs. Caldwell made these delicious cheesy snacks and we all just sat around laughing. It was the most relaxed I'd been in…a really long time. I didn't think about Isabella once. All I thought about was how easy it was to fit in with the Caldwell family.

I smiled over at Matt as he threw his cards down on the table.

He smiled back.

"It's a draw," his mom said.

"What?" Mason said. "No way. We smoked you guys."

We had played boys against girls. And Mason was right, I definitely brought Mrs. Caldwell's team down. There was no way it was a draw.

"A tie," she said.

"Mhm," Mr. Caldwell said and leaned over and kissed her cheek. "Mason, do you mind escorting Brooklyn upstairs for the night? I need to have a word with Matthew."

"Sure." Mason tossed his cards on the table too and stretched.

"A guest room," Mr. Caldwell added.

Mason didn't reply to that comment. So I didn't either. I didn't want to be in some random guestroom. I wanted to be snuggled up to Matt's side. Permanently.

"Goodnight, Mr. and Mrs. Caldwell," I said. "Thanks for letting me stay."

They both smiled at me.

"Of course, dear," Mrs. Caldwell said. "You're welcome any time. I hope you sleep well."

I gave Matt what I hoped was a reassuring smile and followed Mason out of the warm kitchen.

"Night," Mason said over his shoulder before the door closed.

There was an awkward stretch of silence. My thoughts were back in the kitchen. What did Matt's dad want to talk to him about?

"You okay?" Mason asked as we made our way up the stairs.

"Mhm." I didn't know what to fill our silence with. I barely knew him. "My dad likes you," I said. I have no idea why that was the thing that fell out of my mouth. As if it would be a compliment. His family hated mine.

He laughed. "Really? Huh."

"And you were really good in the homecoming game."

He smiled down at me. "Thanks. You should come to more games. There's nothing I love more than my brother embarrassing himself in public."

I laughed, remembering Matt's amazing performance, as we stopped outside of Matt's bedroom. I knew Mason's comment wasn't true. He'd taken Matt away the other night at homecoming. Specifically because he thought Matt was embarrassing himself. Why was he pretending he didn't care?

"Aren't you going to show me to a guest room?" I asked.

"I already cock-blocked Matt once today. No reason to do it again."

"Thanks? I guess?"

He laughed. "You know…I could get used to having a sister. It's kinda fun having someone else around to mess with." He winked at me. "Night, Brooklyn." He turned around, leaving me at Matt's door.

"Goodnight, Mason." I could get used to having a brother. But I'd never get used to having a sister. I looked out over the bannister at the chandelier. And even though I knew the history of this house, I felt safer here than I did at the Pruitts. I retreated into Matt's room and closed the door.

I was finally figuring Mason out. He was kind, but in more of a joking way. Not funny like Rob. Just…hesitant. As if he was scared to get too close to anyone. I wondered why. He was probably the most popular guy at Empire High. He didn't have to lose anyone if he didn't want to.

I wrapped my arms around myself, suddenly cold. Matt's kitchen was comforting. His room without him in it? Not so much. I stared at his nightstand. Were there still pictures of Isabella in there? Was there still a huge box of opened condoms? Was there actually a vampire coffin somewhere tucked away in one of his closets?

I looked over my shoulder at the closed door. Surely I had a few minutes to explore.

CHAPTER 9

Sunday

I pulled one of Matt's t-shirts over my head. He'd told me once that I'd look better in one of his. I hoped he meant it. I folded my mom's squirrel pajamas and placed them on top of Matt's nightstand. There was only one thing I really cared about looking for. I opened the bottom drawer of the nightstand. The envelope full of pictures of Isabella was gone. I breathed a sigh of relief. No more private investigator. No more blackmail. It was done. Matt was free from Isabella's clutches.

I just wasn't sure I was yet. How was my dad going to protect me from her? He couldn't just throw her out. Isabella was his daughter too. I didn't see how any of this could be resolved.

My stomach churned. I had a lot to resolve myself. I needed to talk to Miller. And Felix. I pulled out my phone. It would be easy to send either of them a text. But that seemed harsh. I owed them each an explanation for why I couldn't be with them.

As I stared at my phone, the only person I really wanted to talk to was Kennedy. My dad had said I should let her rest. But I'd let her rest all day. I needed to hear her voice for myself. Just to make sure she was okay. Maybe she'd have some advice for me too. I clicked on her name in my phone.

And waited.

And waited.

I opened the lid of the box of condoms in Matt's nightstand. It looked like there were only a few missing. That was a good sign. I knew he'd been with other girls. But there was something nice about knowing that maybe it wasn't that high of a number.

The phone kept ringing.

I closed the lid and sat down on the edge of the bed. Just when I thought it would go to voicemail I got a groggy, "Hello?".

"Kennedy! Are you alright?"

"I'm fine." Her voice sounded so small. Just like it had after she'd told me about what Cupcake had done to her. The realization hit me hard. Cupcake had drugged her. Getting drugged by Isabella was probably bringing all those feelings back. I imagined her curled up on a ball in her bed, her knees tucked into her chest. It killed me to see her like that last time. And it was my fault she was like that now. I didn't want her to disappear on me again. She was the brave one. Not me.

"I'm so sorry," I said. "I never meant to drag you into..."

"Stop," she said with a small laugh. "You didn't do anything wrong. It was Isabella. God, I feel like such an idiot. I barely remember last night. But I remember drinking with her. I remember for just a minute it seemed like she was actually my friend. I feel so stupid."

"You're not stupid," I said. "Isabella is really good at convincing people of things." She had convinced me to get into that damn limo. And for a few seconds there, she had convinced me I was trash. She'd even tried to convince me I didn't belong in this world. But I did belong. And I wasn't going anywhere. "I wish I was there to hug you."

"Me too." She sniffed. "Are you okay?" she asked.

I blinked fast, forcing my own tears not to fall. I needed to be strong for her. "Yeah, I'm okay."

"That didn't sound convincing at all. What exactly happened last night? The last thing I remember was dancing."

I filled her in on every detail. All of it. Rachel, James, Dr. Wilson, every single thing that happened last night. I was already feeling lighter once I got it off my chest.

"I believe most of what you said. But there's no way I rawred at Robert Hunter."

"Oh that part was absolutely true."

She laughed for real this time. "How am I ever supposed to go back to school after that?"

"Try going back to school after running around outside homecoming in just your underwear."

She laughed again. "Yeah, that would be worse. God, I can't believe I slept through all that. And I can't believe you saw James'…you know."

I laughed. I wanted to say that I hadn't really. That I'd put my hand out to block the scene. But I had seen it. I had stood there like a frozen pervert. I'd never live it down. "I wish I had just been sleeping last night," I said.

"Oh I much prefer your adventure. How do you always end up with an Untouchable erotically bathing you?"

I laughed. I'd forgotten that she'd referred to Matt's washing my hand as erotically bathing. "It wasn't erotic. He's my friend."

"Mhm. A friend who showers with you? Kisses you? Takes care of you when you're hurt? He sounds like a knight in shining armor. And it sounds like he's the opposite of Cupcake down there. Or else you would have said otherwise."

I laughed. James definitely didn't have a mini dong, or however Kennedy liked to put it. And it was true, I liked James. But he wasn't my knight in shining armor. I needed to fill Kennedy in on what happened *after* last night. "I'm back together with Matt."

"Really? How did that happen? The last thing you said about him was that he was drunk. What about Felix? And Miller?"

"Matt waited outside my dad's other apartment all night. He finally showed up when I needed him." I could feel myself getting teary eyed again. Him showing up was all I ever wanted. "He convinced my dad to let me stay at his house until the new security system is set up."

"You're at that creepy mansion?"

I looked around the room. "It doesn't feel as creepy anymore." I hadn't seen a single vampire coffin. "And his parents are really nice." Well, his mom at least. I was still trying to get a read on his dad. It really seemed like Mrs. Caldwell had forced her husband to let me stay. And I was so grateful.

"Well, it can't be any creepier than your dad's place. It's weird that I slept there last night without you. And that I don't even remember it. I woke up to yelling."

"Yelling? Who was yelling?"

"Isabella."

I sat up a little straighter. "What was she yelling about?"

"You."

My heartbeat kicked up a notch. My name in Isabella's mouth couldn't be a good thing. "Was she arguing with someone?"

"No. She was just having a fit. It sounded like she was throwing things. I heard glass breaking. I put one of your pillows over my head to try to drown her out, but it was impossible. I've heard her mad before. I'm used to her wrath. But she sounded terrifying, Brooklyn. I don't think she has any intention of being civil with you."

The blood in my veins turned to ice. "Did anyone try to calm her down?"

"If they did, they didn't do a good job. It went on for like half an hour. Actually, now that I think about it, she must have been on the phone with your dad. Because I definitely heard her say Daddy a lot. Gag."

I felt like I did gag. Or more like I couldn't breathe. Deep breaths. In and out. At least I hadn't been there. I was safe here, right?

"Speaking of your dad, I really don't think he's Satan anymore. He even came to check in on me a little while ago. It was sweet. He apologized to my mom about what happened. He brought us some dinner from this fancy Italian place on the Upper East Side. My mom was so excited. I'm pretty sure she even forgave him, even though she didn't say those words exactly. You know how she is."

"That's good." My dad had been sweet to me too. And it warmed my heart to know that he'd checked up on Kennedy. I'd been away from him for a few hours and I was already forgetting that he was changing. He wasn't what Mr. Caldwell said. And I wasn't a monster either. My dad was just very misunderstood.

I shifted the cellphone to my other ear. "You said Isabella eventually stopped yelling? Did she sound less mad at the end? And what do you mean by being civil with me? What did she say exactly?"

"One second, Mama!" Kennedy yelled. "I have to go. My mom made my favorite rice pudding and it's getting cold. I'll see you at school tomorrow. Stay safe in the vampire mansion!"

"Wait, Kennedy?"

But she'd already hung up the phone. *Shit.* Isabella had no intention of being *civil* with me. Did that mean she was still planning on kicking me out of town? Murdering me or one of my friends? Taking Matt as her own?

I looked down at my phone. It was tempting to call Kennedy back, but she'd sounded happy during our conversation. I wanted her to have a relaxing night with her mom. I just wished I was with her tonight. As much as I wanted to be here with Matt…I wanted Kennedy to know that I was there for her. Because despite what she said, everything that had happened last night was my fault. Isabella wanted to hurt me. And Kennedy had been drugged to cause me pain. I didn't want to put anyone in danger ever again.

God. How was my dad going to keep me safe? How could he protect me and my friends?

I heard a noise in the hall. *Shit.* I went to shove the nightstand drawer shut but a velvet box tucked into the corner caught my eye. I glanced at the door to make sure Matt wasn't coming in. And then I reached into the drawer to grab the box.

It was a jewelry box. I flipped open the velvet top. *Oh. Wow.* There was a huge circular diamond in the middle, surrounded by smaller diamonds on the silver band. I'd touched expensive ball gowns and tiaras, but they were nothing compared to this. It was beautiful. It didn't look new. There were scratches along the band that made it look like it had been worn in love already. For some reason, I thought it would have looked lovely with my mom's blue dress. My heart ached. I'd never know. My dress was gone. And this ring certainly wasn't mine. But God, it was beautiful. I ran my thumb along the glistening band. *Vintage.* That was what Justin would have called it. I liked vintage more than new.

"Do you like it?" Matt asked.

I looked up at him. *Crap.* When had he come in? "Oh. No. I mean yes. It's beautiful. But I'm sorry. I shouldn't have..." I went to put it back in the drawer, but he caught my hand.

"Do you want to try it on?"

"What?"

He pulled the ring out of the box and lifted my left hand. "Just to see if it fits."

My eyes locked with his. He wanted me to try it on? I couldn't. "I..." my thoughts trailed away when he slid it onto my ring finger.

"A perfect fit," he said.

For just a few seconds we were both silent. I wasn't even sure I was breathing. It was so beautiful that it hurt.

"I guess you should just wear it then." His hand slid off mine.

I laughed. "Wait, what? I can't."

"Why? I'll be giving it to you in a few years anyway."

Oh, Matt. My heart was beating faster and faster the longer I wore it. Like it was so happy it was about to explode. "Then we should wait, right? We should..."

"Haven't we done enough waiting? I heard you loud and clear, Brooklyn. I wasn't loving you out loud. What's more out loud than this?"

"This is...this is very loud."

He laughed. "You don't like it?"

"No, I love it. It's the most beautiful thing I've ever seen." I looked down at my hand. But I didn't deserve it.

"It was my aunt's."

I looked back up at him. "Really?"

"My mom gave it to me. To give to the woman I want to marry one day. That's you." The corner of his mouth lifted. "Forever, remember?"

"Matt, I can't..."

He leaned forward and kissed me. Usually our kisses were frantic, like we were running out of time. But this was one slow. Torturously slow. And somehow it was even better than the frantic ones.

"I can't wear this," I said against his lips. "It's an engagement ring, Matt."

"Hmm. True." He pulled back and got down on one knee. "Brooklyn..."

"We can't be engaged. We've already had this conversation. We're sixteen."

"Think of it as a promise then. That one day, I'll make you mine officially. It doesn't matter whether your last name is Sanders or Pruitt. Because you'll be a Caldwell soon. We've also already talked about this. I'm going to take all your firsts."

"Right. You're going to be my first husband." I was smiling so hard it hurt.

He laughed. "I really don't like that joke." He put his hands on my knees and spread them apart.

I swallowed hard.

"Your only husband," he said as he leaned down and kissed the inside of my thigh. My very naked thigh.

Holy shit. I tried to close my legs. It felt too good. It was too overwhelming. But he kept my knees spread apart. If anything, he forced them open wider. And I have no idea why I did it, but I reached out and put my hand on top of his head so he wouldn't move.

He laughed against my thigh and kissed me higher. And higher.

"Matt," I moaned. I stared at the ring glistening on my finger, tangled in his hair.

He wrapped his hands beneath my thighs and pulled me to the edge of the bed, his hands settling on my ass.

Fuck.

His breath was warm on my thigh. His lips soft. His tongue... *God.* My fingers tightened in his hair the higher he went. And I stared at the ring he'd slipped on my finger and I felt...at war with myself. I felt wonderful because of his lips on my skin, but horrible because of the secrets I was keeping from him. "Matt." I pushed on his shoulders. "Stop."

"What?" He lifted his head. And I must have looked horrified because he pushed himself away from me. "I'm sorry. I thought…fuck, I'm so sorry. I thought you were ready." He ran his hand through his hair. "Brooklyn, I didn't mean to…"

"It's not that. I want…I want more of that."

His Adam's apple rose and then fell. "Me too." It looked like he was going to pull me back into his arms, so I slid away from him on the bed.

"But…I…I did something bad." God, I wanted to keep my secrets. I wanted to wear this ring. I wanted to be a Caldwell. I wanted him to keep kissing me. Holding me. Loving me. But he wouldn't. Because I knew if the roles were reversed, I probably wouldn't forgive him. Just thinking about his box of condoms being used on someone else made it hard to breathe. I chose him. I wanted him. But I'd taken too long to figure it out. I closed my eyes and pulled off the ring.

CHAPTER 10

Sunday

Matt caught my hand. "Please don't take it off. I want you to wear it."

He wouldn't in a second. I placed the ring down in his palm and closed his fingers around it. But instead of moving away, I kept his hand wrapped in mine.

"I made a mistake," I said.

"Okay. We can fix it together."

God, why was he so sweet? "I just need to tell you everything, okay? And I need you to listen to all of it. And then if you want me to leave, I will."

"I'm not letting you go back to the Pruitts. You have nothing to worry about. I talked to my dad and..."

"It's not about that. Please, just let me get this off my chest."

He pulled his eyebrows together, but he didn't say a word.

I picked up the story about James where I'd left off before. How he came back to the apartment with me. Washed my cuts. Held me in the shower and let me cry.

"Did you kiss him again?" Matt asked. His voice wasn't angry. He just sounded...defeated.

"No. I promised you I wouldn't, remember?"

He just stared at me.

"At homecoming. You told me not to kiss him again. I promised I wouldn't. That kiss was a mistake. I saw you with Rachel and I was so angry." I pressed my lips together. It didn't matter why I kissed James. It only mattered that I had.

He nodded, even though I knew that night was foggy for him. "Do you have feelings for him?"

"I think I feel close to him because he's sad. He knows what it feels like to be drowning all the time. It was nice to be miserable together." I used James' words to describe it. "But I love you. I only want to be with you."

Matt's hand was still cradled in mine. I held it tighter, afraid he might pull away. But it wasn't necessary. Because he just shook his head.

"Then there's nothing for me to be upset about," he said. "James was there for you when I couldn't be." He ran his tongue along his lower lip, like he always did when he was thinking. "I can't be mad at anyone but myself."

That wasn't how I wanted him to feel. But he was being more understanding than I thought he would be. One of the reasons we'd broken up in the first place was because he'd gotten mad when I borrowed Felix's blazer at school. He wasn't usually so understanding when it came to me hanging out with other boys. But I had to take this as a win. Because there was more to confess.

"That's not everything," I said.

He just stared at me, his dark brown eyes swirling with something I didn't understand.

"While we were fighting, I felt so alone. And I was scared at the Pruitts' apartment." *God, why was I making excuses?* That wasn't what this was about. This was about

Matt and me no longer having secrets. I took a deep breath. "I started seeing someone. He…"

"Was it James?"

I shook my head. "No."

"Was it Felix?"

"No. It's…"

"If it wasn't one of them, I don't want to know who it was."

"But…"

Matt pulled his hand out of mine.

It stung worse than I ever thought it would. I felt so cold when he wasn't touching me. And I had this weird sensation that maybe my father used to be warm too. And that when my mom left his life, he'd turned cold and bitter. I blinked away my tears.

Matt stood up and now I recognized the look on his face. I assumed it was how I looked when I first stepped into Empire High. Broken.

I'd been so worried that he'd break my heart. Why hadn't I protected his?

"Did you kiss whoever it was?" he asked.

"Yes." I held my breath.

"Did you sleep with him?"

"No." I shook my head. "I mean, technically I slept in his bed, but we didn't…"

He winced. "I don't want to hear any more."

"I'm done with everyone else, Matt. The next time I see him, I'll make sure he knows. And I'll make sure to tell Felix the same. I'll even make sure James knows. I love you and only you," I said.

"Okay."

He didn't say he loved me back. And I didn't know what he meant by okay. But it didn't sound like anything was okay. He just stood there, staring at me, a frown on his perfect face.

"Okay." The word was barely audible from my lips.

He kept staring at me. His chest rose and fell. And then he turned away, like he couldn't bear to look at me anymore.

That was a dismissal. He didn't have to say the words. I knew when I wasn't wanted. I slowly stood up. I grabbed my pajamas off his nightstand and pulled them to my chest. My mom's perfume wafted around me. Was this how my mom felt when she walked away from my dad? Like her heart was in a million little pieces?

Matt ran his hand through his perfect golden hair. For just a few minutes, I'd been the one to do that for him.

I clutched the pajamas closer to my chest. My mom had walked away to protect me. But walking away from Matt? That wasn't protecting anyone. It was killing me. Was it killing him too? I stood there for another moment, hoping he'd turn around. But he didn't.

And just like that, I was invisible again. Staring at him from a distance. Wanting him desperately, but knowing I could never have him.

"I'm so sorry, Matt. I should have heard you out right away. I was just so…angry with you. I thought you were keeping what happened with Rachel a secret in part because you didn't want to tell me the truth. And I didn't understand why you didn't trust me with what Isabella had on you. I didn't understand why you kept me in the dark. I would have believed you if you'd been upfront about it.

And I would have kept your secret." I instantly regretted the last thing I said.

"Yeah, you're good at secrets, Brooklyn."

Ouch. I bit the inside of my lip. It hurt because he was right. "I was never trying to hurt you. I was just trying not to…drown."

He didn't respond. He just shoved his hands into his pockets and looked down at the ground.

I didn't want to leave his bedroom. I didn't want to have to leave with Miller. It all felt wrong. But what was I supposed to do? Beg him to let me stay? "Matt?"

He didn't look up.

What was I doing? I wasn't going to beg him. He'd dismissed me. I would have done the same. Just thinking about him kissing someone else made my chest ache. I held the pajamas closer to my chest as if it would prevent my heart from breaking any more. There was nothing else to say. I'd lost my mom and my uncle. And it made me feel abandoned and alone. And I'd just held on to anyone and anything that offered me comfort. Matt didn't understand what it was like to lose everything. Yes, he'd lost his aunt, but it wasn't the same. And even though it wasn't an excuse for my behavior, it had still happened. I couldn't undo it. I couldn't rewind time, even though I desperately wanted to. I'd just lost the best thing I'd ever had. And I was so fucking sorry.

Part of me wanted to close the distance between us and hug him. But he looked so un-inviting. He didn't want me anymore. And I had no one to blame but myself. It felt like I didn't know how to do anything right anymore. He was all I wanted. Why had I messed it up? Why? I walked past him before I broke. He didn't stop me. It stung worse than him removing his hand from mine.

I opened the door, but he reached out and slammed it shut. His body was pressed to my back, caging me in.

"No more running," he said, his breath hot on the back of my neck. "For once, you're going to stay. We're going to fight. And then we'll make up."

"Matt…"

He kissed the side of my neck and I lost the ability to speak. His lips felt so much freaking better than the tears falling down my cheeks. He slid the ring back on my finger as he kissed my neck again and more tears fell.

I thought he was kicking me out. But he wanted me to stay? I tried to turn around but he pulled me against him.

"I don't want to fight with you," I said.

"Too bad." He lightly nipped my earlobe. "Because I'm furious with you."

"Matt, I'm sorry, I…"

"Tell me," he said, cutting me off. "Did he touch you here?" His fingers slid beneath my shirt, skimming the top of my underwear.

I swallowed hard. "No."

"What about here?" His fingers slid beneath the lacy material.

"No." My head rolled back on his shoulder. This didn't feel like a fight. It felt like we were already making up.

"Did you want him? To touch you there?"

"Never."

"Brooklyn." His voice cracked.

I closed my eyes. We definitely hadn't skipped the fight. Or else he wouldn't have sounded so sad. "He didn't touch me like this," I said. "And I didn't want him to."

"Then why did you sleep in his bed?"

"Because I felt alone."

"Imagine how I felt." His fingers slid lower. "You wouldn't answer my texts or calls. You iced me out. I was suffering just as much as you."

He was right. I should have heard him out. I was hurt but I should have cared that he was hurting. "I thought you were keeping a secret to protect your friend," I said. "And when I found out it was because you did something to hurt him? It was hard to believe your side." Especially because I hadn't given him a chance to explain.

"So you ran from me instead of talking? Why is your first instinct to run?"

"I don't know." It was hard talking to him when his fingers were so distracting.

"You do." His lips traced the back of my ear. "Tell me."

I squeezed my eyes shut. "It's hard for me to love people, Matt. Everyone I love leaves me."

His kiss was gentle on my neck. "So why'd you leave me if you knew how much it fucking hurts?"

I was protecting my heart because he kept hurting it. And if I gave it to him like he was asking? I could lose everything. "Because then you couldn't leave me."

"I would never leave you, Brooklyn. I don't know how many times I can say it. I don't know how many times you have to push me away to prove that I'll keep coming back. But I'm not going anywhere. You belong with me."

I nodded. I did. I belonged in his arms. Just like this.

"Do you promise to stop running from me?"

"Yes." His fingers slid slightly lower. *God.*

"I don't want you talking to James anymore."

The segue didn't surprise me at all. I almost expected him to have a few contingencies. I'd proven that I was an untrustworthy flight risk. And if this is what he needed for me to prove I wasn't, I'd give it to him. My friendship with James wasn't worth losing Matt. "I won't. I swear."

There was a long stretch of silence.

"Okay," he finally said. It didn't sound like a dismissal this time.

I tried to turn to face him again but he gripped my waist, keeping me in place.

"Tell me what you want right now." The tip of his nose ran down the side of my neck before he nibbled my shoulder through the thin fabric of his t-shirt. "And maybe I'll give it to you."

I swallowed hard. *Not this again.* Was he hellbent on torturing me? I didn't know what to say. No, that wasn't exactly true. I knew exactly what I wanted. "Touch me." I wanted to skip to the make up portion he promised. I never wanted to fight with him again. I expected an explosion, not a heated conversation where he held me hostage with his hands. He fought unfairly. I'd always give him whatever he wanted like this.

"Here?" He kissed my shoulder where he'd just bitten.

"No," I moaned. "Lower."

"Here?" He kissed farther down on my shoulder blade, his hand not moving an inch.

"No, not there."

"Say it, Brooklyn. Tell me what you want from me." He tugged on my earlobe with his teeth.

"Poke me in the pants." *What? Really? That's what I came up with?* I wasn't even wearing pants.

He laughed, kissing the side of my neck. "As endearing as that is…I want you to tell me that you need my fingers inside of you. Or would you rather have my tongue?"

"All of it."

He finally let me turn around to face him. His eyes weren't cold and distant anymore. He looked hungry. For me.

"I want all of you," I whispered.

He grabbed my ass and lifted me up, slamming my back against his door.

I wrapped my legs around his waist as his lips collided with mine.

"You said you didn't want to do this when I was mad at you the other day," I said between kisses. "Shouldn't we wait until you're not mad at me?"

He kissed me again as he carried me over to his bed and tossed me down on it.

I bounced before sagging into the soft mattress.

"I'm not mad at you." He leaned over top of me. "I'm in love with you. There's a huge difference."

"I'm in love with you too."

"But I do need you to agree to a few rules before we go any further."

I nodded. Sex rules? Was that a thing? Or a safe word or something? Why would I need that? *What is he planning on doing to me?!*

"From now on, you'll kiss only me." He pushed up my t-shirt and planted a kiss on my stomach. "You'll only fall asleep in my arms." Another kiss a little lower. "I will be your first *and only* husband."

I laughed.

He bit my skin in response.

Oh.

"You'll come to me when you're in trouble." He kissed the same spot he'd just bitten. "And you'll give me the rest of your firsts." His fingers hooked in the waistband of my panties. "And you'll never run away from me again. We fight for each other. Always and forever." He pulled my panties down my thighs. "Agreed?"

Fuck yes. I lifted myself up on my elbows so I could look at him. "I promise, Matt."

He kissed the inside of my thigh, making me shiver.

He locked eyes with me as he lowered his mouth. "Now I think it's time we took care of a few of those firsts, don't you think? I think you requested all of it? But let's start slow. I have two things in mind I think you might really enjoy."

I nodded. I had no idea what two things he was talking about. But when his mouth collided with my skin, I knew I wanted everything he could give me. Two things. Ten things. Every single thing. I'd give him all my firsts if they felt this fucking good.

This time when my fingers tangled with his hair I felt more complete than I had in months. More alive. More loved. I wasn't scared. I wasn't alone. I wasn't just barely holding on. I was freaking soaring.

CHAPTER 11

Monday

"Baby."

I woke up to kisses along my clavicle and Matt's fingers in my hair. "Mmm."

"Hey." His hand stopped on the side of my face as I slowly opened my eyes.

I blinked up at his smiling face. He'd kept his 5 o'clock shadow because I'd told him I liked it. He looked so handsome. I reached up and ran my palm along his jaw. "Good morning." We'd never been together like this in the morning. He usually slipped out before I woke up. But I guess that wasn't necessary here.

Matt smiled down at me. "Good morning, beautiful." His thumb dropped to my lower lip. "I like waking up to you."

I smiled up at him. "I like waking up to you too."

He slowly sat up and I realized he was already fully dressed in his Empire High uniform.

"Are you leaving?"

He ran his fingers through his hair. "I actually missed a lot of school last week. Coach Carter said I couldn't play in the game next weekend unless I came in today. I'll stay with you if you want. You know that. But…"

"What? No. You should go. I'll be fine."

"Are you sure?"

"Yeah. I don't want you to have to miss your game. It'll be the first one I'll get to come to as your girlfriend."

He smiled at me. "I'd like that. Maybe you could wear my letter jacket?"

Oh. Isabella had cut up all my clothes. But I didn't think Matt's jacket had been part of the destruction. It had still been packed away in a box. *Thank God.* "I've been dying to wear it. Maybe I should just come to school today too. I think I feel okay..."

"No," Matt said. "I promised your dad I'd take care of you. You still need rest. I even brought you breakfast in bed." He gestured to the tray that was sitting on the bed.

I'd thought I'd smelled bacon. I sat up, keeping the comforter pressed against my chest. That was the sweetest thing ever. "Thank you."

"Take the day off. Relax. Sleep. Whatever you need." He kissed the side of my forehead. "I'll be back after practice."

"Am I allowed to go downstairs?"

He laughed. "Of course. I'm not locking you up here. I just thought you might be more comfortable in my room."

My dad would have tried to lock me up. He *had* tried that.

"There's a TV in the kitchen if you want to watch something. And there's a library if you want to read. My mom's here, so you can just ask her for whatever you need."

I nodded. I liked Matt's mom. Maybe I could just hang out with her today.

"I like that look," Matt said.

"What look?" I smiled up at him.

"The messy hair. Rosy cheeks. My ring on your finger."

I smiled and looked down at the ring. "I shouldn't wear this out of your room though right? Won't your family wonder why I have it?" The last thing I wanted was for the Caldwells to think I was stealing jewelry.

"My dad made it clear he didn't want a Pruitt in the family. I made it clear that you aren't. And that even if you technically are, you won't be for long."

I pressed my lips together. "You told them you wanted to marry me?"

He reached out and brushed a strand of hair out of my face. "Don't worry, I'll tell your dad the same. I know that's one of his rules. To always make my intentions clear."

Yeah, it probably was, but I hadn't read the freaking contract.

"I'll talk to him today," he said. "So yeah…wear the ring. You're mine. And I want everyone to know it."

Matt calling me his always made my stomach fill with butterflies. "As a promise ring, right? That's what you said it was?"

"You can call it whatever you want." He placed a soft kiss against my lips.

"Because that's what it is."

"Whatever you say, Brooklyn. Engagement ring, promise ring, either way…"

I laughed. "But you didn't propose."

"Hmm." He climbed off the bed. "Didn't I?"

"No, you did not."

"I think we remember that differently."

"We're not engaged, Matt."

"The ring says otherwise. And don't you dare take it off. You're mine."

I wouldn't dream of taking it off. "Okay."

"Okay then." He adjusted his tie. "Text me if you need anything." He leaned over and placed a kiss against my lips. "Make yourself at home."

I smiled as he left the room. *Home.* I looked around at the dark red walls. I never would have imagined this place feeling like a home. But it was already starting to. I lifted up a piece of bacon and took a bite. *Yeah, I could get used to this.*

***

It didn't take long for me to get antsy. If Matt expected me to wear this ring everywhere, there were two people I needed to talk to. Class had already started, so Felix had to wait. But Miller was here somewhere. I had to find him.

I wandered out in the hall, avoiding looking at the chandelier. I was a little surprised that Donnelley wasn't standing somewhere with a machete and instructions from Isabella to lop my head off. But he was nowhere in sight. My feet echoed on the stairs. The Caldwell mansion was still scary. But I knew one room that wasn't. I walked into the kitchen and was disappointed that Mrs. Caldwell wasn't standing at the stove humming like last night.

There was a TV hanging under one of the cabinets, just like Matt had said. But I didn't really want to watch anything. The TV reminded me of movies which reminded me of Uncle Jim. And I didn't want to sit in the kitchen and cry. I needed to talk to Miller. What had Mr. Caldwell said about the security last night? That they needed to stay outside?

I turned to the back door and almost screamed when I saw someone there. But it was just…*wait, Rob?* Rob was standing there, smiling at me through the glass. He lifted his hand and waved.

What was he doing here? He was fighting with Matt. And he should have been in class.

But his smiling face made it seem like he did belong here. Had they all made up and I just didn't realize it? I walked over and opened the door. "What are you doing here?"

"Me?" Rob said with a laugh. "What are *you* doing here?"

"Matt invited me?" I wasn't sure why it came out as a question.

Rob smiled. "Yeah, I heard a rumor you were camping out here. I thought I'd come over and see for myself. Wanna hang out?"

"Oh. Um." So they had made up? Or not? It didn't matter, I didn't have time to hang out with him. "I was actually just about to…"

"Come on, Sanders. There's nothing to do in this big house. Besides, there's so many rumors floating around, I'm dying to know the truth. Did you really sleep with James?"

"What? No."

"Then you should probably come and fill me in."

"Come where?"

"To my house. We live just down the street."

I looked down at my squirrel pajamas and slippers. I wasn't dressed to go anywhere. "I can't."

"Why?"

I didn't really care how I looked. It wasn't the slippers or the pajamas. Or even the fact that Matt was fighting with him. Matt only cared if I hung out with James, not Rob. "I can't walk that far." My feet still hurt.

He laughed. "Such a diva." He turned around, leaned over, and patted his back. "Hop on then."

"Rob…"

"Come on, Sanders. You gotta fill me in on what happened so I can stop all those rumors. We can even plan that Isabella prank I promised you. Plus you get a piggy back ride out of it."

I swallowed hard. I didn't want everyone to think I slept with James. If Matt heard that, I could only imagine how mad he would be. And I did really want to pull a prank on Isabella. I wasn't a monster, so revenge was out of the question. A prank though? She deserved at least that. "Can't I just fill you in here? And we could just go with that frog idea you had."

"Nope. I'm not allowed into enemy territory. And you were right…Isabella would probably just kill the frogs."

So the Caldwells and Hunters were still fighting. I bit the inside of my lip. Maybe this was my chance to fix everything I broke. If I could convince him to see Matt's side…Matt would be happy. He'd have his best friends back.

"How long are you going to make me present my ass to you?" Rob said, rubbing his backside seductively. "Get on my back, Sanders."

I laughed. "Okay," I said and climbed onto his back.

"Diva," he said again as he held on to my thighs.

I wrapped my arms around him so he wouldn't drop me. We walked past Matt's pool. I smiled to myself, remembering how Isabella had gotten the nickname Wizzy. I could just imagine a young, hateful tween Isabella trying to swim away from a purple cloud following her through the pool.

I looked around for Miller, but I didn't see him anywhere. "Can we stop by security so I can tell them where I'm going?" Also, I had no idea where the Caldwell security was, and I was hoping Rob knew. It would kill two birds with one stone.

"We have our own security," Rob said.

So much for that.

"So if you didn't bang my brother, I guess that also rules out the threesome rumors?"

"Threesome rumors?" *What the hell?*

"With you, him, and Rachel."

"God no."

He laughed. "Not a fan of Rachel?"

"I'm not a fan of any of what you just said. But yeah…Rachel doesn't exactly like me very much." And I didn't like her. She'd called me a slut and hadn't been very nice to James either. He deserved better.

"She probably doesn't like you because James' tongue was down your throat at homecoming."

I rested my chin against Rob's shoulder. "Yeah. And the fact that she was completely naked when I walked in on her and James."

Rob laughed. "I thought you were the naked one?"

"I had on underwear. And a map."

He laughed again and turned his head, putting his lips dangerously close to mine. "You were wearing a map? What does that even mean?"

I lifted my chin off his shoulder. The last thing I needed was for my lips to somehow end up on another Untouchables'. "I wrapped it around me like a towel. What was I supposed to do? Isabella abandoned me in my underwear."

"Ah, so that part was true. Did she really try to kill you?"

"Yes. And Kennedy." *And I'm pretty sure she still wants me dead.*

"How is Kennedy doing?" he asked.

I smiled. I'd forgotten that I didn't have to worry about Rob kissing me. He seemed much more interested in my friend. "I think she's about as freaked out as me. But she said she was going to school today, so hopefully she's doing alright."

"That's good. So are you actually moonlighting as a prostitute now?"

I laughed. "No."

"Sure about that? I think that kind of work pays pretty well."

"I'm not a prostitute."

"Hmm…that rumor is going to be pretty hard to squash. A few students swore you even admitted it."

God. I had admitted it. I was hoping they'd never put two and two together. "You know the worst part about that night? No one stopped to help me. The only person that was nice was James."

"I would have been nice," he said.

Yeah. He would have been. I put my chin back on his shoulder. Just like he'd helped me breathe during my panic attack.

We walked through another backyard that was just as lush as Matt's. If you could even really call these expanses of property "backyards." Each one seemed more extravagant than the last. There were statues, pool houses, beautiful gardens, and even fountains. A few fences and rich people backyards later, Rob stopped beneath a treehouse and let me slide off his back.

"Home sweet home," he said.

I smiled. There was something adorable about him taking me to his treehouse so I could tell him all about what happened at homecoming. I never had a treehouse growing up, but I'd always wanted one. It had been a long time since I'd felt like a kid. Taking care of my mom had forced me to grow up really fast.

"Girls are allowed," Rob said. "You can go up."

"Well, it's good I'm not breaking any rules," I said with a laugh as I climbed the little ladder. But as soon as I poked my head through the hole in the treehouse's floor, I knew I was about to break a very important rule. James was sitting in the treehouse with his usual frown. But when his eyes locked with mine, a smile stretched across his face.

Nunca. I couldn't be here. I tried to climb back down but Rob put his hand on my ass cheek.

"What are you doing?" Rob asked. "Go up, not down."

"I can't." I'd just promised Matt I wouldn't hang out with James. I wasn't going to break that promise.

Rob's hands shifted on my butt.

What the hell was he doing? I felt myself tense up.

Rob laughed. "Sanders, your ass is as heavy as it is firm. Go up." He shoved me up just as James grabbed my hands to help pull me into their treehouse.

Damn it.

"Hey," James said with a smile. One of the rare real ones. "Are you feeling better today?"

I took a deep breath. "I'm sorry, but I can't be here with you, I…I promised Matt." It was better to be honest.

"You can't be in my treehouse?" James said. "That seems like a strange promise."

I laughed. "No. I can't hang out with you at all."

"Why? Is he scared I'll steal you for myself?"

I guess? Or maybe he just doesn't trust me.

Rob laughed as he climbed up and sat down beside me. "He should be more worried about me. I'm the single one. And now that I've touched your butt, I'm not opposed to touching more." He put his hand on the inside of my knee.

I immediately pulled away from him. *What is he doing!?* I thought he liked Kennedy? I needed to get out of here.

"Actually, I'll renounce my claim on you for the greater good," Rob said and turned to James. "Mom seems hellbent on you marrying a Pruitt. Maybe you should just marry Sanders. What do you think, James? Marry Sanders instead of the troll?"

"You're right, that's not a bad idea," James said. "How 'bout it, Brooklyn? Shall we make it official and get hitched?"

"What?" I laughed even though he seemed pretty serious. Why did the Caldwells and Hunters just keep throwing out marriage proposals like it was no big deal? "No."

"Why? I've already seen you in your underwear, and I liked what I saw. You've already seen my dick and I know you liked that or you would have looked away." He winked at me. "We've already showered together. My current relationship is doomed and so is yours. Let's just make it official and make my mom happy."

What the hell? "My relationship isn't doomed. And neither is yours. You love Rachel."

"And love can't be one-sided." He reached out and tucked a loose strand of hair behind my ear, letting his knuckles graze my jaw. "Besides, I can't get you out of my head. What was it that I said the other night? Let's be miserable together?"

"James..." my voice died away when he moved to be on one knee.

His smile grew a little brighter, as if he was happy with the shocked expression on my face. "I'd like to alter what I said about being miserable together. Let's just be together. I don't think we'd be miserable. Not even a little bit. I think we'd actually be a lot happier together than we are apart. Like when we were together on Saturday night. I liked that. What do you say? Marry me?"

What the actual hell is happening?

CHAPTER 12

Monday

I didn't know what to do. I was completely frozen. Matt was going to freaking kill me.

"What do you say?" James asked, his hand still on the side of my face.

I finally found my voice. "No."

James just smiled. "No you don't like when I touch you like this? Noted." He turned his hand so that his knuckles caressed the side of my jaw instead. It was both soothing and inappropriate at the same time.

"No, not… No. I'm not going to marry you because it'll make your mom happy. That's ridiculous."

"Do it for me then," James said, like what he was proposing wasn't insane. Which it was. Because he was proposing a proposal and apparently every boy at Empire High had lost their minds.

"You don't even like me!" I pushed his hand away.

"That's not true. I told you the other night that I did. And it's the truth that I can't get you out of my head. I've been dreaming about kissing you again."

"Well, stop dreaming that. And try harder to get me out of your head."

"No thanks," he said. "Come on, Rob, help me out here. Don't you think we'd make a great couple?"

"Actually, yeah I do," Rob said. "Look how happy he is, Sanders. He doesn't usually look like that."

I stared at James. He did look happy. The real kind. Not the fake smile that he gave to strangers. Why was he looking at me like that?

I couldn't be responsible for his happiness. I couldn't even handle the weight of my pain. I couldn't possibly bear his too. I shook my head at the same time James' eyes landed on my left hand.

"I guess I'm too late," he said and finally got off one knee. His eyes stayed trained on my left hand.

I clenched my hand in a fist. Of course he'd seen the ring. It was impossible not to see.

"What the hell is that thing?" Rob asked and grabbed my hand.

"It's a...promise ring," I said.

"It looks like a freaking engagement ring to me." He whistled.

I pulled my hand back. "I really need to get going." I couldn't be here with them talking about stuff like this. I was in love with Matt. Period. And if that meant I couldn't be friends with them, then that was how it had to be. Even though I hated when James' smile turned to his usual frown.

"I thought you were too much of a diva to walk?" Rob said.

"Shut up, man," James said and lifted one of my slippers off my feet. "She's hurt. Not lazy." He tossed the slipper at his brother.

Rob's eyebrows pulled together. "Shit. I'm sorry, Sanders." He reached out and ran his thumb along the bandages on my feet.

Why did they both keep touching me? "It's fine," I snatched my slipper back. I didn't want either of them staring at me like I was some kind of dainty damsel in distress. I didn't need saving. The bandages made it look worse than it was. "James can fill you in on what did and didn't happen at homecoming. And you don't need me to plan a prank against Isabella. I'm just gonna head back."

"Hey," Rob said and put his hand on my shoulder before I could move. "I'm sorry, I didn't know you were hurt." He turned his attention to James. "A heads up would have been nice."

"It wasn't my story to tell," James said. His eyes dropped to the ring on my finger again.

I swallowed hard. I didn't want him looking at me like that. Or being so nice. I needed to get out of here.

"Come on, Sanders," Rob said. "Stay. It's gonna be fun. And we definitely need the story about how you got that ring."

I looked down at the beautiful diamond on my finger. It didn't feel right to talk to them about this. I'd already messed up just by leaving Matt's house. "I can't be here. I promised Matt. Please just let me go."

"We won't tell anyone you were here," James said. "Come on, I promise I won't propose again." He lifted up a notebook that had been on the floor. "Isabella deserves to pay for what she did to you. That's what we meant to talk about. So let's just stick with that. Any ideas on how you want to get her back?"

I stared at James for a moment. He'd just lost two of his best friends. He was fighting with Rachel. I certainly wasn't giving him the answers he wanted. And I shouldn't have cared, because Matt didn't want me to. But I did. I cared about James. The more we hung out, the more his cracks were starting to show. And just because Matt had stopped worrying about him, it didn't mean I could shut it off so easily. If Matt wasn't looking out for him, who would? And I'd agreed to come with Rob so that I could try to fix the rift between the Caldwells and the Hunters. If I left right now, I would have just made everything worse. "Just a silly prank?" I asked.

James smiled again. "Yeah. Something to embarrass her in front of everyone."

I leaned back. "As long as it's not revenge." Matt was right. I wasn't and never would be more Pruitt than Sanders. And that meant no revenge. Even if I did want Isabella to die.

"It's not technically revenge," Rob said. "Because we'd already started plotting before Wizzy tried to kill you. Preemptive revenge maybe..."

"Just a prank," James said. "Something epic."

Something epic. Hmm. "You know what would make it more epic? Getting the whole gang back together," I said. "The Untouchables back at it again."

James shook his head. "The Untouchables? I always hated that nickname." He doodled something in his notebook. "Who came up with that? Clearly whoever first said it was dead wrong."

Oh, James. He was trying to hide his broken heart. But random proposals weren't going to fix things with Rachel or bring the Untouchables back together.

"Well, revenge is a dish best served cold," Rob said, ignoring James' comment. "Isn't that a saying? Maybe we could do something with pudding."

I laughed. "And she couldn't kill any frogs that way."

James jotted down the idea.

"You know who probably makes a good pudding?" I asked. "Mrs. Caldwell. I bet if we looped Matt and Mason in on this…"

"Sanders," Rob groaned. "We said we wouldn't talk about your engagement to the enemy. So stop mentioning the enemy's name in our treehouse. This is a sacred place."

"But…"

"No buts. When you hang out with us, you're one of us. When you hang out with them, you're one of them." He made a gagging noise. "No in the middle. Right now you're a Hunter. Be a gross Caldwell later. Unless you want to sleep in my bed tonight instead." He winked at me. "I'll buy you a nicer ring."

James cleared his throat. "I kind of like the pudding idea. Could you imagine how much Isabella would freak if she got that in her hair?"

I tried to focus on James instead of Rob. I couldn't handle any more teasing today. And seeing James smile again made being here feel like less of a mistake. He needed this.

"Or we could shave her head," Rob suggested.

I laughed.

They went back and forth, making me laugh, harder and harder as I looked around the small treehouse. There were toys and comic books on the floor. It looked so much more lived in than James' room had. Pictures lined the wall. Photos of James as a happy little boy. He had the same facial features, in an adorable little boy kind of way. "You used to be so cute," I said and leaned over to look at one.

"Used to be?" James asked. "You're just not looking hard enough now."

I laughed at him and then looked back at the pictures. "Is this all four of the Untouchables as kids?"

"Again with that terrible nickname," James said with a laugh. He leaned over and unpinned the picture from the wall. "But yeah. That was taken one summer when we were little."

"We look ridiculous," Rob said.

I smiled down at the picture. James and Mason both had braces and looked so scrawny, sitting on the edge of a pool. It looked like the pool in Matt's backyard. Rob and Matt looked even scrawnier. Rob was pushing Matt into the pool in the picture and the expression on Matt's face was priceless. The four of them were having so much fun. How could they just let this friendship fade away?

"You can keep it, if you want," James said. "I don't really want it anymore."

I pressed my lips together. Maybe he didn't want it right now. But he would again one day. I'd make sure of it. "Thanks."

"No problem. And I'm still cute."

I laughed. "Sure."

He ran his fingers through his hair. "You'll see, Brooklyn. One day you'll look back at all of this and wish you would have said yes to me."

I smiled. "You never know." But I did. I looked down at the picture. I wanted Matt. And I wanted what was in this picture too. Yes, their friendship had fallen apart. But that just meant it could be put together. I knew that. My heart was being put back together too.

And as I looked down at the picture, it made me want something else too. I could so easily picture Matt and my kids hanging out by the pool. With smiles that big. I'd never thought about kids before. Hell, I was still a kid. But it was so easy to picture it with Matt. Maybe because he seemed to have pushed down the gas pedal on our relationship. And one day, I wanted our kids to be friends with James' kids. And Rob's.

I looked up at James. "I just think that maybe you're all sorry. And that there's no reason to throw away a lifetime of friendship over a misunderstanding."

"Well…if you accept my proposal, I guess I could forgive him."

I rolled my eyes.

He groaned. "Don't do that. I like it too much."

I laughed. "When I roll my eyes?"

"So sexy."

"You're ridiculous."

He laughed. "Yeah, but you like it."

I shook my head. "Can we please focus?"

"Sure thing." He tossed me his notebook.

I looked down at what James had written. *Drop her off in the middle of nowhere. Take her clothes. Point a gun at her head.*

Threaten to kill her best friend. "Best friend" was scratched out with "minion." Make her disappear? A chill ran down my spine. Matt had wanted me to be the bigger person. He didn't want me to stoop to Isabella's level. He'd said I was better than her. But God, I desperately wanted to make her disappear. And I was pretty sure the Hunters had the resources to make it happen.

I should have corrected James. Convinced him that I just wanted it to be a silly prank like I'd insisted before. But I just kept staring at the question mark after the word *disappear*. Like he was asking me for my permission. Like he was offering to do it for me.

And I wasn't sure why, but I wrote down yes and then handed it back to him. His eyes locked with mine. For a second I'd forgotten that his life was just as tangled up in Isabella's as mine. Maybe his mom just wanted him to marry a Pruitt because she liked Isabella. Or maybe it was more sinister like Isabella had said – that the Hunters owed my dad a debt. And they'd paid it with James' future. Either way, Isabella was going to ruin both our lives. Unless we ruined hers first.

James raised his left eyebrow at me.

And I nodded.

"New plan," James said. "I think we all know what we really want here." He tossed his notebook to the side. "We want to make Isabella disappear for good. What do you say, Rob? Got something in your evil genius mind for that?"

"Now we're talking." Rob rubbed his hands together. "Oh! We're going to need pizza for this. Nothing like pizza to plot murder." He pulled out his phone and sent a text. "So what are we thinking, cheese or pepperoni?"

How could Rob think about what kind of pizza we wanted when he just said we wanted to kill someone? Disappear was different than kill. Right?

"Cheese sounds good," James said. "Unless you want something else?" he asked me.

I shook my head. James wasn't freaking out. Apparently he'd meant kill too.

"Perfect," Rob said. "Cheese it is. Now how do you want to kill the troll?"

CHAPTER 13

Monday

Rob didn't need to ask us our opinion. Because before we even had a chance to respond, he told us his whole plan. A plan that was clearly well thought out because it was so detailed. And graphic.

"The key is making sure every inch of her burns so that they can't trace anything back to us," Rob said. "Unless you'd rather use lye. But I really like the idea of fire. It seems like a more graceful way to end it, you know?"

I finally found my voice. "What the fuck, Rob?"

He started laughing. And then laughing some more. He pointed at me, barely even able to breathe. "You should see your face right now."

How was I supposed to look after hearing *that*?

"Your pizza, young Robert," someone said and poked his head through the hole in the floor of the treehouse.

I almost screamed. After hearing Rob's murderous plan, it almost looked like the man's decapitated head was on a platter.

"Thanks, Eric," Rob said and grabbed it from him. "Could we have something to drink too?"

"Already on top of it, sir." The butler slid a tray of sodas into the treehouse with his gloved hand. "Will that be all?"

"Yup."

"Will you be attending classes after lunch?" Eric asked.

"Nah. We need the whole day off. We've had a stressful weekend. Right, James?"

James nodded.

"Very well. Let me know if any of you need anything else. Good to see you again, Miss Sanders."

"You too." I wasn't sure what else to say. *Help me, Rob's a murdering psychopath* probably wouldn't work with his butler.

Eric disappeared down the hole.

"Pizza?" Rob asked and lifted up a slice.

"We can't kill Isabella," I said. "I just meant...make her go away." Twenty four hours ago, I'd wanted her dead. But after talking to Matt... I swallowed hard. I didn't want him to ever think I was a monster too.

Rob laughed. "I know. I just wanted to see your face. I like it when you blush. It's so freaking cute."

What?

"Like you're doing right now."

"You're both ridiculous," I said and shoved his arm.

"Mhm. You're the one that can't keep your hands off me. Do you need me to call Mr. Hill to put a ruler between us again?" He smiled. "See...blushing."

I shook my head. "Okay, this has been super fun. But I really should get back to Matt's house."

"After lunch," James said. "You need to eat." He picked up a slice and handed it to me before I could protest. "Come on. You've lost weight the last few weeks. You gotta eat something."

I pressed my lips together. He'd noticed that I'd lost weight after my uncle passed away? I looked down at my pajama bottoms. I wanted to blame it on the baggy material, but that wasn't it. I'd been sad. It was hard to eat when all I wanted to do was cry. And then everything that happened between Matt and me on top of it? I'd barely had an appetite at all. I never would have guessed James would notice though.

"Please?" James asked. "We won't make any more murder jokes. We'll just plan a prank veering on the edge of revenge that may or may not make Isabella run away from home. I promise."

"Yeah," Rob said. "We're not going to kill anyone. We aren't Pruitts." He lifted his hand for a high-five, but I just stared at him. "Suit yourself," he said and grabbed a soda.

I ate my slice of pizza as they went back to the pudding idea.

"Matt has a really big kitchen," I said. "It would be the perfect place to make that much pudding." I could still fix this.

Rob laughed. "We're going to buy it, Sanders. Who has time to make pudding?"

"I don't know…most people?"

"You're not thinking big enough," he said. "We need *a lot* of pudding. And maybe some dead frogs. That way Isabella can't kill them."

Gross. "Where do you plan on getting dead frogs from?"

"She's super uncreative," Rob said and looked over at James.

"No," James said. "She's just too sweet to think as evilly as us. One of the many reasons I like her."

Rob laughed, but I didn't.

Enough was enough. I'd come here for two reasons, and the second was more important than revenge. "Okay, here's the deal," I said. "I will help with whatever plan that the three of us come up with if you both swear to stop messing with me with all this silly flirting," I said.

"We're not…" James started, but I cut him off.

"And after I help you pull off the most epic prank on Isabella ever, you have to try to make up with the Caldwells."

Rob laughed. "I'm not down with either of those conditions. Especially the first one, Sanders." He winked at me.

"Me either," James said.

God, they were both infuriating. "You need me in order to get access to Isabella's room. There's no prank without me. And those are my conditions."

"Ugh." Rob grabbed another slice of pizza.

"Do we have a deal?" I asked and put my hand out for James to shake. I trusted him more than I trusted Rob. Rob would shout "just kidding" or something. James would make the deal.

"Deal on the second contingency," James said. "I can't make any promises on the first."

"Fine."

He placed his hand on top of mine instead of shaking it. And then Rob threw his hand on top of James'.

"Operation Disappearing Troll on three," Rob said.

I laughed as they both threw their hands up and yelled, "Operation Disappearing Troll!"

"And if Isabella dies in the process, all the better," Rob said.

"That's not funny," I said. But I laughed anyway just because he looked so excited.

"We're basically planning on giving her a heart attack, so it's a possibility," added Rob. "Oh, should we do it right after Thanksgiving? Isabella's always so happy during Thanksgiving break because all her evil relatives are in town."

Evil relatives? I hadn't even thought about my new extended family. Would they all be so horrible?

"Good thinking," James said. "Besides, it gives us more time to plan."

I wasn't so sure more time with the two of them was a good thing.

"What the hell! Are you trying to get Donnelley and me killed?" Miller's head had just popped up through the floor of the treehouse. His face looked so beat up that for just a second, I didn't recognize him.

I jumped, knocking over Rob's soda.

"Shit," Rob said under his breath as he grabbed a napkin. "Who the hell are you?"

"Out," Miller said, ignoring Rob. "Now."

"Miller…" my voice caught in my throat. This was not at all the way I wanted to start our conversation.

"I swear, Miss Pruitt, if you don't get out of this treehouse right now, I'll tell your father that you can't be trusted here."

Miss Pruitt. I hated that he was calling me that. Even more than I hated the idea of having to leave the safety of Matt's house. "I'm sorry," I said to James and Rob. "I have to go." Seeing Miller's bruised face made tears well in my eyes. And the anger in his voice? I deserved it. But it still hurt me. I tried to scramble out of the treehouse before the tears started to fall.

This time James and Rob didn't stop me with proposals or jokes or food. But James did put his hand on my shoulder right before I climbed down.

"Are you going to be okay with him?" he asked.

"Yeah. He's my security guard." I tried to wipe away my tears.

"Okay." James searched my face like he was trying to figure out why I was crying.

I hoped he didn't see the real reason.

"Well…call me if you need anything."

I didn't have James' number. Which was for the best. I climbed down the little ladder. Miller was already walking through the Hunters' perfectly manicured gardens.

"Wait!" I called.

Miller didn't stop.

I tried to run after him but my feet hurt. *Ow.* "Miller!"

He just kept going.

Fuck. I pushed through a fence and tried to run again. Each step was worse than the one before. I stopped and pulled my foot out of my slipper. There was blood on the bottom of the bandage. "Miller," I said, but he was already through some hedges into the neighbor's lawn.

I took another step. I bit the inside of my lip as I made my way past a massive pool house. But as the back of

Miller's head grew farther and farther away, it felt like there was no point. I wasn't going to catch up to him. And clearly he didn't want to talk to me. Just reprimand me.

I sat down under a willow tree and let myself cry. Not for my stupid feet. But for my own stupidity. I hadn't thought about putting Miller's career in jeopardy by going with Rob. I had only been focused on fixing Matt's friendships. But not thinking about Miller was selfish. He'd been there for me when I needed him. And by the look of his face, he needed me now. Instead of seeking him out, I just made his day a million times more stressful by disappearing.

I pulled my knees into my chest. I couldn't seem to get anything right recently. I just kept hurting people over and over again. Before I lost my uncle, I thought I was finally getting my life under control again. But when he died, it was like everything crumbled around me. And I was so tired of hurting all the time. And doing the hurting.

I wasn't sure how long I sat there crying before I heard Miller clear his throat.

I looked up at his bruised face. I wanted to hug him and somehow make it better. Instead, I hugged my knees closer to my chest. "I'm so sorry."

"Are you kidding me?"

I started crying harder. Those words were inadequate. And we both knew it. "I never meant to hurt you."

"You never meant to hurt me?" his voice was harsh. "So dancing with all those guys at homecoming was supposed to make me feel good?"

"Miller..."

"I thought you cared about me."

"I do care about you."

"This isn't caring." He gestured back and forth between us. "This is you rubbing your new relationship in my face when I'm the only one in your life actually trying to protect you."

The only one in my life trying to protect me? What did he mean by that? "But my dad…"

"Your dad?" He put "dad" in air quotes. "Who the fuck do you think did this to my face? I let you out of my sight for a few minutes and he had someone beat the shit out of me."

I swallowed hard. I thought that might have been what happened. "I'm so sorry," I said again, because I didn't know what else to say.

"Are you, Brooklyn? Because you haven't asked me anything about what happened that night. I woke up in a supply closet after your crazy fucking sister injected me with some sedative. I was scared out of my mind when I woke up. Not for myself. Scared for you. And meanwhile you were just fine dancing the night away with Matt."

"Fine? I wasn't fine. Isabella abandoned me in the city in just my underwear! I had to run miles to find the hotel. I was terrified. I *am* terrified." The tears started back up. "I'm still not fine. And I wanted to talk to you right away. But you called me Miss Pruitt…"

"I have to be professional around Donnelley. And everyone else. If Mr. Pruitt finds out I was the one you were sneaking around with… Look what he already did to me, Brooklyn. He'll fucking kill me."

"I thought you were calling me Miss Pruitt because you were mad."

"Of course I'm mad!" He looked up at the sky for a second and took a deep breath. "Fuck," he groaned. "I really cared about you, kid." He lowered his head and locked eyes with me.

Kid. His nickname felt like a knife in the chest. "And I meant what I said…I still care about you."

"Then what the hell is on your hand?" he asked.

I looked down at the diamond on my ring finger. How could I explain this to him? I cared about him. But love? I loved Matt. I only loved him. "I'm sorry, Miller. I…"

"Don't. I don't need to know why you chose him. I don't need the whole *it's me not you* speech. I'm not an idiot." He ran his hand down his face. "If you want to be part of this world, that's fine. But I'm not going to let myself get killed because of you. I'm done."

Done? I cringed and pulled myself to my feet. "What do you mean done?"

"I can't be your security guard. I can't watch you every day with him. Don't make me do that, Brooklyn."

I blinked fast, forcing my tears not to start again. I couldn't make him stay. But I hated that he had to go. "Okay."

He reached out and touched the side of my face. "I'm sorry."

For a second I just stared at him. "What are you sorry for?" I was the one that had ruined us.

"I shouldn't have left you during the dance. This is all my fault. I'm so fucking mad at you right now. But I'm even madder at myself." He leaned down and scooped me up into his arms. "I know you're hurt. I'm sorry I made you run after me."

I didn't blame him for any of that. I was just sorry that he was quitting because of me. He needed this money for school. And despite what he said, all of this was my fault, not his. It was my fault he'd walked away from me during the dance. It was my fault he was hurting. All of this was my fault.

"Couldn't you stay?" I asked. "And just be assigned to someone else?"

"I think I need a fresh start, kid," he said.

Okay. I rested my head against his chest and breathed in his familiar scent. I knew I'd needed to end things between us. I just didn't know it would make me feel like I was sinking all over again.

Miller carried me all the way back to Matt's. He carried me through the house, up the stairs, and to what I assumed was the guest room I was supposed to be staying in. He put me down on the edge of the bed.

There were boxes scattered around the room.

"What is all this stuff?" I asked.

"Some of the new clothes Justin sent over for you. And a few things that weren't damaged." Miller opened up one of the boxes. "I knew you'd want these back." He pulled out my mom's blue dress and my Keds.

"What?" I stood up. "How?"

"I went back to get them for you. I know how much this dress and these shoes mean to you."

Instead of taking the dress out of his hands, I threw my arms around him. "Thank you. For everything. For taking care of me when I had no one else. For being my shoulder to cry on."

He placed a kiss on my forehead and unwound my arms from his waist. "Take care, kid."

My heart wasn't as healed as I wanted to believe. Because it felt like it just ripped down the middle as Miller walked out of the room and out of my life.

But I knew a broken heart kept beating. Mine seemed to ache all the time, but I was still here. *Ow.* I pressed my hand to my chest. It would eventually stop hurting. It had to.

CHAPTER 14

Monday

Mrs. Caldwell was humming at the stove. By the smell of cinnamon in the air, I was beginning to understand why Matt always smelled like scrumptious dessert. As much as my stomach wanted me to stay, I'd been trying to get Matt away from the dinner table for what felt like hours. Apparently Matt and Mason always did their homework sitting at the kitchen table together. It was wonderful that there was so much family time in this house. But not when I needed to tell Matt about this afternoon.

"Can we go upstairs for a bit?" I asked. The class notes Matt had brought me from school remained untouched on the table. I needed to talk to him before I could focus. God, he was going to be so mad at me.

"Someone's anxious for alone time," Mason said with a laugh. "I'm guessing last night went well?"

I leaned closer to Matt. "Please?" I whispered, trying to ignore Mason.

"Oh, Brooklyn," Mrs. Caldwell said as she came back to the table carrying a pan of something with a perfectly golden crumble on top. "I meant to ask you this afternoon...but I couldn't find you."

Shit. I didn't want my whereabouts to come out like this. Did she know I was with the Hunters?

"I was hoping we could do a girls' night," she said and started dishing out the dessert.

I breathed a sigh of relief.

"Maybe Friday night?" Mrs. Caldwell asked.

I glanced at Matt. He was smiling. And I was pretty sure he was just pretending to read the notes in front of him. I wondered if this was his idea or his mom's. It didn't matter either way. I was excited to get to know his mom better. "That sounds great," I said.

"You can invite all your friends too. It'll be so much fun. And it'll give us a chance to get to know each other better."

All my friends? The only girl friend I had was Kennedy. "Sure." It came out as more of a question than a direct answer.

"Wonderful. About how many friends do you think you'll invite? I'll need a head count to figure out what we should do."

She wanted to get to know me. And now the first thing she'd learn was that I didn't have very many friends. I cleared my throat. "I can ask my friend Kennedy to come."

Mrs. Caldwell smiled. "Anyone else?"

"Um…no. That's it."

"You know what? That's even better. More than a handful is a crowd anyway. And maybe you boys can have James and Robert over? I feel like I haven't seen them in ages."

For just a second everyone was silent.

"Maybe some other night," Mason said and scooped some of the dessert on a plate.

Wait. Did Mrs. Caldwell not know about their falling out?

Mrs. Caldwell laughed. "I feel like our fridge is overflowing. I'm used to the boys coming over for dinner at least a few nights a week. Invite them over for dinner tomorrow then." She stood up. "I'm going to go book a few things for our girls' night!" She looked so excited as she walked out of the kitchen.

"Your mom doesn't know that you guys are fighting?" I asked.

"There isn't much to tell," Matt said.

"There is if they're usually here all the time. What are you going to tell her when they don't come over for dinner tomorrow?"

"That they were busy."

"Eventually she's going to catch on…"

"Which means we'll never have to have an awkward conversation," Mason said. "Just let them slowly disappear from all of our lives."

"You can't just delete friends from your lives." Everyone was making this so much harder than it needed to be. It was all a huge misunderstanding. Without even realizing it, they were letting Isabella dictate their lives.

"It's already done," Matt said. "They wouldn't hear me out."

"But…"

"And James kissing you was the final straw. I'm never talking to either of them again."

I swallowed hard. God, he was going to hate me. "Can we please go upstairs for a few minutes?" I asked.

Mason laughed. "Insatiable."

I grabbed Matt's hand and pulled him away from the table before Mason could make any more jokes about our sex life. By the time we reached Matt's bedroom I practically shoved him inside. I closed the door and locked it. When I spun around, Matt's arms were caging me in.

"You know I like when you just ask for what you want," he whispered against my ear. "I was just waiting for you to tell me your wildest fantasies."

My heart started racing. "In front of your brother?"

"You could have whispered all the unspeakable things you want me to do to you." He traced his tongue along the side of my ear.

It took every ounce of restraint not to grab his face and pull his lips to mine. "As much as I want to do more of…that…I need to talk to you first."

"Or we could talk after." His fingers skimmed across the waistline of my leggings. "I've been thinking of you all day. Thinking about what I did to you last night."

God.

His fingers dipped beneath my waistband. "Thinking of you alone in my bed."

"I hung out with James!" I wasn't sure why I screamed it. It was like the secret was burning a hole in my chest

Matt's fingers froze on my skin.

"I didn't mean to," I said. "Rob came over and was talking about all the rumors swirling around. And he said that he wanted me to help him clear them up. I didn't want there to be rumors about me sleeping with James, which apparently there are. And I thought I was just going to hang out with Rob. But when I climbed into his treehouse James was there and then…"

"Are you kidding me?" Matt pushed himself away from the door. "You promised me…" he glanced at the clock on his nightstand "…less than 24 hours ago that you wouldn't hang out with James anymore. What the hell?" He didn't sound mad. Just disappointed. Somehow that was even worse.

"But that's what I'm trying to explain. I didn't mean to hang out with James. I was going with Rob and…"

"Jesus, Brooklyn. I'm fighting with Rob too. You're supposed to be on my side."

"I am on your side."

"Well it doesn't really look like it."

His words stung. But I knew I deserved them. "I'm so sorry. It won't happen again." I'd be able to follow through on the prank without seeing the Hunters. That's what phones were for. I could still fix everything.

"And you're not supposed to leave the house," Matt said. "We don't know where Isabella is. Do you have any idea how dangerous it was to go to the Hunters' house?"

"I was just trying to fix your friendship…"

"I asked you not to see James. How is you hanging out with him fixing anything? You looked me in the eyes and promised." Now he sounded mad.

I knew I was in the wrong. But I hadn't meant to do anything bad. "I didn't know James was going to be there." And now our conversation was going in circles and not getting any better. I was just trying to be honest with him.

Matt sat down on the edge of his bed.

I hated when he was mad at me. I hated fighting with him. Unless it was the kind of fighting we did last night, in which case…I wish we were doing that instead. But he didn't seem to be offering that. "I'm sorry that it happened. But I wanted to make sure I told you the truth."

"The truth?" He looked up at me. "The truth is that giving you that ring meant something to me. I even went to your dad's place today to tell him about my intentions with you. I'm all in with you. I've told you that. But you're making it really hard to trust that you're all in too."

"I am all in with you. James is just a friend and I won't see him anymore, I swear."

"Did he try to kiss you?"

"No. And even if he did I would have turned him away. We just talked. Matt, I don't want him. I want you."

"What did you talk about?"

I knew he was trying to be reasonable. He was giving me a chance to explain. But if I told him about the prank, he'd make me call it off. I didn't want to give up on my one chance of fixing his friendships.

"Did he hit on you at all?" Matt asked when I didn't respond.

Fuck me. "Yeah, but he was just joking around. And I didn't flirt back. They were both just being weird."

He ran his fingers through his hair. "Rob too? What did they say?"

Withholding the prank was one thing. But what if James joked about his fake proposal at school tomorrow? I wasn't going to blindside Matt. That was the whole reason I told him about the treehouse in the first place. James promised he wouldn't say anything. But I didn't know enough about James to trust him.

I took a deep breath. "James kind of…proposed. But he was kidding." *I think.*

"What?"

"Rob said something about how his parents want James to marry a Pruitt. They were just joking around."

He ran his hand down his face. "I know that I messed up. I gave you every reason to run into someone else's arms. But not today. Not now. I was trying to be understanding, but this…it's like you're purposely torturing me."

"I'm not trying to hurt you."

"Brooklyn, you freaking got proposed to today by someone that wasn't me." He abruptly stood up. "And just before homecoming you were sleeping in another man's bed."

"You said you forgave me…"

"It doesn't mean I forgot about it!" He turned away from me. "Fuck."

I hated when he couldn't even look at me. I knew I'd made a mess of things, but I wasn't running anymore. I walked up to him and grabbed both sides of his face so that he'd look at me. "I only love you. And who cares if James' parents want him to marry a Pruitt? I'm not a Pruitt. I'm a soon-to-be Caldwell."

Matt reached out and hooked his arm around my waist. "You finally agree that you're wearing an engagement ring?"

I glanced at the ring on my hand and then back at him. "I mean, it's a promise to be engaged, right?"

He pressed his forehead against mine. "You're going to be the death of me, Brooklyn."

I closed my eyes. "Don't say that." I squeezed my eyes tight. It felt like I was cursed. Like everyone that was important to me died. If anything ever happened to Matt…

"I can't lose you too." I opened my eyes as if seeing him would prevent him from slipping away.

"You know what I mean. You're driving me crazy." His lips drew a fraction of an inch closer to mine. "No more hanging out with James. Or Rob."

"As long as you promise not to hang out with Isabella." I wasn't sure why I was cutting a deal with him. I should have just agreed. But there was still something bothering me about the night Isabella had a gun to my head. Besides the fact that she had literally been trying to kill me. She'd been trying to get rid of me so that she could be with Matt. She was in love with him. And he needed to know that if he didn't already.

Matt pulled back. "I can definitely promise you that. I hate her, Brooklyn."

"Yeah. But she loves you." I felt better just by getting it off my chest. I'd needed to know if he loved her too. Even a little bit. I knew he thought Isabella was a disease. But what if he thought she was a sexy disease? Like…well, I couldn't think of any sexy diseases. Maybe Isabella was the first.

He tucked a loose strand of hair behind my ear. "I strongly doubt that Isabella loves me."

"She was blackmailing you because she didn't want you anywhere near me. She wanted you for herself."

He started to shake his head.

"I'm serious, Matt. She told me. Me loving you is part of the reason she hates me. And I remember the way she touched you right here in this room. Like she'd done it a thousand times before…"

"She was blackmailing me. I was trying to keep her calm while I figured out a way to get out of it."

By letting her touch you? I took a deep breath. It didn't matter. He'd forgiven me for what I'd done. And I could let that go too. As long as it didn't' continue. "I just need to know that you don't like her back."

"I swear I don't like Isabella. I loathe her."

And her whole family. My family. But I'd meant what I said. I was going to be a Caldwell soon enough. And I wasn't going to let Matt's opinions of my new family bother me. I barely knew any of them. But I knew Matt. I stared into his eyes. "She said she could date you before she married James. And that maybe she'd keep you as a houseboy."

"Is that like some kind of man servant?" He laughed. "It doesn't even matter." He cradled my face in his hands. "I love you, Brooklyn. I've only ever loved you."

"You promise?"

"I'll only ever love you, baby."

I stood up on my tiptoes, sealing my own promise to him with a kiss. *I promise to only ever love you too.*

CHAPTER 15

Tuesday

Matt smiled as I walked downstairs in his varsity jacket. It was one of the few things that Isabella hadn't managed to ruin. And I'd be lying if a small part of me wasn't excited to rub this jacket in her face at school today.

"Now it's official," Matt said and pulled me into his arms.

"The ring didn't do it?" I smiled up at him. I knew he was probably still a little upset with me. But he didn't look upset right now.

He dropped his head, letting his lips graze against mine. "My ring on your finger and my jacket on your shoulders? Either would have been a win. But both?" He kissed me slow. I was still getting used to his slow kisses. I loved these kisses more than the frantic, secretive kisses he used to give me. Because these meant more. These were real.

"Are you sure you're up to going to school?" Matt asked.

"Yeah. I don't want to just sit around all day again." I pressed my lips together because we both knew I'd done a lot more than that yesterday. "And I also need to talk to Felix." Really? That was what I thought would be good to mention right now?

Matt sighed and shook his head. "What are the odds that he's going to propose to you in gym today?"

I laughed. "Slim to none. And I told you, James was just joking around." *I'm pretty sure.*

"He's trying to steal you away from me because he's an ass."

Yeah. Maybe. But James had also promised to try to fix things with Matt after our Isabella prank. I just needed to make sure I didn't have to meet up with the Hunters anymore in order to pull it off. I was going to fix everything. And Matt would be happy then. And so would James. It was a win-win for everyone.

I looked up at Matt's face. He didn't look upset. He looked…uneasy. Like he was worried today was going to be a disaster. But he had nothing to worry about. I slid my hand into his. "Trust me, there's no way James could ever steal me away from you."

"Yo," Mason said through a bite of granola bar. "Come on, we're gonna be late. Morning, sis," he said and winked at me before making his way out the ornate front doors.

"Well, at least he knows you're off-limits," Matt said as I pulled him outside.

"I'm off-limits to everyone but you. The ring and the jacket, remember?"

"Promise not to take them off?"

"I promise. But I'll have to take the jacket off in gym." I took every promise very seriously now. And I wanted to make sure he knew it. "I don't think Coach Carter would like it if I was running around on the track…" my voice trailed off. I couldn't run today. I was wearing my thickest socks and walking still hurt a little. "Actually, I guess I won't be participating in gym today."

"You're sure you don't want another day to rest?"

"No, that's ridiculous."

"We're good, man," Mason said as Miller approached us. He lifted up a pair of keys. "I'll drive them."

"She comes with us or doesn't leave at all," Miller said.

Wait…Miller? Miller was waiting by a brand new SUV. Miller and the SUV were both a surprise. He'd said he was going to quit.

"I'm a good driver," Mason said. "Most of the time I don't even speed."

"Miss Pruitt, let's go," Miller said, ignoring Mason.

"What's going on?" I asked, letting Matt's hand fall out of mine.

Donnelley poked his head out of the passenger window. "Like the new ride? It's top of the line. Safest vehicle in its class. Bullet-proof windows and everything."

Bullet-proof windows? What the fuck? Did that mean Isabella still had a gun?

"Miss Pruitt, you have to drive with us to school," Miller said. "Your father insists." He opened up the back door.

Mason shrugged. "Are you coming with me or going with them, Matt?"

"I'll stay with Brooklyn," Matt said.

"Suit yourself. See you guys at lunch." Mason hopped into his convertible and sped off.

I couldn't ask Miller what was going on. So I did the only thing I could do and climbed into the back seat. Maybe he just hadn't gotten a chance to talk to my dad yet. But if my dad had sent this car…he must have had a chance. Right?

The ride was silent and awkward. Maybe only awkward for me and Miller. We'd said goodbye. I'd assumed I'd never see him again.

Matt didn't seem to find it weird at all though. But then again, he had no idea Miller was the guy I'd been seeing.

The closer we got to school, the more uneasy I felt. I'd been so excited to walk into school with Matt that I hadn't thought about the fact that more had changed than just our relationship status. A few weeks ago, James would have been driving Matt to school in his Benz. A few weeks ago, Isabella hadn't pointed a gun to my head. A few weeks ago, I had been Matt's dirty little secret. But now everything was different. And there was a lump in my throat getting bigger by the second.

"We'll be here waiting after school," Miller said as he pulled up outside Empire High.

We'll? As in him again?

"Will you need a ride after football practice, Matt?" Miller asked. "I can have someone sent for you."

This was too weird. I unbuckled my seatbelt.

"Nah, I'll catch a ride with Mason. Thanks for driving us," Matt said.

"And Miss Pruitt?" Miller added. "If Isabella does anything at all to you, please notify either of us right away."

"Like what?" My voice was so small, I wasn't sure Miller or Donnelley had heard me.

But then Donnelley turned around to look at me. "She's not supposed to talk to you at all. Mr. Pruitt and her are still negotiating the specifics, and until something is signed she's not allowed to have any contact with you. She understands this. So if she talks to you at all…you text us right away and she'll be removed from school."

"She'll be expelled?" I asked.

"No. This is a family matter. One of us will come escort her out for your safety."

My safety? I nodded. This was a good thing. Isabella wasn't allowed to speak to me. That was great. Except…the knots in my stomach didn't feel great. Since when did Isabella ever do anything she was supposed to? "Okay," I said. I had a feeling I'd be texting them in no time. I followed Matt out of the SUV.

Matt threw his arm over my shoulders as we made our way up the front steps. He waved at one of his football friends and then kissed the side of my forehead. "Today is going to be a great day," he whispered in my ear. "Don't worry about Isabella. Let's just enjoy this moment. No more wasting time."

It was what I'd always wanted. For him to love me in public. What was I doing worrying about Isabella? I wouldn't let her rob me of this moment. And Matt knew how much wasted time weighed on me. He'd said the exact right thing to get me out of my head.

He held the front door for me and the hallway hushed. Everyone was staring at us as Matt walked me to my locker. I wasn't sure if it was because of the prostitute rumors, the fact that Isabella had tried to murder me, or that Matt was holding my hand. Probably a combination of the three.

Matt seemed to think it was the last one, because when we reached my locker, he pulled me against his chest and kissed me, showing our relationship off to the whole school. I didn't care about the rumors swirling around. For the first time at Empire High, I felt safe. As long as I had Matt - really had him - everything would be fine. And I did. His hand slid dangerously close to my ass and I laughed.

I heard a few whistles. A few laughs. A few cheers for Matt. And then the hush was gone.

"Nothing for them to whisper about now," he said. "By the first bell, everyone will know you're mine. And everyone will know not to mess with you," he said a little louder for the benefit of the passersby.

"Brooklyn!" Kennedy yelled. She almost toppled me over in a hug, but Matt was there to keep us both upright.

"What is on your hand?" she said with a gasp. "Oh my God." She looked at Matt's smiling face and then mine. "What is going on?"

"It's a promise ring," I said at the exact same time that Matt said, "We're engaged," loud enough for anyone near-by to hear.

I laughed and Matt smiled down at me.

"What? Well, which one is it?" Kennedy lifted up my hand to stare at the ring. She didn't wait for me to re-spond. She just threw her arms around me again. "It doesn't even matter. I can't even remember the last time I saw you this happy. And I'm so happy for you. Did you know that Matt and Mason sat with me at lunch yester-day?" She pulled away from her hug.

"No, I didn't know that," I said and smiled up at Matt.

"I'm going to let you two catch up," Matt said. "See you at lunch?"

I nodded. I couldn't stop smiling.

He leaned down and gave me one last kiss.

I heard the flash of Kennedy's camera capturing the moment.

Kennedy waited for him to walk away before continuing. "I'll definitely get that one developed for you," she said and looked up from the screen. "You guys are so adorable."

I opened up my locker to hide my face. After what she'd been through this weekend it felt inappropriate for me to be smiling so hard. But she seemed to be in a good mood. A great one, actually. She snapped another picture as I pulled out my books for first period.

"You said they sat with you at lunch?" I asked.

"Yeah, well, obviously Cupcake doesn't sit with us anymore. And Felix wasn't in school yesterday. Matt and Mason saw that I was sitting alone so they invited me over to their table. It was really nice. But I wonder what will happen today now that the Hunters and Isabella are back in school. Who do you think will claim the Untouchables' table? I really hope it isn't her."

I lifted my gaze to where Kennedy was looking. Isabella had just walked in. Her normal minions were nowhere to be seen. All I could hear were her high heels echoing in the hall. I swore people jumped out of her way, but I was probably imagining it. She didn't look at me at all. Her demon eyes were trained on something at the end of the hall. A pitchfork perhaps to match her red, dress-code inappropriate, heels. But right before she passed by us, she turned her head and smiled. At me. A real, horrifying smile. Her smile grew as she drew a line across her throat with her index finger like she was planning on beheading me.

I gulped. Did that warrant a text to Miller? Technically Isabella hadn't said a word.

"Wow," Kennedy said. "Subtle much?" She laughed.

"How are you laughing right now?" I asked. "She still wants to kill me."

"Laughing is better than curling up in a ball and crying. Trust me…I already did that all weekend."

I winced.

Kennedy sighed and leaned her back against the lockers. "There's no point in being scared of her. Your dad promised she wouldn't hurt me again."

He'd promised me the same. But he wasn't here at school with me. I closed my locker. "But what if she…"

"Drugs us or kidnaps us? Worrying about it won't do us any good."

That was true. But it wasn't as simple as worrying about a grade or something. It was life or death when it came to Isabella.

"I can't believe how wrong I was," Kennedy said. "When I told you boys like Matthew Caldwell don't end up with girls like us. How did he propose?"

"It's a promise ring. We're not engaged. That's crazy."

"He's crazy for you. But spill it."

"I was snooping, actually. I found the ring in his nightstand. And he told me to try it on. That's really it."

She snapped another photo. "Sixteen and engaged. The life of the elite, I guess. Do you think you'll have one of those elaborate engagement parties?"

"I don't think so." We walked toward her homeroom.

"Well if you do, make sure Justin plans it. I want to hang out with him more. And if you don't make me your maid of honor?" She drew a line across her throat like Isabella had. "Joking," she said and laughed on her way into class.

A chill ran down my spine, and it wasn't from what she'd said. I turned around. Isabella was standing on the other side of the hall. That same horrifying smile on her face. Had she been standing there the whole time just staring at me? I turned and ran to my homeroom despite the fact that my feet still hurt.

CHAPTER 16

Tuesday

Everywhere I went, Isabella was there. She even came into my English class with the pretense of handing in a late assignment to my teacher. But I didn't buy it. Because she'd stared at me the whole time with that same creepy smile as earlier. I was used to having her minions keeping their eyes on me when she had been blackmailing Matt. But it was like she didn't trust their intel now. Like she needed to watch me for herself. And there was nothing more horrifying than her evil, smiling face.

Felix wasn't in gym class. I'd waited for him by the doors, but he never came. Kennedy said he'd been absent yesterday, and he must have been absent again today. Unless he was avoiding me. I'd hoped to talk to him before the whole school knew about Matt and me. But I'd missed my chance. I sat down on the bleachers and sighed. At least I didn't have to participate today.

It wasn't just my mind spinning or my chest aching. All day my stomach was upset, worried about my talk with Felix and avoiding Isabella as best I could. But Felix wasn't here. And Isabella was somewhere in the school. I didn't have anything to worry about out here. No creepy half-sisters or awkward conversations. Sitting on the bleachers in gym class was the first time all day I'd been able to breathe easy. I watched as a few of my other classmates ran on the track.

I looked down at Matt's varsity jacket. The cool autumn wind blew, and I was happy to finally have something warm. I leaned my head back on the bleachers behind me. The sun on my face was as warm as the jacket. My eyelids felt heavy. I yawned and tried to keep them open. It was like my body had been on high alert all day. And now that I was outside, breathing fresh air, I realized how exhausted I was. I yawned again.

I must have fallen asleep, because the next thing I knew, Coach Carter was blowing his whistle, signaling the end of class. I sat up and ran my fingers through my hair. God, I felt a million times better.

Maybe Isabella had always been around that much and I just hadn't realized before. It was a small school. There really wasn't any way to avoid her.

Fresh air and sunshine had been the cure to my paranoia. Coach Carter blew the whistle again. I went to stand and realized that there was a piece of paper underneath one of my Keds. It must have been litter from the last game. I lifted my foot and grabbed the piece of paper so I could toss it. But then I saw something written in bright red ink.

The countdown is on. Your bloodline is about to run dry.

That wasn't red ink. I stared at the words. Was it written in…blood? I dropped the note.

Shit. I leaned forward and watched the paper flutter beneath the bleachers. What the hell was that? My heart was pounding out of my chest as I got up and started running toward the gym.

I knew it was Isabella. Who else would leave a threat like that under my foot? But she wasn't in my gym class. I stared at the other students running back up to the gym. It had to have been one of them. Right? And the only one I really knew was Cupcake.

"Cupcake!" I yelled and tried to catch up to him, but my stupid feet still hurt.

It was like he heard me and started running faster.

By the time I reached the gym he was already running up to the boy's locker room. *Son of a bitch.* A few students turned and started laughing at me as I walked toward the girls' locker room. Luckily I didn't need to change, because the laughter and pointing only got worse in there. I grabbed my backpack out of my gym locker and got out of there as fast as I could.

Had they seen Cupcake leave the note? Was that why they were laughing? But the laughter continued to swirl around me in the hall too.

I kept my eyes on my shoes as I hurried to lunch. The last thing I needed was for Isabella to catch me in the hallway. I'd thought more about death in the past year than I ever thought I would. But today I wasn't concerned with someone else dying. I was concerned about my own life.

The crowded cafeteria made me breathe a little easier. And I made a mental note to remember to write in my new journal. Today was a good example of how Isabella was the reason I was getting panic attacks. Maybe my dad would believe me with written proof. It was Isabella and only Isabella that made me panic.

I glanced over at the Untouchables' table, wondering if that was where I should be sitting. But Isabella was perched there with her minions surrounding her. Her eyes locked with mine and she burst out laughing. All of her friends turned too, like their evil minds were in tune with their master's.

I quickly looked away. I didn't want to see them all smile in unison. Or worse...do that thing where they pretended to slice their throats with their hands. My heart was pounding in my chest. *Please don't let Matt sit at that table.* If he did...there was no way in hell I'd be joining him.

I caught a glimpse of the Hunters a few tables over, laughing with some guys I didn't know. James looked up at me. I thought he might wave. Or laugh at me like everyone else seemed to be doing. But instead he just lowered his eyebrows slowly. Like the sight of me here pissed him off.

I turned away. I didn't care why James was frowning or why everyone else seemed to be laughing. Jokes about me being a prostitute didn't make me laugh. Besides, I had more important things to worry about. Like the fact that Isabella was 100% still planning on killing me.

Matt would know what to do. I scanned a few more tables until I found the Caldwells. Matt and Mason were both sitting at my usual table. They'd brought a few football players with them. Kennedy was already sitting there too and she waved me over. I slid into my usual seat, but it felt anything but normal with the laughter behind me only growing.

Matt looked down at me. He opened his mouth to say something, but Kennedy cut him off.

"Is that some kind of weird new fashion statement?" Kennedy asked.

"What?" I looked down at Matt's varsity jacket.

"Not that. You look amazing in your fiancé's jacket. I'm talking about the bullseye symbol on your forehead."

I lifted my hand to my forehead, and when I pulled my fingers down they were bright red. The exact same red as the note. *What the hell?* "Am I bleeding?"

Matt grabbed my hand. "No. It's…lipstick? Maybe?" He stopped me when I went to reach for my forehead again.

"Why is there a bullseye on my forehead?" I looked over at Isabella who was laughing with her minions.

"You didn't do it?" Kennedy asked.

"Why would I put a target symbol on my forehead in red lipstick? I fell asleep in gym and there was this crazy note…"

"I can get it off," Kennedy said. She poured some of her water bottle onto a napkin, leaned forward and started blotting my forehead.

"Did you say something about a note?" Matt asked.

At the exact same time, I looked over at Isabella. That creepy smile spread over her face as she stared back at me. She slowly shook her head and then lifted her finger to her lips. I was far away from her, but I could practically hear the chilling "shh." And I was pretty sure there was an "or else" attached to it based on the wicked glint in her eye and the way she ran her fingers across her throat again.

I swallowed hard. What was she planning on doing if I told someone about the note? I thought about what Miller had said. To text him if Isabella talked to me at all. But she hadn't technically said a word to me. And she'd made it seem like she would definitely kill me if I told anyone.

"Baby," Matt said. "If Isabella's bothering you..."

"No. Nothing like that." I tried to focus on my own table and not on Isabella's. I didn't want her to slit my throat for tattling on her. "It's just lame that she claimed your table," I said. My cover up was as lame as the fact that Isabella stole their table, but I didn't know what else to say.

"I know, it sucks," Kennedy said. "I can't believe Isabella won the Untouchables' table. Shouldn't you guys walk over there and kick her to the curb?"

"We'd rather be sitting here with you two," Matt said and smiled down at me. "It's just a stupid table." He pushed some of my hair away from where Kennedy was scrubbing my face. "Was it Isabella who drew that on your forehead?" he asked.

I shook my head. It wasn't a lie. I didn't actually think she'd done it. For some reason, I'd blamed Cupcake, but that didn't make any sense either. He was the one with a bullseye on his junk, and if I ever got an opportunity I was going to kick him right there for what he'd done to Kennedy.

"Well, it's gone now," Kennedy said and handed me the napkin to wipe off the lipstick from my fingers. "So whoever did it can stop laughing," she said a little louder so that the students around us would get the hint and stop laughing too.

"Thanks," I said as I scrubbed my fingers. "Can we just talk about something else?" I looked back over at Isabella's table. The Caldwells should have been there.

And if not them, the Hunters should have claimed it as their own. But Isabella? She wasn't untouchable. She was just an asshole.

Isabella's evil grin spread over her face again when she saw me staring.

I turned away. God, what the hell was she looking at me like that for? She was about to do something awful, right? That was the only explanation.

"How has the rest of your day been, minus the whole bullseye thing?" Matt asked.

Horrible. Isabella keeps watching me. It feels like my heart is going to beat out of my chest. I swallowed down the lump in my throat. "It's been okay." I started bouncing my leg up and down. *Maybe I should just leave.* Isabella was always the freaking worst at lunch.

Matt put his hand on my knee to stop it from bouncing. "You heard what your bodyguards said. If she's bothering you, all you have to do is text them."

"She hasn't actually spoken a word to me. She just keeps…smiling." That wasn't exactly an incriminating offense. And technically it probably wasn't her who left the note. Or the one that had written on my forehead. But who the hell else could it be? I hated Cupcake, but he didn't hate me.

"Well, she also did that thing," Kennedy said and pulled her fingers across her throat. She lolled her head to the side and stuck her tongue out.

"She did what?" Matt asked, looking more upset by the second.

I took a deep breath. "It's fine. She hasn't even come near me. I'm not scared of her." I tried to sit up a little straighter. But I wasn't feeling brave at all. Because I was freaking terrified. *Shh. Or else.*

"Oh my God," Kennedy said. She was staring over at Isabella's table.

I turned to follow her gaze, just in time to see Isabella plant a kiss on Cupcake's lips. *What the fuck?* Cupcake plopped down in the seat next to Isabella. He was smiling too, but it didn't look evil. Just cocky and idiotic…the same way he always looked.

"Is she serious?" Kennedy said. "It's not enough that she steals the Untouchables' table, she has to make me look like an idiot too?"

"Ignore her," I said. But that was easier said than done. Because Isabella was getting exactly what she wanted. Tons of attention. She'd taken the most prestigious table. She'd stolen Kennedy's boyfriend. She was on an insane power trip. And now she had a new minion to do her bidding. A minion who wasn't scared of drugging people. *Fucking Cupcake.*

I watched Isabella stand up and walk over toward us.

Shit. What was she doing?

"And now she has to rub it in?" Kennedy groaned.

I cringed as the sound of Isabella's heels clicking drew closer and closer.

"Hello, Matthew," she said in her fake sugary voice as she put her claws on Matt's shoulders.

He turned to look up at her. "Isabella, you have five seconds to get your hands the fuck off of me."

"Or what? I thought you loved when I touched you." She trailed her fingers down his bicep.

I was going to be sick.

Matt caught her hand and pushed it off. "You're insane. If you haven't heard the rumors, which I'm sure you have, I'm with Brooklyn. You're done controlling my life. And contrary to whatever lies you want to tell, you and I were never a thing, Wizzy."

"Oh snap," Kennedy said.

Isabella laughed. "Yes, I've heard the rumors. You know Brooklyn slept with James, right? And then he even proposed." She tilted her head to the side. "Wow, she has a ring and everything. She must be so excited to be Mrs. James Hunter one day." She glared at me.

Matt stood up. "Let's make one thing very clear. You're not allowed to talk to my girl. Ever again. I won't allow it, and it's against your dad's rules too. Brooklyn, text your security."

"I'm not talking to *her*," Isabella said. "I'm talking to *you*, Matthew. I haven't broken any of Daddy's rules. I'm absolutely certain of it. Talking to you isn't talking to the trash. Oh, but I'm also talking to the trash's friend." She turned her attention to Kennedy. "Hey, girl. I heard you slept well this weekend." She laughed.

"Since when has drugging people been funny?" Matt said. "Wait. Don't answer that. Just…don't talk to Kennedy either. Did you really not get the hint when we ditched our usual table? We're done. With you. And the Hunters. And anyone else who messes with our family."

"Your family?" Isabella scoffed. "That trash goblin isn't your family. You're a Caldwell for goodness sake."

"You should watch your tongue," Mason said. He tilted his neck to the side, cracking it. "From here on out, Brooklyn is untouchable. She has your dad's security now.

And she has us. So you better run along back to your minions and go mess with someone else."

Matt and Mason both had my back. And they were right. I had the safety promised to the Pruitts and the Caldwells. I was the untouchable one. And Isabella was just…a demon person.

I wanted to tell her that. I wanted to say something. *Anything.* But it was like my lips were frozen shut. *Shh. Or else.*

"Wanna bet?" Isabella said. "Because I have a feeling that she won't be with us for much longer. The poor girl literally had a target on her forehead when she walked into the cafeteria. I think her time is running out. Or maybe someone else's is."

God. What the hell did she mean by that? I knew she was planning on cutting my head off. I got the message loud and clear. But someone else's too?

Isabella looked down at her watch like something terrible was about to happen any second.

I was definitely going to be sick.

There was static on the speaker system and all of us looked up.

"Brooklyn Sanders, please come to the principal's office immediately."

The words made my heart race. The last time I'd been called to the principal's office…

"Hmm," Isabella said. "Looks like someone else from her family just died. Pity. I wonder who it was this time. Hopefully no one too important." She turned on her heels and walked away.

What? It felt like my heart was beating in my throat. Kennedy was here. And they would have called for her if something had happened to her mom. Matt and Mason were here. But she'd been talking about my bloodline. The only other family I had was…was Isabella's family. *Dad.*

She wouldn't have.

She couldn't have.

What the hell did she do?

"I repeat, Brooklyn Sanders to the principal's office."

I stood up, almost falling into Matt. He tried to steady me, but I pulled away.

She wouldn't have.

She couldn't have.

"Brooklyn, it's probably nothing bad," Matt said. "She was just messing with you."

But I was already running.

CHAPTER 17

Tuesday

Isabella wouldn't have hurt her own father. That was insane. *But she's insane.* I heard Isabella's laughter echoing around in my head. I picked up my pace, ignoring my feet burning. *Please be alive. Please.*

Matt caught up to me in the hall, grabbing me by the waist. "Hold on a second, Brooklyn."

"I can't." My tears burned the corners of my eyes.

"You're okay." He held me so tightly that it almost hurt. Normally it would have been comforting. His strong arms were like a safe haven for me. But right now, I couldn't breathe. I squirmed in his grip. I was running out of time.

"Matt." I could barely get his name out. All I could hear was a clock ticking down in my head. What had Isabella done? "She killed my dad." The words bubbled up from my throat. And then I couldn't stop them. "She killed him." I kept saying it over and over again.

"Isabella didn't kill anyone, baby. It's okay. You're okay." His breath was warm in my ear. It was usually as comforting as his arms around me, but right now I couldn't breathe. His breath was too warm. His arms were suffocating me. It was too much.

"She's having a panic attack," James said.

I wasn't even sure where he'd come from.

"You need to give her room to breathe," James added. "It's okay, Brooklyn, just take a deep breath."

"I think I know what I'm doing," Matt said. "You're just making it worse. Get out of here."

"You're the one making it worse," James said. "Get off of her."

"I swear to God, James. Leave us alone." Matt held me even tighter.

"I can't breathe," I gasped.

Matt let me go, like my words singed his skin. He was staring at me like I was broken. Like he broke me.

"Brooklyn," James said and put his hand on my back. "Take a deep breath."

He wasn't supposed to be the one comforting me. I kept my eyes on Matt. He was hurt. And I wasn't sure if it was because he thought he hurt me. Or because it seemed like I wanted James to help me calm down. I didn't want this. I didn't want any of this.

"Breathe," James said.

I couldn't handle James' gentle touch. Or the look of torture on Matt's face. Instead of taking a moment to catch my breath like James suggested, I started running again. I knew what I needed. And I needed my dad. I needed him to be alive and healthy. I needed to get Isabella's words out of my head.

I burst into the principal's office.

The school receptionist gasped.

No. Please, please, no. I couldn't lose anyone else. I couldn't. I was gasping for breath as I put my hands on the desk to steady myself.

"My word, what's going on?" she asked.

I tried to catch my breath. "Aren't you supposed to be telling me that? Where's my dad? Is he okay? Is he hurt?"

"Dear, your father's been waiting for you outside. Didn't Isabella give you my note? Your father called this morning to let me know he wanted to take you out of school for lunch. I saw your sister walking by the office and gave her the early dismissal note."

What? "He's alive?"

"Of course. He's right outside. He's been waiting for a while, that's why I made the announcement. I was just on the phone with him…"

I ran out of the principal's office. I heard yelling down the hall. James and Matt's voices echoing in the empty hallway. I cringed. I didn't want them to fight. *I don't want any of this.*

I pushed through the front doors of Empire High. My dad was leaning against his town car, his cell phone pressed against his ear. He looked up at me as I ran down the stairs.

"I'll have to call you back," he said and ended the call as he ran over to me. "Princess, what's wrong? What happened?"

I threw my arms around him and sobbed. And sobbed. And sobbed. I clutched at his perfectly pressed suit like he was my lifeline. "I can't lose you," I said through my tears.

He ran his hand up and down my back. "I'm not going anywhere. I promise, princess."

He couldn't promise that. No one could promise that. My whole body shook as I cried. But he didn't seem to care that I was wrinkling his expensive suit. Or crying on his silk tie.

"I thought she killed you," I said. I was finally catching my breath as he held me.

"What? Who?"

"Isabella. She said she was going to end my bloodline. I thought…I thought…"

My dad snapped his fingers at the bodyguard standing next to him. "Call Miller. Get him to remove Isabella from the school immediately."

"Yes, sir," he said. He was already pulling out his phone.

"No." I tried to clear my thoughts when all I could think about was that my dad was okay. "You can't. She'll kill me."

"Isabella's not going to hurt you." He gently ran his fingers through my hair. "I promise."

Another promise that I wasn't sure he could keep.

"You're shaking. Should I call Dr. Wilson?"

"No," I mumbled into his chest as I tried to catch my breath. "You can't take Isabella out of school."

"Take a deep breath," my dad said. "Can you do that for me?" He ran his fingers through my hair, just like my mom used to do when I was upset.

I knew students were probably looking out the window at the weird new girl hugging her dad. And I didn't care one bit. They could call me a prostitute behind my back. And draw targets on my forehead. And refuse to speak to me. But it didn't matter what they did. Because I was the lucky one. I knew how fortunate I was to have a living parent that cared. And I'd hug my dad on the steps of Empire High whenever I got a freaking chance.

"Just breathe," my dad said.

Eventually his words and his fingers running through my hair got my heart to stop racing. And my lungs filled again. I looked up at him. "Isabella didn't actually say to me that she was going to end my bloodline. She didn't speak to me all day. There was this note written in lipstick but I thought it was blood. It talked about the bloodline thing. And I freaked out. She had Cupcake draw a target on my forehead. And she kept running her fingers across her throat whenever she stared at me like she was going to kill me. The school receptionist gave her the early dismissal note to give to me. And she just used the opportunity to mess with my head. I thought she'd killed you. But she didn't actually speak to me. Please don't take her out of school. It's just going to make everything worse. You taking my side always makes everything worse."

He shook his head and then looked up at the sky like he was searching for an answer to his problems. But there was no solution up there for his demon daughter. He slowly exhaled and then looked over to his bodyguard. "Text Miller back. Tell him to abort." Then he looked back down at me. "Let's go to lunch. We'll figure out a solution together, okay?"

I nodded.

He kissed my forehead and then ushered me into the car. "You're sure we shouldn't stop by Dr. Wilson's office?"

"I'm sure." I didn't want to spend lunch in a doctor's office. I wanted to spend it with him.

"Well, make sure to write about this in your journal," he said.

"Dad."

His eyes always softened when I called him that.

I wanted to tell him that I'd keep writing in the journal. That maybe something else was stressing me out. But it just wasn't true. "I don't need to write it down. I've only ever had a hard time breathing when Isabella threatens to kill me. I'm sorry," I added when I saw the look on his face.

"Princess, it's okay." He put his hand on top of mine. "I believe you. I'm sorry I pressed it. I was just hoping..." his voice trailed off. "We're going to figure this out. I promise."

I wanted to believe him. But the more promises he made, the less I believed any of them.

***

I expected for us to go to his country club. Or some swanky restaurant that had a huge waitlist. Instead, my dad's town car stopped at a small corner diner.

The inside was just as adorable as the outside. There were black and white checkered floors and red booths. The heat was turned up for the cool autumn day and the smell of grease hung in the air. It reminded me of a diner back home. My mom and I used to go to it all the time for milkshakes. Especially when I had bad days at school.

The hostess greeted him by name with a friendly smile.

Wait. He comes here frequently? I glanced at him out of the corner of my eye. I thought there were house rules about carbs or something. Or was it junk food? God, I needed a copy of those rules.

The hostess showed us to a booth and asked if he'd like his usual. He ordered two.

I couldn't help it. I just stared at him as she walked away.

"This is one of my favorite places," my dad said.

"But it's..." my voice trailed off. "It's not very much like your apartment."

"I know, it's refreshing right? I used to come here with your mom all the time."

I pressed my lips together. First the hidden apartment that had belonged to my mom. Now a diner they used to go to together? There were forgotten pieces of my mom scattered all over the city. And I was pretty sure my dad was the only one who remembered where they all were. "You kept coming here after she left?"

"Actually, I bought it," he said as he leaned back in the booth.

"You bought it?"

"It was a good investment opportunity." He straightened the salt shaker so that it was perfectly in line with the pepper shaker, as if that was more interesting than our conversation.

"That's the only reason?"

He stopped fidgeting with the seasonings. "I didn't want them to change anything."

I shook my head. "I don't get it. If you loved my mom that much, why did you let her leave?"

"My business is dangerous, Brooklyn. It was better..."

"I know. You've said that before. But you have enough money and resources to do whatever you want." I gestured to the literal diner he bought to preserve his memories of my mom. "You said you can protect me. You could have protected her." *You could have protected us.* If he'd stayed in my life, my mom might still be alive. There might have been something he could have done. Some procedure or…something. We'd needed him.

"She wanted to go. I had to respect her decision."

I didn't press him. I could tell that it had killed him to let her go. It may have killed my mom too. "I'm sorry. We don't have to talk about that. Why did you want to have lunch?"

"I wanted to give you an update on the new security system. Everything is already in place. But…"

"Coffee for you too, hon?" a waitress asked. The smell of fresh coffee swirled through the air as she poured a cup for my dad.

I'd always liked the smell. But never the taste. "No, thanks," I said.

She hurried off as quickly as she'd come.

My dad wrapped his hand around his mug. "Your mom never liked coffee either. Just the smell of it." He smiled at me.

I didn't know if he knew how hard these conversations were for me. The things I knew about my mom mixed with his memories. I wanted to hear everything but at the same time none of it because it made me miss her so much that it hurt.

"You look so much like her," he said.

I looked down at the table. I didn't want to cry anymore today.

"Brooklyn, I know I let your mom down. I've spent half my life missing her. I've been given a second chance to do this right. And I'm not going to make the same mistake twice. I'll do whatever it takes to protect you."

When I'd first met him, I thought he hated me. But now I was pretty sure I was his only family member he even got along with. He loved my mom. And he loved me too.

I knew I didn't know him that well. But I did know that I needed him. Who else would keep me safe from Isabella?

CHAPTER 18

Tuesday

I bit the inside of my lips until the tears that were threatening to spill went away. "You mentioned that the new security system is in place?"

"I was hoping to give you the good news that you could come home," said my dad. "But with Isabella...I don't...I'm not sure it's for the best."

"You mean you're scared she'll hurt me if I come back?"

"I honestly don't know."

I swallowed hard. He was always so certain. How was he not confident in his ability to control Isabella?

"And then there's the issue of your health. If Isabella really is setting off your panic attacks...it would be best to eliminate her from your life as much as possible. She'll be going off to college next fall. Then you'll be perfectly happy and healthy coming back home. But until then, we need to discuss some more suitable alternatives. My second apartment..."

"Can't I stay with Matt?"

"I'm not on the best terms with Matthew's father. I'm not sure if they'd be open to that arrangement. Plus the apartment has all the highest security..."

"I don't want to be there all alone."

"Of course not. I'd never let you be alone. Miller and Donnelley will always be with you."

I couldn't even imagine what Matt would do if he found out I was supposed to basically be living with two other guys. Especially if he knew that I'd been involved with one of them. "Please, Dad. If I can't live with you until next fall, please let me stay at the Caldwells' until then. I don't think they mind me being there. I could get a job to help pay for food and…"

"It's not about the money. I agreed for you to go there on a temporary basis. Not for a whole year."

"But…"

"And then there's the issue of school itself. Until Isabella graduates, I think maybe homeschooling would be best. I've been researching a few of the best online options and of course we could have private tutors. Then you won't have to see Isabella at all."

"What? No."

"It's the safest option."

"But I don't want to be in that apartment all day and all night. That's not a solution. That's…that's locking me away." This conversation was reminding me of the way he'd first treated me. Like I didn't belong in his world. But screw that. I belonged just as much as Isabella. I was his blood too. He was acting like he wanted to hide me from the world. Like he was embarrassed of me. And I was sick and tired of everyone making me feel like I was trash. "Is that the deal you offered my mom if she stayed? That she could be in that apartment as long as she never left?"

"I didn't bargain with your mother. I bought her that apartment because I loved her. I never asked her not to leave. Because she was never mine. You are. I'm trying to protect you."

"That's not the way to protect me. You can't just keep me separated from the rest of the world. That's not a solution."

"I can't guarantee your safety at school. Just look at what happened today."

"I belong at Empire High just as much as Isabella does. If she gets to keep going, so do I. Or maybe you should lock her up in an apartment and homeschool her because she's the one causing problems. Not me."

He took a deep breath and leaned back in the booth. "As you may have seen…I've been having a hard time controlling Isabella's actions. Finding loopholes to the rules has always been one of her favorite activities. And it's been worse since she's found out about you. I can't control her."

"But you can control me?"

"I need to keep you safe. I can't let anything happen to you too."

I swallowed hard. "Counter proposal. I stay with Matt. And I keep going to Empire High."

"That's not a solution. Isabella will…" his voice trailed off. He pressed his fingers to his forehead like he was fighting off a headache. "I don't know what she'll do. That's the whole problem."

He looked defeated. And I realized that maybe my dad's promises were futile. Because he'd admitted he couldn't control Isabella. I wondered if maybe a part of him was as scared of her as I was.

"One thing you should know about me," I said. "I learned a very important lesson when my mom got sick. Time is limited. And I made a promise to myself to live each and every moment to its fullest. I won't stay locked up in an apartment. I won't stay home from school. There's nothing worse than not living each moment you have." Isabella wasn't going to control my life. There wasn't a chance in hell that I'd let her. That's why I'd stayed here. To prove that she couldn't break me. That I belonged here just as much as she did.

"And I'm sorry that Mr. Caldwell doesn't like you," I added. "But I think he's warming up to me. So I'll ask him and Mrs. Caldwell myself if I can stay for a year. I'll figure out what they want for room and board and I'll make sure I work to give it to them. And I'm going to keep going to Empire High because it's where my uncle wanted me to go. I'm not going to let Isabella steal a year of my life from me. Because that's exactly what she wants."

Each word that fell out of my mouth made me feel more determined. I nodded, like I was giving myself a pep talk. I was staying in New York. I was done hiding. Someone needed to knock Isabella off her high horse.

My dad raised his eyebrow. "I guess there's no changing your mind?"

I tried to sit up a little straighter. *Nunca.* "No."

"Don't worry about the Caldwells then," my dad said. "I'll talk to them myself. Besides, Matthew's made it very clear that we're all to be family soon enough. Let me see the ring." He put his hand out.

I placed my hand into his.

"It suits you," he said. "Are you sure this is what you want?"

I nodded.

"Very well. I'll have some more paperwork for both of you to fill out." He dropped my hand and took a sip of his coffee.

"Speaking of paperwork. Can I have copies of all the documents I've signed?" It was like a fire had been lit under my butt. Remembering the promises I'd made to myself after my mom's death reminded me to stop being stagnant.

"Of course."

Wait, really? That was easy.

"I'll make sure Miller gives you copies by tonight. I'm glad that you're being thorough. I was a little worried you signed the relationship agreement a tad too quickly."

I didn't want him to know that I hadn't really read either of them. I cleared my throat. "Speaking of Miller. He mentioned that he was leaving. But he's still here." I hoped that was vague enough.

"Much like you, Miller signed documents when he started working for me. All of my employees are family. It's a mutual understanding. You don't quit on family."

The way he said it made a chill run down my spine. But Miller was an employee, not family. Surely he could quit. That didn't make any sense. But I was worried questioning it any further would just put suspicion on Miller. I'd have to talk to Miller about it later. Besides, I had a few more questions while I was feeling brave enough to ask.

"Isabella mentioned that the Hunters owed you a debt. And that James has to marry her to pay it off. Is that true?"

My dad laughed. "I didn't realize you'd have so many questions for me this afternoon." He smiled. "As for Isabella…she has a very active imagination."

That isn't exactly a no.

"Oh look," he said. "Our food is here."

I looked up as the waitress dropped off a few turkey sandwiches with all the fixings and…chocolate milkshakes. Just like my mom and I used to order.

I wanted to see the menacing man I always expected him to be. But I didn't see it. I saw a man who loved my mom fiercely. A man who lost. He wasn't a monster. I couldn't believe any of the lies Isabella tried to spread. She was a loophole ninja. She was trying to play me. But I wasn't her puppet.

My dad's response did bother me though. "So Isabella was lying about her and James?"

"The Hunters came upon rough times several years back. It was actually the start of a joint business venture. Completely unrelated to any of our children. I would never force either of my daughters to marry someone they didn't want to. Especially for money," he said with a laugh. "I mean, look at you. I told you that Mason was a better option. His whole future has been laid out in front of him. But I can tell you're happy with Matthew. And even if he might not provide for you as well, I gave him my blessing. I just want you to be happy, princess."

"I don't need him to provide for me. I'm happiest in places just like this."

My dad smiled. "I know. But you don't have anything to worry about regardless. Your inheritance is now sizably larger than either of the Caldwell boys anyway. If anything, Matthew is a step below you."

I would never describe Matt that way. "You know I didn't ask for any of that."

"Which is precisely why I'm giving it to you." He pushed my milkshake forward. "Aren't you going to try it? I swear it's the best in the city."

I smiled and took a sip. It tasted just like the ones at the diner back home. I watched my dad take a bite of his sandwich. Sitting in this diner with him felt normal. He didn't feel like a stranger anymore. He felt like a freaking lifeline.

"I do have one more question," I said. I'd found out what the locked room at his secret apartment was for. It was filled with my mom's things. But there was a locked room in his actual apartment too. And I wanted to know what was in it. "What's in the room down the hall from my bedroom at your apartment? The one with the new security key code? Is that filled with my mom's stuff too?"

He dabbed a napkin across his lips. "No. That's…" his voice trailed off. "You know what? I think it would be best if I showed that to you in person. The next time you come over, okay?"

"Yeah. Okay." How bad could it be if he was willing to show it to me? I was breathing easier already. I'd asked every single question I'd had for him.

"Tell me more about your relationship with Matthew," my dad said. "Is it progressing toward intimacy? I know you mentioned before that it wasn't, but we need to be safe with these things."

Oh God. Not the sex talk again. "Everything's good, I promise."

He nodded. "Good, good." He took a sip of his milkshake.

For a minute neither of us said anything at all. And I really hoped that was the end of the conversation. But then he started talking again.

"But do you mean good as in you are being sexually active?"

"Dad." Wasn't this a weird thing to bring up in public? I looked over to see if any of the waitresses had heard him. Fortunately they all seemed busy.

"Okay, we don't have to discuss it any further. But, Brooklyn, if you're planning on moving in that direction with Matt, I think it's better to stay in front of all of this. If you're okay with it, I'd like to go ahead and set that appointment with Dr. Wilson sooner rather than later. It's better to just get it out of the way, don't you think?"

"Sure." If he was going to keep pressing the issue of birth control maybe it was just better to get it over with. "Do you mind if I do it alone though? This whole thing is very awkward."

"Oh. I mean, yes, if that's what you want. But if you're uncomfortable talking about it with me, then maybe you aren't ready to…"

"It's fine. Really." Just because I didn't want to talk about sex with my dad didn't mean I wasn't ready to have sex. I didn't even think I'd be comfortable having this conversation with my mom.

"Okay. I won't mention it again." He smiled.

I took a huge bite of my sandwich. Now that the question was out there…was I ready to have sex? I knew Matt was. He said he was waiting for me. And I knew he loved me. I was all in with him. So shouldn't I go all the way with him?

"Are you getting excited for the holidays?" my dad asked.

It was a normal question to ask in the fall. But I honestly hadn't been thinking about it at all. This would be the first time I didn't celebrate Thanksgiving and Christmas with my mom. "Mhm," I said, even though my heart wasn't really in it.

"I know it's several weeks away, but no matter what's going on with Isabella, I'd like you to come over for Thanksgiving. It's always a pretty big celebration for us. We have family coming in from out of town that I want you to meet. And you can invite whoever else you want. I just…it's a day for family. And I want you to be there. Besides, Isabella's always in a lovely mood around Thanksgiving."

The Hunters had mentioned Isabella being cheery during the holidays. I couldn't really imagine a sweet and charming holiday Isabella. But it had to be better than a gun slinging Isabella. "Yeah. That would be nice."

He smiled. "It's so easy to see your mother when I look at you. But I see a lot of myself too. You go after what you want and you get it. You should consider applying to the business school of whatever college you plan on going to."

"Did you study business in college?"

He nodded. "I used to think that Isabella would take over the family business one day. But I'm seeing everything a little differently now."

I couldn't help but smile. I still didn't know exactly what it was he did. But it was the first time I truly thought that being a Pruitt maybe wasn't such a bad thing. And no matter how hard I fought it…I was a Pruitt. I belonged here. I just needed to prove it to Isabella too. And I think James and Rob were right. Pudding seemed like a pretty great way to put her in her place.

CHAPTER 19

Tuesday

"Are you sure you don't want to come with me to the club?" my dad asked as we pulled up outside Empire High. "I can give you that golf lesson I promised you."

"Can we do it another day?" My dad and I had stayed at the diner for hours talking about my mom, holiday traditions, and what I wanted to study in college. And despite how tempting it was to ditch my final class of the day and take him up on his offer…I wanted to go back to school. I knew Matt would be worried about me if I didn't show up for entrepreneurial studies. Plus, if I was supposed to take over the family business one day, maybe Mr. Hill could actually teach me a few things.

"Of course, princess. We'll do it another day," he said and patted my knee. "Enjoy your last class. And call me if you need anything at all. Or if Isabella talks to you. Or does something that doesn't involve talking, like getting someone to leave you a threatening message." He raised his eyebrows at me.

"I will, I promise." I unbuckled my seatbelt and climbed out of the car. I waved goodbye as his car sped off.

I looked up at the ornate wooden doors of Empire High. For the first time, I was going to walk through them knowing that I belonged. I wasn't there because my uncle was a janitor anymore. And I wasn't a dirty little secret. I belonged in this world.

I walked up the stairs and pushed through the doors. Isabella had tried her best to knock me down. All those embarrassing moments in lunch. Literally pointing a gun at my head. Making me feel inadequate. But all she'd done was make me stronger. Isabella could have people paint targets on me all freaking day. It wouldn't stop me from taking her down.

I kept my head held high as I walked toward my locker. The bell rang, signaling the end of the class I'd just missed. Students filled the halls. When I reached my locker, Matt was already waiting for me.

"Hey." I gave him the most reassuring smile that I could. The last time he'd seen me, James' hands were on me, trying to help me breathe. Matt had looked like he was in so much pain. I would have texted him if I had my phone, but I'd run out of school with none of my things.

Instead of reaching out for me, he pushed his hair off his forehead. It was like he was scared to touch me.

"I'm so sorry about lunch," I said. "I didn't mean to freak out..."

"Brooklyn, I'm the one that's sorry. I thought I was helping earlier. I thought..." He shook his head. "I didn't mean to hurt you."

"You didn't hurt me." I grabbed his hand. "I promise you didn't hurt me."

"You said you couldn't breathe."

"It was just a panic attack. It was nothing."

He nodded even though he didn't look very convinced. "I didn't even know that you got panic attacks," he said. "I had no idea what was going on. Why didn't you tell me?"

"I was kind of hoping they'd just go away."

He lowered his eyebrows slightly. "What if James hadn't been there?" he asked.

I shook my head. "He didn't fix anything. I just needed to make sure my dad was okay. And he is. Isabella was messing with my head, like you said."

"So everything's good now?"

"Yeah. Everything's fine."

He took a deep breath. "You really scared me, baby." He pulled me into his arms. "You can tell me anything, you know."

"I know."

"So what should I have done? In that situation?"

I leaned back so I could look up at him. He didn't need to make anything right. But I'm glad he wanted to take care of me. "Maybe if you could just kind of rub your hand up and down my back and remind me to breathe?" I tried not to wince. It was exactly what James had done. I hoped Matt didn't remember.

He dropped his forehead to mine. "I can do that," he said, his cinnamon scent surrounding me. "How often do you get them?"

I sighed. "Just when Isabella scares me."

"So a lot then?" he said with a laugh.

I gently hit his arm.

"We should probably get to class," Matt said. "We don't want to piss off Mr. Hill."

No we do not. "One sec." I opened my locker and grabbed my entrepreneurial studies book. I usually looked forward to class to see Matt but dreaded it because of Mr. Hill. But Mr. Hill had actually been a little nicer to me recently. He hadn't made me read out loud in ages. The last time he'd called me out at all was when I was dancing too close to Rob at homecoming. I wanted to think it was because he was friends with my uncle. But maybe me suddenly having tons of money played a role too.

We made our way to class with my hand in his. It was the first time I'd been to class with him like this. It was only several weeks ago that I stared at the back of his head and daydreamed. And now we were engaged. *Engaged.* That hadn't really sunk in yet. *I'm freaking engaged to Matthew Caldwell.*

"No way," Matt said when I went to my normal seat. "Sit next to me."

"Won't Rob be mad that I stole his seat?"

Matt shrugged. "Yeah, I don't really care what the hell he thinks. You're sitting with me." He pulled the desk slightly closer to his and I laughed.

Rob walked in right when I sat down.

He smiled at me and stopped right next to his old desk. "Did you seriously steal my seat, Sanders?"

"I can move…"

"I'm just messing with you," he said with a wink. "If it were anyone else, I'd complain. But now I just get to stare at you during class, so it's a win-win for me." He sat down in my old seat and whistled. "Yeah, this is a great view."

Matt turned around. "I swear to God…"

"Did you hear something, Sanders?" Rob asked. "It sounds like there's a really high-pitched little girl complaining about something, but I don't see anyone…"

"Can't you guys just kiss and make up already?" I asked.

Rob laughed.

Matt didn't.

"I knew you were funny," Rob said. "One of the many reasons why I think we'd make a much better couple. Isn't dating the high school football star a little cliché? Soccer's a much sexier sport, Sanders. It has international appeal. We could travel the globe together." He gave me another flirtatious wink.

Was he trying to start a fight?

"If you haven't noticed the ring on her finger, she's mine, dipshit," Matt said.

"I don't know…yesterday when we were hanging out she said it was just a promise ring. As far as I'm concerned, promises are just declarations that are begging to be broken. What do you say, Sanders? Meet me in the treehouse at midnight?"

Yeah, he was definitely trying to start a fight. Somewhere in all that ridiculousness were fighting words. And I needed to put a stop to it right now because Matt looked like he was about to strangle Rob. "I'm happy with Matt," I said. "Which I made clear yesterday. So I won't be meeting you in your treehouse. And also like I said yesterday…I'd appreciate it if you stopped flirting with me. I know you're just trying to get under Matt's skin."

Rob put his elbows on his desk and leaned forward. "I love a girl who knows how to take control."

"Is there a problem back there?" Mr. Hill asked.

Shit. Shit, shit, shit. He was going to make me read out loud for the entire period. I could feel myself sinking in my seat.

"No? Great. May I continue then?"

"Of course, Mr. Hill," Rob said.

Mr. Hill squinted at him and then cleared his throat. "Very well."

So he's not going to punish me? Thank God. Just as I started to breathe a little easier, Mr. Hill started talking again.

"As you know from the syllabus, there is no midterm per se in this class. But I will need a status update on your projects. I expect them by the end of the week."

Oh, crap. How were we supposed to finish our group project when Rob and Matt were fighting? James had given us a pretty good head start on the website. But we still had to figure out exactly what was going to make our fitness site unique.

I glanced over at Matt. He was staring at the board, but it didn't look like he was paying attention at all.

I needed to make sure he knew I was all in with him. I didn't want him to have any more doubts. I picked up my pen and jotted him a note:

How do you think your parents would feel about me moving in until Isabella goes off to college? Or more importantly...how would you feel about that? Would you get sick of me after a year?

I tore out the sheet from my notebook, made sure Mr. Hill wasn't looking, and slid it onto Matt's desk.

He read it and a smile spread across his face. "Are you serious?" he whispered.

"My dad said it was okay," I whispered back. "If it's okay with your parents, I mean."

"I don't think they'd mind at all. My mom already loves you."

I smiled.

"And what about you?" I whispered. "You want me to stay?"

"Are you kidding? Of course I do."

"I'm not going to ask again," Mr. Hill said. "Is there a problem back there?"

"Sorry, Mr. Hill," Matt said. "It was all me."

"Great, Mr. Caldwell. Then how about you pick up on page 107 then? Second paragraph down."

Matt gave me a small smile and then opened up his book and started reading. And reading. And reading. He seemed to take the punishment a lot better than me. Where I stumbled over the words, he read them perfectly.

I rested my chin in my hand as I watched him talk. He was really good at public speaking. I knew that he wished he could take over his dad's company one day. But maybe he had more to offer than that. Maybe it was a blessing in disguise that his dad wanted Mason to take the reins. What careers needed good public speakers? Politics, for sure.

I smiled to myself. In the blink of an eye I could almost see our future. He could be the mayor of New York. I could take over my dad's business. Matt and I could rule this town. Us against the world.

Sometimes thinking of the future made my chest hurt. I used to be scared of not having one. Of my life being cut short. But I wasn't my mom. I wasn't my uncle. I was healthy. Dr. Wilson had confirmed it. And if I could get these stupid panic attacks under control, I'd be perfectly content. I wasn't going to die young. I had my whole life ahead of me. My whole life with Matt.

The bell rang and Matt slammed his book shut.

"Next time don't talk during my class, Mr. Caldwell," warned Mr. Hill.

Matt rolled his eyes and looked over at me. "You're welcome," he said.

"What? You were talking too. It's about time someone got in trouble other than me."

He laughed. "I know, I was just messing with you." He shoved his book into his backpack. "Do you have time for a quick visit to the auditorium before you get whisked away back to my house?"

"What exactly are we going to do in the auditorium?"

"Just because I'm loving you out loud now, it doesn't mean I don't get to love you in private anymore. See you in a few," he said and tossed a note on my desk.

I looked down at his familiar scrawl.

Baby,

Meet me in the auditorium in five minutes?

Love,

-Matt

P.S. I've spent a lot of time waiting for you in the auditorium. I hope my future wife doesn't leave me hanging anymore.

I was smiling so hard it hurt. I looked up and Matt was already gone from the room. I folded up the note and slipped it into the pocket of the front of my blazer. It was the first note he'd ever signed. And he'd called me baby a few times, but for some reason seeing it in writing made my heart race.

"When are we going to meet up to do more planning on Operation Disappearing Troll?" Rob asked.

I almost jumped. I hadn't realized he was still in the classroom. "I can't, Rob. We'll have to plan the rest of the prank via text. Here." I wrote down my cell number on a piece of paper and handed it to him.

"James isn't going to be happy about this. I'm pretty sure this breaks our deal. No prank means me and James don't have to talk to the Caldwells."

"I'm still going to help with the prank. The deal is still on."

"If you say so." He pulled out his phone and put in my number. "I don't know why you're so concerned about all of us being friends again anyway. We're not fighting because of you. We're fighting because Matt's a snake."

"He's not a snake. You never gave him a chance to explain what happened with Rachel. You're being unreasonable." I pulled my backpack over my shoulder. I was done with this conversation. If Rob and James wouldn't listen to one of their lifelong friends, why would they listen to me?

"Hey." Rob grabbed my wrist before I could walk off. "I heard you had another panic attack. You okay?"

I was pretty sure he was the snake. Obnoxious one minute and then able to be sweet the next. But I didn't think he was doing it to be manipulative. Deep down in Rob's sarcastic way, he actually did care about me. Or else he never would have helped me through my first panic attack. "Yeah, I'm okay. Thanks."

"You don't need to be scared of Isabella. James and I have your back." He let his hand slowly fall from my wrist, his fingers trailing down my palm. "See you tomorrow, Sanders."

I shivered. "Wait. Rob?" If he really had my back, he could do me another favor. "Can you please stop pushing Matt's buttons on purpose?"

He shrugged. "But they're so easy to push."

"Please?"

"Anything for you, Sanders," he said with a wink.

Instead of going to my locker to get my things, I went straight for the auditorium. The last time I'd met Matt in the auditorium, I'd been scared out of my mind. And angry. God, I had been so angry at him. But this time? I loved him so much it hurt.

The heavy door closed behind me with a thud. The smell of old wood wafted around me, reminding me of our first kiss. The kiss he'd stolen. He didn't have to steal anything from me now.

"Matt?" I whispered into the darkness.

Okay, this time was scary too. But not because I was expecting some terrible prank. It was just because the Empire High auditorium was really freaking creepy. "Matt?" I said a little louder.

I laughed as he wrapped his arms around me from behind.

"God you're beautiful," he whispered into my ear.

"It's pitch black in here."

"It's not like I forget how beautiful you are in the dark." He kissed the side of my neck. "You drive me crazy, baby."

I turned in his arms and tried to make out his face in the dark. "Do you really think I can move in for a whole year? My dad said he'd talk to your dad…"

"It's fine. I promise. I'll let my parents know tonight, okay? Now, where were we?"

I laughed, but he silenced me with a kiss.

Not just any kiss. One of his frantic ones. Like we were running out of time. I had been getting used to his slow ones. The ones where we had all the time in the world. But right now…we didn't. His football practice was starting any minute. And God, I'd be lying if I said I didn't love when he was a little wild. It reminded me of our start. I wasn't a dirty little secret anymore. But maybe I kind of liked being treated like one sometimes. Sneaking around with Matthew Caldwell was the most thrilling thing in the world.

He backed me up until my back hit the auditorium door. He pushed up my skirt, bunching it around my waist.

"What are you doing?" I gasped.

His fingers slid underneath my tights.

"Matt someone could come in…" I moaned instead of finishing my sentence. *Fuck.*

"Do you know what causes panic attacks?" he whispered as his fingers drove me insane.

God. I dropped my head back against the wooden door. How did he expect me to answer him like this? My fingers dug into his strong shoulders.

"Stress," he said and gently kissed my neck. "And I think I know how to make my girl relax."

CHAPTER 20

Friday

"No way," Kennedy said when we were ushered out of our car on 5th Avenue.

I was just as surprised as she was. We were in the fashion center of New York, standing right outside the world famous Odegaard boutique. I had never been here before, but I'd remembered Justin mentioning it. He worked for the head stylist of Odegaard – Diane Cartwright. Who just so happened to be my personal stylist too thanks to my dad. *I wonder how pissed she is that all those clothes got destroyed by Isabella…*

"For girls' night we're getting makeovers!" Matt's mom said.

Kennedy opened her mouth but no words came out.

"I've rented out the whole store for the evening," Mrs. Caldwell said. "We have a hairdresser and a makeup artist coming. And of course we have to go shopping. Plus you two will need costumes for our annual Halloween party next weekend. My treat, of course."

Wow. When she mentioned that all girls' nights involved shopping, I kind of figured we'd end up at the mall or something. But Mrs. Caldwell was always dressed flawlessly. This made perfect sense. I'd seen Matt, Mason, and even Mr. Caldwell around the house in pajamas. But never Mrs. Caldwell. "Mrs. Caldwell, you don't have to…"

"I want to. That's why it's my treat. Come with me, girls." She walked through the ten-foot-tall glass doors and greeted the person standing there with a kiss to each cheek.

Kennedy and I both looked at each other. "I feel like I'm going to be arrested just for stepping foot in there," she said.

I laughed. "This is surreal, isn't it?"

"It's freaking amazing is what it is!" Kennedy grabbed my arm. "I mean…makeovers?! At Odegaard? That's not even a thing! This isn't real life!"

I laughed.

"And I've heard rumors about the Caldwell annual Halloween party. It's supposed to be *epic*. They go all out. Apparently last year there were even fire dancers."

I wasn't sure how fire dancers related to Halloween at all. But the Caldwell mansion was perfectly suited for a Halloween party. There definitely wasn't much decorating they needed to do. That's why I mainly hung out in the warm and cozy kitchen and Matt's room. I barely even went in the guestroom I was supposed to be sleeping in. I just went in every now and then and pushed around the sheets.

"Girls, what are you waiting for?" Mrs. Caldwell said and waved us inside. The woman she'd been chatting with had disappeared through another set of doors.

I forced myself not to spin around. The air even smelled fancy inside, kind of like how when you walked into a department store and got sprayed by one of the perfume sellers. Only…nothing like that at all. Because it didn't even look like a store. There were marble walls and a chandelier. It was more like the entrance of a five-star hotel than a boutique.

Where are we? Kennedy was right. This wasn't real life.

I heard someone squeal and turned to see Justin walking over to us.

"Ladies!" he said. "I saw that you were on the schedule tonight so I took the overtime hours. You're so welcome."

"Ah, Justin!" Kennedy said and gave him a hug. "I didn't know you worked at Odegaard."

"I know Odegaard backward and forward. I'm Diane Cartwright's personal assistant. And tonight I'm yours." He winked at her. "Great to see you again, Brooklyn." He gave me a hug and a kiss on the cheek. "And Lori. You look fabulous as always." He grabbed her hand and kissed it.

"Thank you, Justin," she said with a laugh. "I didn't realize you knew Brooklyn and Kennedy."

"Please. I know almost every woman on the Upper East side. How did the three of you become friends?"

Mrs. Caldwell put her hand on my shoulder. "You're looking at my future daughter in law."

"No." Justin gasped and then grabbed my hand. "Yes! I knew I'd be planning your wedding soon. Wow, what a ring." He fanned himself with his freehand.

I laughed. "It's pretty, isn't it?"

"Pretty doesn't cut it. That must be at least 2 carats. Tell me you've picked a date for the wedding. I need to pencil you in as soon as possible. I want yours to be my first wedding as an official wedding planner."

"I mean…we don't know when it'll even be." *God, he looks so excited.* "But I did promise you…"

"If you weren't engaged, I'd kiss you right now. Lori, she's a keeper. I've never met such a sweet girl in this city."

Mrs. Caldwell smiled. "Yes. I can tell why my son loves her so much."

I so badly wanted her to like me. Matt always said she already loved me. And she was always perfectly lovely. But I was pretty sure if I came home from school one day and told my mom that a boy was moving in and that we were engaged, she would have freaked out. I kept waiting for the other shoe to drop. But Mrs. Caldwell was still smiling. *I wonder how old she was when she got engaged to Mr. Caldwell.*

"I'll pencil you in for every Saturday in the fall for the next few years," Justin said. "Fall weddings are the best. Trust me. And speaking of events…what's the theme of this year's Halloween party, Lori?"

"Characters from old movies," Mrs. Caldwell said. "The classics."

Kennedy looked so excited. "Can I be Jasmine from Aladdin?"

Mrs. Caldwell laughed. "I meant like from the 50s or 60s…" her voice trailed off. "Oh, my. I'm feeling my age around you two. I guess something from the 90s does work as an old movie for you," she said with a laugh. "Jasmine it is!"

Kennedy smiled.

"And what would you like to be?" Mrs. Caldwell asked me.

I pressed my lips together. I wanted something conservative enough to work around Matt's parents. But also sexy for Matt. And now only Disney princesses were swirling around in my head. "I don't know," I said with a laugh. "What do you think I should go as?"

"What about the girl from Clueless?" Kennedy asked. "Not because you're like her. Just because of the blonde thing. And you already have a school uniform to wear."

"Kennedy, that defeats the purpose of shopping," Justin said. "Neither of you are leaving here without a perfectly tailored Halloween costume."

She laughed. "Right. Sorry, I'm used to working with what I have."

"Tonight we splurge," he said and looped his arm through hers. "Follow me, ladies."

He led us through a set of doors and into a giant room that looked like it would be more suitable for wedding dress shopping than anything else. But it was filled with fancy clothes instead of wedding dresses.

We wove through the clothes and mannequins to one of the changing areas. All of them were empty. *I guess Mrs. Caldwell really did rent out the whole place.*

"Oh, and Brooklyn, your order is almost ready. Diane is just putting the finishing touches on a few things."

"Your order?" Mrs. Caldwell asked.

"You didn't tell her about all your clothes?" Justin asked. He shook his head. "That wench of a sister she has cut all her clothes to bits. The little horror. Some of them were one-of-a-kind pieces. And now they're all in literal pieces in the garbage."

"What?" Mrs. Caldwell looked over at me. "Isabella did that?"

I really didn't want to talk about Isabella right now. I'd had to deal with her all week at school.

"You should hear about all the other stuff she's done," Kennedy said. "She poured milk all over her blazer once. She's tried to sabotage her relationship with Matt on several occasions. She leaves Brooklyn threatening notes at school, and I'm pretty sure they're written in blood."

"It's lipstick." *I think*. The notes hadn't stopped. But I wasn't scared of Isabella. As far as I was concerned, she could choke on the red lipstick she used to write the notes. I'd kept my dad updated on everything she'd done. Or that she made Cupcake or one of her minions do. Isabella hadn't acted on any of her threats. She was just trying to scare me out of town.

"Oh and there was that one time when she tried to kill both of us," Kennedy said. "That was loads of fun."

"No," Justin gasped.

"Yeah, at homecoming. She drugged me and then abandoned Brooklyn naked in the middle of the city."

"I was wearing underwear," I said. I could feel my cheeks turning red.

"What?" Mrs. Caldwell said and turned to me. "Why didn't you tell me any of this?"

"I...I thought you knew," I said. "Didn't Matt tell you?"

She pressed her lips together. "No. No he did not."

That was news to me. Why wouldn't Matt tell his mom about Isabella? "Why did Matt tell you I was staying with you?"

"Because of the issues with your father."

I bit the inside of my lip. That made sense. His parents hated my dad. It was a good excuse for me to move in with them if I hated my dad too. But because I was trying to escape a psychopath? That made me a considerably worse houseguest. I didn't blame Matt for lying. I was just relieved I was able to stay with him. But a heads up would have been nice.

"I'm sorry..."

"No reason to apologize, sweetheart," Mrs. Caldwell said. "It doesn't matter why you're staying with us, I'm happy to have you. I just feel bad because I already invited Isabella to the Halloween party. This is a disaster. She's already RSVP'd. I can't take it back."

"Of course you can," Justin said. "Go snatch her invitation and rip it to shreds just like she did to Brooklyn's clothes."

Mrs. Caldwell laughed. "If only it was that simple. The last thing I need is to upset the Pruitts." She seemed to realize what she said and shook her head. She wrung her hands together and I wasn't sure if it was because she was worried about how I'd react to her comment, or if she was actually worried that there would be some kind of repercussions for upsetting my father.

"It's okay," I said. "Isabella's not allowed to talk to me. It doesn't matter if she's at the party."

"Really?" Mrs. Caldwell looked so relieved.

"Yeah, it's fine." I didn't love it. It basically meant Isabella would have full access to the only place I truly felt safe. I might as well have been living with her.

"Just make sure to lock your bedroom door," Justin said with a laugh. "Now where were we." He snapped his fingers. "Sandy from Grease. That tight little black number. You'd look divine, Brooklyn."

"That's perfect!" Kennedy said.

Mrs. Caldwell smiled. "Oh, I love that movie. You really would make a perfect Sandy."

I'd watched Grease with my mom half a dozen times. She always used to stand up and make me dance with her to all the songs. I didn't know whether I was smiling or about to cry. "Yeah, that sounds good to me."

Justin clapped. "This is going to be perfect. Fingers crossed Halloween doesn't end with you naked and alone in the middle of the city."

I half laughed half groaned. "I will never get in a car with Isabella again. It'll be fine."

"It's showtime," Justin said and spread his hands. "Let the shopping begin!"

CHAPTER 21

Friday

Kennedy disappeared behind a rack of clothes and I followed her out of earshot of Justin and Mrs. Caldwell. The clothes were all glamorous. But I really didn't know a thing about fashion. I'd leave all that to Justin. What I really needed was to talk to Kennedy. We used to hang out all the time, and now that I was living at Matt's we didn't get to see each other nearly as much. And there was a question I needed to ask her that I didn't want anyone at school to overhear.

"Hey, have you heard from Felix at all?" I asked.

She shrugged. "No. Why?"

"I really need to talk to him. I've texted him a few times, but he never responds." Besides, it would be better to talk to him in person. Even though he hadn't been to school all week, I assumed he had probably heard the rumors about my engagement ring. Everything that happened at Empire High seemed to travel like wildfire. Except for Felix's whereabouts.

"Felix's parents mostly live abroad and sometimes he disappears for a couple weeks at a time when he visits them," said Kennedy. "I don't think he gets international texts."

"Oh. So he's visiting his parents?"

"Yeah, probably. What do you need to talk to him about?"

"I just want to clear the air."

Kennedy lifted up a pair of pants that could only be described as genie pants. I wasn't even aware that pants like that were made outside of costumes. But the material was definitely not cheap polyester.

"Do you think he still likes you?" Kennedy asked.

"I don't know." *Not if he's heard the rumors.* I really, really wanted to talk to him in person before he heard about Matt. "Do *you* still like him?" I'd been dancing around this question with her ever since we'd met. She'd denied it. She'd changed the subject. She'd laughed. But I never quite believed her.

"Nunca. Have you read all those contracts your dad gave you yet?"

Nice try, Kennedy. I wasn't letting her off the hook that easily. "No, I'm still going through them." I'd been through the whole dating one. There wasn't really anything weird in it. And for some reason it made reading the other considerably less appealing. "Just a nunca on the Felix thing?"

"Yeah, it's a nunca from me. These would be perfect, wouldn't they?" Kennedy asked and held up the genie pants.

"Yes...but let's circle back to my question real quick. Are you sure you don't still like Felix?"

"And these would be great for your costume," Kennedy said and pulled out a pair of leather leggings.

They would indeed be perfect. But she was avoiding the question. "Kennedy, I think if you have feelings for Felix..."

"Oh, are we talking about boys?" Mrs. Caldwell asked. "Tell me everything."

Kennedy laughed. "There's not much to tell. Brooklyn keeps trying to set me up with this boy at school. And I keep telling her I'm not interested. Rob on the other hand? I very much like him."

"Robert Hunter?" Mrs. Caldwell asked. "Well, that's perfect. He'll be at the Halloween party too. I've always wanted to play matchmaker."

"He will be?" I asked. Did Matt and Mason know that?

"Of course. The Hunters come every year. Robert and James practically grew up in our house. They're over all the time. The last few weeks have been so busy for them, I haven't seen them much. But they all already RSVP'd. It'll be so good to see them."

"Mhm," Kennedy said and glanced at me. Her face screamed *what the hell is happening?*

I shook my head as discreetly as possible.

"I'm going to figure out a way to give you and Robert a moment alone at the party," Mrs. Caldwell said. "Oh, the hairdresser is here. Do you two have any idea what you want to do for your new hairstyles?"

I kind of liked my hair the way it was. But Mrs. Caldwell looked so excited. And I was trying to prove that I belonged in this world just as much as Isabella. I thought about all the girls at Empire High. "Maybe add some layers?"

"That's a great idea," Kennedy said. "It'll give your hair more volume. And I've always wanted to try highlights."

"This is going to be so fun," Mrs. Caldwell said. "Let me go check in with the hairdresser. I hope she brought those books of hairstyles. I always love flipping through those."

"Does she not know that her sons are at war with the Hunters?" Kennedy asked.

"No. Matt and Mason think that by not mentioning Rob and James that they'll just disappear. As if erasing a lifetime of friendship just happens. Especially because their parents are friends. I think." I didn't really know that for a fact. But they were neighbors. Where I grew up, all neighbors were friends. So, it was probably true.

"So Isabella *and* the Hunters are coming to this party," Kennedy said. "This is going to be kind of amazing."

I laughed. "It's like a ticking time bomb."

"As long as I'm not the one that explodes, I'm happy to watch all of it unfold."

My phone buzzed.

"You talk to your man," Kennedy said. "And make sure you try these on." She shoved the black leather leggings into my arms. "They're going to be perfect for your costume. I'm gonna go ask the hairdresser to make me look like J-Lo."

I laughed and pulled out my phone. But it wasn't Matt. The text was from an unknown number: "Hey, Brooklyn. Can we talk? I can meet you out back by the pool. See you in an hour?"

I looked up at Mrs. Caldwell and Kennedy laughing. I didn't have time for Rob's shenanigans right now. He'd been texting me from a different number every night this week, trying to trick me into weird meetings with him. Usually the texts were funnier than this. But I still knew it was him.

I typed out a quick text. "I'm not home, Rob."

My phone buzzed right away. "It's not Rob. It's James."

I was used to the funny texts from Rob. But now that I knew it was James? It didn't seem so light anymore. What did James want to talk about? He didn't mention Operation Disappearing Troll. Was it about something else? I bit the inside of my lip. It didn't matter. I promised Matt. "I'm still not home," I wrote back.

He texted back right away. "But I like being miserable with you."

My stomach twisted into knots. Matt said he didn't care about James' wellbeing anymore. But he did. I knew he did. And he'd want to make sure that James was okay, even if they were fighting.

"Are you okay?" I texted.

"No. I'm miserable. And it's loud here."

"Where are you?"

"I don't know. Some club."

A club? That meant he was drinking. Or worse. "What club? Where?"

"Are you coming?"

"James, tell me where you are."

"I like when you're bossy. Come make me feel better."

Yeah, he was definitely drunk. Or high. Or something. I had no idea what his current elixir of choice was. "James, give me the address."

"Call me and I'll give it to you," he texted back.

Damn it. "Fine. One second."

I walked over to Mrs. Caldwell and Kennedy. They were flipping through books of different hairstyles. I hung the Sandy leggings on the back of one of the chairs.

"I need to make a call real quick," I said. "I'll be right back."

"Wait," Kennedy said. "What do you think of something like this?" She flipped around the hairstyle book she was holding. The model in the picture had these beautiful chestnut highlights in her hair.

"That would look amazing on you," I said.

"Yeah?"

"Absolutely," Mrs. Caldwell said. Then she turned to me. "Don't go too far, sweetheart. Not past security, alright?"

"Mhm." I made my way out of the private room. The grand entrance was completely empty. I pressed on James' number.

"Hey," he said. But I could barely hear him over the music blaring in the background.

"James, where are you?"

"Where are you?"

I shook my head. "I'm out."

"Are you with Matt?"

"No. I'm out with his mom. Tell me where you are."

"I like Mrs. Caldwell," he said. "She's nicer than my mom. Everything Matt has is better than what I have."

Oh, James. "Can you please tell me where you are?"

"What are you and Mrs. Caldwell out doing?" he asked, ignoring me.

"We're getting makeovers."

The music got a little quieter, like he'd shut himself in a bathroom or something. "You don't need a makeover, Brooklyn. You're perfect just the way you are."

I bit the inside of my lip. He wasn't supposed to be saying stuff like that to me. "James…"

"How do you know if someone loves you or your money?" he asked.

"I don't know."

"Yes you do. Because you love Matt for Matt. You don't care about his money. You're not like Rachel."

"I thought you two made up?"

"Yeah. But I don't want to be with her anymore. She doesn't love me. People in love don't cheat."

"People make mistakes." I'd certainly made plenty of them.

"I want to be with you," James said. "Like in the shower. It was like you needed me. I think I like being needed. Rachel doesn't need me. She just wants the life I can give her."

"James…"

"I won't kiss you. I just want to sit with you. I can't remember the last time I was as happy as I was that night. Just sitting."

"If I remember correctly, you also got your…*you know*…bitten. It couldn't have been that great of a night."

He laughed. "That part was not the best. But my dick is fine, if that's what you're wondering."

"I wasn't."

He sighed. "I'm so fucking tired."

Something about the way he said it made it seem like he wasn't sleepy. More like tired of his life.

"Can you please tell me where you are?"

"I'm going to get the fuck out of this city as soon as I can. Is everyone in Delaware as nice as you? Maybe I'll move there."

"Not everyone. But in general...yeah, people seem friendlier."

"Yeah, maybe I'll go there. One day. I don't know. I'm tired. You know?"

No, I didn't know. That was the problem. All I knew was that I was worried about him. Ever since Matt told me he was scared James might try to hurt himself, I'd been worried. More now than before. Because it seemed like now I was the only one looking out for him. "Tell me where you are, James."

"I'm in a bathroom."

"That's not helpful."

He laughed. "I meant what I said when I proposed. I don't think we'd be miserable together. I think you make me happy. I think you're the only one that makes me happy."

"Don't say that." My stomach twisted into more knots. It wasn't fair for him to put his happiness on me. I couldn't be his person.

"Why shouldn't I say it? It's true." He sighed. "And you understand my misery too. I like drowning with you. Fuck. I want you even more because I can't have you."

"Just because we aren't together doesn't mean we can't be friends. I'm a pretty great friend, James."

"Friends with benefits?"

"Just friends," I said.

"Right. The kind with lots of benefits."

I laughed. "Please just tell me where you are."

"Will you come? And just sit with me for a few minutes? I won't tell Matt."

It didn't matter if he would or wouldn't tell Matt. I couldn't do that. "I'm going to make sure you get home safe."

That seemed to be enough for him. Because he finally gave me the address. I jotted it down and hung up the phone.

The SUV that drove me everywhere was still right outside. I walked out onto 5th Avenue and tapped on the glass.

Miller rolled down the window. "Yes, Miss Pruitt?"

I hated when he called me that. "I know this is a weird request, but is it possible for one of you to go pick up my friend? He's drunk and he needs a ride home. I don't really trust anyone else to make sure he gets home safely."

"What's the address?" Donnelley asked.

"He mentioned that he was in a bathroom in this club." I handed him the piece of paper I'd written the address down on.

"That's close by," Donnelley said. "I can swing by real quick. What friend?"

"James Hunter. He has brown hair and dark brown eyes and..."

Donnelley laughed. "I know Mr. Hunter. I'll make sure he gets home safely."

Miller lowered his eyebrows. It looked like he'd been trying to ignore me the whole time, but the name bothered him enough to actually make him show emotion. I hated that Miller had seen James kiss me. I hated that we were in a situation where we still had to see each other every day. I hated that I'd hurt him.

"Miller, will you stay here?" Donnelley asked.

"Yeah. Sure." Miller climbed out of the car and slammed the door.

The SUV drove off and I breathed a little easier. Donnelley would make sure James was safe. I looked over at Miller. I hadn't had a moment alone with him all week. Not since he'd told me he was quitting.

"James Hunter, huh?" Miller asked. "Remember when you told me you hated guys like Felix Green and Matthew Caldwell?" He looked so sad. "Now you hang out with all of them. And you're engaged to one of them."

"Miller..."

"It's fine. Just an observation, kid." He leaned against the wall outside Odegaard. "You should probably get back inside."

"I don't want you to hate me."

He lowered his eyebrows. "I don't hate you. I just hate seeing you with other guys. And I hate that I don't have any way out."

"I asked my dad about you quitting. He said you two had a mutual understanding..."

"A mutual understanding?" He raised both eyebrows. "Is that what he said?"

"Yes." It came out as more of a question than a response.

"Did he throw the term *family* around too?" he asked.

"Yeah, actually."

"I'm not that psychopath's family."

I winced. First Mrs. Caldwell was worried about upsetting my dad with the whole Isabella invite. And now Miller was calling him a psychopath? I swallowed hard. They'd never seen the side of my dad that was sweet and caring. This was all a big misunderstanding.

"I'm sorry," he said. "You know what I meant."

"No, actually, I don't. Miller, if you really want to quit I'm sure he'd let you. You just have to talk to him."

Miller shook his head. "I did talk to him."

"Well, I can talk to him…"

"You really are trying to get me killed, aren't you?"

"Of course not. Just let me…"

"There's no out for me, Brooklyn."

"But…"

"You saw what he did to me when I let you out of my sight." He gestured to his face. "I know too much. If I try to leave, he'll kill me. I don't know what kind of lies that man is feeding you. But he's not who you think he is."

I didn't even know what to say. I knew my dad was dangerous. I knew that and yet…I didn't really. I'd seen him be kind and sweet more times than I'd seen him be mean.

"There's no out," he said again. He closed his eyes like he was exhausted and rested his head on the wall behind him.

I swallowed hard. I wondered if he was as tired of life as James. And I hated that I couldn't help either of them. "Miller, I'm sure my dad would listen to me if I asked him to let you quit."

"Right, because complaining to his daughter is a great way to sway a man like him."

"A man like him?"

"Brooklyn, what do you think your dad does?"

"He's a businessman." That was what my dad had told me. That he owned a lot of family businesses.

"Your father is a mobster, Brooklyn."

A mobster? I shook my head. "That's not..."

"He threatens people for a living. He kills people when they cross him. He's made a lot of enemies in this town. Including your fiancé's parents. Compared to some of the people your father is mixed up with, Isabella isn't even that big of a threat." He kicked at some trash on the sidewalk. "There is no out. Not for me. And definitely not for you."

I wanted to laugh it off. To tell Miller all the reasons why he was wrong. That he was exaggerating. But actually, that all made a lot of sense. Except for the fact that Miller hadn't seemed all that scared of my dad in the beginning. "But if he's so awful...why did you ever kiss me to begin with?"

"I'd never broken his rules before. I didn't know the consequences. But I never plan on breaking them again."

So he was stuck here? For how long? Months? Years? Forever? I shook my head. I wanted to tell Miller that I'd talk to my dad. But he'd just told me not to.

"I don't regret kissing you," Miller said. "But if your dad ever finds out…I won't just lose my job. I'll lose my life, Brooklyn. So you gotta stop looking at me like that."

I didn't know how I was looking at him. Like I wanted to hug him? Like I was about to burst into tears? *There is no out.*

CHAPTER 22

Friday

"Is everything alright?" Mrs. Caldwell asked.

I looked in the mirror to see Mrs. Caldwell in the reflection as the hairdresser was straightening my hair.

I was worried about James. I had no one to talk to about it. And now Miller's warning was stuck in my head and wouldn't go away no matter how much we shopped. I was trying to have fun. But I couldn't seem to shake the warning. *There is no out.* I cleared my throat and looked down at my lap. "Mhm."

Mrs. Caldwell sat down in the chair next to mine. "Was that Matt on the phone?"

"Oh, no. I'm not upset about anything with Matt."

She gave me a warm smile. "So you are upset?"

Damn it. Mrs. Caldwell knew my dad. Wouldn't she know the truth? There was a reason why she'd allowed me to stay in her house when she thought it was because I didn't want to stay with my dad. But I didn't know her well enough to ask her a question like that.

Instead, I looked at my reflection in the mirror. "I'm sorry that Matt didn't tell you the real reason why I needed a place to stay."

Mrs. Caldwell smiled. "It doesn't matter why you're staying with us. What matters is that you're safe in our home. What matters is that my son loves you." She reached out and squeezed my shoulder. "You know…we haven't really gotten a chance to talk about wedding details. Have you and Matthew discussed a possible date?"

"No, not really." I laughed. "We'll have to wait until at least after college at the earliest."

Mrs. Caldwell looked…disappointed? I didn't know her that well, but she didn't exactly look happy with my response.

"I mean, we're a little young, don't you think?" I added.

"I think age is just a number. And I've never seen my son this happy before. You already feel like part of the family. Why not make it official?"

That was sweet. But a small part of me wondered if she wanted me to make things official with Matt because of my new last name. And the fact that the Caldwells wanted nothing to do with the Pruitts. Because we were…mobsters? I shook away the thought. It was ridiculous. *Mobster.* The word rolled around in my head. I didn't know what to think of my dad. But the more I thought of the obsessive security, the way he treated his staff, the secrecy, all the contracts…it all seemed more than what a normal businessman would need.

"I don't know anything about planning a wedding," I said. I hadn't really thought about any of the details. Just that I knew for sure I wanted to be with Matt for the rest of my life.

"That's what I'm here for. And Justin seems to be keen on being your planner. Talk to Matthew. Let's get a date in the books."

I nodded. But I couldn't even imagine planning a wedding right now. It felt like Miller had just dropped a bomb on my lap. And I had schoolwork. And Isabella was still trying to kill me. And… My thoughts trailed off. What was I even thinking? I loved Matthew Caldwell. His mom was right. What was the point in waiting? Waiting was wasting time. And I wasn't one to do that.

"I'll talk to Matt," I said.

She smiled. "Wonderful. Oh look, they're all done. You look stunning, sweetheart." She gestured toward the mirror.

I stared at my reflection. The changes were subtle, but they were there. I looked like I belonged at Empire High. I bit the inside of my lip. But was that really what I wanted?

When I had decided to stay in New York instead of getting on a bus and going home, I'd told myself Isabella couldn't dictate my life. That I belonged here just as much as she did. Now I looked the part. But I wasn't sure if it was what I wanted anymore. I didn't care about revenge. Or getting even with her. All I cared about was Matt. And he liked me because I was different. Now I just looked…the same as everyone else.

"You look amazing," Kennedy said as she sat down in the chair on the other side of me. She was looking perfectly glamorous with her new highlights.

"Yeah?"

"It's like you only…even more perfect."

I laughed. "It's not too much?"

"What? No? Matt's going to love the new you."

I hope so.

***

I carried my bags of clothes up to the guest room I was supposed to be staying in. Then I wandered into Matt's room. He wasn't there, so I walked down the hall to Mason's room. I knocked and let myself in.

The two of them were playing videogames.

Mason cursed at something on the screen. He didn't even look over his shoulder to see if it was me before he started talking. "Brooklyn, we've talked about this. You gotta knock. What if I had a sexy guest?"

I laughed. "You never have guests." I'd learned a lot about Mason recently. Yes, it was true that he was a total player. But he never brought whatever girls he was currently sleeping with to the house. I was pretty sure he didn't want to give his mom a heart attack. And despite the fact that he was a total womanizer, he treated me like I was the sister he never had. There was a heart of gold under his tough exterior. And for some reason it made me happy that I was one of the only ones that got to see it.

Mason laughed and turned to look at me over his shoulder. "Damn." His eyes wandered down my body.

The way he stared at me used to bother me. But I'd also learned that he was a good guy. And he'd never step on his brother's toes when it came to me. The fact that he called me "sis" all the time helped.

Matt's gaze followed Mason's.

It felt like my heart was going to beat out of my chest.

They were both just staring at me. And I didn't know if it was a good kind of stare or a bad one. "We got makeovers," I said to break the awkward silence. I did a little spin when they still said nothing. And then I immediately felt more awkward because my skirt was so short and spinning made it rise up even more. *Screw me.* I walked over to the couch and sat down in the empty spot between them. "Someone just blew up," I said and gestured to the screen.

"Shit," Matt said. He hit something on his controller and then tossed it to the side.

Mason laughed. He stood up and stretched, dropping his controller on the couch too. "I'm gonna go get a soda. You guys want anything?"

"We're good," Matt said.

"I'll literally be back in five minutes. And this is my room. So don't fuck on my couch." He tossed a pillow at Matt's head, but Matt caught it before it hit his face.

I laughed, but it caught in my throat weird. I didn't know what Matt was thinking. And his silence was unnerving.

"You look…different," Matt finally said when Mason closed the door. His fingers traced my thigh right where my new thousand-dollar skirt stopped.

I swallowed hard. I'd only cut off a few inches, but the layers in my hair and the new makeup definitely made me look different. "A good different or bad different?"

"I liked you exactly the way you were," he said.

Crap.

His fingers slid higher up my thigh. "But I think you get more beautiful every day. With or without makeup. Or a new haircut. You're beautiful, baby."

I wasn't sure why, but his words made tears pool in the corners of my eyes. "So why do you look mad?"

"Because your skirt is too short." His fingers bunched my skirt up as he pushed me backward. My back hit the couch cushions as he leaned over me. "And your heels are too high." He grabbed my leg, hoisting it over his shoulder and kissing the inside of my thigh.

Fuck.

"And your shirt is cut too low." His nose traced the curve of my exposed cleavage. "Only I should be allowed to see you like this. So you either need to go change into pajamas right the fuck now. Or wait for me in my room just like this. On the bed. With your legs spread."

I could barely breathe. And it wasn't just the naughty words coming out of his mouth. He was staring at me with so much intensity. Almost like his gaze could burn my exposed skin.

"And maybe lose the thong." His thumb rubbed against the lacy fabric. "I tend to tear things when I get impatient."

Jesus.

"So which will it be? A fun night in pj's playing videogames? Or…"

The door started to open.

Matt pulled me back to a seated position, tugging my skirt back into place. But he couldn't take away the flush in my cheeks. Or the fact that I was practically panting.

"Do you want to play too, sis?" Mason asked as he walked back in. He jumped over the back of the couch and sat down.

"Actually, I'm feeling a bit tired." I turned to Matt and winked at him. "Goodnight, Mason."

He gave me a quick side hug before I stood up. “Night.”

I left his room and hurried to Matt’s. Did he really want me to sit on his bed like that? Or was he just saying it to make me blush? And if he did mean it, did he want me to keep my high heels on? It seemed weird to put my shoes on his bed. But they were new…

Screw it. I pulled off my underwear and climbed onto his huge bed.

I didn’t get a chance to decide how to pose because his door opened a second later. I hadn’t even reached the middle of his bed. I froze on all fours and stared at him over my shoulder.

He groaned. “What are you trying to do to me?” He moved so fast. I blinked and his hands were on my waist, pulling me against him. I could feel his hardness through his sweatpants. And I was very aware of the fact that it was the only material between us.

He grabbed my shoulders, pulling me up so that my back was pressed against his front. “When you dress like this it makes me want to fuck you.” He kissed the side of my neck. “But I don’t want to fuck you, Brooklyn.” His kisses trailed down to my shoulder. “I want to make love to you. And you’re making it very hard for me to be patient.” He let go of me and took a step back. “Let me find you something to cover up with before I lose my mind.”

What? “But…” my voice trailed off as he grabbed one of his t-shirts out of a drawer. “What if I’m ready?”

His hand paused on the drawer.

I swallowed hard. I loved him. I loved him so much that just thinking about him when we were apart made my chest hurt. I wanted to marry him. I wanted to have his children. I wanted us to be us forever.

I leaned over and opened up his nightstand drawer. And I pulled out a condom from his annoyingly large box of them. I placed it on the bed beside me and pulled my shirt off over my head.

His Adam's apple rose and fell.

I pushed off my skirt too. And I was just reaching down to take off my heels when his hand caught my ankle.

"I can do that," he said. He slowly undid the strap and let one shoe fall to the ground. And then the next. He kissed the inside of my ankle, his lips trailing up my leg torturously slowly. Until they stopped at the top of my thigh. "Are you sure?" he asked. His voice sounded tight, like he was having trouble keeping control.

I loved his fingers. I loved his tongue. But I wanted all of Matthew Caldwell. Not just pieces of him. All of him.

"I'm sure. I love you. I couldn't be more sure."

He moved on top of me. "I love you." He kissed my forehead. "I love you." He kissed the tip of my nose. "I'm so fucking in love with you, Brooklyn."

I grabbed the back of his head and lowered his lips to mine. He kissed me senseless. He'd told me that he'd be all my firsts. First kiss. First touch. First taste. First love.

My fingers dug into the muscles of his back. *God, but this?* This first was everything.

CHAPTER 23

Saturday

I was pretty sure Matt agreed that this first was everything too. Because he kept wanting to do it over and over again. Not that I was complaining. But I was sore. I wasn't sure how I was going to walk around his house today without anyone catching on to what we'd done all night long.

I tried to move my leg and groaned. *Ow.*

Matt laughed.

I opened my eyes and looked up at his smiling face. His head was propped up on his hand and he was staring at me.

"Were you watching me while I slept?" I asked.

He reached out and tucked a loose strand of hair behind my ear. "Maybe?"

"Do you know how creepy that is?"

"I like looking at my girl. What's wrong with that?"

I didn't bother trying to hide my smile.

"You better get used to me staring at you all the time. You signed up for a forever of it."

I laughed and propped my head up on my hand too. "About that…what are your actual thoughts about getting married. For real?"

"I told you I want you to be Brooklyn Caldwell."

"I know. But…when exactly were you thinking you wanted that to happen?"

"Brooklyn Sanders, are you asking me to marry you?"

I laughed. "Never mind." I started to sit up.

"Hey."" He grabbed me around the waist and pulled me on top of him.

I straddled him as his hands found my hips.

"You mean you want to pick a date?" he asked.

"Do you?"

"We could fly out to Vegas tonight."

I laughed. "Stop it, I'm serious."

"I'm serious too."

"You're not serious." I splayed my hands on his chest. "You're crazy." I shouldn't have said anything. We were too young. He thought I was just messing with him. "Are you hungry? I'm starving." I tried to move, but he kept his hands locked on my thighs, holding me in place.

"I'm crazy in love with you, Brooklyn. I wasn't joking about Vegas. But we never really talked about what kind of wedding you wanted. Do you want the whole shebang? The white dress?" His hands ran down the sides of the t-shirt I'd borrowed from him. "The flowers? All that?"

Honestly I had never really thought about it before. All I knew was that Matt was everything I wanted and needed. And I could so easily picture walking down the aisle toward him. I nodded. "I do want all of that."

"And when do you want it?"

"I assumed you were thinking after college?" I asked.

"I wasn't thinking after college."

"You weren't?" I stared down at him.

"No."

The way he was staring at me made my heart race. I swore it was beating so loudly that he could hear it. "Then when were you thinking?"

He smiled up at me. "I asked you first, baby. When do you want to get married?"

"Well, I heard the fall is a great time for a wedding." At least, that's what Justin had said. And I trusted him.

"It's fall right now," Matt said.

"Is it?" I laughed as he tickled my side. "Stop it!"

Somehow I wound up beneath him, his body pressed against mine.

"The fall is pretty busy with school and football practice," he said.

True. Justin acted like my fairy godmother, but I wasn't sure he actually had magical powers. A fall wedding would have to wait for a long time. "Which is why you do want to wait till after college?"

He shook his head. "I was thinking more of a winter wedding."

"The winter after we graduate from college?"

He laughed. "No. This winter. We could do it during Christmas break. And if we do it at the start of break, then we'll even have time for a honeymoon." He smiled down at me.

I couldn't help but smile back. "This winter? Is that really what you want?"

"No, I want to marry you in Vegas tomorrow." He leaned down and kissed the side of my neck. "But I can wait till the winter if that's what you want." His kisses slowly trailed down my neck. "I like the idea of you in a white dress saying I do."

"Yeah?"

"Mhm." He lightly nipped at my earlobe.

"Okay. Let's do it this winter." A fall wedding may have been Justin's dream, but it wasn't mine. I didn't care what season I married Matt. I just wanted to marry him. And now I was already picturing snow in our wedding pictures.

He kissed me slowly. "I'll make sure you have the wedding of your dreams. But the only thing I really care about is having you."

Something about the way he said it reminded me of James' fears about Rachel just wanting to be with him for his money. And I needed Matt to know that he didn't need to ever doubt me. "Matt?" I grabbed both sides of his face so he'd be looking down at me. "I love you. For you. I know you can give me the wedding of my dreams and everything I could possibly ask for, but I don't want you to ever think that's why I want you."

He let his forehead drop to mine. "I know. But it doesn't matter if you don't need it. I'm going to give you everything you've ever wanted."

***

As far as I was concerned, we were never leaving this bed.

Matt had breakfast sent up and I'd been lazily brainstorming ideas for our wedding in the journal I was supposed to be using to track my panic attacks.

"How many bridesmaids do you want?" he asked.

"Well, Kennedy of course. What about you? How many groomsmen?"

"I'll just ask Mason."

I stared at him. He couldn't just ask Mason. James and Rob were his best friends too. He needed to make up with them before our wedding or he'd always regret it.

"Actually, there's a girl that's always nice to me in my English class," I said. There wasn't. "Maybe I'll ask her too. And I could always ask Justin. I think he'd say yes. So I actually want three. Who will your other two be? It would look silly if it wasn't even."

"I can ask Brett and Jason."

"Who are Brett and Jason?"

"A couple of my football friends. They danced with me on the homecoming float when I was serenading you."

I laughed. "Really? Brett and Jason? There aren't two other people you want to ask? Two more important people in your life?"

"Nah. Can't think of anyone."

Come on. "Actually, I want two more, I think. So you'll need to choose two more too."

"I'll ask Jeff and Mike too then."

What? Who even are these people? I set the notebook down. "Two more."

"Brooklyn…"

"You have to make up with the Hunters, Matt. They're your best friends. Not Brett and whoever."

"Brett, Jason, Jeff, and Mike didn't kiss you though. And they don't think I'm a liar."

"You can't have a wedding without your best friends by your side."

"The last time I checked, the only person I really need there is my girl."

Darn him and his stupid charming smile. "You're really not going to try to make things right with them?"

"I've apologized to James a dozen times, Brooklyn. For something that I didn't even do. I tried to make things right. I don't know what else I could have done. You're making it seem like I don't care, but this is on them. I didn't cut them out of my life. They cut me and Mason out."

"I know. I'm sorry. But after all those things you confessed to me about James' problems...aren't you ever worried about him?"

"Of course I'm worried about him. But what can I do if he won't even talk to me?"

That was a fair point.

"It's really sweet that you care about this, Brooklyn. But I'm done caring. I just want to know you have my back. That you believe I didn't do anything wrong."

Well, technically he did do something wrong. He should have told James what happened right away. But I got why Matt kept it a secret. He was trying to protect James, not hurt him. Matt was a good person. And I needed to stop worrying about the Hunters and start focusing on the man right in front of me. Marriage meant sticking up for each other.

As soon as I had a minute, I'd text Rob and tell him the prank was off. I wouldn't talk to Rob or James again until *they* made things right with the Caldwells. It wasn't really my fault that they weren't friends anymore. I was done meddling. I just wanted to be happy with Matt.

And I didn't need revenge against Isabella anymore. I didn't need to worry about fitting in. Because I already found my place. Right here.

I snuggled into Matt's side. "I do believe you. And I'll always have your back. Now that you mention it, I think I do just want one bridesmaid. So maybe just Mason for you then?"

"Sounds good to me." He kissed the side of my forehead.

I felt so comfortable and safe in Matt's arms. And for some reason it reminded me about how uncomfortable I was with my new family. I had no idea how we were going to have a happy wedding when our families hated each other.

"Matt, why did you tell your mom I was staying with you because I didn't want to live with my dad?"

"Because I knew it was an easy way to make her say yes."

I laughed. "You're very good at getting what you want."

He didn't respond. He just lifted up my notebook to look at some of our wedding ideas.

"But it was easy to make her say yes because your parents hate my dad, right?"

He set the notebook back down on my lap. "I don't know if I'd say hate. They just don't see eye to eye on how to run a business."

"And that's why they had a falling out?" I asked. "Is that all you know?"

"My dad doesn't exactly loop me in on his business decisions."

I knew this was a sore subject for him. He wanted nothing more than to take over the family business one day, but his father wouldn't even entertain the idea.

I sat up so I could face Matt. "I heard this rumor and I don't know if it's true." There was no way I was going to mention Miller. "And I know I should just ask my dad, but he's so evasive when I ask him questions. So I just need you to tell me if it's true." I swallowed hard. "Is my dad a mobster?"

Matt laughed. "I don't think so. He just..." his voice trailed off. "All I really know is that he does some shady stuff with his business. And my parents wanted no part in it. But a lot of their friends do business with him still. Like the Hunters."

Shady stuff. Even though my dad denied it, Isabella said the Hunters owed the Pruitts a debt. "That kind of sounds like mobster stuff to me."

He lowered his eyebrows. "Yeah, I guess it kind of does, doesn't it? No wonder my parents want nothing to do with him."

I nodded. "And he kind of acts like one, right? With all the bodyguards. And security systems. And how he won't even really tell me what exactly he does. He said it was better that my mom left because he couldn't keep her safe. And didn't you see my bodyguards' faces? He had someone do that to them when they broke the rules. He...he...I think maybe my dad's into some really bad stuff. And when we had lunch the other day he was talking about me taking over the business one day..."

"You can't do that," Matt said. "I don't know if he's a mobster or not, but like I said...he does shady stuff. Illegal stuff. You just said yourself it was dangerous."

"I know. I wasn't really thinking. I just...he seemed proud of me. I don't know, it was stupid."

"Nothing you do is stupid." He pulled me onto his lap. "You should just ask him flat out. Or I can ask my dad..."

"No, I don't want you to involve your dad. He's already being really nice for letting me stay here. I'll ask my dad about it."

Matt pushed a loose strand of hair behind my ear. "Let's forget about whether or not our parents are friends. Our wedding isn't about them. It's about us."

I nodded. He was right. And yet...it kind of felt like the wedding was about me becoming a Caldwell as quickly as possible. "Are you sure you don't want to marry me just so my last name isn't Pruitt?"

"I want to marry you because my eyes always gravitate to you in a room. I'm only happy when I know that you're happy too. You're the only one that puts me in my place. You're different than all the other girls I've ever met. You're pure. You understand me. You're so strong. When you cut me out of your life, I realized that I'm only really living when we're together. You're funny and smart and you even get along with my brother, which is rare."

I laughed.

He reached out and cupped my cheek in his hand. "I can't keep my hands to myself when I'm around you. I love you, Brooklyn."

That was more than enough for me. I'd only been looking for a little validation and he'd given me a ton. This wasn't about him not wanting me to be a Pruitt. This was about him desperately wanting me to be his. And I already was.

CHAPTER 24

Monday

I picked up my pace on the track. My feet finally felt back to normal and running made me feel back to normal too. Or maybe it was just the new Odegaard sneakers Mrs. Caldwell insisted on buying for me when I told her I liked running. Either way, it was so easy to breathe when air was flowing all around me. Normally running helped clear my head too. But no matter how much time ticked by on the track, I kept coming back to one thing. Or rather one word. *Mobster.*

I knew I needed to talk to my dad. But it was weird to just call him up and ask. I needed to meet with him in person. *Mobster.* I shook my head. I wasn't a character from a crime movie. Did mobsters even really exist anymore? And certainly mobsters weren't as nice as my dad. Although, no one saw the side of my dad that I did. I doubted even Isabella did.

Just thinking about her made me look over at the bleachers. Cupcake had been following me around more and more recently. Today he was sitting on the bleachers with a few friends and just…staring. I wanted to believe that he was just checking out my new outfit and hairstyle. But I knew the truth. He was spying. Reporting back to Isabella. I tried to not let it bother me. But I certainly wouldn't be closing my eyes around him again any time soon. I didn't need another target painted on my forehead.

Every day I'd been getting threatening notes. And every day I'd given them to Miller to pass on to my dad. The look of concern in his eyes terrified me. It made me thankful that I could take sanctuary at Matt's house. But this weekend at the Halloween party, she'd be there too.

"Hey, newb!"

I stopped on the track and turned to see Felix running up to me.

"Felix!" I hadn't seen him since homecoming. I'd sent him texts and tried to call. Kennedy had mentioned he might be abroad visiting his family. I hadn't realized how much I'd missed him until I saw his smiling face. I ran over to him, throwing my arms around him, almost knocking him to the track.

He laughed. "Good to see you too," he said.

"I missed you."

"Yeah, you said that in your texts. Which pretty much flooded my inbox as soon as I landed at JFK." He kissed my cheek.

And I realized I was too close to him. Much too close. I unwrapped my arms from around his shoulders and stepped back.

"Sorry about that," I said. "I just really needed to talk to you." I was glad I got to participate in gym today. He didn't seem to know about me and Matt yet. At least, he wasn't looking at me like he did. And if I'd been sitting on the bleachers wearing Matt's varsity jacket, this conversation would have gone very differently.

"You look different," Felix said.

I could feel my cheeks turning red. Was it that obvious that I'd had sex?

But then Felix reached out and lightly tugged on my ponytail. "New haircut?"

I laughed. Of course he meant that I looked different because of my makeover. It was almost the exact same thing Matt had said on Friday night. I'd bought the makeup that the makeup artist had used on Friday. And I'd tried to recreate the look as best as possible for school today. But I didn't want to ask Felix if he thought it was a good or bad different. Honestly, I hoped Felix thought I looked terrible. "Yeah, new haircut."

"And shoes." His eyes dropped to my sneakers. "Damn, are those Odegaards?"

"Yeah." I lifted them up to show him the signature blue soles.

He smiled. "You look good, newb. Very Empire High."

"Thanks." *I think?* I could feel my cheeks flush again. He wasn't supposed to be staring at me like that. I needed to tell him what was going on. "So about what I wanted to discuss with you..."

"I have news for you too. And I think you're going to be excited. At least, I hope you are." He shoved his hands into his sweatpants. "I was having trouble getting a hold of my parents. And I knew it couldn't wait. I flew out to go see them in order to get their permission for you to move in."

What? I just stared at him. That was not at all what I'd expected him to say. I thought he was just on vacation with his parents. Not trying to help me. "Move in?"

"With me," he added with a laugh. "I know you don't want to stay at the Pruitts' place. I thought your dad might agree since you'd still be in the same building. What do you say, newb? Roommates?"

It was sweet. Terribly, awfully sweet. And I was a monster. I swallowed hard. I was a monster, apparently just like my dad was. Just like Isabella was. God, I even had the same stupid haircut as Isabella's stupid monster friends. No, I wasn't a mobster that was going to get someone to repeatedly punch Felix in the face. But I was basically about to do that to his heart. "Felix..."

"I know you just want to be friends right now. Separate rooms, I promise. For now," he added with a wink.

Fuck. "You haven't been in contact with anyone since homecoming? You haven't heard...anything at all?"

"No. I couldn't get international calls and texts while I was in England."

I didn't even really know where to start. Why did he have to be so wonderful? There was a lump in my throat that wouldn't go away. And I could feel tears welling in my eyes. *He's going to hate me.* "I'm so so sorry."

"Well, that doesn't sound good. You hate that word. You must have done something really bad."

I hated that word when it didn't make sense. Like when people said they were sorry about my mom dying. But in this case? I couldn't give him enough sorrys. The last time I'd seen him, Matt and I hadn't even been together. I'd flirted with Felix at homecoming. I was such an idiot.

"I thought you'd be happy about the invite, newb. I never meant to make you cry."

Shit. I wiped my face.

"Oh."

I'd never heard him sound so serious before. I froze. *The ring.* He'd seen the ring.

He laughed even though it sounded forced. "Matt?" he asked and then sighed. He pulled one of his hands out of his pocket and scratched the side of his jaw. "I left to find you a better place to live. I didn't realize he'd be offering you something too."

"Can I just start from the beginning?" I couldn't seem to make my tears stop. I hated hurting people. Especially Felix. All he'd ever done was be nice to me. He'd spoken to me when Matt kept me invisible. He'd freaking flown out of the country to make sure I didn't have to live with Isabella. And the worst part was that I did love him. I loved Felix Green. I just wasn't in love with him.

"Let's run," he said. "I really feel like a run."

Okay.

***

I filled him in on everything that happened after he disappeared at homecoming. Isabella's insanity. Me running around New York in my underwear. Me actually getting close to my dad. Cupcake dating Isabella. Me dating Matt. Me getting engaged to Matt. Isabella's threatening notes. All of it.

Felix stopped and leaned over to catch his breath. "Fuck."

I wasn't sure which thing had upset him. Probably all of it.

"So you're engaged to Matt?" He was still staring at the ground.

"I'm sorry."

He laughed and looked up at me. "I get it now. Why you hate the word sorry. Newb, you can't be sorry if you love him. You can't be sorry for being happy."

"Of course I can. If it hurts you."

He stood up straight and pushed his sweaty hair off his forehead. "I don't want you to be sorry for being happy. I just want you to be happy."

I pressed my lips together.

"You are, right? He makes you happy?"

I'm so freaking happy. I nodded.

"Well…good then."

"Yeah?"

"What else am I supposed to say? You're wearing his ring, newb. I think I'm pretty much out of the race. I mean…not this one." He gestured to the track. "You only ever run with me."

I smiled. I knew he was trying to joke around, trying to make things feel a little more normal between us. But Felix and I had never really been just friends. There had always been a *maybe* between us. Now that I was engaged, though, there couldn't be a *maybe*. But I hoped we could still be friends. "I don't want this to mean we don't hang out anymore. I want us to be friends. I still want you to sit with us at lunch and…"

"Is Matt okay with that? Because I don't really feel like having to beat his ass again."

I laughed. I probably wouldn't have worded their fight that way. "He'll be fine with it. He has to be. You're one of my best friends, Felix. One of my only friends."

Felix looked over at Cupcake. "Did he really draw a target on your forehead?"

"I don't know if it was him. But I'm pretty sure."

Felix shook his head. "I knew I never should have gone into business with that asshole."

I bit the inside of my lip. He had gotten into business with Cupcake because of me. Another thing to add to the ever-growing list of things I'd messed up.

"Felix, I'm so..."

"It's fine, newb. It's better that I'm out of distribution. Hell, I think I'm done with the whole thing. I might just sell Cupcake my client list. I don't want to be my parents. I had to fly halfway across the world for them to even talk to me. They're dicks. I don't want to be anything like them."

"Really?" I couldn't help but be excited. Felix was too good for that business. "You're going to stop selling altogether?"

He laughed. "A very smart girl once told me that I'm better than that."

"You are better than that."

He looked back over at Cupcake. "Besides, I don't want to work with someone like him. I talked to him about what happened with Kennedy. He swears it went down differently than..."

"Kennedy wasn't lying."

He winced. "I didn't say she was. I believe you. I believe her. But he..." He shook his head. "Kennedy should talk to someone about what happened. Cupcake isn't going to listen to me. And he should pay for what he did to her."

"She doesn't want anyone else to know."

"Maybe I could talk to her?"

"No. I promised I wouldn't tell anyone. I shouldn't have even told you. Please don't say anything."

"But someone needs to…"

"Please, Felix."

He pushed his hair off his forehead. "Okay. I won't say anything. But what if he does it again?"

Isabella. Cupcake was dating her now. I knew she was terrible. The literal worst human being I'd ever met. But shouldn't I warn her? About what Cupcake was like?

Felix and I both looked at each other.

"I'll try to talk to Kennedy again," I said. "To see if she'll come forward. And in the meantime…I guess I should warn Isabella? Somehow without telling her about what happened with Kennedy."

"I wouldn't blame you if you didn't warn Isabella," Felix said.

"Yeah, but I'd blame myself if he did something to her. Maybe I'll write a menacing letter to her about it in red lipstick."

Felix laughed. "Dump Cupcake or else?"

I smiled. "Yeah, something like that."

Coach Carter blew the whistle, signaling the end of class.

"Think you can run faster than me now that you got fancy new kicks?" Felix started running backward.

I laughed. "Yes." I sprinted past him.

"Shit," he said with a laugh as he caught back up to me.

CHAPTER 25

Monday

Felix and I walked into the cafeteria together. "Save me a seat?" Felix asked. "I want to go talk to Cupcake real quick. But I definitely don't want to sit at that table."

I laughed. "Yeah, no problem." I watched him walk over to the Untouchables' original table. I wanted to go over to Isabella right away and somehow warn her about Cupcake. But Cupcake was sitting right next to her. I couldn't exactly do it in front of him.

"Everything okay with that?" Matt asked as I sat down next to him at our table.

"With Felix or Isabella?"

"Both?" He smiled. "You look worried. What's wrong?"

"Everything is fine with Felix. I told him about us. And he just wants to be friends. For real this time."

"That's good," Matt said and pulled me onto his lap. "So you're worried about Isabella then?"

It was weird. I was nervous to have to go talk to Isabella about Cupcake. But it wasn't really a decision. I had to do it. Despite everything, I'd never forgive myself if Cupcake did something to her. But that awkward conversation wasn't what was bothering me.

"I didn't receive any notes from her today," I said.

"Maybe she finally got the hint that they're not going to make you stop coming to school."

"I guess." I was used to the threatening notes though. Not getting any? Somehow it seemed more menacing. I looked back over at Isabella's table. It was just her, Cupcake, and Felix now. Where had all her minions disappeared to?

"I brought your salad," Matt said.

"You're the best." I kissed his cheek.

The flash of a camera made me turn to Kennedy. "You two are so ridiculously cute," she said.

I smiled up at Matt. It was so weird being snuggled up to him in the cafeteria. When school had started, I'd never imagined we'd wind up here. Only in my dreams.

"What's your costume for the Halloween party?" Kennedy asked Matt.

"It's a surprise." He reached around me to grab a fry off his plate.

"Wait, you're really not going to tell us?" I asked.

He laughed. "All you need to know is that I'm going to make an entrance."

I shook my head at him. He was the ridiculously cute one.

"Oh, I can't wait," Kennedy said. "Your annual Halloween party is always one of the biggest events of the year."

"Well, I think Brooklyn and I are going to try to top it this year," Matt said.

I could feel my cheeks turning red.

"We picked a date for our wedding," he added.

Kennedy opened her mouth and then closed it again. "Shut up. For this year? When?!"

I laughed. "Saturday, December 22nd."

"This is amazing."

"And I had a question to ask you," I said. "Will you be my bridesmaid? Or maid of honor? Or whatever you want to be called? You're my only one."

Kennedy squealed. "Do you seriously even have to ask? Yes!"

Matt held me even closer.

"What made you decide to do it so close to Christmas?"

"It gives us more time to celebrate during winter break," Matt said.

That had been the original reason. But the more we'd talked about it, the sweeter Matt's reason was. He knew the upcoming holidays were going to be hard on me. Just thinking about not waking up and celebrating Christmas morning with my mom made tears come to my eyes. The wedding was the perfect way to keep myself from not getting upset during the holidays. And we were creating a new family. The two of us. It would be hard to be sad during Christmas when our toes were in the hot sands of the Bahamas.

"You two are the best couple ever," Kennedy said. "Are you going to eat all of those?" Kennedy asked and pointed to Matt's French fries.

"Kennedy, if you want French fries, you should just order them," he said with a laugh. "Why are you always stealing mine?"

"Because I like green beans too. I just want a mix."

Matt laughed and shoved his tray into the middle of the table.

"You gotta keep him," Kennedy said. "He's the best."

"I plan on it."

"Hey guys," Felix said and sat down next to Kennedy.

"What were you doing talking to the enemy?" Kennedy asked as she stole another fry.

"I'm selling Cupcake my list of clients. I'm done selling."

"Really?" Kennedy's whole face lit up.

I wasn't sure I'd ever seen her quite this happy. Maybe she'd finally admit she liked Felix now that he wasn't going to be a drug dealer anymore.

I looked over at Isabella's table and was surprised to see her sitting all alone. It was a sight I never in a million years would have thought I'd see. And I couldn't think of a better time to go talk to her than now.

"I'll be right back," I said and stole one of Matt's French fries too.

"You guys really need to get your own fries," Matt said.

"It's way more fun to just steal yours." I kissed his cheek and climbed off his lap. I didn't tell him I was going to talk to Isabella, because I knew he'd try to stop me. I'd explain it to him later. Right now I just needed to get it over with as quickly as possible.

Isabella smiled at me when I sat down across from her. "I'm not supposed to talk to you, Sissy."

"I just need to tell you something."

"Regardless, Daddy will be mad if he knows we spoke."

"I won't tell him."

She dropped her fork on her tray. "Let me make this clear then. *I* don't want to talk to *you.* So you should probably run along back to your boy toy."

"Matt's not a boy toy." *Whatever that is.*

"Yes he is. You're only with him to grate on my nerves. And you're failing. Because I know for a fact that he doesn't even like you. He'll come crawling back to me soon enough. Just you wait and see."

Fuck off. "We're getting married."

She laughed. "No. You're not."

"Actually we are."

"You're adorably absurd," she said. "You'll be gone soon enough."

The way she said it made a chill run down my spine. "Look, I didn't come over here to argue with you. I came here to warn you about your new boyfriend..."

She laughed. "Cupcake and I aren't exclusive. I'm only casually seeing him to annoy your friend. You see..." She leaned forward like she didn't want someone to overhear our conversation. "I'm going to break you, Sissy. And I'm going to do it by breaking everyone around you. I'm going to make it so that I'm not the only one that wants you out of this city. Every. Single. Person that you call a friend? Or lover? They're going to hate you soon. I made sure of it. Starting with Matt." She looked down at the watch on her wrist. "Tick. Tick. Boom."

I laughed because I didn't know what else to do. Her words made my chest hurt. And my lungs feel tight.

"So is that all?" she asked. "Because I'm in the middle of lunch and you're making me lose my appetite."

"Isabella, I came over here to warn you that…"

She held up her hand to stop me. "Oh, darling. No. You came over here so I could warn you. And I just did. So leave, garbage person." She flicked her wrist to dismiss me.

I took a deep breath. It didn't matter that she was hateful. She was still a person. And technically she was my sister. "Isabella, I know for a fact that Cupcake uses drugs to take advantage of people."

She laughed. "I know. He was the one that gave me the idea to drug Kennedy at homecoming. He's such a catch. Actually, the more I think about it, the more I think we should go steady. Don't you think? Just for a while of course. Because I'll be dating Matt as soon as you get the hell out of my city."

I clenched my jaw so tightly that it hurt. "You're such a bitch." I'd texted Rob yesterday to let him know the prank was off. But this conversation really made me want to go back on that decision. How could she laugh about drugging Kennedy? What was wrong with her?

She laughed again. "Daddy doesn't like it when we curse. I'll be telling him about that offense."

Damn it. I was trying to warn her. And all I was accomplishing was getting myself upset. "Just be careful with Cupcake. I don't want you to get hurt."

"That's funny. Because I do want to hurt you. Which is exactly why I'm winning this game."

God, this conversation was pointless. I'd warned her. And I'd had enough. I stood up, but Isabella grabbed my arm with her freezing cold fingers.

"You should probably go out in the hall," she said. "You have about five minutes before the bell rings to announce the end of lunch. And based on how long my friends have been gone…you'll probably need more like twenty minutes to undo the damage. Oops."

"What damage?"

"You're wasting precious time. The longer you dilly dally, the easier you're making it on me." She looked down at her watch again. "I think Matt and you will be over by the end of the day at this rate."

Fuck. I practically ran out of the cafeteria. I didn't even look over at my lunch table to see if anyone had noticed me leaving. But as soon as I stepped out into the hall, I prayed that no one was following me.

Shit.

There were printouts of me covering every inch of the hall. Taped to lockers. Scattered all over the hallways of Empire High.

Shit!

They were everywhere, covering practically everything in sight. Even the water fountain had pictures. All the images were a little fuzzy, but they were all of me. In my underwear at the hotel. From the night Isabella had tried to kill me. She must have gotten them from the security cameras.

And there were hundreds. Thousands. *What the hell?* There were pictures of me running around the hotel with the makeshift map dress. And there were a lot of me holding James' hand in the hall as we both sprinted away from Donnelley. Actually, most of them were of me and James together. Half-naked. Holding hands. *God.*

But it wasn't just the nudity that was upsetting. It was the words written on every single one of them. They were advertisements for my prostitution services. My phone number was on each one. Some even had those little tear-able tabs at the bottom so you could easily take it and give me a call later.

I grabbed one of those and tore it from the wall. I grabbed another and another. I heard laughter and turned around.

Cupcake was standing there with a stack of more printouts in his hands.

Matt was going to freak out when he saw these. I could feel tears blinding my eyes as I tore down another picture. And another. I tried to grab some of the printouts off the floor but there were too many.

"Cupcake, what the hell?!" I yelled.

He laughed and threw his hands up into the air, sending hundreds more flyers fluttering down onto the ground. "What? I didn't do anything. You're selling *your* services, Brooklyn. Pretty sure you're the only one that looks guilty here."

I looked down at one of the printouts in my hand. *For a good night, contact Brooklyn Sanders. She's been entertaining all the boys of Empire High and comes highly recommended for a very affordable price.* I looked up and Cupcake was gone.

What the actual fuck?!

Oh God. I do look guilty. It didn't matter that the pictures were all of me in my underwear. Isabella had made it look like I was trying to sell my body. No one was going to believe me over her. I ripped off another picture from a locker as the tears burned my eyes. I tore down handfuls of them. But there were too many.

The bell rang, signaling the end of lunch.

Screw me.

CHAPTER 26

Monday

The first thing I heard was the laughter as I tried to pull more pictures off the lockers. I grabbed more printouts, but it was no use. There were too many of them.

"She's such a whore," Isabella said from somewhere behind me. "I can't believe she's sleeping with James *and* Matt. And now she wants to take on even more clients?" She laughed. "Oh my, it even says she's affordable. I bet her going rate is a dollar."

All her minions laughed.

I tried to ignore them as I got down on my hands and knees to pick up some of the printouts from the floor.

"Slut," someone said.

"I knew she was a prostitute."

"One of the cheap ones too." More laughter spread through the hall.

"She's even on her knees right now."

My tears burned my eyes as I crawled around on the Empire High floor.

"Baby?" Matt's voice in the hall made my tears run even faster down my cheeks.

I tried to pull more of the pictures into a pile on the floor. Not that it mattered. He'd seen them. He'd seen me in my underwear holding James' hand. And even though

I'd told him about what happened that night, seeing it was a million times worse. "I'm sorry," I choked.

"Come with me," Matt said. He grabbed my hand to pull me to my feet.

"I'm so sorry…"

He pulled me toward the closest bathroom. I tried to ignore the rude words being thrown our way. Matt seemed to be handling it better than I was. I thought he'd be pissed, but he was so calm.

"Look, she's holding someone else's hand now," some guy said.

Matt ignored him, sidestepping to pull us closer to the bathroom.

But then the guy added, "I wonder how much her escorting services go for?"

And it was like Matt snapped. He let go of my hand so fast that I didn't know how he had time to wrap it around the guy's neck. "Say another word about my girl and you won't be able to recognize yourself in the mirror." Matt shoved the guy backward, slamming him against a locker.

I swallowed hard. I guess he wasn't as calm as I thought.

"Show's over!" Mason said from somewhere behind us.

I turned to see him hit his fist against a locker a few times to get everyone's attention.

"I said show's over!" he yelled. "Everyone get to class."

Matt pulled me into the closest bathroom and locked the door behind us.

I could still hear the laughter in the hall. I thought Matt would be pissed. I thought he would have screamed at Isabella and started to pull the pictures down too. But he had been eerily composed until that guy had basically called me a prostitute. He seemed calm again now as he pulled me into his arms.

"Are you okay?" he asked. "Can you breathe?"

His words just made me cry harder. He was angry. But he was more concerned about whether or not I was having a panic attack.

"Baby, look at me." He grabbed both sides of my face. "Are you okay?"

"Of course I'm not okay. Isabella is trying to freaking ruin my life. She wants you to leave me. She said she was going to turn everyone against me. I can't handle being on edge all the time. I feel like I'm about to lose my mind."

"Isabella can do whatever the fuck she wants. But she'll never tear us apart. And she'll never break you down. Do you hear me?"

I nodded. I wanted to believe him. But Isabella was hellbent on ruining us. On ruining me. And it wasn't a fair game. Instead of fighting fire with fire, I'd stopped fighting altogether. I swallowed hard.

"Are you sure you can breathe alright?" he asked.

"I'm okay." I shook my head. I wasn't okay. Not really. "Isabella's framing me. But I didn't put those pictures up, Matt. I didn't..."

Matt winced. "I know you didn't. Come here." He pulled me back into his arms.

"She's never going to stop," I said.

He didn't respond. He just held me for a few minutes in silence. Until the laughter in the hallway died away.

"Give me your phone," he said. "Enough is enough. You're supposed to call your security detail if Isabella ever does something. You can't let this one slide."

I didn't want to stop Isabella with my dad's help. That always made everything worse. I wanted to freaking fight back myself. But Matt and I had already had this conversation. He'd said I was better than Isabella. And I wanted to show him that I was. I didn't want to stoop to her level. I didn't want to become her. So I pulled my cell phone out of my blazer pocket and handed it to him.

He lifted the phone to his ear. "Hey, it's Matt. There's been an incident with Isabella." He tried to give me a reassuring smile. "Some inappropriate pictures. She's upset, but no, I've got it covered." He looked over at me and pulled the phone away from his ear. "Do you want to go home for the day?"

I shook my head. I refused to let Isabella drive me away from school. Her games weren't going to make me leave.

"No, she's okay," Matt said.

I noticed that there was a hole in one of the knees of my tights. *Crap.* That didn't look good when there were jokes going around about me being on my knees.

"Thanks," Matt said and hung up the phone. "They said they'd pull her out of school for the rest of the day. Not sure what will happen after that."

"Okay."

I watched Matt loosen his tie. He pulled off his blazer and rolled up the sleeves of his uniform dress shirt.

"What are you doing?" I asked.

"I'm going to go get my varsity jacket for you to wear the rest of the day so people know that you're mine and only mine. Do you want me to grab anything else from your locker?"

That wasn't what he was about to do. Well, maybe it was. But it didn't look like the only thing he was planning. I grabbed his arm. "I don't want you to fight my battle for me."

He lowered his eyebrows. "It's our battle, Brooklyn. We're a team. And no one - *no one* - talks about my fiancé like that."

"If you want me to be the bigger person, you have to be too."

"The things they were saying..." his voice trailed off.

Yeah, I'd heard it too. I'd seen it written. And now literally everyone at Empire High had seen me in my underwear. Holding James' hand. Isabella was trying to make it seem like I was with James so that Matt would dump me. But Matt had said we were fine. So I should have been able to drop it and move on. Maybe it was the Pruitt blood in my veins. Or the fact that I had a mobster father. But all I wanted to do was make Isabella pay for this.

Hell, I wanted to roll up my sleeves and punch Isabella in her stupid face. But Matt said that wasn't me. And it wasn't the Matt I fell in love with either.

"I've been patient, Brooklyn. When you told me what happened between you and James. When you told me you were seeing someone else when we were fighting. I've been trying so hard to be understanding. But the things our classmates are saying about you? I've been patient with you, but I don't need to be patient with them. No one should ever talk to you like that. And what kind of person would I be if I didn't go out there and defend you? I can only take so much. I'm about to snap."

I could see that. I knew he had a temper. And I knew that my behavior had tested him. I didn't want him to lose control because of me. I took a deep breath. "Well, your fiancée doesn't want you to get kicked out of school." I put my hands on his chest. "You said it yourself. Isabella's not going to break us. And if you want me to be better than her, you have to be better than all of them too. Because I know you are."

He ran his hand down his face and sighed. "Fucking Isabella."

I laughed. "I think you meant…fuck Isabella."

He laughed too. "You are better." He ran his thumbs beneath my eyes to remove the rest of my tears. "And I'm trying to be better for you too."

"I'm really sorry about the pictures of me and James…"

"I don't care about some stupid pictures. I know you're not in love with James."

I smiled up at him. "No, because I'm very much in love with you."

The corner of his mouth ticked up.

"How long do you think it'll take for someone to remove all those pictures?" I asked. The thought made tears come to my eyes again. My uncle would have had to clean up that mess. He would have seen the pictures of me in my underwear and all those nasty words. The thought made me mad all over again.

"I'm going to go talk to the principal and make sure he knows what actually happened," Matt said. "And I actually am going to go get my jacket out of your locker for you to wear. Stay here, okay?"

I nodded.

He placed a kiss against my lips. "Us against the world, Brooklyn."

I watched him walk out of the bathroom and I leaned against one of the sinks. *Us against the world.*

My phone buzzed and I pulled it out. There was a text from Rob: "So what's the going rate, Sanders?"

I groaned and texted him back. "Bite me."

"Oh, I'm planning on it. And we both know I don't need to pay you for it."

I rolled my eyes and set my phone down. Rob was funny, but I wasn't ready to laugh about this yet. Not when there were literally thousands of pictures out in that hall advertising my prostitution services. I pulled my ruined tights off and threw them in the trash.

Another text came through: "Please tell me Operation Disappearing Troll is back on?"

I bit the inside of my lip. I was angry at Isabella. I was so freaking pissed. My phone buzzed again.

"And if so…I really need those blueprints to the Pruitts' apartment."

I actually laughed. I had no idea why our pudding prank needed blueprints, but Rob seemed to really think it did. He'd been bugging me to get them for weeks but would never say why he needed them. It was tempting to just tell him to do whatever the hell he had planned. But I wasn't going to stoop to Isabella's level. I wouldn't give her the satisfaction. And I wouldn't go against my promises to Matt.

"I haven't changed my mind," I texted back.

"Really? Wait, you are at school today, right? If not, my going rate joke probably landed a little flat."

I laughed. "I saw the pictures. But I'm not going to stoop to her level."

"Suit yourself, Sanders. It's just a prank, though. It's not like we're going to get her half naked in front of tons of people. That would just be pure evil." There was a winky face at the end of his text.

I shook my head. Yes, Isabella was evil. But she'd have to do something a lot worse than this to make me break.

CHAPTER 27

Saturday

Justin sprayed my hair with hairspray for what felt like the millionth time. I tried not to cough. Even though my hair was a little too long to pull off the perfect Sandy Halloween costume, I thought it looked pretty great. Justin walked off to pack the hairspray back into his bin.

"What do you think?" Kennedy asked as she lifted up her genie lamp. She rubbed the side of it seductively.

I laughed. "You seriously look just like Jasmine. Now we just need to get Rob to agree to be your Aladdin."

Her smile was so big. "Thank you for all this." She looked down at her outfit.

"I didn't do anything. It was all Mrs. Caldwell."

"Yeah. But you're her future daughter in law. It's all about connections in this town, haven't you heard?"

I laughed. "What do you think of my outfit?" I asked and spun in a circle. "Is it too much?"

"No, it's perfect."

I ran my hand down my skintight leather pants. Last weekend, these had seemed like a good idea. But now I kind of wished I'd picked one of Sandy's girl-next-door outfits instead of this one. "Are you sure it's not too…"

"Prostitutey? No. And screw all them anyway. Let them talk. Everyone's just jealous because as soon as Isabella graduates, you're going to be the new queen of Empire High. And then no one will ever be able to say a bad word about you again."

I didn't know about all that. But once Isabella, James, and Mason graduated...I couldn't think of who was more popular than Matt. And like Kennedy said, it was all about connections in this town. By association, Kennedy and I would be at the top of the totem pole. The rumors swirling around school about me being a prostitute hadn't completely stopped. But no one ever said anything when Matt was by my side. And he made sure to be glued to my side in the halls of Empire High. Isabella had even been surprisingly well behaved the rest of the week. I hadn't gotten a single evil note from her.

Besides, everyone was way more excited about the annual Caldwell Halloween party than stupid rumors. There was a buzz in the air all week long. Tonight was going to be so much fun. Decorators and caterers had been in and out of the house all morning, transforming the Caldwells' house into the haunted mansion it was meant to be. I was so excited to see how it had all come together. Two hours ago Justin had locked us in the guest bedroom I was supposed to be using, but it felt like we'd been waiting in here forever. I was dying to explore before the party began.

"And the last touch - the perfect heels," Justin said. "High enough to lift your ass, but low enough to dance the night away."

I laughed. "You get me."

"It's my job to get you."

"Speaking about your jobs." I leaned down to strap on my heels. "I talked to Matt. And it's going to be hard for us to plan a wedding for the fall because of school."

"Oh," Justin said. "Right, of course. I completely understand. It was silly for me to even mention it." He started putting all the makeup into his travel bin. I'd never seen him look so dejected before.

I tried to repress my smile. "Which is why we decided we should get married in the winter. This winter," I added.

His hand froze on a curling iron.

"Will you help us?" I asked. "I know it's last minute, but…"

He screamed. At the top of his lungs. And then he was lifting me up in the air and twirling me around.

His laughter was infectious.

"I don't know if you're joking," he said as he set me back down on my feet. "But you can't take it back now. My fragile heart would shatter into a million fabulous pieces."

"I'm serious. We want to do it on December 22nd. And I can't imagine planning it without you."

"December 22nd? Done. But we need to hurry." He grabbed both my hands. "I have so much to do. Wedding dress shopping this week, yes?"

"Okay."

"Do you have any idea what style dress…" his voice trailed off. "Never mind. We both know you need me for this."

I laughed. "I absolutely do."

"What about the location? Do you have a place in mind? I'll need to call them ASAP."

"There's this restaurant in Central Park that Matt used to go to with his family as a kid. Right by a pond. And there's these fairy lights that come on at night." I pictured Matt getting down on one knee and asking me to be his girlfriend right on the bridge by the restaurant. He'd pulled out a hot dog instead of a ring. I was smiling so much it hurt. "I don't know the name of the restaurant but Matt does..."

"It's done. Don't worry about it. I've got this. I promise. This is the big break I've been waiting for. And I'll make everything perfect, I swear to you. Every last detail. You can rely on me."

"I trust you."

He screamed again. "I need to go. I have a million things I need to do. December 22nd?" He pulled out his phone. "Oh thank goodness it's a Saturday. Saturday weddings are the best. Anything else you girls need for tonight?" He was already pulling his makeup cases into his arms.

"We're good," Kennedy said. "Go plan the wedding of my best friend's dreams."

Justin did a weird salute before practically skipping out of the room.

"I love him," Kennedy said.

"Me too. And if anyone can pull this off in less than two months, it's him."

"I can't believe you'll be hitched in less than two months! Shotgun wedding," Kennedy said with a laugh.

My face turned red. I hadn't told Kennedy that I'd slept with Matt. It felt...wrong to talk to her about it. Her first time had been stolen from her. And I didn't want to tell her about how perfect Matt had been.

"Your face is bright red. Oh my God, wait. You're not actually pregnant..."

"No!"

She laughed.

And now I had made it awkward. How was I supposed to tell her about my first time now? I'd kept it a secret for over a week.

"Your face is still red," she said. "Wait, have you two taken the next step?" She laughed. "I'm ridiculous. Of course you have. You're freaking getting married! Why didn't you tell me?"

I sat down on the edge of my bed. "I'm sorry. I didn't know how to tell you. I feel so guilty..."

"Guilty?" She sat down with me. "Why on earth would you feel guilty for being happy?"

God, it felt like I'd been carrying around this weight with me forever. "When I moved to New York it was like my life was over. I was so sad all the time. Like this part of me was missing. And now all I do all day is smile..."

"Brooklyn." Kennedy pulled me into her side. "Your mom would have wanted you to be happy."

"I know. I just..." my voice trailed off. "I miss her and Uncle Jim so much. I shouldn't be this happy without them. I still miss them so much. But Matt's love...I don't even know how to describe it. He just lifts me up."

Kennedy rested her head on my shoulder. "You've been through so much. There's nothing wrong with holding on to something that makes you smile."

I swallowed hard. I knew that. But it felt good to hear it out loud. "And I feel awful talking about our relationship in front of you because of what Cupcake did..."

"I'm okay," Kennedy said. "And I never want you to keep something from me because of what he did. That's just letting him take more away from me. I always want you to be able to tell me everything. So spill it. Tell me about your first time."

I filled her in on the details. And despite what she said about being okay, I saw the hurt in her eyes. I'd seen glimpses of it ever since she told me what had happened with Cupcake. Mostly she did seem okay. But I knew she was putting on a brave face.

I remembered that time that Miller asked if I wanted for him to "take care" of Cupcake for me. I pressed my lips together. I'd talked to my dad a few times on the phone, but I hadn't gotten the courage to flat out ask him if he was a mobster. Because honestly, I was pretty sure I already knew the truth. "You know...if you really want revenge. I can probably make something happen."

"What do you mean?"

"This is going to sound really strange. But I'm pretty sure my dad's a mobster. And if I told him that Cupcake messed with you...he'd...rough him up a little. Or something. Actually I don't even know if I need to tell my dad. I think I could just ask Miller or Donnelley to do it."

She opened her mouth and closed it again. "There's a lot to unpack there."

I laughed.

"Wow, it all makes sense now," she said.

"What does?"

"Why my mom couldn't get the judge to honor Uncle Jim's will. There was no logical reason why you shouldn't have been living with us. I mean, we thought something sketchy was going on. But your dad really must have everyone in his pocket. And the way he always gets everything he wants. Oh and all those security guards." She shook her head. "He's a freaking mobster!"

"Oh God. He really is, isn't he?"

"Is he coming tonight?" asked Kennedy. "I bet he's planning on dressing like himself and he's going to look just like Al Pacino from The Godfather."

Yeah. There really wasn't any denying it. "He's not coming. But you're right. I definitely see the similarities now."

"Your life is surreal. How does Matt feel about marrying a mobster's daughter?"

I shook my head. "I was a little worried at first. Matt's made it pretty clear since we've met that he thinks the Pruitts are toxic. And I know he's excited for me to not have the last name Pruitt anymore. But we fell for each other before I knew who my dad was. It doesn't really change anything. Matt and I have been through so much already…nothing is going to break us."

Kennedy smiled. "You two are perfect together. Meanwhile, I'm sitting here debating whether or not I should snap my fingers and off Cupcake."

I laughed.

"I'm just kidding. I'm not crazy. I don't want any mobsters attacking Cupcake. I don't need revenge. That's just not me." She laughed. "I can't even imagine doing something like that. I'm not Isabella."

For some reason, her words made my stomach churn. That's what Matt wanted. A girl who didn't need revenge. And I was trying to be that for him. But sometimes, all I wanted to do was text Rob and tell him that the prank was back on. Just thinking about when Isabella made fun of my uncle and me made my blood boil. And the pictures of me in my underwear all over school. Or when she poured milk down the front of me. There was also the time she literally put a gun to my head. Or...*God.* I took a deep breath. The list was endless. And I needed to let it go. *I'm not like Isabella. I'm a Sanders, not a Pruitt. I don't need revenge.*

"Speaking of the devil herself, is Isabella actually coming tonight?" asked Kennedy. "I can't imagine what on earth would possess Isabella to think that was a good idea."

"I have no idea. But knowing my luck...she'll be here. Trying to flirt with Matt. Or doing something else terrible."

"She can't do anything terrible to you here. You have the Pruitts' security *and* the Caldwells' security. If she makes one mean peep about you, they'll kick her out on her ass."

"I hope so."

"I know so." Kennedy stood up. "The party is going to start any minute. Come on, we need to go explore. I hope they have fire dancers this year!" She grabbed my hand and pulled me toward the door.

I was excited about the party. But the knots in my stomach didn't go away as we stepped out into the hall. I knew Kennedy was right. Isabella couldn't get away with doing anything to me here. But I had a really bad feeling about tonight. And the fake blood dripping from the bannisters didn't really help.

CHAPTER 28

Saturday

The decorations made me feel like I was at the Pruitts' apartment instead of at Matt's mansion. Or maybe it was just the haunting music and the creepy vibe in the air. I was used to the Caldwells' house feeling warm and safe, despite its décor. But there was a definite chill in the air tonight. And I had a feeling Isabella was already here.

I didn't know how the fake blood was constantly dripping from everywhere. It had to be water fountains with red dye, but it looked so real. I leaned forward to inspect some of the red water.

"You girls look stunning."

I jumped.

Kennedy screamed.

And Mrs. Caldwell laughed. "It's just me."

"You scared us half to death," Kennedy said. She was clutching her genie lamp to her chest like it could protect her from monsters. "But you look amazing, Mrs. Caldwell."

She smiled.

I was pretty sure Mrs. Caldwell was dressed like the woman from Psycho. *After* she'd been murdered in the shower. She'd somehow made her hair look wet, she had a bath towel wrapped around her, and fake blood was splattered on the side of her neck. Some of the blood was on the towel too. She really did look terrifying. I wondered if most people were going as horrifying things like her. If so, tonight was definitely going to be scary.

"Have you two seen all the decorations in the ballroom yet? I think we've topped last year for sure." She glanced at her watch. "I better go check in with the caterers though. I'll be back in a bit for our big plan regarding a certain someone's crush on Robert." She winked at us and hurried off.

"I'm seriously regretting telling her I liked Rob," Kennedy said as we ducked beneath a spider web. "What on earth do you think she has planned to push us together?"

I stepped around a pond in the foyer with red water in it. "A blood bath?"

Kennedy laughed and then screamed as a skeleton swung down from the ceiling on our way to the ballroom.

"God." I pushed the skeleton to the side. "I'm going to have a heart attack tonight." And then I screamed when a fog machine kicked on.

Kennedy grabbed my arm. "We should have had Matt walk with us."

"He told me to wait for him in the ballroom. Something about making an entrance."

"I thought he was joking about that. You really have no idea what he's dressing up as?"

I shook my head. "Are those eyes following us?" I pointed to a row of portraits that weren't normally in the hall.

"This is giving me the creeps." Kennedy stepped closer and then backed up, hitting me. "Yeah, there's definitely people behind those. Stop staring at us!"

One of the pictures blinked and we both screamed. Kennedy started running down the hall.

"Wait for me!" Something popped out of a coffin leaning against the wall. But I was running too fast to even see what it was.

Kennedy stopped and I almost ran into her.

"Oh wow," she said. "It's even more amazing than I'd heard."

The "Enter if You Dare" sign above our heads looked like it was written in blood. But beyond the double doors into the ballroom was a completely different vibe. The whole ballroom floor was covered in fog. There was a huge thing that looked like a witch's cauldron in the corner. But it was actually a stage for the DJ. The smoke was bubbling from the top of it, pouring out over the room, reaching towards every corner of the ballroom.

There were lights running up the sides of the walls that looked like floating ghosts. Every inch of the ceiling was covered in interwoven spider webs. And black crystal spiders hung down from them. The bar in the corner had rows and rows of goblets filled to the brim of some red signature drink. Gold candelabras held tall white candles that were dripping wax. And the bar itself was a nod to the old Hollywood theme. It was wrapped in what looked like huge video film, each piece of film splattered with red shiny fake blood. There was a pumpkin patch in the corner filled with white pumpkins with gold stems that looked like they doubled as seats for when people grew tired from dancing. All of it was hauntingly beautiful.

"Maybe I won't have a heart attack after all," I said with a laugh. "It's almost pretty."

"It really is. I bet this is how your wedding is going to be. Like so over the top amazing. I can't even wait!"

I hoped my wedding reception didn't look just like this. It was still a little scary. I didn't want the main theme of my wedding to be horror.

Guests started coming in through the doors behind us. There were gasps of appreciation. And the DJ started with some light music as waiters dressed as zombified old-fashioned movie attendants flooded the floor holding trays of hors d'oeuvres. I tried to avoid the zombie waiters because they looked like they really did just rise from the dead to come eat human flesh.

"Look, there's Felix!" Kennedy said and waved him over.

He was wearing the signature bandana of the boy from Karate Kid on his forehead. But otherwise he was just wearing a gray sweatshirt and a pair of worn jeans.

"You two went all out," he said and gave us each a hug. "You look great, newb. And Kennedy, you look amazing."

I looked back and forth between them. He'd said I looked great. But he said Kennedy looked amazing. *Amazing!* Had she caught that too? I knew that Kennedy *said* she liked Rob. But I was pretty sure she *loved* Felix.

Kennedy shrugged. "Thanks, weirdo. I'd tell you the same, but you barely even tried." She waved her hand in front of his sweatshirt.

"Hey, the karate kid wore a sweatshirt at some point in the movie," Felix said.

"Are you sure about that?" she asked.

He laughed. "No, I'm not positive. You got me." He looked up at the spider webbed ceiling. "This is insane." He let his gaze drop back down to me. "So this is your new home, huh?"

"At least until Isabella graduates. I don't really know what will happen after that." It was strange that Matt and I hadn't talked about it. We were going to be married. A fact that I was still getting used to hearing out loud. So then what? I thought about the apartment that my dad had saved for me. That seemed like a good place to go. Would Matt's parents let him move out? Would my dad allow it?

My dad. I bit the inside of my lip. I hadn't seen my dad all week. Just a few phone calls with him checking in. I figured dropping the news about my wedding date would be better done in person. So I hadn't gotten a chance to tell him yet. But I really needed to soon. Justin was probably already calling him for details. *Shit.* My dad approved of Matt as a second choice to Mason. I still got the feeling that he was hoping I'd change my mind though. And the whole mobster thing? I felt the distance between us. And not telling him that we'd picked a date wasn't helping anything. I wished he really would walk through the doors dressed like Al Pacino in The Godfather. At least then it would confirm my suspicions and I could actually talk to him.

"Earth to Brooklyn," Kennedy said and waved her hand in front of my face.

"What?"

Kennedy laughed. "Do you want a drink?"

"No, you two go ahead. I'm gonna wait for Matt."

I watched Kennedy and Felix walk over to the bar. I kept my eyes trained on the door. My thoughts were all colliding in my head. And I kept getting shivers down my spine. I turned around, but no one was even looking at me. When I turned back to the door, I watched Rob, James, and Rachel walk in.

Rob was dressed like Rocky. He even had a bruise around his eye and boxing gloves. James and Rachel were dressed up as…well, I wasn't really sure. James had on a tuxedo with a white jacket. And Rachel was in some ridiculously revealing bikini. My guess was they were going as…themselves? I really had no idea what movie their outfits could be from. I hoped I was disappearing in the fog. But Rob's smile and the fact that he was walking over to me said differently.

"Happy Halloween, Sanders. You make a damn fine Sandy. Leather should be your new go-to."

"Thanks. You don't look so bad yourself." My eyes wandered down to his exposed six pack. I'd officially seen all the Untouchables without their shirts now. It felt like I'd just accomplished some kind of weird Empire High scavenger hunt.

He smiled.

Fuck. Why was I staring at his abs? "How long did it take to put all that eye makeup on?" I tried to hide my smile.

He laughed. "You really know how to throw punches." He lifted up his hands that were covered with boxing gloves and then lightly tapped one beneath my chin. "One of the many reasons why I love you."

Stop it. I looked over his shoulder, but there was no sign of Matt. "I think you should focus on finding your Adrian."

"I'm not really looking for an Adrian right now. More like a one-night admission to my boxing ring, if you get my drift."

Well that wasn't good. Kennedy wanted Rocky and Adrian love. Not a gross one-night stand.

"How about it?" he asked. "Just one night of you and me before you marry my brother? It's better to get me out of your system now."

I laughed. "Doubly hilarious. You're not in my system. And I'm not marrying James."

"I don't know…Brooklyn Hunter has a better ring to it than Brooklyn *Caldwell.* Ugh." He shuddered.

"James is literally standing right over there with his girlfriend." I looked over at them. James already had a glass of something in his hand and I cringed.

"Yeah, but Rachel Hunter sounds terrible."

I shook my head.

"Speaking of terrible things. I need those blueprints to the Pruitts' apartment."

"I told you that the prank was off."

He sighed. "But it's going to be so fun. I mean… pudding. So much pudding."

I laughed because I couldn't help it. I wanted to pull the prank on Isabella. I really did. But I'd promised Matt I wouldn't be like Isabella. And that I wouldn't hang out with the Hunters. "I know. But I can't do it. I'm trying to be better than her."

"Anything you do is better than her. One because you're beautiful. Two because you think you're as funny as me. And three because I know I'll eventually corrupt you. Just text me when you change your mind. Make sure the blueprints are in the text." He leaned forward and whispered in my ear. "Your ass looks amazing by the way."

My face was bright red as he pulled away.

He groaned. "Oh and reason four. I want to rip your clothes off when you blush. Huh. I guess those were four reasons why I like you. Save me a dance?"

"You don't like me." God, he was just like his brother. "You're just trying to mess with Matt. And no, I'm not going to dance with you."

"You playing hard to get just makes me want you even more."

I folded my arms across my chest. "You're ridiculous."

"That makes your boobs look even better."

I looked down. I was basically pushing up my push up bra. *Damn it.* I dropped my arms.

Rob laughed. "Text me those blueprints. Later, Sanders."

I rolled my eyes as he walked away. Why was he so confident that I was going to turn to the dark side? *I'm not Isabella.* I bit the inside of my lip. But I kind of did understand why he thought I'd cave. Isabella kept doing terrible things to me. There were only so many times she could embarrass me before I snapped. My promise to Matt was the only reason I hadn't retaliated. Every bone in my body wanted to just freaking slap her.

Or maybe Rob just thought I could be swayed because I was literally wearing the Sandy costume from when she embraced her wild side. But I didn't want my wild side to be behaving like a mobster's daughter.

My thoughts came to a stop when the only other mobster's daughter I knew walked in through the doors. I was pretty sure my jaw dropped to the floor when I saw Isabella's costume. Yeah, there was only so much more I could take. I felt tears pool in the corners of my eyes. *Fuck my life.*

CHAPTER 29

Saturday

"Puta mierda," Kennedy said as she joined me by my side.

I'd only ever heard her say that once before. And she'd told me that the meaning was nothing worth repeating. *Puta mierda indeed.*

Isabella was dressed exactly like me. Or, Sandy, rather. And no, not exactly. Her costume was so much more…everything. Her high heels were taller. Her top was cut lower. More of her midriff was showing. Her hair even had more volume, which I shouldn't have been upset about, but I really freaking was. It was probably a wig. But it didn't matter how she'd done that with her hair. She was the perfect Sandy. I was pretty sure every guy's head had turned to look at her when she'd walked in.

I felt myself shrinking, trying to blend into the fog on the floor.

"Do you want me to spill my drink down the front of her?" Kennedy asked as she took a sip from her goblet.

"No." I turned away from the door. "God, how did she figure out that I was dressing up as Sandy?"

"I guess the odds of it being a coincidence are pretty slim."

"There's no coincidence when it comes to Isabella."

"I swear I didn't say anything," Kennedy said.

"I know. I wasn't implying that you did. I just..." I sighed. "This really sucks."

"At least you know what she had up her sleeve for tonight. Don't let her bother you. She's just trying to get under your skin."

Well, she'd succeeded.

"You need a distraction," said Kennedy. "And I have the perfect one. Guess what Felix just told me?"

"What?"

"That it's actually official. He's done with his drug business. He sold his list of clients to Danny Zuko."

I must have looked confused because she pointed to the door.

I turned to see Cupcake who was dressed up as Danny Zuko from Grease. He was wearing the classic white t-shirt and leather jacket. He even had an unlit cigarette dangling out of the corner of his mouth. *They did a couples costume? Why didn't I think of that?*

But it was better that Matt wasn't dressed like Danny Zuko. Because he'd be a hotter Danny Zuko than Cupcake. And it would be clear to everyone that the hotter Danny should be with the hotter Sandy. Was that Isabella's plan? To somehow woo him away with a couples costume square off? If so, she was going to be disappointed. Because I had no clue who Matt was dressing up as.

Crap. What if he was dressing up like Danny Zuko to surprise me?

"Oh no. She's coming this way. Come on," Kennedy said and pulled me toward the pumpkin patch.

But it was no use. Isabella's demon eyes had lasered in on me and there was no hiding. Even though we tried to hide behind the big pumpkins and the giant cauldron.

"Are you running from me, Sissy?" Isabella asked.

I tried not to groan as I turned around. "What? No." I stepped away from the fog tumbling down from the cauldron.

"Good evening, Kennedy," Isabella said. "You better watch your drink tonight. Who knows what someone might try to slip into it."

Kennedy laughed, even though it sounded forced. "Go to hell, Wizzy."

Isabella glowered at her. "You can call me Sandy for the night. What do you think of my outfit?" She did a stupid little twirl. "Oh no." She put her hand to her cheek in mock surprise. "Sissy, are you dressed up like Sandy too?" She leaned forward and squinted at me like it was hard to tell. "How utterly embarrassing for you. Don't tell me Matt's dressed like Danny? That would be...such a travesty for you. Especially if he and I win best costume together."

So that was her game? She wanted to win best costume with my fiancé? Kennedy was right. Isabella could go to hell.

"And if you think this is bad," Isabella said, "then just you wait. Because I will definitely be wearing white to your wedding. Not that you'll ever make it to the altar."

I swallowed hard. She didn't necessarily say that I'd be dead. But she was staring at me like I'd be dead. "Dad won't let you do anything to me. And he won't let you wear white at my wedding."

"You call him Dad now, huh? How quaint. I don't know, Sissy. I'm the one living at home. While you're out on the street."

I'd hardly call living with the Caldwells being out on the street. I jumped when I heard a little bark.

"Sir Wilfred, bad dog," Isabella hissed when her evil little dog pranced over to me.

Who brought a dog to a party? He was going to get trampled. I went to pick him up but Isabella beat me to it. She pulled Sir Wilfred to her chest.

"Bad dog," she said again. "How many times do I have to tell you to not mingle with trash? Stupid mutt."

Sir Wilfred whimpered in her arms.

I pressed my lips together. Sir Wilfred was growing on me. Every time Isabella was mean to him, I loved him a little more. And I hated that she treated him just like she treated me. It looked like he was shivering in her arms. Probably because her hands were so freaking cold. Or maybe he was just scared of her like I was.

"Isabella, there's a gate in the backyard. Why don't you let Sir Wilfred play out there during the party?" I would have offered to let him stay in my room. But then all my clothes would somehow get cut up. I reached out and petted his cute little furry head.

"Sir Wilfred is not a peasant," she snapped and pulled him away from me. "God, now he's dirty." She dropped Sir Wilfred back onto the ground like he was diseased from my touch.

This had to be animal cruelty. "Isabella, I don't think Dad would..."

"Let me just stop you right there. Daddy doesn't care what you think. At all. He loves me most. And he'll always believe me over you."

I couldn't pull a prank on her. But I could stand up to her. She may have been a better Sandy. But that didn't mean she was better than me. And it certainly didn't mean our dad loved her more. He couldn't possibly. And it was about time I pushed her off her high horse. But I didn't have time to think about what to say. Because suddenly Old Time Rock and Roll started blaring through the speakers right behind us.

And Matt literally slid into the ballroom in his socks. He was wearing a dress shirt without any pants.

He didn't dress up as Danny Zuko!

"Oh my God, he's doing the *Risky Business* dance!" Kennedy said.

Matt spun around and pretended to sing into a candlestick. Then he ran over to one of the huge fake pumpkins and jumped up on it.

Everyone was cheering and clapping. I saw a flash out of the corner of my eye. Kennedy was snapping pictures of the whole thing.

I stepped around Isabella to get a better view.

Matt jumped off the pumpkin, landing on his knees. The fog on the ground dispersed around him as he pretended to play an air guitar.

And when he got up, he locked eyes with me. He tossed the candlestick to the side of the room before sliding across the floor, grabbing me around the waist, and dipping me low.

Everyone was whistling and applauding like crazy.

And I was laughing so hard that it hurt. I kept laughing as he lifted me back up and pulled me into his chest.

"You look beautiful, baby," he whispered in my ear.

"You're not wearing any pants," I said through my laughter.

He stepped back, keeping our fingers intertwined. "Huh. How 'bout that?"

"You're amazing." I smiled up at him. Matt had all the confidence in the world. And I was pretty sure if anyone else had dressed up in the same outfit as him, he wouldn't have cared. "That was quite the entrance. I thought you were lying about needing one."

He laughed. "I know how much you like when I make a fool of myself."

"You never make a fool of yourself. Everyone in this room loves you. But I love you most."

He smiled down at me. "*I* love *you* most."

I stood on my tiptoes to kiss his cheek, but he turned his head and captured my lips with his. A few people whistled again. Matt was definitely winning best male costume. And I didn't care if I won too. I'd already won, because I had him.

"Come on," Matt said. "Let's dance." He grabbed my hand and Kennedy's hand and pulled us onto the dance floor.

He didn't acknowledge Isabella's Sandy costume. I wasn't sure if he just didn't notice because he was too busy dancing with me and Kennedy. Or because he really cared about Isabella so little. Either way, it was a win for me.

Matt broke out a weird robot dance move and then pointed to Kennedy. She moved her arms robotically too and then pointed at me. I took a few straight-legged steps and bent over, doing the best robot I could.

And the three of us couldn't stop laughing.

Matt was a great dancer. Me? Not so much. But I'd never had so much fun. Tonight couldn't be more different than homecoming. That disaster of a night, I'd been torn between Matt, Miller, Felix, and even James if I was being honest. But tonight? I only had eyes for Matt. I didn't just have a boyfriend now. I had a fiancé. I was going to marry the boy pretending to rain water on my head in the middle of the dance floor. And I'd never smiled so much in my life.

A slow song switched on and he pulled me in close.

"Brooklyn, you're the most beautiful girl in the room."

I was tempted to look to see where Isabella went.

It was as if he could tell because he put his hand on the side of my face. "Always."

I smiled up at him. And I realized I almost forgot to tell him the good news. "Justin agreed to help us with our wedding."

Matt smiled. "That's great. I know you really wanted his help."

I literally couldn't do this without Justin. I had no idea what needed to be done. And Justin knew everything. "I'm going dress shopping in a few days."

"Can I come?"

I laughed. "No you can't come dress shopping with me. It's bad luck."

"I think the two of us have had enough bad luck. Just smooth sailing from here."

"You think so?"

"I know so. Hey look." He nodded his head toward his left.

I followed his gaze. Kennedy and Felix were slow dancing together. *Finally!* "They'd make a cute couple, wouldn't they?" I asked.

"*And* it would mean Felix would stop flirting with you."

"He's already stopped. We're just friends. I only have eyes for a certain someone who isn't wearing any pants in public."

Matt laughed. "Speaking of pants…are you hungry? I'm starving."

What kind of segue was that? He'd had me laughing so much all night that my cheeks actually hurt. "I'm starving." I had completely forgotten about eating tonight. "Let's go track down a zombie." I grabbed his hand and pulled him over toward one of the waiters.

Matt had no sooner lifted up one of the hors d'oeuvres when Kennedy came over and grabbed it out of his hand.

"Thanks, I'm so hungry," she said and stuffed the whole thing in her face.

"What is it with you and always stealing my food?" Matt said. "There's trays of them going around everywhere. Get your own, woman."

"But it's so much easier to take yours," Kennedy said.

They both laughed.

I remembered when Kennedy had insisted that Felix, me, and her were the three amigas. That hadn't exactly worked out. But Matt, me, and her? Yeah, we kind of were. I was glad that they got along so well. Because I wasn't sure what I would do without either of them. Together they had somehow pieced my broken heart back together.

Someone tapped on the microphone and we looked up at the cauldron stage.

Mrs. Caldwell was standing up there in her towel with even more fake blood dripping down her shoulders than before. "We hope everyone's having a great night!"

Adults and kids alike cheered.

"The votes are in, and it's time to announce the winners of our costume contest!" She lifted up two gold envelopes.

I looked up at Matt. "I didn't see anywhere to vote."

"Because we were dancing. There was a voting box over by the pumpkins."

Shit. What if Isabella had won by just a few votes?

"And the first winner is..."

My heart felt like it was beating in my throat.

Mrs. Caldwell tore open the envelope. "...Robert Hunter as Rocky!"

I could hear Rob laughing from somewhere.

"Seriously?" Matt said. "He's just half naked."

I laughed as I looked at Matt's pants-less legs. "You're one to talk."

He smiled down at me.

"But seriously...you definitely should have won. You even put on a performance."

"Right?" Matt spun in a circle.

I shook my head at him. I did believe he should have won. But I was secretly glad he hadn't. Because the odds of Isabella winning over me were very high. And James had told me Isabella had rigged the homecoming voting. I wouldn't have put it past her to do again. But now if Wizzy won, she'd have to dance with Rob. Which would be hilarious because they hated each other.

I held my breath as Mrs. Caldwell opened the second envelope.

"And the second winner is Kennedy Alcaraz as Princess Jasmine!"

"Oh my God, really?" Kennedy said as she grabbed my arm.

I laughed. Kennedy looked amazing. And she deserved to win. But I kind of thought that maybe it was Mrs. Caldwell that had rigged the voting this time. To get Rob and Kennedy together. Mrs. Caldwell was diabolically wonderful. Or maybe Kennedy and Rob had actually won and it was fate.

I looked up at Matt. I was becoming quite the believer in fate.

"Let's get Kennedy and Robert up here for a dance!" Mrs. Caldwell said into the microphone.

"I can't believe this is happening!" Kennedy said. She released my arm from her grip and made a beeline to the stage.

I looked around, hoping to see Isabella's reaction to losing. But I didn't see her in the crowd. My Sandy lookalike was gone. I breathed a sigh of relief. Hopefully she'd left when she'd realized that no one wanted her here. And hopefully it would be the last event at the Caldwell mansion she was ever invited to.

"Do you want to get out of here?" Matt whispered in my ear as Kennedy and Rob started dancing.

I looked up at him. "We live here."

"I just want to steal you for a few minutes. Or maybe more like thirty minutes. We'll see what happens." He pulled me toward the ballroom doors before I even had a chance to respond. But I knew what was on his mind. I'd be lying if I said it wasn't on my mind too.

CHAPTER 30

Saturday

I was holding Matt's hand so tightly that I was sure I had to be hurting him. But he just laughed as we ducked under spider webs in the hallway.

I screamed as a vampire popped out of the coffin.

"It's all fake," Matt said as he tucked me into his side.

"Even the blood?"

He put his fingers through one of the fountains. "It's just red food dye."

I knew that. And yet…it was all still creepy. "Your house was pretty much made for Halloween parties. I'm surprised this isn't always the décor in here." I jumped when a spider fell from the ceiling.

"Are you really scared?" Matt asked.

"I'm terrified." I held his hand even tighter.

He stopped in the middle of the hall and pulled me to his chest. "You have nothing to be afraid of. Not when you're with me, Brooklyn."

A fake scream echoed from somewhere down the hallway and I flinched.

Matt walked me backward until my butt collided with the side of a smoke machine. "I've got you," he said as his lips brushed against mine. "And I'll never let anything bad happen to you."

It didn't seem nearly as scary in this hallway when I focused on him. Tonight had been perfect. *He* was perfect. Halloween was quickly becoming one of my favorite days of the year. "So this is what you wanted to steal me away from the party for?" I asked. "To make out behind some spider webs?"

He laughed. "No, not exactly. I was hoping I could get you pants-less like me."

"Very smooth."

He winked at me and then pulled me away from the fog machine. We started running down the hall. I only flinched one more time, which I considered a win.

"I can't run in these shoes!" I yelled to him.

We were both laughing as he picked me up and ran out into the foyer. He didn't waste any time as he carried me up the stairs to his bedroom. He somehow managed to open the door while holding me. And he kicked it closed. He skipped the lights, carried me right to the bed, and threw me down into the middle of it.

And my excitement quickly turned to disgust. "Matt, why is your bed so wet?" I blinked, trying to make my eyes adjust to the dark room. Oh God, it smelled gross too. What was that?

"Huh?" He leaned over me. "What the fuck?"

My hands were definitely wet. But I couldn't see a thing. *Ew.* My back was wet too. *Oh crap, all the curls in my hair!* I reached up to touch the back of my head and realized my mistake. Whatever was on my hands got even more into my hair. *Gross.*

"Let me go get the lights." Matt crawled off of me. He flicked the lights.

The first thing I noticed was that his hands and forearms were covered in...blood? "Matt!" I screamed. There was even some blood splattered on his shirt. I looked down at myself and screamed even louder. I was covered in it too. I wanted to laugh it off. The house was oozing with fake blood. But this wasn't water with red food dye. It was thick and sticking to my hands. The whole bed was soaked in it. It was everywhere.

"What the fuck?" Matt said.

I crawled backward on the bed and my hand touched something soft. I looked down and screamed again. There was a dead dog in Matt's bed. No, not any dog. A sob escaped my throat. It was Isabella's dog, Sir Wilfred. Her adorable little puppy had his stomach sliced open. *Oh God.* His guts were pouring onto the bed and his white fur was matted with blood. I covered my mouth with my hand so I wouldn't puke. But the blood smeared across my face, spreading the horrid smell of blood right under my nose. I was going to be sick. I started gagging, but nothing came out.

Matt ran over to the bed and pulled me off, holding me tight. "Don't turn around," he said as he led me away from the bed and toward his bedroom door.

It was a little too late to protect me from seeing Sir Wilfred dead on his bed. I hadn't just looked at the poor dog, I'd practically bathed in Sir Wilfred's blood. How could someone do this to a sweet little animal? My stomach rolled. I looked up at Matt as he opened the door. And I realized he wasn't staring at the bed. He was staring at the opposite wall. I turned to see what he was looking at.

On the wall above his dresser were the words, "You're next," written in Sir Wilfred's blood.

You're next.

The words rolled around in my head.

Isabella's going to kill me.

My heart started racing. *You're next.* As much as Matt's arms comforted me, I didn't need Matt right now. I needed my dad. He was the only one that knew what to do with Isabella. I needed to get to Miller or Donnelley so they could call my dad. I pushed myself away from Matt and ran out the door.

"Where are you going?" Matt yelled as he ran after me.

I barely stepped out of his room when I ran straight into Freddy Krueger. I screamed so loud that I was pretty sure they could hear me in the ballroom downstairs. Freddy Krueger grabbed me. "What the hell is going on?" he yelled down at me. His scarred face looked even more grotesque in real life.

"Get off me!" I screamed and tried to shove him off.

He just gripped my arms harder.

"Miller!" I yelled at the top of my lungs. "Donnelley! Help me!"

"Jesus, Brooklyn, it's me," Mason said and pulled his mask off. "What's going on?"

I breathed a sigh of relief, which only made the blood fill my nose. I pointed behind me and then made the mistake of covering my mouth again, smearing more blood on my face.

Mason stared into the room. "What the fuck is that?"

"How long have you been up here?" Matt asked. "Have you seen anyone go into my room?"

"The only person I saw go in was Brooklyn like twenty minutes ago."

"I was downstairs twenty minutes ago," I said.

Mason shook his head. "But I saw you..."

"Isabella's dressed like me. I mean, she's dressed like Sandy." God, she hadn't just dressed like me to annoy me. Well, I was sure that was a fun bonus. But she'd done it so she could sneak into Matt's room and murder her poor dog on his bed. Isabella had done a lot of terrible things to me. But this was fucking insane. And I didn't need the evidence that a person dressed like Sandy had gone into Matt's room twenty minutes ago. I knew it was her. "It's Isabella's dog," I said. "It was Isabella. She wants to kill me." Saying the words out loud made it even harder to breathe. This wasn't a game. I'd tried to ignore Isabella ever since homecoming. But it wasn't working. Not fighting back was going to get me killed.

"Shit," Mason said.

Matt clenched his hands into fists. "I'm going to fucking kill Wizzy. Stay with Brooklyn." He turned to go find her.

I wanted to call after Matt, but he was already running down the stairs.

"Shit," Mason said again, his eyes still trained on the words on the wall.

I felt a little safer with Mason standing here with me. But I didn't need a babysitter. I wanted to find Isabella too. I was going to fucking kill her first. I ran after Matt.

"Wait!" Mason called.

I reached the bottom of the stairs before I realized there was no air in my lungs. I pressed my hand against the wall.

"Are you okay?" Mason asked as he lightly touched my back.

"No." Tears started to stream down my face.

"Here, sit down," Mason said as he pulled me down to sit on the step.

I leaned forward. I wasn't sure if I was going to throw up or faint.

Mason abruptly stood up. "Isabella!" he yelled.

I looked up to see Isabella standing in the foyer. She smiled at me and then disappeared back into the spooky hallway. Mason took a few steps toward her and then stopped and looked back at me. I knew why he wasn't running after her. Matt had asked him to stay with me.

"Go," I said. "I'm fine."

He cursed for the millionth time tonight and then took off running.

Matt and Mason could take care of finding Isabella. I needed to find Miller. I needed my dad. He was the only one who would know what to do with her once the Caldwells found her. I pushed myself up. My legs were shaky as I made my way toward the front door. My security was still forced to stay outside. And they'd be out there somewhere. I opened up the door.

James was standing on the front step. He immediately pulled something out of his mouth and threw it onto the ground, grinding it into the gray stone with the heel of his dress shoe. Smoke swirled around his face and he coughed. He waved his hand through the air, trying to disperse it.

"Oh. It's just you," he said with a laugh. But then he lowered his eyebrows as he took in my appearance. "What the hell happened to you?"

"Isa…" I gasped for air. "Isabella."

He grabbed my hand without waiting for a response, pulling me into his chest. "Just breathe," he whispered into my ear.

My tears felt hot on my cheeks as the cool autumn air blew around us. For just a few minutes, James held me. Until I was able to catch my breath.

"Oh God, I'm getting blood all over your tux."

James laughed. "I don't care about my tux. But why exactly are you covered in blood?"

I made sure not to wipe my face as I pulled away from him. "We went upstairs and found Isabella's dog dead on our bed with the words, 'You're next,' written in blood on the wall."

"We?" James asked. "You mean you and Matt?"

I wasn't sure why that was the part that he was questioning. I nodded.

"And he left you?"

"He left me with Mason. But then Mason saw Isabella and I told him to go after her."

James ran his fingers through his hair. "Are you okay?" He shook his head. "Sorry, that was a stupid question."

I tried to blink away my tears.

"We should probably take a shower real quick to get you cleaned up," he said.

I laughed, which made him laugh too. "What are you dressed as?" I asked.

He looked down at his ruined white tux jacket. "James Bond. From *The Man With the Golden Gun* specifically."

Oh. That made sense. And Rachel was one of his Bond girls. "Where's Rachel?"

"Dancing. I just stepped out for a second. I needed some air."

Air? I wasn't blind. I'd seen all the smoke in the air out here. "What were you smoking?"

He shoved his hands into his pockets. "What does it matter?"

"It matters to me."

He smiled. "Because I matter to you? Last time I checked, you turned down my proposal."

"That doesn't mean I don't care about you."

"I'm Rachel's problem. Not yours." He sat down on the step.

I didn't really know how to respond to that. "So are you two good?"

He exhaled slowly. "You mean do I think she actually likes me instead of just wanting my money?" He shrugged. "I don't know. But it doesn't make me like her any less. I don't know how to quit her. She's like a freaking drug."

I nodded. I didn't really understand, because I never did drugs except that one time I accidentally had pot cupcakes. But I was more addicted to Matt than I think I even knew.

We both sat in silence.

I was glad James was staying with Rachel, even though his words were slightly disturbing. I wanted him to be happy. But as I thought about happiness, I realized that there was one thing holding me back from it. Isabella.

She'd always be standing in my way. And I needed to make a stand. Enough was enough. I wasn't going to suffer the same fate as poor Sir Wilfred. I was not going to be *next*.

"I want to do the prank," I said into the cool autumn night.

James smiled. "Yeah?"

I nodded. I didn't tell him that I wished that Isabella was just dead. Hopefully an innocent prank would get this feeling out of my stomach. I just needed Isabella to know I wasn't rolling over. I wasn't going anywhere.

"You sure? I thought you didn't want to stoop to her level."

"I'm not threatening to murder her. Although I don't know why Rob keeps asking me for blueprints to my dad's apartment."

"Who knows."

"But it's still just the pudding thing, right?"

James nodded.

I took a deep breath. Pudding. It was just a silly prank. But it meant I was fighting back. "And the deal is still on? About trying to make up with Matt?"

"A deal's a deal, Brooklyn."

I put my hand out for him to shake.

He looked down at my bloody hand, shrugged, and shook it.

CHAPTER 31

Saturday

The front door opened and Matt was standing there looking…super pissed.

Crap. I stood up and stepped away from James. "Did you find Isabella?" I asked.

"Yeah, we found her. The cops are on their way. I was looking all over for you."

I knew he was talking to me, but he was staring daggers at James. And James was wearing a cocky smile. Apparently he had no intention of helping me out and telling Matt that we were just talking.

"I'm sorry," I said. "I came out to find Miller and I ran into James."

Matt lowered his eyebrows slightly. And I wasn't sure if it was because of the mention of Miller or James. But he didn't know that I'd been with Miller. *Right?*

I felt like I needed to give him a better explanation. "I was having another panic attack."

Matt's eyes softened. "I'm sorry I ran off." He pulled me into his arms. "I wanted to make sure we caught Isabella."

I nodded against his chest. I knew he was trying to remain calm. Because I could hear how fast his heart was racing.

People started coming out the front door.

"The party's over," Matt said to James.

That was a "get lost" if I ever heard one.

James laughed.

God, the last thing I needed was for them to fight again.

"Cool," James said. "Later, Brooklyn." He started to walk down the steps.

I held Matt tighter and hoped he wouldn't read into James' words. I needed the calm, supportive Matt right now. Not the angry one that got into fist fights. Matt's heart was still stammering in his chest, but he just held me.

"I'm sorry," I said again. "James was out here and I was having trouble catching my breath."

"It's okay." Matt rested his chin on top of my head.

Red and blue lights lit up the sky as more people rushed out the front door. Yeah, the party was definitely over early.

"Come on, let's get inside. It's freezing out here." Matt grabbed my hand and pulled me back into his house. I nestled myself into his chest. He held me tightly as he ran his hand up and down my back. We stood like that in the middle of the foyer until the final guests were gone. The red and blue lights flashed through the open door of the Caldwell mansion. Someone turned on the lights in the foyer, making everything a lot less spooky. Although the red and blue flashes didn't feel reassuring.

"There you guys are," Kennedy said and wiggled her way underneath one of Matt's arms too. "We were looking all over for you, Brooklyn."

"I know, I'm sorry," I said.

"Where were you?"

"Outside. I needed some air." I didn't bother to mention that I'd been looking for Miller or the fact that I ran into James. None of that mattered now. All that mattered was that we had eyes on Isabella. She was pretending to sob in the corner. At least, it seemed fake to me. She had nothing to cry over except for the fact that she'd been caught.

I watched a cop walk into the house and start talking to Mr. and Mrs. Caldwell. Mason walked over and let them know that he saw Isabella go into Matt's room. Isabella's dramatic sobs grew louder and I tried not to roll my eyes.

The police officer approached Isabella and she started screaming at him.

"I'm not the one that you should be questioning," Isabella said. "That little family-stealing psycho murdered my dog!" Isabella yelled, pointing at me. "She's been out to get me ever since she found out we were related. She's completely lost it." Isabella pretended to sob again.

The police officer sighed. It seemed like he knew it was fake too. "Ma'am, if you could please calm down..."

"Calm down?" cried Isabella. "She's the one with blood literally on her hands."

I winced. *Damn it.* She was right. Even though Matt and Mason had caught Isabella before she snuck out of the house, they hadn't exactly caught her red handed. I was the one with blood on my hands. And Mason had seen what he thought was *me* going into Matt's room. There wasn't any evidence against Isabella. There never was. Honestly, Isabella was right. I looked guilty. Not her.

"This is ridiculous," Matt said. "I'll be right back." He walked over to the police officer.

Kennedy hugged me harder. "Are you okay?"

"No, not really."

"Matt told me what happened. Did she really kill her own dog?"

I nodded. I didn't want to talk about this. Just thinking about Sir Wilfred made me want to throw up. "Distract me. How was your dance with Rob?"

"Great. But if I'm being honest?" She looked over her shoulder to make sure no one was listening to us. "Well, how big of a distraction do you want?"

"A huge one."

Kennedy took a deep breath. "You were right. I've had the biggest crush on Felix since freshman year and he's finally being nice to me. I know I should have told you, but..."

I squeezed her so hard that she actually yelped. "I knew it."

She laughed. "You're getting blood all over me."

"Oh my God, I'm so sorry." I took a step back but she just pulled me back into another hug.

"It's okay," she said. "I guess it's what I deserve after not being honest with you."

"I think he likes you too," I said. "He said you looked amazing tonight."

She laughed. "He did, didn't he?"

"Sweetheart," Mrs. Caldwell said as she walked over to me. "Here, you should take my towel." She started to undress.

What is she doing? I tried to protest, but I was relieved to see that Mrs. Caldwell was wearing a very chic strapless dress underneath her bath towel. Because of course she was. Mrs. Caldwell was always prepared for everything. Meanwhile, I had rolled around in dog blood. I swallowed hard. I wrapped the towel around myself and tried not to think about the fact that I now looked a hell of a lot like the woman that got knifed to death in the shower in Psycho. Definitely more than Mrs. Caldwell had earlier.

The police officer walked over to us. "Miss Pruitt is sticking to her story that you were the one that killed the dog, Miss Pruitt." He scratched the side of his head as he stared down at his notes. "I hate Halloween."

"So you think I murdered my half-sister's adorable puppy and then rolled around in his blood for fun? And then wrote, 'You're next,' on the wall in his blood? Why would I do that?"

He looked down at his notepad. "According to her...because you hate her."

Yeah, I freaking do hate her. But I'm not a dog killer! "She's been out to get me ever since she found out we were related."

The officer just stared at me. "That's exactly what she said about you."

"This is ridiculous," Matt said. "My brother saw Isabella go into my room..."

"No, he saw someone dressed as Sandy go into your room," the officer said. "And no one else saw a thing. And we don't have enough evidence to make an arrest."

It looked like Matt was about to punch him in the face. And the last thing I needed right now was for Matt to wind up in prison. I grabbed his hand. He slowly unclenched his fist.

"Princess!" my dad said as he came rushing into the foyer.

"Dad!" I said.

And at the exact same time, Isabella called, "Daddy!" But she could choke on her words, because my dad came rushing over to me.

"Are you alright?" He grabbed both sides of my face.

I nodded. But just him being here and taking care of me made tears come to my eyes all over again. I glanced at Isabella out of the corner of my eye. The expression on her face was priceless. It looked like her head was about to explode. But I wasn't having a competition with her over who our dad loved most. I was trying to get her freaking locked up before she killed me.

"What happened?" my dad asked, his hands settling on my shoulders.

I hadn't realized how my story might sound to my dad. Me going into Matt's room? Lying on his bed? But I didn't care what he thought right now. I just needed him to know what Isabella had done. "Isabella murdered Sir Wilfred on Matt's bed. She dressed like me so she could get away with sneaking into his room. There was blood everywhere. And she wrote, 'You're next,' on the wall in Sir Wilfred's blood. She's telling the cops that I did it. But I swear I didn't. I would never hurt an animal. I would never do something like that."

My dad looked shocked. And hopefully it was about the Sir Wilfred thing and not the fact that it was pretty clear I was sleeping in Matt's bed.

He turned to the closest cop. "I can handle this from here," he said.

"But, sir…"

"I said I'll take care of it." My dad snapped his fingers and then pointed to the front door.

And the cops…left. They just turned around and walked out of the house. *Oh God.* It was true. He was a mobster. And he had the police in the palm of his hand. For just a second I was scared of him too. But then he grabbed Isabella by her bicep and pulled her over to me.

"Apologize to your sister. Now," he added.

"But, Daddy, I didn't…"

"We both know that you did. Now if the next words out of your mouth aren't, 'I'm sorry, dear sister,' you'll be spending the rest of your senior year abroad."

"But, Daddy!"

"Do it. Or else."

Isabella locked eyes with me. "I'm sorry, dear sissy." She said it with so much venom, she might as well have said, "You're next, fuck face."

My dad snapped his fingers again. Donnelley grabbed Isabella and pulled her toward the front door.

"Daddy!" she screamed.

My dad cringed and then straightened his tie as he walked over to Mr. and Mrs. Caldwell. "I'm so sorry about your party, Max," he said, extending his hand to Mr. Caldwell.

I looked over at Matt's father. He'd abandoned his fake knife that was pretty much the only way anyone would know he was the crazy guy from Psycho. His arms were folded across his chest. And he did not look pleased.

He looked like he had the first night he met me. Like he couldn't believe a Pruitt was standing in his house.

"You're sorry?" Mr. Caldwell said, not shaking my dad's outstretched hand. "Isabella killed a dog on my son's bed and then wrote..."

Mrs. Caldwell grabbed his arm and cleared her throat.

Mr. Caldwell took a deep breath. "What I meant to say is, perhaps Isabella should no longer be allowed on our property."

"I couldn't agree more," my dad said. "It won't happen again. But in regards to what she wrote on the wall...I'm almost certain that she was talking about Brooklyn and not your son, so you don't need to be so alarmed."

"So alarmed? If that's true, Isabella threatened your other daughter. And that in no way comforts me when we've extended the invitation for Brooklyn to stay at our house."

"I can guarantee that Isabella will stay off your property."

"Not just our property," Mr. Caldwell said. "She'll no longer be invited to any events hosted by our family either, no matter the location. Or the circumstances. Including the wedding this December."

Oh fuck.

CHAPTER 32

Saturday

"What wedding?" my dad asked.

"Matthew and Brooklyn's of course," Mr. Caldwell said.

"This December?" My dad shook his head and then looked over at me. "You'll have to cancel the plans, Max. There's no way my daughter is marrying your son this winter. They're sixteen years old. And I won't let you push your agenda on my kid. Have you lost your damned mind?"

"Do not insult me in my own home, Richard."

"Dad, can I talk to you for a minute?" I asked.

My dad cleared his throat and walked away from the Caldwells without another word. "Not a chance in hell, Brooklyn," he said as he made his way to the front door.

I grabbed his arm. "It's what I want."

"You can't be serious. They're clearly pushing the wedding date up so that they're not housing someone with my last name."

Honestly, I'd thought the same thing. But it made no difference what Matt's parents' motivations were. I knew Matt didn't care about any of that. I'd asked him flat out. "It's what I want," I said again.

"You're not old enough to know what you want. An engagement? Fine. I humored it. But you can't marry that boy."

That boy? The way he said it made me want to slap him. Matt wasn't just some boy. He meant everything to me. "Why?"

"Because I said so."

That wasn't a good enough reason. "Do you have any idea how scared I was tonight? Matt's the only one that makes me feel safe. I need him. He helps me breathe through my panic attacks. Which I'm still getting because I'm terrified all the time. And that's not going to change. Isabella's never going to stop. And if his parents want us to get married so they feel better about my staying here, who cares? I don't see what's so terrible about me having a last name that's not associated with a mobster."

For just a second my dad looked angry. The way he looked when Isabella and his wife upset him at our first family dinner. If there was a glass of wine nearby, it 100 percent would have been thrown against a wall. But the anger was gone in a flash. He just looked...defeated.

"Is that what the Caldwells have been telling you while you're living here?" he asked.

"No." *It was Miller.* "I just put two and two together."

He took a step closer to me and lowered his voice. "Don't throw that term around lightly, Brooklyn. And a new last name isn't going to make you safer. Or change what you are. As soon as everyone found out I had another daughter, you were put in harm's way."

"Who do you mean by everyone?"

"There's been unrest amongst the families these past few months." He looked over at the Caldwells. "Rumors have been swirling."

"What rumors?" I asked.

"It doesn't matter."

Actually, it kind of did. But I was more focused on what it seemed like he was confessing to me. "So it is true? You are a mobster?"

He sighed. "I married into it. And I don't fault you for trying to marry out."

Wait, Isabella's mother was the real mobster? Suddenly it made sense why my dad had needed my mom to leave the city. If Mrs. Pruitt was anything like her daughter, she probably would have had my mom killed.

"But make no mistake, Brooklyn," my dad said. "You're part of my family no matter what your last name is. There's no way out. And it's not Matthew keeping you safe. It's me."

There's no out. I swallowed hard. It's exactly what Miller had said.

"But if you feel safer marrying Matthew so that he'll be by your side at all times..." he raised his eyebrow at me. "It didn't elude me that you were in his bed this evening."

I could feel my face turning red.

"But given the circumstance, I'll let it pass. This time."

I felt like I was sinking under his harsh gaze.

"I assumed you'd want to get married after college." He shook his head. "This seems all a bit fast. Is this really what you want, princess?"

"Yes."

"Then I'll allow you to marry him. Or Mason. Are you sure you wouldn't rather tie the knot with him?"

God, when would he let this go? *Probably when I walk down the aisle.* "I love Matt." And only Matt. I'd dated enough men in the past two months to know who my heart was with.

"Very well. I have two contingencies though."

I nodded and looked up at him.

"First, you and Matt will be moving into your mom's old apartment as soon as you're married. I won't have you staying here any longer than necessary. Clearly it's unsafe."

Because of Isabella. But I didn't think my dad wanted to argue anymore tonight. "Okay, I'll talk to Matt about it."

"And second, you will let me pay for the whole thing, yes?" A smile spread over his face. The father I was growing to love was the one talking to me now. Not the scary mobster one.

"Really?" I couldn't help but smile back.

"Of course, princess." He kissed my forehead. "Anything for you, you know that." He looked over at the Caldwells and sighed. "Not my choice of in-laws, but I'll make it work. I'll go have another word with them to help smooth this over." He walked over to the Caldwells and started having a much more civil conversation with them.

"Sorry about that," Matt said as he pulled me back in his arms. "I know you hadn't had a chance to talk to your dad about the wedding yet. Were you able to change his mind?"

"Mhm." I pressed the side of my face against his chest and I actually saw Mr. Caldwell laugh at something my dad said. "But he did have one contingency. He wants us to move into my mom's old apartment after we get married." I pulled back so I could look up at him. "I know we haven't talked about what we were going to do after…"

"Are you kidding?" Matt dropped his forehead against mine. "I'd love to live with just you. A little more privacy sounds pretty great to me."

And a state-of-the-art security system to keep my evil half-sister and the apparently discontent *families* out. Whatever that even meant. It didn't matter. None of it did. As long as I had Matt by my side everything would be fine.

But there was one thing about my conversation with my father that weighed on me. And it wasn't fair to marry Matt without being honest with him.

"I was right," I said. "He is a mobster."

Matt sighed. "Yeah, we kind of figured, didn't we?"

That wasn't really the reaction I'd expected. "So if we get married…that kind of drags you into this mess."

"If we get married? There's no *if*, baby. Nothing would make me not marry you."

I breathed in his exhales. "But he told me it's dangerous. I don't want to put you in danger."

"Hey." Matt cradled my face in his hands. "This isn't about our families. It's about us. I want to marry you. And that's all that matters."

"It kind of matters." *There's no out.* "It's a family business. I'm a Pruitt."

"Yeah, and I'm a Caldwell, but I'm not the future CEO of MAC International. Let our older siblings take care of the family businesses. We can go wherever we want. Do whatever we want. Be whoever we want to be." He pushed a loose strand of hair behind my ear.

"As long as I can be Brooklyn Caldwell I'll be happy."

Matt smiled. "And as long as I can call you my wife, I'll be happy."

He was freaking perfect. "Can we please get out of these clothes now?" I asked.

Matt laughed. "And into the guest bed."

Oh my God. I didn't bother telling him that my dad disapproved of our sleeping arrangements. I couldn't not sleep beside Matt. The sound of his heart beating while I was snuggled up to his chest was the only way I was able to fall asleep. He'd held me close every night after my uncle passed away. He held me tight every night since I moved in. When I was in his arms, I felt whole. And no one, not even Isabella, was going to break me again.

CHAPTER 33

Wednesday

I ran my fingers along the velvety couch and looked up at the chandelier above my head. There was only one way to describe the wedding dress boutique – pure elegance. It was like Odegaard, only the wedding equivalent. And I was already feeling uncomfortable knowing that these dresses probably cost more than the down payment of my mom's house back in Delaware.

A super stylish woman in a black dress walked over to us. "Hi, I'm Sarah, and I'll be your bridal consultant today. Which one of you is the bride?"

I stood up to shake her hand. "That would be me. I'm Brooklyn."

"It's so nice to meet you. And who is with you today?"

"This is my maid of honor, Kennedy. My future mother-in-law." I gestured to Mrs. Caldwell. "And my Justin." I laughed. "He's my wedding planner."

"Nice to meet all of you," Sarah said. "Are you ready to get started?"

She didn't say it, but it seemed like she was thinking we must be waiting for someone else. Like my mom. I found myself blinking away tears. "Yes, let's do this."

Sarah smiled. "What silhouette are you leaning towards?"

"Oh, um." I looked over at Justin.

He laughed. "We need the full treatment, Sarah. We're going to try one of every style to see what she's most comfortable in. And then we can narrow it down from there. Sound good, Brooklyn?"

I nodded. I was so glad he was here.

"Great," Sarah said. "And when is your wedding?"

"It's December 22nd," Justin said. "So we need to make a decision today."

Sarah stared at him for a second. "Wait, you mean *this* December 22nd? That's less than two months away. I don't know if we're going to be able to turn something around that quickly."

"Sarah." Justin said her name with the most serious expression on his face. "We both know that your designers always make exceptions under certain circumstances."

Sarah looked over at me and then back at Justin. "Yes, under very limited circumstances. But rush orders start at..."

"Her father let me know that her budget is $15,000," Justin said.

My budget is what?

Kennedy's jaw dropped.

I was pretty sure I looked as shocked as Kennedy. And Sarah. Sarah was probably thinking there was no way I could afford that. I was wearing a pair of jeans and Matt's varsity jacket. She probably thought I couldn't even afford to be in the store.

"And when I say $15,000 is the budget, I mean it's the minimum," Justin added and smiled over at me. "Your dad wanted to make sure you knew you could get anything you wanted," he said and winked at me. "I'm loving him more and more every day. He's making this wedding very easy on me."

At least $15,000? That was too much. I wanted to run out of the store and go over to Goodwill to find something second hand. I wasn't a designer dress kind of girl.

Sarah cleared her throat. "Well, the rush won't be a problem at all then." She looked embarrassed. "Do you want to head back with me, Brooklyn, and we can get started?"

I nodded.

"And if you all would like to look around for dresses you think Brooklyn would look good in, please feel free."

Justin squealed with excitement and got up right away and started looking through the dresses. Mrs. Caldwell and Kennedy laughed and joined him as I followed Sarah.

***

There didn't seem to be a style that I liked yet. The problem was that I loved dancing with Matt and all the dresses felt…too heavy. Or too big. They were all just too much everything. It seemed like the more expensive the dress, the more it weighed.

Sarah was just unzipping me from a poofy dress when there was a knock on the dressing room door.

"It's just me," Justin said from the other side. "And I have the perfect dress for our beautiful bride."

I held the current one against my chest as Sarah opened the door.

Justin was smiling and holding up a dress. "This is the one," he said. "I can feel it." He shoved it into Sarah's hands and walked away with a sassy strut.

It was hard to tell how it would look on. But as soon as Sarah zipped up the back and put the clips on for it to fit my frame better, I was…speechless. It was long-sleeved with sheer and lace embellishments down the arms. The bottom was loose and flowy. And the best part? Even though it was tight enough to accentuate my waist, it was comfortable.

"What do you think of this one?" Sarah said.

There was a lump in my throat and I wasn't sure why. I think a part of me was still worried I didn't really belong in Matt's world. But in this dress, I looked like I belonged beside him. "He's going to love it," I said with a laugh as I brushed away my tears.

"Let's go show everyone." Sarah opened the door and I slowly followed her out, holding up the soft, flowy material so I wouldn't step on it.

I walked up onto the platform and dropped the fabric so that it pooled perfectly around my legs. Everyone stopped talking.

"Brooklyn," Kennedy said. "You look so amazing."

"A ten out of ten from me," Justin said. "You're simply glowing in that dress."

I smiled and turned to look in the mirror. I really was glowing. It was like this dress was made for my body.

"That's definitely the one," Kennedy added.

"Here," Sarah said as she clipped a veil into my hair. She spread the sheer fabric across my shoulders. The lace accents matched the dress perfectly. I felt like a princess.

And I could picture my wedding day better than I ever could before. Walking down the aisle towards Matt's smiling face. Saying "I do" and promising him forever. I could see it all so clearly.

The only person who hadn't said a word was Mrs. Caldwell. I glanced at her in the mirror to see her reaction. She'd grabbed a tissue and was blotting her eyes. I turned around to face her. "Mrs. Caldwell?"

She laughed and continued to blot her eyes. "Oh, I'm sorry, I'm a mess." She tried to wipe away the rest of her tears.

I would never describe Mrs. Caldwell as a mess. But the fact that she was crying had me worried. "Do you not like it?"

She laughed and stood up. "Brooklyn, you look stunning."

"Really?"

She nodded. "Matthew's going to love it."

"Then why are you crying?" I said and tried to laugh through my own tears welling in the corners of my eyes. But it was no use. The tears started falling down my cheeks.

"Because I was just thinking about how much I've always wanted a daughter. And I know that the circumstances that led you to New York were awful. But I'm so grateful that you met my son." She stepped up onto the platform with me and squeezed my hands. "I know your mom and uncle can't be with us on your wedding day. And I wasn't lucky enough to meet either of them. But I have a feeling they would have said you looked beautiful in this dress too."

I nodded through my tears. It was exactly what I'd needed to hear. I looked back in the mirror, ignoring my tear-stained face. My mom really would have loved this dress. If she'd ever gotten married, I could picture her wearing something just like this. Something light and flowy that she could dance the night away in. I smiled, remembering the way that we used to dance around the kitchen. It was like a little piece of her was in this dress. And I think it's why I loved it so much.

I'd wondered what my mom would have thought about me getting married so young. But she'd fallen in love with my dad when she was a teenager. And she'd fallen in love with me too. She was brave and strong and knew exactly what she wanted. I wasn't sure I was nearly as brave or strong as her. But I was trying to be. And I did know exactly what I wanted. Matt.

CHAPTER 34

Wednesday

I wasn't sure how Matt and I could get any closer. But as the days turned to weeks, and the weeks to months…we were completely inseparable. I didn't even feel like myself unless we were touching. Which was why I always practically ran to lunch.

I spotted Matt laughing with Mason at our usual table. It still felt surreal to me that I was dating Matthew Caldwell. I wasn't sure when that feeling would disappear. *Hopefully never.*

"Hey," I said when I reached the table. I leaned down to kiss Matt on the cheek. But he grabbed me around the waist and pulled me onto his lap. Yeah. It was so much easier to breathe when we were close.

Kennedy snapped a picture of us. "I'm going to make you the most amazing pre-wedding album," she said.

"Pre-wedding album?" Matt asked. "Is that even a thing?"

"It is when I have thousands of pictures of the two of you being ridiculously adorable." She stole one of the fries off his tray and he didn't even complain. "I can't wait for Friday's Thanksgiving. Are you sure you don't need us to bring anything?"

"Nah, my mom said to just come hungry," Matt said.

Kennedy and her mom were both coming to our second Thanksgiving on Friday and I was so excited. I'd already agreed to go to my dad's tomorrow to celebrate with his family, so the Caldwells had been so sweet to change their celebration to Friday so that Matt and I could attend both. And I was thrilled when Mrs. Caldwell had extended the invitation to Kennedy and her mom too. She'd dubbed it "Friendsgiving," and she was going all out as usual.

It was going to be a perfect, relaxing long weekend. Just as soon as real Thanksgiving was over. I was excited to spend time with my dad. But I hadn't stepped foot in his apartment since homecoming. I'd be entering Isabella's turf, and both she and I knew it.

"Are you nervous about tomorrow?" Kennedy asked. "Entering Wizzy's lair once again?"

I looked over at Isabella. She'd calmed down over the past month. She'd only left me one threatening note in my locker a day now. Sometimes two. But at least there weren't any dead animals. I'd never be able to forgive her for that. Matt and I had buried Sir Wilfred in the Caldwells' backyard. And I felt guilty the whole time since I'd originally hated the little guy. God, just thinking about his body on Matt's bed made me feel sick to my stomach.

"No, I'll be fine," I said. "I'll have Matt there with me." I smiled up at him. "Honestly, I'm mostly nervous about meeting my new extended family." And I was a little nervous about the prank James, Rob, and I were planning on pulling on Isabella. But they promised they had everything covered. I just had to sit back and laugh. And hopefully get the Caldwells and Hunters to finally make up.

"What if all your new relatives are as terrible as Isabella?" Kennedy asked. "Yikes."

"What'd I miss?" Felix said and sat down next to Kennedy.

The two of them weren't dating. *Yet.* But Kennedy was finally civil with him. And I'd give it another few weeks before one of them caved and confessed they were madly in love with the other. Because now that I knew for a fact that Kennedy liked Felix? It was obvious. I hoped it was obvious to Felix too. Because I wasn't going to meddle anymore.

"We were just talking about Thanksgiving," Kennedy said.

"Oh, I can't wait till Friday," Felix said. "Thanksgiving always sucks with my parents out of town. But this year I'm going to eat so much turkey."

Kennedy laughed.

I was so excited that Matt had calmed down about my friendship with Felix. It was even Matt's idea to invite him over on Friday. I almost felt confident saying that Felix and Matt were friends now. Maybe they'd make it official soon too...with a handshake or something. Not the way Felix and Kennedy were going to make it official.

"What time did you say I should come over?" Felix asked.

"You can come over whenever, really," Matt said. "Brooklyn has an appointment in the morning, but she'll be back before noon, right?" He looked over at me.

My dad had finally made me that appointment to get birth control. I was surprised it took him as long as it had. Especially since he'd basically found out I was sleeping with Matt on Halloween. "Mhm," I said, hoping no one would ask me any questions about it. A gynecological exam hardly seemed as fun to talk about as Thanksgiving.

"And we can always just play video games before dinner's ready," Matt added.

"Awesome," Felix said. "Are we talking Xbox or..."

Mason leaned over. "Of course we're talking Xbox. And we're going to kick your ass."

"Oh, game on," Felix said.

They all laughed as the bell rang, signaling the end of lunch.

Matt's fingers intertwined with mine as we all walked out into the hall. But all of us stopped when we saw two cops standing outside the cafeteria.

One of them stepped forward. "Felix Green, you're under arrest for the possession of drugs on school property."

Felix laughed. "What?"

"We found drugs in your locker," the cop said.

"That's not possible."

"Mr. Green, you need to leave the school grounds immediately," the principal said. "You're hereby expelled. An investigation..."

"An investigation? But I don't have any drugs in my locker..." Felix's voice trailed off as the cop held up a bag of white powder.

"You need to come with us right now," he said.

The sound of laughter made me look behind me. Freaking Cupcake. With his arm around Isabella and a huge grin on his face. I knew without a doubt that he was behind this. They both were. Isabella winked at me and my heart sank.

Her words from several weeks ago came back to me. "*I'm going to break you, Sissy. And I'm going to do it by breaking everyone around you.*"

Felix seemed to have come to the same conclusion on who had set him up, because he yelled, "What the hell, Cupcake?"

Cupcake shrugged his shoulders. "I didn't do anything. You can thank Brooklyn for this. I saw her on the phone earlier. She probably turned you in."

What? I took a step forward, but Matt grabbed my arm to hold me back.

Felix didn't even look over at me. "Fuck you, Cupcake. Brooklyn had nothing to do with this and you know it."

"I'm not so sure about that," Isabella said. "This is all definitely happening because of her. Nothing like this ever happened before she moved to the city. It's a shame she doesn't just leave."

They were doing this because of me. *God.* She was trying to destroy everyone around me.

"He must have put the drugs in my locker," Felix said and pointed to Cupcake. "He set me up."

"Mr. Green, I'm not going to ask you again, you need to leave the school grounds immediately," the principal said.

"But I didn't do anything."

The cop grabbed his arm.

"It was Cupcake!" Felix yelled. "He's selling drugs on school property. He's putting them in his gross sugar cakes. He had to be the one that planted drugs in my locker. You should be arresting him."

Cupcake just laughed. "I haven't done anything wrong."

"You haven't done anything wrong? You fucking raped Kennedy, you disgusting piece of shit." Felix lunged at him, but the cop caught his arm.

No. No, no, no. Oh, shit!

There was an audible gasp from the students around us. But Kennedy's gasp was the only one I was focused on. Tears pooled in the corners of her eyes as the cop handcuffed Felix and dragged him away from Cupcake.

"Everyone get to class!" The principal yelled. "Now!"

"How could you?" Kennedy said as students rushed past us. "You promised you wouldn't tell anyone. I told you I liked Felix. How could you do this to me?"

"Kennedy, I'm so..."

"Sorry? I don't care if you're sorry. You promised."

"I know, it just kind of came out at homecoming..."

"He's known since homecoming?! Are you freaking kidding me?"

"I was just trying to help. I was so worried about you."

"Save it, Brooklyn. I always have your back. Always. And the one time I ask you to have mine, you don't."

"Kennedy..."

"I was barely holding on as it was. You know that. And I was finally excited about something. But this whole time Felix was just being nice to me because he felt bad for me?"

No. "Of course not."

"You think he'd actually like the poor girl from the wrong side of the tracks?" She tried to wipe away the tears that were pouring down her cheeks. "My life isn't a fucking fairytale like yours, Brooklyn. God, Felix probably still likes you. Because everyone always just likes you. No one will ever want me."

"Kennedy, that's not true. Someone will want you."

"Someone? Just not Felix? You sabotaged me. You knew I liked him and you ruined everything. He'll never look at me the same. And God, I really can't freaking look at you right now." She ran off toward the bathroom.

I went to follow her, but Matt grabbed my hand. "I think you should give her a second to cool off."

Isabella laughed as she walked past us. "Two down," she said. "That was easier than I thought. Only one to go." She placed her index finger in the center of Matt's chest.

Matt grabbed her hand to push it away.

"Funny," said Isabella. "We're already holding hands."

Matt dropped her hand like it had burned him.

"No matter. I still have a month to ruin this relationship. See you on Thanksgiving, Sissy." She blew me a kiss and walked away, her high heels clicking loudly on the floor.

"I didn't mean to," I said through my tears. "I thought Felix would talk to Cupcake and fix it. I thought…"

"Why'd you tell Felix and not me?" Matt asked.

"I didn't mean to tell anyone. It just kind of slipped out at homecoming…"

"At homecoming, yeah I heard you. Which means you kept it from me for weeks, Brooklyn."

"I wasn't keeping it from you. Kennedy asked me not to tell anyone."

"But you told *him*."

God, he sounded so pissed. "I'm sorry."

Matt took a deep breath. "Maybe next time you need help with something you should ask your fiancé instead. Then maybe none of this would have happened."

"You weren't my fiancé then. We weren't even together. Matt..."

"Because you wouldn't come talk to me. You just broke up with me without even letting me explain my side. We only ever fight when you don't talk to me. And when we got back together you looked me in the eye and promised me no more secrets. So what the hell is this?"

"It wasn't my secret to share."

"Well apparently it was, because you shared it with Felix." He shook his head. "I'm not having this argument with you in the middle of school. We can talk about it later. Or not, since you don't like letting me in." He left me standing in the middle of the hall as he walked away.

"Matt!" I yelled after him. But he was already pushing out the front doors of Empire High. *God, what the hell had I done?* I ran after him and down the front steps. "We also said we wouldn't run away!" I called after him.

He froze at the bottom of the steps and turned around. He looked so sad, and I hated that I'd done that to him.

I ran down the rest of the stairs. "Please, I don't want to fight with you," I said.

He didn't say a word.

"When Kennedy told me what Cupcake did to her…I didn't know what to do. It felt like I had this secret that I couldn't keep in. And I would have told you, but I already felt so guilty about letting it slip to Felix. Please, I can't handle you hating me too."

Matt reached out and ran his thumbs beneath my eyes, wiping away my tears. "Kennedy doesn't hate you."

"It sure seems like she does."

"She doesn't. And I could never hate you either."

"It sure seems like you do."

He dropped his forehead against mine. "You drive me fucking crazy. But that's because I love you. Not because I hate you. I could never hate you, baby."

I breathed in his cinnamon exhales. "I really am sorry." I wrapped my hands around his torso. Now the prank tomorrow was looming over my head. I should have told Matt about it weeks ago. I shouldn't have kept it a secret. Hell, he may have even helped me plan it. I had no idea. But I couldn't tell him right now when he was already upset with me. It felt like he was slipping away from me, so I just held on to him tighter. Tomorrow everything would be better. Isabella would be put in her place. And hopefully the Hunters would make up with the Caldwells. Matt would understand. He had to.

"Me too."

"Why are you sorry?" I asked.

"For snapping. With all the wedding planning and playoffs coming up… I'm trying so freaking hard to stay calm for you. I don't want to stress you out, but it's just so hard sometimes."

I knew he was doing that. He was worried about my panic attacks. He'd been so understanding and patient with me ever since we got back together. But I didn't want him to put that weight on his shoulders. I wanted him to feel free to react however he needed to. The last thing I wanted was for him to be stressed out instead of me.

"Take a deep breath," I said and rubbed his back.

He laughed. "I'm not having a panic attack, baby."

"I know." I looked up at him. "But it helps with stress too."

"There's other things that are better for stress."

I laughed as his hands slid to my ass. Yeah, I guess that would work too. But a better idea had just crept into my head. I knew exactly what to do to make sure Matt wasn't stressed out.

CHAPTER 35

Thursday

"It's a Thanksgiving present," I said and pushed the wrapped package toward Matt.

He smiled at me. "There's no such thing as a Thanksgiving present, baby."

"Open it." I tapped my hands on the top of the big box. I was so excited to see his reaction.

"You're so beautiful," he said, his eyes transfixed on my face instead of the huge wrapped gift in front of him.

"I swear, if you don't open it, I will," I said.

He laughed and looked back down at the box. "How did you even get this huge box up here?"

"Oh my God, Matt just open it!"

He smiled and tore the wrapping paper on the side. He pushed back the rest of the paper.

It was just a generic box. And when he went to lift the flap I held my breath. *Please like it. Please don't be upset.* This could go one of two ways, and I just really hoped he loved it.

He didn't say anything as he stared down at the contents of the box.

Oh no. He hates it.

He reached down and lifted up a paintbrush. "You got me painting supplies?" His eyes locked with mine.

"You said you used to love to paint with your aunt. And that you didn't have as much time recently. But now that you don't have to chase me around anymore, you have a little more free time." *He really does hate it.* Maybe it was too soon. When he'd told me about his aunt's death, the story of them painting together had stuck with me. I liked things that reminded me of my mom. But that didn't mean Matt wanted to be constantly reminded of his aunt.

God, what had I done? "I'm sorry." I grabbed the brush out of his hand and tossed it back into the box with the canvases and paints. "I thought it might help with your stress, but it was stupid. I'm just making it worse." I closed the lid.

"What? No, baby, I love it." He opened the top of the box back up and pulled out the unassembled easel.

"You do?"

He started putting the easel together. "I have a much better idea than going to Thanksgiving at your dad's house," he said.

I just stared at him. I thought he was upset. But now he just looked super excited. "And what's your idea?"

"I'm going to finish putting this together. And you're going to get naked and lie on the bed so I can paint you."

I laughed. "As wonderful as that sounds…we have to get going. I promised my dad we'd be there and I'm already nervous enough without being late. But maybe we can do that tonight? You really like it?"

He put the easel down on the ground. "I love it." He pulled me into his arms. "I love you." He placed a gentle kiss against my lips. "You're going to be my muse."

I laughed. "So just tons of nude portraits of me, huh?"

"You can wear clothes in some of them if you want. Definitely not necessary though."

"You're ridiculous." I placed my head against his chest. "And I love you so much it hurts." Truly. It felt like everything hurt today. My heart most of all. I was sure that Kennedy was never going to speak to me again.

"She'll call you back, baby."

I didn't even know how he knew I was thinking about Kennedy. It was like he could read my mind. "What if she doesn't?"

"She will."

Kennedy hadn't answered my dozens of texts and calls. I hated that it was a holiday and Kennedy and I weren't speaking. I was so sorry. I never should have told anyone her secret. Especially when she'd specifically asked me not to. And now the whole freaking school knew. But I knew she was most upset about Felix knowing. God, Felix. I didn't know if Felix was sitting in a jail cell. But he hadn't answered my calls or texts either, and I was assuming the worst. Matt's lawyers were supposed to help, but it was a holiday. It didn't seem like they'd have any news until at least tomorrow.

"Do you think I should tell my dad about Felix?" I asked. "It kind of seems like he has the cops in his pocket. He might be able to help."

"That's not a bad idea. But I'm sure my parents' lawyers will update us soon."

"Yeah. I hope so."

"Come on, the sooner we get Thanksgiving number one over with the sooner you can be naked."

Even though Matt seemed eager to get back, it took me forever to drag him out the door. And my stomach was twisted in knots.

"I still don't understand why I was invited," Mason said as we stood in the hall outside the Pruitts' front door.

I wanted to tell him that I had no idea why either. But apparently my dad was rather persistent when it came to the fact that he thought Mason was a better suitor. I actually hadn't known Mason had been invited until this morning.

"Mom and Dad were invited too," Matt said. "But they're busy getting ready for tomorrow."

Mason laughed. "That's a great excuse. I should have just told Mr. Pruitt I was washing my hair."

That was a weird joke, but it made me laugh regardless. "It's not going to be that bad," I said and knocked on the door. *I hope.*

"But we're missing the game," Mason said.

"The Giants aren't even playing, Mason." It hadn't taken me long to figure out that the Caldwells were huge Giants fans. They watched the games together as a family every Sunday.

"Yeah, but the Cowboys are playing. And we need to make fun of them."

"Cowgirls," Matt coughed into his hand.

I laughed. "I'm sure they'll have the game on somewhere," I said. But I wasn't really sure. I'd never seen a TV in the Pruitts' place. I assumed no television was one of the many rules I still hadn't read.

"Princess," my dad said as he opened the door. He pulled me into a hug. "Welcome home." He kept his arm around my shoulders as he shook Matt's hand. "And Mason, I'm so glad you could join us today." He shook his hand too.

"Mhm," Mason said. "Do you have the game on?"

My dad laughed. "Of course. I need to introduce Brooklyn to a few people. But Isabella can show you to the living room."

I honestly couldn't even remember where the living room was. But the last thing I wanted was for Isabella to show them anything. "I can show them real quick," I said.

Isabella appeared from somewhere at the sound of her name. Like a witch. "Not necessary, Sissy. I'm more than happy to show them."

I'm sure you are.

"Happy Thanksgiving," she said as she slipped her arm through Matt's and practically dragged him away from me.

"Come with me, princess," my dad said. "I want you to meet the family."

I looked over my shoulder to see Matt pushing Isabel la's hand off his arm.

Not today, Wizzy.

***

I couldn't remember anyone's names. I thought this was supposed to be an intimate family dinner. But there had to be at least 40 people here. And I was beginning to wonder if every uncle I met was actually a relative or not.

"Dad," I said as he pulled me away from a girl that I knew for a fact was related to Isabella. Because they looked almost the same and she was rude to me. "Remember my friend Felix Green?" I asked. "Who lives in this building?"

"Of course."

"Someone planted drugs in his locker at school. He got arrested and the principal is threatening expulsion. Could you maybe…help him get off?"

He smiled down at me. "You want me to take care of it?"

"Yes." I knew it came out as more of a question than a direct answer. But the way he'd said *take care of it* gave me pause.

"It's not so bad to have connections," my dad said.

That was true. I just wasn't sure his connections were on the up and up.

"Anything else I need to know about what happened with Felix before I make a call?"

"No, he's innocent." Several weeks ago, he wouldn't have been. But Felix was trying to be better. His past mistakes shouldn't ruin his future. There was one piece of information that my dad needed to know though. "I guess you should probably know that Cupcake and Isabella framed him."

My dad looked down at me. "Cupcake?"

"Joe Dickson. He's a kid from school. I think Isabella is sort of dating him. I'm almost positive that they put the drugs in Felix's locker. Isabella said something to me a little while ago about breaking everyone around me. I think she's trying to make everyone hate me so that I leave town."

"When were you planning on telling me this?"

"Today?"

My dad sighed. "Princess, it's of vital importance that you tell me everything Isabella says to you. Do you understand?"

I nodded.

"I mean it. Every single thing."

"I will." I honestly wasn't worried about Isabella right now. Well, minus the fact that she'd probably been hitting on Matt for the past 30 minutes. "So you'll help Felix?"

He smiled. "I'll take care of it."

"Thanks, Dad."

"If you'll excuse me for a moment. I need to have a conversation with Isabella about this…Cupcake. It's the first I've ever heard of him."

Crap. I wasn't trying to get Isabella in trouble today. I knew my dad required weird relationship contracts and stuff. Isabella was going to be furious with me. But would it really make anything worse? The psycho already wanted me dead.

CHAPTER 36

Thursday

I turned down a hall that I thought lead to the living room. But it was the one that went to the library. How did I not know where the freaking living room was? I turned around and ran straight into James.

"Hey," he said with a smile.

"Hi." God, I couldn't be alone with him in a random hallway. If Matt saw us together he'd be so beyond pissed.

"Sorry, I didn't mean to startle you," James said. "I just saw you going to the library and figured it would be a good place to talk."

He clearly knew this apartment better than I did. "I don't really have time to chat right now. I left Matt with Isabella. Do you have any idea where the living room is?"

He laughed. "Back that way to the left." He pointed over his shoulder.

"Great." I tried to step around him, but he stepped the same way, trying to let me pass, and we both laughed.

"Actually, while I have you, I did want to give you something." He pulled out something from his pocket.

And for just a second I had a terrible feeling that he was about to propose again.

"What's with the face?" He held up a thumb drive. "It looked like you were worried I was about to pull a prank on you instead of Isabella."

Yeah, something like that. "Sorry. What is that?"

He handed the thumb drive to me. "Your completed project for your entrepreneurial studies class."

"Wait, *completed* project? You were only supposed to do the coding."

He shrugged. "I figured with Matt and Rob fighting it would be hard for you to finish. Now you don't have to worry about it."

Wow, that was really nice. "Thanks, James. But that wasn't necessary."

"It was no problem." He gave me one of his real smiles. The ones it seemed like he reserved just for me.

"But it wasn't necessary. You and Matt are about to be friends again," I said. "Because the deal was…"

"That we'd talk to him." James shrugged. "Doesn't mean we'll magically be friends again. He kissed my girlfriend."

"And you kissed me."

"True. And I don't feel an ounce of remorse. It was a great kiss."

I could feel my cheeks getting red. "Well, don't say that when you talk to Matt. How about you try apologizing instead?"

"That wasn't part of the deal, Brooklyn. You just said we had to talk."

"You know what I meant."

"Did I?"

"James!"

He laughed. "I'm just messing with you. I'll talk to him. I'll be nice and everything. I promise."

"There you guys are," Rob said and ran over to us. He seemed out of breath, which was weird because I knew he was in great shape. Soccer players had to be.

What had he been doing?

"Everything's all set for the prank," Rob said. "Last chance to back out, Sanders."

I took a deep breath. Isabella was never going to stop messing with me unless I stood up to her. And it was a hell of a lot easier having James and Rob's help to do it. This was my one shot to put her in her place. In front of her whole family. And it seemed like my only chance of fixing the Untouchables too. "No. I want to go through with it."

"Good," said Rob. "Because I had to work my ass off to get everything ready. You two were no help. Especially you, Sanders. You never gave me the blueprints, so I had to go on a crazy hunt to find the person that renovated this place several years ago. And then I had to bribe them to get the layout." He shook his head. "It took hours. You're welcome."

"What?" Our prank was simple. And it all happened in the dining room. He knew exactly where that was. "Rob…you didn't need blueprints." I felt like we'd had this conversation a hundred times over text already.

"Yeah I did." He winked at me.

"No, you didn't."

Rob laughed. "So much pudding."

I shook my head. "I thought we agreed on just a little bit of pudding."

"Right. That's what I meant. Pudding ratios are all about perspective."

Okay. At least I knew what the prank involved, or else I'd be worried that he had something else up his sleeve. But I knew for a fact there was no pudding up his sleeves. He was wearing a white dress shirt. That would have been a disaster.

"So you've got everything covered?" I asked.

"Mhm," Rob said. "I even moved around a few place cards so that I could sit right next to the troll."

James laughed.

"Great." I took another deep breath, forcing myself not to back down from this. "Let's do this."

Rob put his hand out. James put his hand on top of his brother's.

"Do the thing," Rob said and nodded toward their hands.

I laughed and put my hand on top of theirs.

"Operation Disappearing Troll on three," Rob said.

All three of us yelled it and laughed.

I couldn't wait to see Isabella's face.

***

I was pretty sure Rob had moved around more than a few place cards. Because he also had me sitting between him and James. And Matt was sitting across from us. Like some kind of weird spectator of the awkwardness. *What the hell?*

Rob tapped the seat beside his. "Sanders sandwich."

Not happening.

"Ignore him," Matt said. He grabbed my place card and switched it with Isabella's evil cousin, Poppy, so that I'd be sitting next to him and that the Hunters would be forming a very snooty sandwich instead.

"No, not Poppy," James said. "She's the worst." He tried to switch her place card with someone else's just as Poppy walked into the room. James quickly switched it with his own and slid into the seat next to his brother.

Poppy seemed happy about her spot. But Isabella didn't look nearly as pleased when she walked into the room and saw the seating arrangement. Apparently she wasn't excited to sit next to Rob.

"No way is this right. James, switch with Rob," Isabella said.

"Nah," James said. "I'm good."

Isabella huffed.

And Matt actually laughed. Almost like he would have when all the Untouchables were still friends. It was the first time I'd seen him not hostile with them in ages.

Mason sat down next to me and laughed too. I was very much aware of the fact that I was still a Sanders sandwich…just between the Caldwells instead of the Hunters. I was exactly where I was supposed to be. I would have been perfectly comfortable if Rob hadn't kept winking at me.

"Is something wrong with your eye?" I asked Rob.

"Nope." Rob lifted up the bowl of chocolate pudding in front of him. "Pudding, Wizzy?"

"Bite me."

"But it's a Hunter family tradition. The Thanksgiving pudding of...prosperity and health. If you don't eat any, you'll have a year of bad luck."

"Stop talking to me or you'll have a year of bad luck," she said.

Rob winked at me again.

Stop it.

"What's going on?" Matt asked as he looked back and forth between me and Rob.

"Nothing," Rob and I both said at the same time.

Great, now it didn't sound like nothing. I looked down the long dining room table, searching for a good distraction. There were dozens of people here. Surely someone could say something to shift the focus off me and Rob. I sighed with relief as my dad stood up at the head of the table. He lightly tapped his knife against his glass, easily silencing the room.

"Thank you all for coming tonight," he said. "Once a year we all get together to celebrate our family. And tonight we have a new addition. Princess, I am so lucky that you've found your way back into my life."

Everyone turned to stare at me. And despite what my dad said, I didn't feel like part of the family. I felt like an intruder. Especially with the way Isabella was staring at me. And Poppy. And even a few of the "uncles."

I tried to focus on my dad instead of on all the haters.

"And I expect everyone to welcome you with open arms," he said.

It sounded more like a threat than a toast. I gulped.

"A toast. To family. To new beginnings. To a wonderful year ahead." He lifted up his glass. "Happy

Thanksgiving, everyone." He tapped his glass against his wife's.

For just a second my eyes locked with Mrs. Pruitt's. She was staring at me in the same way that Isabella always did. Like my time had come. And I saw her in a whole new light now. She was the real mobster. My dad had married into this mess. Was she the one controlling the strings? Was that why there was unrest with the families? Was that why everyone was staring at me like I didn't belong?

Matt tapped his glass against mine. "To family," he whispered in my ear.

I tried to take a deep breath. It didn't matter if this family hated me. The family I was marrying into didn't. "To family," I said and leaned forward to kiss his cheek. Matt was my real family.

Everyone started clinking glasses and drinking their champagne.

I turned to watch Isabella take a sip of hers. And I couldn't help but smile. It was game time.

CHAPTER 37

Thursday

The first signs of Isabella's discomfort were her wiggling in her chair. I swore I even saw a gleam of sweat on her forehead.

I didn't think anyone else noticed.

But when her stomach started gurgling? A few people at the table started to look over at her.

"Are you feeling alright?" Rob asked. He looked so freaking happy.

"I'm fine, twerp," Isabella said. She lifted her champagne flute and downed the rest.

Oh no.

Rob's eyes grew round.

"Oh, shit," James said under his breath. And then he just laughed.

I don't think any of us had expected Isabella to drink all of her champagne. That wasn't part of the plan.

"You okay?" Matt asked me. He put his hand on my thigh. "You look a little pale, baby."

"Yeah, I'm fine." But I wasn't. I was pretty sure my stomach suddenly felt as upset as Isabella's was about to. I just wanted a little payback. Not a *real* accident. Just a teensy tiny threat of an accident would have been enough for our prank to work.

"How much did you put in there?" I tried to mouth silently to Rob.

He just shrugged. But it looked like he was about to burst out laughing.

Oh God. Rob had really had to encourage me about the laxatives part of the plan to begin with. But he insisted that they were necessary. I never thought she'd down the whole glass. This was bad. Really, really bad.

Isabella's stomach gurgled even louder.

Poppy leaned forward to see where the noise was coming from.

Isabella grabbed her napkin and wiped off her forehead.

She looked…sick. Damn it, this wasn't part of the plan! She was just supposed to feel uncomfortable and stand up to excuse herself. Simple as that. But Isabella didn't move at all. She just kept sitting there, her stomach gurgling more and more.

Her cheeks puffed up like she was going to barf, but she swallowed whatever it was back down. But the air still had to come out of somewhere. So she farted. Loudly.

My mouth dropped open.

Someone's fork clattered onto their plate.

"Excuse you, Rob," Isabella said.

"That wasn't me," he said. "That was all you, Wizzy."

"No it was not." Her stomach gurgled again. It looked like she was dying to get up. But now if she did, it would basically be a confession that she was the one that farted.

It didn't matter though. Because she farted again, even louder this time.

Okay, maybe it was a little funny. I pressed my lips together so I wouldn't giggle.

Isabella's face contorted with pain. There was no way to explain her way out of this. Everyone had to know it was her.

"If you'll excuse me for one second," Isabella said. "I think I left my…curling iron on." She grabbed her stomach.

Rob laughed. "You better hurry, Wizzy. You don't want another accident like that pool one. I can think of a pretty endless list of new and improved poop-themed nicknames."

She elbowed him in the neck as she stood up.

"Ow," Rob said.

Isabella farted again so loudly that every single person at the table had to have heard it.

I tried my best not to laugh. This was horrifying. And maybe we had taken it a little too far. But it was kind of hilarious too.

Poppy gasped as Isabella walked by. "Oh my God, Isabella. Gross!" she said.

"What?" Isabella looked down at the back of her dress where Poppy was pointing.

Rob had slipped some of the chocolate pudding onto Isabella's seat right before she'd sat down. That was the prank. All of it. Get her to stand up in the middle of dinner and make it seem like she'd pooped her pants.

"I didn't…" Isabella said, just as she farted again.

Poppy started laughing.

A few other people at the table did too.

Tears started streaming down Isabella's cheeks. I wasn't sure if it was because she was embarrassed though. It just looked like it was really painful to hold in her bowel movement.

"It's not..." her voice trailed off as she put her hand on her ass to cover up the pudding stain as another huge fart ripped through the room. And then she screamed at the top of her lungs and ran out of the dining room, her hands trying desperately to cover her fake poopy butt...but failing.

It had gone too far. I hadn't meant to make her cry. But when I saw Rob barely holding back his laughter, I couldn't *not* laugh. And once I started, I couldn't stop. Everyone thought Isabella had actually shit herself. The prank had worked. It was freaking amazing. And it felt so good to see her being the butt of a joke for once.

"She was crying, Brooklyn," Matt said. "Why are you laughing at that?"

I covered my mouth. How did he not see the irony in his words? Isabella always laughed when she made me cry. And I couldn't even count on one hand how many times she'd publicly humiliated me. This was hilarious. I was actually shocked that he wasn't laughing. "She pooped her pants," I said, leaning into what it looked like.

Matt just stared at me like he didn't even recognize me.

My laughter died in my throat. This had been exactly what Matt was talking about. Him not wanting me to stoop to Isabella's level. I wasn't the kind of person who laughed at other people's tears and embarrassment. So why was I? Really, what was wrong with me? And yet…another glance at the Hunters had me laughing all over again.

"Come on, man, it was kind of funny," Mason said.

I smiled up at him.

He winked at me. "Karma, right?"

Yeah, something like that. At least one Caldwell brother understood. Really, how was Matt not even a little amused? Isabella had made his life a living hell too. This was justice. "She laughs all the time when I cry," I said to Matt.

"Yeah. Because she's an asshole. You're not."

Asshole. Just thinking about the amount of poop coming out of Isabella's asshole right now made me giggle again. "Asshole," I said with a laugh.

And for some reason that finally made Matt smile. "Fine. Maybe it's a little funny. But only because you find it so hilarious." He kissed the side of my forehead. "This is like the whizzing in the pool thing all over again."

Right? It was the perfect prank. And now James and Rob would talk to Matt and Mason. They'd all make up And everyone would have a great night. Except for Isabella. But I didn't really care. As far as I was concerned, she deserved it. Besides, she'd be down in a few minutes to try to prove to everyone that it had only been pudding on her skirt.

I looked across the table. I thought Rob and James would still be laughing, but now James looked as pissed as Matt originally was. Rob was whispering to him and waving his hands around. James stood up. It looked like he was going to run out of the room, but Rob grabbed his arm to stop him. "Just wait for it," Rob said.

"Have you lost your mind?" James pulled his arm out of Rob's grip.

"Wait for it," Rob said. He looked so excited.

There was a loud cracking noise. For a second I thought someone had dropped a dish. But then I saw a piece of drywall falling onto the table.

"Shit," James said.

I looked up at the ceiling to see the cracks expanding right above the dining room table. And then brown goo started leaking through the cracks.

Oh God.

Mrs. Pruitt screamed and everyone started backing away from the table.

Shit literally started raining down from the cracked ceiling in big gross globs. There was a loud cracking noise and an explosion of poop fell from the ceiling, covering all the food on the table.

Poppy took some shit right to the face and screamed at the top of her lungs. She started sobbing, wiping the poo from her cheeks.

"Richard, do something!" Mrs. Pruitt yelled as a chunk of drywall landed in the center of the dining room table. One of the chandeliers fell and she screamed again as the crystals shattered.

Someone slipped backward on the mess, slamming into the china cabinet, sending glass and broken china in every direction.

Another crack made the ceiling finally collapse.

And Isabella fell through it.

On a toilet.

With her dress pulled up around her waist.

Everyone started screaming and running around, slipping in the shit and colliding with each other.

What the fuck is happening?

The toilet landed right in the center of the table on top of the Thanksgiving turkey. The table snapped in half and Isabella screamed at the top of her lungs.

More poop splattered everywhere as the toilet hit the ground. A water pipe burst, spreading everything literally everywhere. Poop seeped into the carpet. It hit a few of the guests. I even had to dodge some of it.

What the hell?!

I heard someone barfing in the corner of the dining room.

"Don't look at me!" Isabella shrieked as she unsuccessfully tried to cover herself. Another fart ripped through the room.

And then Rob started laughing so loud. He put his finger through some of the shit on the table and licked it off.

For a second I almost started throwing up too.

But then Rob winked at me.

Oh no. It wasn't poop. It was pudding. I was pretty sure I was one of the only people that knew it. And now I knew why Rob said he needed blueprints of the apartment. So that he could make sure to set this up just right. And why he kept joking around about an abundance of pudding.

So.

Much.

Pudding.

"Do something, Richard!" Mrs. Pruitt screamed again. "Someone do something!" She put her hands out as some of the water from the burst pipe shot in her direction. She tried to dodge it and slipped in the pudding, landing face first in the mess.

I gasped. *Oh God.*

My dad stepped forward to try to help Isabella off her porcelain throne, but he slipped on the pudding too. He grabbed the arm of the guy next to him and they both tumbled into the pudding, one of them knocking into the broken china cabinet. And this time the cabinet toppled forward, smashing into the dining room table.

The second chandelier fell to the ground and as someone went to dodge it, they somehow hit the turkey carving fork. It sailed through the air and stuck into the family portrait. Right in the middle of Isabella's painted forehead. The forked dragged down, ruining the portrait as everyone continued yelling and running around.

Holy shit.

Rob leaned across the broken table, not caring at all about his dress shoe stepping in the brown goo, since he knew it wasn't poop. "Good one, Sanders," he said and lifted up his hand.

I just stared at him. *This wasn't part of the plan! Put your hand down, you crazy person!*

I heard another person vomiting.

"I'm going to kill you!" Isabella screamed at me. "I'm going to fucking kill you, you monster!"

I didn't do this. I backed up, knocking into Matt. He grabbed my arms to steady me.

"You're going to fucking die, Brooklyn!" Isabella screamed.

"Isabella," I said. "I didn't..."

"Shut up, you bitch! I'm going to kill you in your sleep! How could you do this to me?"

Matt's hands fell from my arms.

I turned around. "Matt, I didn't..." my words trailed away. How was I going to explain this?

Matt looked over at Rob, who still stupidly had his hand raised in the air for a high five.

"Best prank ever," Rob said. "A classic Hunter, Sanders mess around."

No. No, no, no!

"That was definitely worth all the planning," he said. "Don't leave me hanging, Sanders."

What the hell, Rob?!

Matt looked down at me. "I can't believe you." He stepped away from me like I was poisoned.

"It's not what you think," I said.

He just shook his head and walked out of the dining room.

"Matt!" I yelled and ran after him. "Wait!"

Matt stopped at the Pruitts' front door. "What the hell is wrong with you, Brooklyn?" For weeks he'd kept his cool. Trying not to stress me out. But it was like something snapped inside of him. He was seething, his chest rising and falling as he tried to hold himself together. It looked like he was going to explode. "Were you seriously hanging out with the Hunters behind my back to plan...that?"

"Yes. I mean, no. I didn't know..."

"You didn't know that you were hanging out with Rob and James behind my back?"

I didn't even know what to say to that. Tears started falling from my eyes and I tried to wipe them away.

"You promised me you wouldn't," he said. "You promised me you were on my side."

I wasn't sure whether he was going to punch the wall or cry. "I am on your side, Matt. I did this for you. I wanted you guys to be friends again."

"You made Isabella shit herself and fall through the ceiling to make me friends with those dickwads again? How does that make any sense?"

"It was pudding." My voice sounded so small. How could I make him understand this? My mind seemed scrambled as I searched for the right words. I wasn't even sure what I could say to fix this. The way he was looking at me…it was the same way he looked at Isabella. Like I was a monster.

"We just talked yesterday about no more secrets," he said. "And you were hanging out with them this whole time. And that?" He gestured toward the dining room. "We talked about revenge. And I told you that you were better than this. You're not supposed to be like them!"

What did that mean? "I'm not. I'm…"

"Give me a break. You're just like Isabella. You laughed at someone's pain. You plotted to hurt someone. I was marrying you to fucking save you from becoming a Pruitt. And you became one anyway."

His words made my chest hurt. "I didn't ask you to save me." *I asked you to love me.* "And I'm not like them. I didn't know it was going to go this far. It was just supposed to be laxatives and a little pudding on her chair. That was it. I just wanted her to stop messing with me."

"She fell through the freaking ceiling half-naked!"

"But I didn't know that was going to happen! And you can't stand there and tell me that she didn't deserve that after everything she's done to me." *She deserved worse.*

He shook his head. "I can't even look at you right now."

It was the exact same thing Kennedy had said to me yesterday. I grabbed his arm. "Matt, I'm sorry. I didn't mean it. If you'd just give me a second to explain." None of this was coming out right. "I didn't mean to."

"You didn't mean to talk to James and Rob behind my back? Or you didn't mean to lie about it? Or you didn't mean to keep this crazy revenge plot from me? Or you didn't mean to lie about keeping secrets? Or you didn't mean to stoop to Isabella's level and publicly humiliate her when I thought you were the bigger person? Which thing didn't you mean?"

God, what had I done? "All of it." I tried to blink away my tears.

"My mom was wrong. You can't marry out of this crazy family. They're toxic. All of them."

Is he calling me toxic? I tried to wipe away my tears. But I couldn't stop crying. Because he was staring at me like I was a stranger. Like I was toxic. Like I was a Pruitt and not a soon-to-be Caldwell. *Isabella's a disease.* Those were some of the first words he'd ever said to me. I'd known that's what he thought. That the Pruitts were all toxic. I just prayed he didn't lump me in with the rest of them.

"You're not the person I thought you were." He grabbed the doorknob.

"Yes I am. Please just stay and hear me out."

"Like you heard me out when you believed I'd sleep with my best friend's girl? You didn't give me the time of day."

Matt. My chest ached not just because he was angry. But because what he was saying was true. "I'm sorry…"

"I fought for you. For us. I tried to be patient and understanding about what you were up to all that time you weren't speaking to me. But we're together now and you still look me in the eye and lie and keep secrets and sneak around behind my back. How the hell am I supposed to be understanding about that? You don't care about my opinion at all. You don't care about me."

"Of course I care about you." My tears were falling so fast that he was blurring in front of me. How could he think I didn't care? I loved him so much that it hurt. "Yes, I planned a stupid little prank to get back at Isabella, but I never meant for it to go this far. And I was doing it to fix your relationship with James and Rob."

He shook his head. And he didn't say it. But I knew what he was thinking. That I did it because I was a Pruitt. That their blood was in my veins. That I was a monster.

I couldn't think straight. Nothing was coming out right. But I was crying too hard. And I could feel so many eyes on me from the dining room. I couldn't breathe. "You have to believe me," I choked.

"That's the whole problem, Brooklyn. You haven't given me any reason to believe a word you say." He opened the door.

"Matt, you promised you wouldn't walk away."

"I guess we're both liars." The door slammed shut behind him.

CHAPTER 38

Friday

I guess we're both liars. The words kept rolling around in my head as I stared up at the ceiling of my bedroom at the Pruitts'. I hadn't slept at all. My whole body ached. My heart most of all. The prank was supposed to fix everything. But if anything, the Hunters and Caldwells just hated each other even more. And everyone hated me.

Matt wasn't speaking to me. Kennedy still wasn't answering my texts. I'd yelled at Rob and James, even though James swore he didn't know about that part of the prank. They were probably mad at me now too. As far as I knew, Felix was still in jail because of me. And Mason was pissed at me too. He'd left shortly after Matt and told me not to bother to come back to the house.

Even Isabella had called me a monster. I didn't care about her opinion. But that one did hurt. A monster had called me a monster.

Miller and Donnelley were both stationed outside my room to make sure Isabella didn't make good on her promise of killing me in my sleep. But what would it have mattered if she had? No one would miss me. Everyone would be better off if I was gone.

I wiped away my stupid tears as I looked at my phone. I'd left dozens of calls and texts for both Matt and Kennedy. And my screen was still blank. I just stared at it, waiting for something to come through.

But why would it? I was a liar. They'd both said so.

I was a monster.

I was a Pruitt.

I sat up and pressed on Matt's name on my phone again. I'd tried to explain it a million times already, but one more time wouldn't hurt. It rang once and went to voicemail.

He'd rejected my call. He'd seen it was me and ignored it. Even though he had to know how much I was hurting too. His silence literally made my chest ache. I tried not to cry as the voicemail switched on.

"Matt, it's me." Of course it was me. Who else would leave him so many repetitive voicemails? "Can you please call me back? I know you're mad. And I would be too. But you have to believe me. I never meant for it to go that far." I ignored the tears rolling down my cheeks. How could he ignore me right now? He wasn't supposed to cut me out. He was supposed to be by my side. Always. He promised me.

"How could you compare me to Isabella? How could you think that I'm like her when you know me better than anyone else? And how could you ignore me when I'm hurting?" I wiped away my tears with my fingertips. "I gave you so many second chances when we first got together. All I'm asking for is one. I think you owe me that after everything we've been through." Didn't he see that? How could he treat me this way? I was still crying, but they were angry tears now. And I didn't bother to wipe them away. "You're a hypocrite, Matt. You're a fucking hypocrite."

I hung up the phone and let myself cry. Because I was pretty sure yelling at him instead of apologizing was something that Isabella would have done too. *I'm not like her. I'm not. God, maybe I am.*

There was a knock on my bedroom door.

"Princess, can I come in?" My dad walked in. He gave me a small smile. "How are you feeling this morning?"

I felt my bottom lip start to tremble. "I messed everything up, Dad."

He rushed over and put his arms around me. "Nonsense. You didn't do anything wrong."

He was one of the only ones that believed me when I said I didn't know about the whole prank. It was just supposed to be a stupid fake poop prank. I hadn't meant to do any structural damage to the apartment. Or ruin Thanksgiving.

"Everyone hates me," I sobbed into his chest.

"I don't hate you." He leaned back so he could look down at me. "You're an angel, Brooklyn." He cupped my face in his hands. "My angel."

That was kind of him to say. But it wasn't true. I was a freaking demon.

"Everything is going to be fine. I promise," he said.

I shook my head. "How is everything going to be fine? I upset everyone in my life except for you." What if Matt never spoke to me again? What if Kennedy didn't? I was going to be all alone again. I couldn't start over again with no one. I couldn't do it. Despite what Matt said, I wasn't strong. And who knew if he'd even meant that. Because he'd said it himself...he and I were both liars.

"Do you know what you need?" my dad asked. "A spa weekend. I'll call some people in. That's what Isabella always does when she's upset."

I'm not Isabella. God, or am I?

"Or maybe something else?" he said with a smile. "Name it, and we can do it."

"You said you'd teach me how to play golf. Could we do that?" I'd never taken him up on his offer to go to his country club. And a little father daughter time might help lift my spirits.

"Well, you won't be able to this weekend. But soon, of course."

"I can do it this weekend. I'm pretty sure I'm uninvited to Friendsgiving. And I could really use the distraction. I'm just going to be sitting around the house bored."

He lowered his eyebrows, as if my response confused him. "You'll be resting, yes. That's just what you need." He patted my knee.

I wasn't sure if that was true. I didn't want to rest and get pampered. I just wanted Matt back. "I really didn't mean for it to go that far last night," I said.

"I know, princess. But it was good to see a little fire in you." He smiled at me.

"You're happy that I made Isabella and all that pudding fall through the ceiling?"

He laughed. "Between you and me? I'm glad you stood up for yourself."

At least he understood. And he didn't look at me any differently. I disgusted everyone else. But my dad thought

I was an angel. Maybe that was the whole problem. Maybe his views were skewed because he was used to living with Mrs. Pruitt and Isabella. Anyone was better than them.

But better than them wasn't good enough. I looked down at the ring on my finger. I was a Pruitt. Matt didn't want me to be who I was. His parents didn't want me to be who I was. But if I wasn't me, then who the hell else was I supposed to be? I thought I was finally fitting in to my new world.

"I don't want to become Isabella," I said and sniffled.

"Brooklyn, you are your mother's daughter. You're…you. You can't possibly be someone else. Who's filling your mind with things like that? Matthew?"

I pressed my lips together.

"You deserve someone who believes in you enough to know that you're special. You are. I've never met anyone so caring and generous."

I wasn't sure what I'd done yesterday was in any way caring or generous. I had no idea why he'd chosen those two words to describe me. And I didn't tell my dad that Matt stopped believing in me because I'd given him a reason to. Because I was a liar. "Thanks, Dad."

He patted my knee. "Now, I'd love to keep chatting, but it's just about time for your appointment."

Oh, I'd completely forgotten about that. "Dad, I really don't feel like going anywhere today."

"Dr. Wilson came here of course. Come on, you wanted to see what was in that room down the hall anyway, right?"

What did that have to do with Dr. Wilson? "Um, yeah, okay." Maybe it would be good to move around. Besides, I didn't want to be alone right now. Talking to Dr. Wilson would at least keep my mind preoccupied.

I walked out of my room and tried to hide from Miller's judging glare. Although…he didn't look so disapproving this morning. He just looked…sad. For me? Because of me? I had no idea. I could add him to the list of people that hated me right now.

His eyes locked with mine. "You don't have to do this," Miller mouthed silently to me. "You can still back out."

What? Why was everyone so concerned about whether or not I was on birth control? It was no one's business but mine. I just turned away from him. I didn't have the energy to fight with him right now. All the fight in me was gone.

We stopped outside the locked room down the hall and my dad started to type in the code.

"Do you think that maybe everyone was better off before I got here?" I asked. That was the question I kept coming back to. Before I came to New York, the Hunters and Caldwells were friends. Kennedy had never dated that creep Cupcake. Miller was probably happy. Felix hadn't been in prison. And my uncle wouldn't have had to waste his final few months on this earth taking care of me. I swallowed hard. I was the worst.

My dad shook his head. "How can you possibly say that?"

"Because it's true."

"You saved my life. In more ways than one. Truly, Brooklyn. You are my angel. And I'm so grateful every day that you walked into my life."

"Really?" I blinked back my tears. It was exactly what I needed to hear. Maybe I had made one person's life better. And even though I had been wary of my dad at first, he'd made my life better too. I didn't know what I'd ever do without him now. Maybe when my mom was pregnant he hadn't wanted me. But he wanted me now. And today I really needed to feel wanted.

"Really." He kissed the top of my head and pressed enter on the keypad. The door made a weird hissing noise and he opened it.

The room was blindingly white. I blinked a few times, waiting for my eyes to adjust.

"Oh good," my dad said. "You're already here." He shook Dr. Wilson's hand.

I looked around the white room. There was a bed, a chair, and lots of weird machines. It kind of looked like a hospital room. I shuddered. I hated hospitals. And I knew my dad hadn't asked me much about how my mom had died, but he knew she'd gotten sick. Why would he think I wanted to see this room? I'd basically lived in a hospital room like this the past few years. And why the hell did he even have a room like this?

"It's good to see you again," Dr. Wilson said. "How about you lie down for me and we can get started?"

"Why do you have a hospital room in your home?" I asked and turned to my dad.

"It's hard to make time to go in for all my checkups," my dad said. "With work and everything."

I wondered if the Caldwells had a hospital room in their mansion. I hadn't come across it while I was there. I stared at one of the machines as I lay down. It didn't look like any that had been in my mom's hospital room.

My dad sat down in the chair beside the bed and grabbed my hand. "I know you said you didn't want me in here with you," my dad said. "But I'm going to stay for as long as I can. I don't want you to do this alone. Is that okay with you?"

He was being extra nice today. He knew I was feeling down. I squeezed his hand. "Yeah, you can stay."

"I can't thank you enough for doing this," my dad said.

"It's no problem."

He lifted my hand and kissed it. "Really, princess." Tears were welling in the corners of his eyes.

I wasn't sure why he was so emotional about this. It was just birth control. *Ow.* I looked over to see Dr. Wilson injecting something into my arm. He'd already given me shots when we'd first met. Did I really need any more? I bit the inside of my lip. I needed a distraction. "What are all those machines?" I asked.

My dad gave me a strange look. "They're for my dialysis. I need it three times a week. It was getting exhausting going to the hospital so frequently. So Dr. Wilson helped set all this up."

Wait, what? "Dialysis?" I tried to sit up, but my body felt all weird and tingly. "What's dialysis for?" I'd heard about it before, but I couldn't place it.

My dad shook his head like he was confused by my question. "My kidney failure."

"Your kidneys are failing?" I was pretty sure he needed those. *No. No, no, no.* It was suddenly hard to breathe. It felt like the room was closing in on me. *He's dying. No, he can't be dying. He can't leave me too.*

"You know that, princess. It was in the agreement you signed."

"What?" My thoughts were starting to blur together.

"In section 72 B. Where you agreed to give me your kidney."

No. No, I didn't agree to that. I tried to say the words out loud but they didn't come out for some reason. This wasn't happening. I didn't want this. I felt like I couldn't breathe. "Dad," I was finally able to gasp.

"I'm right here." My dad reached forward as my mind got even fuzzier. He ran his fingers through my hair like my mom always used to. I closed my eyes and imagined it was her.

"Thank you," my dad whispered. "Thank you for this."

I was pretty sure I was sobbing, but I couldn't feel my tears on my cheeks. Everyone hated me. And my dad just wanted me for my kidney. I'd trusted him. I'd fucking trusted him. But he didn't love me. He'd never wanted me.

God, how could I ever think otherwise? He'd popped up out of the blue and forced me to live with him not because I was his daughter, but because I was a fucking match for his failing kidneys? All the blood work. All the being overly worried about my health. All the safety precautions. Him swearing he wouldn't let Isabella ever hurt me? I thought he was being a good dad. I thought he loved me.

I couldn't feel my tears, but I saw them fall from my chin and onto my shirt. I remembered Miller being surprised I'd signed the contract. I remembered how excited my dad was when I'd finally given him the signed papers. I was his angel? Fuck that. And fuck him. I was just an organ donor.

My dad never wanted me. I'd known that. I'd known it and I still let him in. Of course he didn't love me. Of course he didn't want me. No one wanted me. No one.

I couldn't breathe. All I could think about was how much everything hurt. My heart ached.

My mom had been right. My uncle had been right. Mrs. Alcaraz had been right. Even the Caldwells had been right. My father was a monster.

And maybe I deserved this. Because Matt thought I was a monster too. I was toxic. I was a disease. I'd made so many mistakes. I'd betrayed Kennedy's trust by telling Felix about Cupcake. And I'd betrayed Matt by doing the prank and talking to the Hunters. I'd even betrayed the Hunters by completely throwing them under the bus for the whole prank. I wanted to think that everyone would eventually be able to forgive me.

I'd called Matt a hypocrite. But I guess that was me. Because I'd never be able to forgive Cupcake for what he did to Kennedy. Or how he and Isabella set up Felix. It seemed like everyone in my life betrayed everyone else. But this? My dad betraying me in this way? I'd never forgive him. Never. He was supposed to love me unconditionally. He was supposed to be my dad. I just needed one person to believe in me. To want me. To love me.

My dad's face blurred in front of me. I'd thought he loved me. I'd thought Matt loved me too. Why did no one ever love me?

I pictured my mom singing to me as we danced in the kitchen. It was like I could actually hear her voice. And then the image in my mind morphed and I was holding her cold hand in her hospital bed. Watching the life drain from her face.

She was the only person that ever loved me for me. The only person that saw the good in me. The only person worth fighting for. And she was already gone.

For one last second, I felt her fingers in my hair. And her song in my ear. My heart felt like it was breaking in two. But I knew that wasn't true. Because it was already shattered.

CHAPTER 39

Friday

Matt

I looked down at all my missed calls and texts from Brooklyn. She probably had an equal number of them on her phone now because she'd ignored all my calls and texts this afternoon.

I was pissed off last night. Fuming. Not just because I'd seen a side to Brooklyn I'd never seen before. But because she'd lied. She'd looked at me and lied to my face while she was out sneaking around with James and Rob behind my back.

How the fuck was that supposed to make me feel? James had proposed to her. And if she didn't see that he was trying to steal her away from me, then she was blind. Or maybe she was hoping he would.

I sighed and ran my hand down my face. She had every reason to be mad at me too though. And I had a feeling I knew why she wasn't calling me back. I'd basically told her I was marrying her to help get her away from her crazy fucking family. And that it was pointless because she belonged with them.

She'd lied. She'd made me feel like shit. But I'd been the asshole. And I hated that I'd made her feel like shit too.

Thinking about shit made me picture the destruction of the Pruitts' dining room. I shook my head. What a mess. But if anyone deserved to fall through the ceiling on a toilet, it was Isabella. Brooklyn was right about that.

"Are you going to call her?"

I looked up to see Mason leaning against the doorjamb.

"Mom's already wondering why Brooklyn didn't come home with us last night," he said. "You definitely won't be able to evade her questions if Brooklyn doesn't show up for Friendsgiving."

"What do you think I've been doing in here all afternoon?" I tossed my phone down on my bed.

"I don't know? Jerking off?"

"Funny. Brooklyn's not answering my calls."

"Huh. If you ask me, she seemed pretty sorry last night. I'm surprised she isn't answering."

"Yeah, I know. But I shouldn't have left her at the Pruitts. And I shouldn't have said all that stuff about her being like them. She's probably super pissed off at me."

Mason shrugged. "No one wants to be compared to a Pruitt."

I wasn't even sure that was the worst part. Brooklyn had gone behind my back in order to pull that prank on Isabella. If she had come to me and told me that she really needed to stand up to Isabella, I would have helped her. But Brooklyn must have felt like she couldn't rely on me. And now I'd given her even more reason to doubt me.

"I'm going to go there and try to talk to her. Can I borrow your car?" I asked and stood up.

"Much better plan than calling," said Mason. "But I don't mind driving."

I laughed. "You're coming with me? Voluntarily? To the Pruitts'?"

"You said a lot of stupid shit last night. You're going to need a wingman."

Fair enough.

"And I'm pretty sure if I stay here Mom's gonna make me help in the kitchen. And no one wants that."

Another good point.

Mason slapped my back as I walked through the door. "It's gonna be fine."

"Yeah. Maybe we should stop and get flowers though," I said. "Just in case." Not that I knew what flowers were her favorite. I'd bought her every type of flower I could find after her uncle passed away. I got it stuck in my head that if I found the right kind, she'd smile. That hadn't worked. But holding her as she fell asleep in my arms *had* worked. She smiled a lot in her dreams. Recently I'd been getting her to smile more when she was awake too. And I couldn't believe I'd stood there yelling at her when all I cared about was seeing her smile.

***

I knocked on the Pruitts' door. I'd gotten a bouquet of red roses. Sometimes when my dad made my mom angry, he'd come home with a dozen roses for her. If it worked for him, hopefully it would work for me.

Mason gave me a thumbs up.

The bodyguard that always hung around Brooklyn opened the door. His eyes were red and puffy like he'd been crying.

"Oh. Um. Hey," I said. "Can I speak with Brooklyn?"

He wiped under his nose with the back of his hand. And then held the door open for Mason and me to come in. "Mr. Pruitt's been expecting you. He's in his study." He gestured toward the large wooden office doors.

Okay. "But will you tell Brooklyn that I'm here? Friendsgiving starts in less than an hour and we really have to get going."

The guy looked like he was about to start crying again. "Just go talk to Mr. Pruitt."

Before I could ask any more questions, he walked away.

Weird. I hoped he was okay. Brooklyn was always so nice to her security team, but they always just made me feel uncomfortable. Like they hated me for some reason. I walked over to Mr. Pruitt's study and knocked on the door.

"Come in."

I pushed open the door and froze. Mr. Pruitt was sitting behind his desk in a wheelchair. His arm was attached to an IV. His face was completely drained of color. Except for his eyes. They were red and puffy just like the security guard's. He looked like death.

"Matthew," he said, his voice hoarse like he hadn't used it in a long time. "There's been…an incident."

"What kind of incident?" It was like all the blood rushed to my ears. I could hear my heart pounding.

Mr. Pruitt looked back down at the picture of Brooklyn he had on his desk. "Brooklyn…she…" his voice trailed off as a sob escaped his throat. He tried to reach for a tissue from his desk, but his arm gave out.

"What the hell is going on? Where is she?"

Mr. Pruitt just shook his head. "We didn't know how weak her heart was until it was too late."

Too late? Too late for what?

"I'm sorry," he said. "I'm going to miss her just as much as you."

What the fuck was he talking about? I didn't realize I was stumbling backwards until I ran into Mason. Mason grabbed my arms like he was expecting me to fall over.

But this was just a sick joke. Brooklyn was fine. I'd just seen her last night. She'd just left me dozens of messages. There was no incident. I pushed Mason off of me and ran out into the foyer. "Brooklyn!" I yelled.

My voice echoed in the empty foyer.

"Brooklyn!" I ran up the stairs. "Brooklyn, please just talk to me!" I ran down the hall to her bedroom. "Brooklyn?" The room was empty. I ran back out into the hall. Where the fuck was she? I started opening up random doors. "I'm sorry, baby. Please just talk to me."

"I told her she wouldn't live to see her wedding day," Isabella said.

Her words sent a chill down my spine. I turned to see her standing in the middle of the hallway with a huge smile on her face.

She had no clue what she was talking about, though. Brooklyn was fine. "Get out of my way, Isabella." I walked past her. "Brooklyn, where are you?!"

"Those morgue people came and took her away hours ago."

Panic was starting to settle into my chest. "Brooklyn!"

"They just wheeled her cold, lifeless body out," Isabella said. "Like a bag of trash. Because that's what she was."

I lunged at her. I didn't realize or care that anyone was watching us, but two bodyguards grabbed me before I could wrap my hands around Isabella's throat.

Isabella laughed.

"Get off me," I yelled. "Brooklyn, where are you?!"

"Exactly where she belongs," Isabella said. "Six feet under with her whore mother."

I ripped my arm away from one of the security guards and grabbed the front of Isabella's sweater.

She screamed at the top of her lungs.

"What did you do?" I yelled.

The security guards pulled me away.

This wasn't happening. This wasn't real.

"I didn't have to do anything," Isabella called after me as I was being pulled down the steps. "I had a wonderful plan, but I didn't even have to use it. She died because she was weak."

"Don't you dare fucking call her that." I tried to lunge up the stairs again, but Mason stepped in front of me.

"She died in surgery," he said.

I shook my head back and forth. "No. What the hell are you talking about? She wasn't having surgery today."

"She'd agreed to give her dad her kidney. There were complications."

No. "She would have told me if she was doing that." I just kept shaking my head as the tears started to fall down my cheeks. "She's okay. She's alive. I'll call her again. I'll just call her. You'll see." I fumbled with my phone in my pocket. All the missed calls and texts were blinking back at me.

Mason put his hands on my shoulders. "They didn't know her mom died of heart disease. Mr. Pruitt seemed shocked when I told him that. They were under the impression that it was cancer like her uncle."

No.

"She's gone, Matt. Her heart gave out on the operating table. She didn't make it."

"She's not gone." What the hell was he talking about? Surgery? She just had a doctor's appointment. Not a freaking surgery. "Brooklyn!" I yelled.

"I'm sorry, Matthew," Mr. Pruitt said.

I turned around. Mr. Pruitt was in his wheelchair in the middle of the foyer. His IV wheeled in right beside him. "I owe her everything. She saved my life."

You fucking prick. "She never agreed to any surgery!"

"She did. She signed the papers. I have a copy of them in my office if..."

"One of your contracts? They're a million pages long. No one reads those things, you psychopath."

He looked at me like I'd slapped him. "I can't change what happened now. It's done."

How could he talk about his daughter like she was just a finished business transaction? "This is a joke, right? This is all a joke?" But I didn't have the energy to call out her name again. Because no one was looking at me like this was a joke. *She can't be dead. She can't be.*

Mr. Pruitt pulled Brooklyn's ring out of his pocket. "She would have wanted you to have this back." He held it out to me.

If Brooklyn was alive she wouldn't have taken it off. She'd promised me forever. She'd promised. I didn't want the ring back. I just wanted her.

He grabbed my hand and pressed the ring into my palm. "I'm sorry. I'll be in touch with the funeral arrangements. I know she would have loved for you to give a speech." Mr. Pruitt snapped his fingers and one of the bodyguards wheeled him away.

I looked down at the ring in my hand and it became blurry through my tears. "This isn't real. She can't be dead. She can't be."

I wanted to run around the house looking for her. I wanted to see her laughing at one of my jokes. Or even crying because I was being an idiot. I just wanted to see her face. I needed to see her face.

Mason hugged me.

This isn't real. I closed my eyes and opened them again. But I was still standing in the middle of the Pruitts' foyer, Brooklyn's ring digging into my palm.

Brooklyn was gone. And the last thing I'd ever said to her was that she was a liar.

I looked down at the rose petals all over the floor. I wasn't even aware that I'd dropped the bouquet. What the fuck had I even brought them here for? Flowers couldn't fix anything. They couldn't bring her uncle back. And they couldn't bring Brooklyn back either.

My whole body felt numb.

"It's going to be okay," Mason said.

How was anything going to be okay? Brooklyn was dead. And she'd died thinking that I hated her.

CHAPTER 40

Wednesday

Matt

I was still numb. I'd gone from rage to despair. I'd called the cops on Isabella, convinced that she was somehow behind it. I'd hired a private investigator, thinking maybe Brooklyn was still alive and out there somewhere alone and scared. Hell, I'd even thought I'd seen her in the street. But I'd just scared some random girl half to death when I grabbed her arm. From rage to despair, all the way back to…numb.

I looked over at the coffin. I wanted to climb inside and stop breathing. I wanted to stop feeling this hollowness in my chest. I just wanted my fucking girl back.

Someone in the church cleared their throat.

And I realized I'd just been standing up here saying nothing. "I was supposed to marry Brooklyn next month," I said into the microphone. The mic made a squealing noise, like it was rejecting the past tense words that didn't make any fucking sense coming out of my mouth. "And I don't really know what to say about our ending, when all I was thinking about recently was our beginning." I swallowed down the lump in my throat.

"I wrote my vows to her a few weeks ago. Before…this." I looked over at the coffin again. How could she be dead? How was this happening? I took a deep breath and pulled out the folded up piece of paper in my pocket. I stared down at the words that I'd planned to say to her on our wedding day.

"I don't know anything better to say than how I feel about her." The words started to blur in front of me, but I knew them by heart anyway. "Brooklyn. When I first met you, you thought you were invisible. But I always saw you. The first thing I loved about you was how your eyes lit up whenever you saw me. Like I was the only one that could make you happy."

Happy? Fuck. I destroyed her. I wiped the tears out of my eyes. I had to get through this. I had to let her know.

"But you were the one making me happy. You were a breath of fresh air in this city. I was infatuated with you before we ever spoke. And I fell harder for you every single day since you first let me in. And I know that I'll keep falling harder every day from here."

I dropped my head. "I know you're scared of time. But I'm giving you all of mine. Every second. I'll cherish you, Brooklyn. I'll keep you safe." I choked on my words.

"I know that we're young. But you've taught me that the one thing in this life we can't waste is time." I shook my head. "Baby, I can't imagine my life without you. I'd be lost if we weren't together. I'm only happy when I know that you're happy too. And it took me being an idiot, but I know for a fact that I'm only really living when we're together. And I don't want to go another day without you by my side."

I took a deep breath. "I promised to be all your firsts. First kiss. First love. First husband." When I'd written these vows, I could picture her smiling at that. An inside joke that not one damn person would understand but her. And she wasn't fucking here to laugh with me. "And there are so many more firsts we'll get to experience together. First child…" my voice cracked. I couldn't read this part. I couldn't make myself think about all the firsts that had been ripped away from us. I wiped my face and skipped to the last paragraph.

"Brooklyn Sanders. Or Pruitt. It doesn't matter what your last name was. Because you're a Caldwell now. My wife." I tried to steady my voice, but it was impossible. "My home. My heart. My best friend. And the love of my life. I promised you that I've only ever loved you. And that I will only ever love you. And I'm standing here today, doubling down on that promise, baby. Because I will love you and only you until the day I die."

I promise. I walked down from the altar and past the pew where my family was sitting.

I heard my mom call my name, but I kept walking. No one could say anything to fix this. And I couldn't sit here and listen to any more speeches about how much other people would miss Brooklyn. Because they wouldn't miss her like I would. They didn't love her like I did. I was all she had. She'd told me that. I was supposed to be her rock. And she'd died thinking I hated her.

I knew what it felt like to not be able to breathe now. Because my lungs fucking hurt every second of every day that Brooklyn wasn't beside me. It was like the pain was eating me whole. Or maybe it was the regret.

How was I supposed to keep going without her? I couldn't imagine a world where she was gone. I thought

I'd known what the pain of a short life felt like when I'd lost my aunt. But this? It was like a knife twisting in my chest.

I pushed out the doors of the church. The cool autumn breeze rushed past me. And like everything in this world, it reminded me of her. And how she'd told me how she and her mom used to rake leaves and jump in them every fall. I'd never even gotten the chance to do that with her. She couldn't be gone yet. There was still so much we had to do. I wanted to wake up from this nightmare. How was this the end? I sat down on the front steps and put my face in my hands. How was I supposed to keep going without her?

Someone put their hand on my shoulder.

I looked up to see Mason sitting down beside me. He didn't offer any words. Because what could he say?

James and Rob joined us a second later.

"Matt?" James said. He stepped in front of me. He wiped the tears off his cheeks and shook his head. "I gotta tell you. Brooklyn didn't know how far the prank was going to go. I didn't even know."

"It was my fault," Rob said. He wiped a tissue under his nose. "I just thought it would be funny. I wasn't trying to mess with your relationship, Matt. I swear."

I nodded. Rob always took jokes too far. He didn't have to explain that to me, I'd seen plenty of his pranks firsthand.

"And she really was just trying to get us all to be friends again," James said. "We made a deal. That if she helped us with the prank, we'd try to sort things out with you guys."

I knew that too. I'd listened to all the missed voicemails. And read all the texts that I'd originally ignored. Brooklyn had explained everything.

I thought about the last voicemail she left me. She'd been crying. And she called me a hypocrite. Her last words to me. *You're a fucking hypocrite.*

And mine to her? I'd told her I didn't believe in her. And called her a liar. And walked out instead of having a conversation with her. I'd left her feeling alone, when being alone was her greatest fear. Having no one that loved her. And time. Time and not having enough of it. It felt like there was a knife in my chest twisting every time I thought about her. Did she die thinking I didn't love her? Was that the last thing she remembered of me?

"It's okay," I said. It wasn't. I forgave James and Rob for the prank. I did. But what they'd roped Brooklyn into doing had set me off. That prank caused me to say those terrible things to Brooklyn. My last fucking words to her.

So I hated James.

I hated Rob.

But I hated myself the most.

Rob sat down next to me. "I feel awful. I should have told her about the rest of the prank. She was so mad at me. I never meant to upset her. I thought…I don't know what I thought. Well, I thought she'd think it was funny. But she wasn't laughing. And I hate that she was mad at me at the end."

James nodded. "That look on her face after you left, Matt. She was so mad at us. I felt awful. I never meant to hurt her. I really liked her. She was perfect. For you. She was perfect for you. And I'm really sorry that I interfered at all. I never should have flirted with your girl. I'm just…I'm really fucking sorry, Matt."

I looked down at my shoes. I couldn't even look at him. I'd been waiting for him to apologize to me. But the wound felt too fresh. He'd flirted with her brazenly right in front of me. Like it was all a game. Nothing felt like a game anymore. "It's okay," I finally said. It wasn't. But I didn't have the energy to hold a grudge right now. I just needed my friend back.

"I told her not to follow you after the prank," Mason said. "I was so cold to her." He grabbed a tissue out of his pocket. "I feel like a dick."

"You guys have nothing to feel guilty about," I said. I was the one that was guilty. Not them. She'd relied on me. I was the one that let her down.

"Do you want to talk about it?" James asked.

I shook my head.

"Maybe another time? You guys could come over later. Like old times." He smiled, but I could tell it was forced. There was no going back to old times now that Brooklyn was gone. And we all knew it.

"I can't talk about it." I couldn't voice what I'd done. My horrible last words to her. Saying it out loud would make it feel more real. I hated that she thought I hated her. I hated that I'd let her down.

They all waited like they thought I'd change my mind.

"I can't, you guys."

"Okay," Rob said. "Then we won't talk about it." He put his hand out. "Let's all promise to never talk about her again. Not until Matt's ready to."

"Yeah." James put his hand on top of Rob's. "We all fucked up."

Mason put his hand on top of James'. "If we hadn't been fighting, there wouldn't have been a prank. And we never would have said those things to her." He shook his head like he felt guilty too.

I just stared at the three of their hands. They could feel bad about how they'd treated her, but they'd never feel as guilty as I did. And maybe they could just turn off a switch and never think of her again, but I couldn't. I loved her.

"So we won't talk about her until Matt's ready?" Rob asked.

Mason nodded.

James looked like he was going to start crying again. "Yeah."

They all turned to me. Maybe it would help them not to talk about her. But it wouldn't help me. It wasn't that I didn't want to. I just…couldn't. I couldn't talk about her without falling apart. I placed my hand on top of theirs anyway though. Because it was what Brooklyn would have wanted. She'd been trying to fix us. This was the first time we'd talked in weeks. She'd want this.

"Friends again?" Rob asked.

I hated them. But I nodded. I'd pretend to be their friend until I could actually be their friend again. Maybe once I could forgive them for making Brooklyn think I hated her before she died. Maybe once I forgave myself.

"Friends on three," James said with a smile.

I shook my head and threw my hand up when they did. I watched Rob and Mason walk back into the church.

"I really am sorry," James said. "She was a great girl."

"I thought we weren't supposed to talk about her."

He nodded. "For now. But whenever you're ready to talk about her again, I'm here."

I wouldn't be taking him up on his offer. It wasn't that I just blamed him in part for the horrible last words I ever spoke to Brooklyn. He'd also robbed time from us. His girlfriend had kissed me. Not the other way around. And I'd tried to keep the secret to protect him. Because I was fucking worried that he'd take his own life. But he was still standing here breathing. And Brooklyn was dead.

I'd wasted weeks of my time with her, keeping her a secret, hurting her feelings...because of my loyalty to him. So he couldn't fucking stand here and tell me he was here for me. *I* was the one who had been there for *him*. Not the other way around. James wasn't my friend.

"I really am sorry," he said.

I knew he meant it. And I knew that Brooklyn wanted me to forgive him. Fuck. I took a deep breath. I had to let it go. I knew he was sorry. And honestly? I was sorry too. I was sorry I hadn't told him right away when Rachel had kissed me. I was sorry that we'd stopped being friends in the first place. Brooklyn was right. I couldn't just cut him out so easily. James was like a brother to me.

I expected James to walk back into the church with Mason and Rob. Instead, he sat down next to me. Maybe he was the one worried about me now.

I'd forgive him eventually. I knew I would. One day I'd be able to call him my friend and mean it. But that day wasn't today. It was better that we just sat in silence. It was nice of him to stay though. It made me feel a little less alone. He knew I needed him. And wasn't that all friendship really was? After all, time was limited. Just like Brooklyn had said. I didn't want to waste any more of it by fighting with James. And I just really needed my friend back right now.

"She loved you," James said.

The past tense made the knife in my chest twist again. But they were still somehow the exact words I needed to hear. Brooklyn did love me. And I'd always love her. I just nodded. Because there was nothing else to say.

CHAPTER 41

Wednesday

Matt

Felix gave me another hug before walking away from the gravesite. I didn't know exactly when we'd become friends. But Brooklyn, me, Kennedy, and him always hung out. I was glad someone had gotten all his charges dropped. But I didn't know how to hang out with him and Kennedy without Brooklyn. I didn't know how to do anything without Brooklyn.

A few more people gave me hugs. And I waited until I was the last one standing by Brooklyn's grave. Just me and her.

I watched the last black car drive off and then I sat down on top of the fresh dirt. "Hey," I said into the silence. I wasn't sure what I was doing. But I wasn't ready to walk away from this spot just yet. All I could picture was Brooklyn being cold. And scared. And alone. I needed her to know that I was here.

"I love you." I wouldn't use the past tense with her. Not now. Not ever. "You know that right? How much I love you, baby?"

I wiped away the tears from my eyes. "You had to have known that." I shook my head. "You were right about me though. I am a hypocrite. I deserved that."

I stared down at the dirt. It was like I was waiting for her to say something back. I would have killed to hear her voice again. See her smile. Hear her laugh.

"I'm sorry that I let you down," I said. "I'm so fucking sorry." I wiped away the tears that were dripping down my chin.

How was I supposed to let her go? My whole heart was hers. She was the only person that I ever wanted to hold. She was it. She was everything. She'd always be everything to me.

I pulled her ring out of my pocket. I'd meant what I wrote in my vows. She was it for me. I pushed aside some of the dirt with my hands. And I put the ring down and scooped the dirt back into place. I wouldn't be needing that ring for anyone else. It belonged here with her.

I knew our last words to each other were harsh. But she didn't stop loving me. I knew that. She loved me. And just because she was dead, it didn't mean that love just disappeared. She was still all that I thought about. I still woke up reaching out for her. I still turned around expecting her to be there. How was I supposed to ever let go of her? I wasn't just in denial. I physically couldn't do it.

I patted the dirt where the ring was. She was all the firsts I'd ever experience. I wouldn't marry someone that wasn't her. I wouldn't have kids with someone else. I wouldn't grow old with someone other than her. I would never be able to do it. She was gone. But I didn't want to love anyone else. Ever.

I felt like she was so far away from me. I lay down on the dirt to be even closer to her. "I promised you forever. I meant it, baby."

I closed my eyes and pretended she really was beside me. If I'd gotten just a few more moments with her, I'd tell her how much I loved her. How sorry I was. I closed my eyes tight. I couldn't believe the last thing I said to her was that she was a liar. She wasn't the liar. I was. I'd promised myself I'd make her an Untouchable. And I'd failed.

"Matt?"

I opened my eyes. Kennedy was standing at the foot of Brooklyn's grave. The sun was starting to set behind her. I must have fallen asleep. I sat up and brushed the dirt off the side of my face. "What are you doing here?" I asked.

"Same as you, I think." She patted Jim's tombstone. "Hi, Uncle Jim," she said, and then sat down beside me. "I needed to talk to her."

I nodded. The only concession I'd gotten from Mr. Pruitt was that Brooklyn be buried next to her uncle. She wouldn't have wanted to be in some gaudy Pruitt mausoleum. She belonged here. With someone that loved her. I cleared my throat. "Do you want me to give you a second?"

"No, not really." Tears started streaming down her cheeks. "Matt, I messed up. The last thing I ever said to her was that I couldn't even look at her. I told her that her life was like a fairytale. A freaking fairytale? No one I know has ever experienced as much pain as she had. Her life wasn't a fairytale. She thought I hated her. That I thought she was a bad friend."

"She knew you didn't mean it."

"But I still said it. And I ignored all her calls and texts. She died thinking that I hated her. And I can't stop crying."

I wrapped my arm around her shoulders. "Me too."

"You can't stop crying either?" She tried to laugh, but it came out forced.

"Yeah, that. But we had a fight before she died. I told her she was a liar. And that she'd never given me any reason to believe in her. I can't stop thinking about what I said. I know exactly how you're feeling."

Kennedy started crying even harder. "I just want to tell her that I'm sorry. And that she was the best friend I've ever had. And I don't know what I'm going to do without her."

"Me either."

We were both silent as we stared down at the ground. I didn't know what to say to her because I felt the same guilt. But I did know what Kennedy needed to hear. "She knew that we loved her." She had to have known.

"It's silly," said Kennedy, "but I was going to sit here and reminisce with her. Remind myself about all the good times to convince myself that she did know." She handed me a photo album. "But since you're here, I think you should have this. It was going to be my wedding present to the two of you."

I opened it up and saw a picture of Brooklyn smiling at the camera. Page after page of her laughing and smiling…at me. Just the way I remembered. Her whole face was lit up. I smiled when I saw pictures from the homecoming game. Shots of me dancing like a fool and

Brooklyn grinning with joy. Pure joy. I'd made her feel that.

"I know it's a cheap gift," Kennedy said. "But I..."

"It's perfect," I said. I didn't have any pictures of Brooklyn. And for some reason, it was like her face had started to get blurry in my head. I needed this. "Thank you," I said.

"This isn't right." Kennedy sniffed. "She'd been through so much. And she was finally happy. No one so kind and wonderful should be allowed to only have such little happiness in their whole life. It's not fair."

No, it wasn't. But life wasn't fair. If it was, Brooklyn's mom and uncle would still be alive. But if Brooklyn's mom was still alive, I never would have met Brooklyn. She never would have moved to New York. She'd still be alive.

This city was what killed her. Mr. Pruitt killed her. And there wasn't a single thing I could do about it. Because Brooklyn's name was on those papers, signing away her kidney to her sick dad. And Mr. Pruitt owned the cops. And the lawyers. He was the untouchable one. Not me.

"I'm really glad she had you," Kennedy said. She pointed to one of the pictures of Brooklyn and me at the Halloween party dancing.

I wished I could have rewound time to that night. I would have held her close and not let go. I would have insisted we leave town. Get away from her crazy family. But I didn't do that. I'd thought I could keep her safe. I'd been wrong.

I wanted to blame anyone but myself. Because all I could feel was guilt swallowing me whole. I'd said terrible things to her. I hadn't answered her calls. I'd let her stay in that monster's home instead of bringing her back with me. And I'd pretended she was a dirty little secret. When in reality? She was my whole fucking world.

We sat there in silence. I wasn't even sure how long. We just sat and sat. She didn't say a word as I cried. So I didn't say a word about her tears either. I think we both just needed to be close to Brooklyn. And it was nice that there was someone else that seemed to care as much as I did. Brooklyn was loved. And she'd always be loved.

"It's getting late," Kennedy said. "We should probably get going."

I closed the photo album. I could barely see it in the encroaching darkness anyway. "You go ahead."

"You're staying?"

I stared at her. "Where else am I supposed to go?" My whole life was here. I couldn't fathom moving from this spot. I just…I couldn't. Not now. Not tonight.

Kennedy nodded. "Okay. I'll stay too."

"You don't have to…"

"She would have wanted me to. She would have wanted me to make sure you were okay."

My stupid tears started up again. "I'm not okay. I don't know how to be okay."

"I know." She grabbed my hand and squeezed it. "So I'm just going to stay too. We can be not okay together. For however long it takes."

Forever. I would forever not be okay.

My friends didn't understand. They thought not talking about Brooklyn would help. And maybe it would help them. But it wouldn't help me. It seemed like Kennedy was the only one who understood. I couldn't let Brooklyn just fade away. I wouldn't. "I don't ever want to forget about her. And no one else understands. I can't forget her. I can't stop loving her."

"We won't," Kennedy said. "We won't let her just become a distant memory. We can't."

I opened up the photo album again and squinted down at a picture of Brooklyn smiling at the camera. It was hard to see it in the dark. Like there was a haze around her perfect face. Like she was already slipping away. *I'm never letting you go, Brooklyn. I'll never stop loving you.* "Never," I said. *Never.*

Kennedy put her head on my shoulder. "Nunca."

WHAT'S NEXT?

Matt thinks Brooklyn is gone. But…is she?
Find out now in *Matchmaker*!

Or download *Matthew Caldwell: The Untouchable* to find out what Matt was thinking when he first met Brooklyn!

To get your free copy of Matt's point-of-view, go to:

www.ivysmoak.com/ehb-pb

A NOTE FROM IVY

I've had so much fun reliving high school. Well…in some ways at least. The last few chapters of this book wrecked me. I knew what needed to happen, but I was still sobbing at my keyboard for days writing and editing the end of this book. For everyone who has already read The Hunted Series, you knew going into these books that Matthew Caldwell was single as an adult. And I hate that tragedy was part of his journey.

My heart is broken.

But I truly believe that broken hearts can heal. Matt healed Brooklyn's heart. And there is someone out there that will heal Matt's in the future.

Yes, the future!! We're skipping ahead to find Matt's happily ever after. It'll take place right after This is Love in the reading order. So if you haven't read The Hunted and Light to My Darkness series yet, make sure to catch up today. Plus seeing adult James is going to have you dying to see adult Matt too.

Matt. Oh my heart. All I know about Matthew Caldwell is that he deserves his happily ever after. And it's coming. I promise.

Ivy Smoak

Ivy Smoak
Wilmington, DE
www.ivysmoak.com

ABOUT THE AUTHOR

Ivy Smoak is the USA Today and Wall Street Journal best-selling author of *The Hunted Series*. Her books have sold over 3 million copies worldwide.

When she's not writing, you can find Ivy binge watching too many TV shows, taking long walks, playing outside, and generally refusing to act like an adult. She lives with her husband in Delaware.

TikTok: @IvySmoak
Facebook: IvySmoakAuthor
Instagram: @IvySmoakAuthor
Goodreads: IvySmoak

Recommend *Betrayal* for your next book club!

Book club questions available at:
www.ivysmoak.com/bookclub

Printed in Great Britain
by Amazon

30189702R00223